FIC
DUMAS
v. 1

HWLCFN

Chicago Public Library

R0406899613
The last Vendee

C0-DXA-305

LITERATURE AND LANGUAGE DIVISION
LITERATURE INFORMATION CENTER
THE CHICAGO PUBLIC LIBRARY
400 SOUTH STATE STREET
CHICAGO, ILLINOIS 60605

PORTRAIT OF DUMAS.

The Last
Vendee

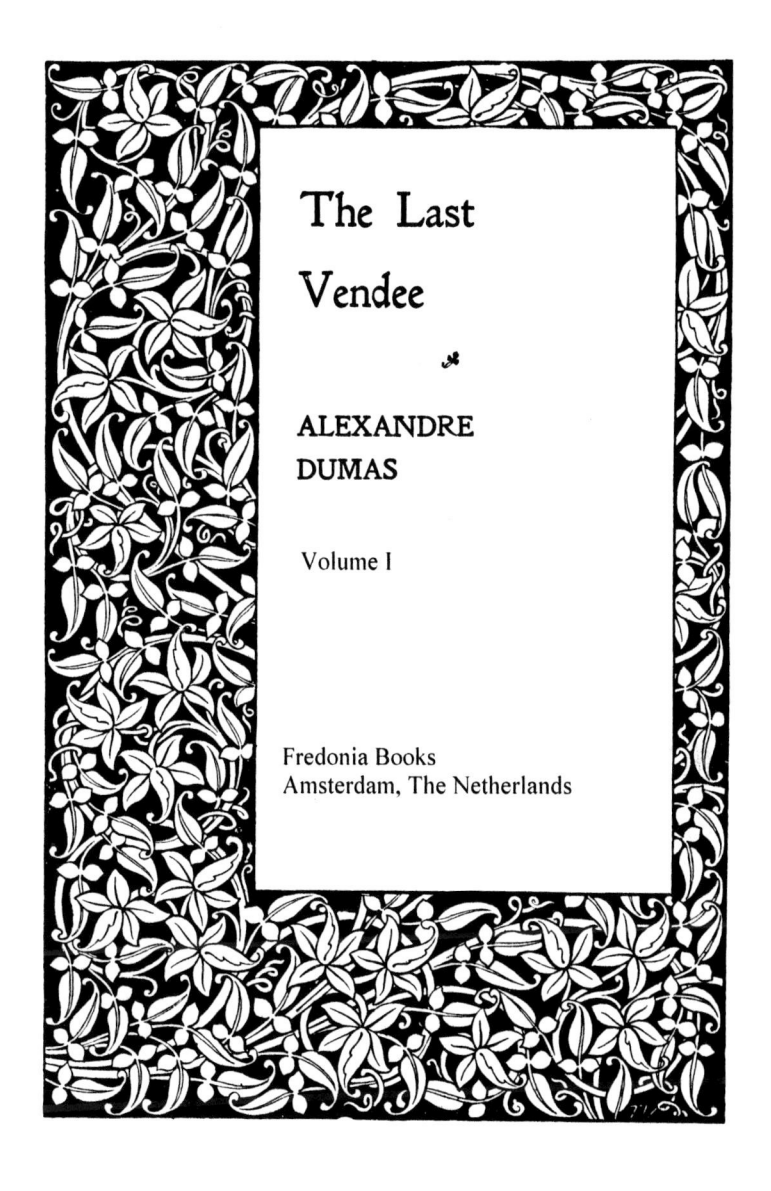

ALEXANDRE
DUMAS

Volume I

Fredonia Books
Amsterdam, The Netherlands

The Last Vendée; or
The She-Wolves of Machecoul
(Volume I)

by
Alexandre Dumas

ISBN 1-58963-173-0

Copyright © 2001 by Fredonia Books

Reprinted from the 1894 edition

Fredonia Books
Amsterdam, The Netherlands
http://www.fredoniabooks.com

All rights reserved, including the right to reproduce this book, or portions thereof, in any form.

In order to make original editions of historical works available to scholars at an economical price, this facsimile of the original edition of 1894 is reproduced from the best available copy and has been digitally enhanced to improve legibility, but the text remains unaltered to retain historical authenticity.

THE LAST VENDÉE;

OR,

THE SHE-WOLVES OF MACHECOUL.

VOLUME I.

CONTENTS.

		PAGE
I.	CHARETTE'S AIDE-DE-CAMP	9
II.	THE GRATITUDE OF KINGS	18
III.	THE TWINS	26
IV.	HOW JEAN OULLIER, COMING TO SEE THE MARQUIS FOR AN HOUR, WOULD BE THERE STILL IF THEY HAD NOT BOTH BEEN IN THEIR GRAVE THESE TEN YEARS	34
V.	A LITTER OF WOLVES	42
VI.	THE WOUNDED HARE	50
VII.	MONSIEUR MICHEL	58
VIII.	THE BARONNE DE LA LOGERIE	66
IX.	GALON-D'OR AND ALLÉGRO	76
X.	IN WHICH THINGS DO NOT HAPPEN PRECISELY AS BARON MICHEL DREAMED THEY WOULD	86
XI.	THE FOSTER-FATHER	95
XII.	NOBLESSE OBLIGE	104
XIII.	A DISTANT COUSIN	114
XIV.	PETIT-PIERRE	124
XV.	AN UNSEASONABLE HOUR	137
XVI.	COURTIN'S DIPLOMACY	148
XVII.	THE TAVERN OF AUBIN COURTE-JOIE	156
XVIII.	THE MAN FROM LA LOGERIE	165
XIX.	THE FAIR AT MONTAIGU	177
XX.	THE OUTBREAK	184

CONTENTS.

		PAGE
XXI.	JEAN OULLIER'S RESOURCES	196
XXII.	FETCH! PATAUD, FETCH!	207
XXIII.	TO WHOM THE COTTAGE BELONGED	214
XXIV.	HOW MARIANNE PICAUT MOURNED HER HUSBAND	222
XXV.	IN WHICH LOVE LENDS POLITICAL OPINIONS TO THOSE WHO HAVE NONE	227
XXVI.	THE SPRINGS OF BAUGÉ	235
XXVII.	THE GUESTS AT SOUDAY	247
XXVIII.	IN WHICH THE MARQUIS DE SOUDAY BITTERLY REGRETS THAT PETIT-PIERRE IS NOT A GENTLEMAN	256
XXIX.	THE VENDÉANS OF 1832	263
XXX.	THE WARNING	269
XXXI.	MY OLD CRONY LORIOT	276
XXXII.	THE GENERAL EATS A SUPPER WHICH HAD NOT BEEN PREPARED FOR HIM	285
XXXIII.	IN WHICH MAÎTRE LORIOT'S CURIOSITY IS NOT EXACTLY SATISFIED	291
XXXIV.	THE TOWER CHAMBER	298
XXXV.	WHICH ENDS QUITE OTHERWISE THAN AS MARY EXPECTED	306
XXXVI.	BLUE AND WHITE	316
XXXVII.	WHICH SHOWS THAT IT IS NOT FOR FLIES ONLY THAT SPIDERS' WEBS ARE DANGEROUS	327
XXXVIII.	IN WHICH THE DAINTIEST FOOT OF FRANCE AND OF NAVARRE FINDS THAT CINDERELLA'S SLIPPER DOES NOT FIT IT AS WELL AS SEVEN-LEAGUE BOOTS	339
XXXIX.	PETIT-PIERRE MAKES THE BEST MEAL HE EVER MADE IN HIS LIFE	347
XL.	EQUALITY IN DEATH	362
XLI.	THE SEARCH	874

		PAGE
XLII.	IN WHICH JEAN OULLIER SPEAKS HIS MIND ABOUT YOUNG BARON MICHEL	385
XLIII.	BARON MICHEL BECOMES BERTHA'S AIDE-DE-CAMP	398
XLIV.	MAÎTRE JACQUES AND HIS RABBITS	405
XLV.	THE DANGER OF MEETING BAD COMPANY IN THE WOODS	420
XLVI.	MAÎTRE JACQUES PROCEEDS TO KEEP THE OATH HE MADE TO AUBIN COURTE-JOIE	431

THE LAST VENDÉE;

OR,

THE SHE-WOLVES OF MACHECOUL.

I.

CHARETTE'S AIDE-DE-CAMP.

IF you ever chanced, dear reader, to go from Nantes to Bourgneuf you must, before reaching Saint-Philbert, have skirted the southern corner of the lake of Grand-Lieu, and then, continuing your way, you arrived, at the end of one hour or two hours, according to whether you were on foot or in a carriage, at the first trees of the forest of Machecoul.

There, to left of the road, among a fine clump of trees belonging, apparently, to the forest from which it is separated only by the main road, you must have seen the sharp points of two slender turrets and the gray roof of a little castle hidden among the foliage.

The cracked walls of this manor-house, its broken windows, and its damp roofs covered with wild iris and parasite mosses, gave it, in spite of its feudal pretensions and flanking turrets, so forlorn an appearance that no one at a passing glance would envy its possessor, were it not for its exquisite situation opposite to the noble trees of the forest of Machecoul, the verdant billows of which rose on the horizon as far as the eye could reach.

In 1831, this little castle was the property of an old nobleman named the Marquis de Souday, and was called, after its owner, the château of Souday.

Let us now make known the owner, having described the château.

The Marquis de Souday was the sole representative and last descendant of an old and illustrious Breton family; for the lake of Grand-Lieu, the forest of Machecoul, the town of Bourgneuf, situated in that part of France now called the department of the Loire-Inférieure, was then part of the province of Brittany, before the division of France into departments. The family of the Marquis de Souday had been, in former times, one of those feudal trees with endless branches which extended themselves over the whole department; but the ancestors of the marquis, in consequence of spending all their substance to appear with splendor in the coaches of the king, had, little by little, become so reduced and shorn of their branches that the convulsions of 1789 happened just in time to prevent the rotten trunk from falling into the hands of the sheriff; in fact, they preserved it for an end more in keeping with its former glory.

When the doom of the Bastille sounded, and the demolition of the old house of the kings foreshadowed the overthrow of royalty, the Marquis de Souday, having inherited, not great wealth, — for nothing of that was left, as we have said, except the old manor-house, — but the name and title of his father, was page to his Royal Highness, Monsieur le Comte de Provence. At sixteen — that was then his time of life — events are only accidental circumstances; besides, it would have been extremely difficult for any youth to keep from being heedless and volatile at the epicurean, voltairean, and constitutional court of the Luxembourg, where egotism elbowed its way undisguisedly.

It was M. de Souday who was sent to the place de Grève to watch for the moment when the hangman tightened the rope round Favras's neck, and the latter, by drawing his last breath, restored his Royal Highness to his normal peace of mind, which had been for the time being disturbed. The page had returned at full speed to the Luxembourg.

"Monseigneur, it is done," he said.

And monseigneur, in his clear, fluty voice, cried: —

"Come, gentlemen, to supper! to supper!"

And they supped as if a brave and honorable gentleman, who had given his life a sacrifice to his Royal Highness, had not just been hanged as a murderer and a vagabond.

Then came the first dark, threatening days of the Revolution, the publication of the Red Book, Necker's retirement, and the death of Mirabeau.

One day — it was the 22d of February, 1791 — a great crowd surrounded the palace of the Luxembourg. Rumors were spread. Monsieur, it was said, meant to escape and join the *émigrés* on the Rhine. But Monsieur appeared on the balcony, and took a solemn oath never to leave the king.

He did, in fact, start with the king on the 21st of June, possibly to keep his word never to leave him. But he did leave him, to secure his own safety, and reached the frontier tranquilly with his companion, the Marquis d'Avaray, while Louis XVI. and his family were arrested at Varennes.

Our young page, de Souday, thought too much of his reputation as a man of fashion to stay in France, although it was precisely there that the monarchy needed its most zealous supporters. He therefore emigrated, and as no one paid any heed to a page only eighteen years old, he reached Coblentz safely and took part in filling up the ranks of the musketeers who were then being remodelled on the other side of the Rhine under the orders of the Marquis de Montmorin. During the first royalist struggles he fought bravely under the three Condés, was wounded before Thionville, and then, after many disappointments and deceptions, met with the worst of all; namely, the disbanding of the various corps of *émigrés*, — a measure which took the bread out of the mouths of so many poor devils. It is true that these soldiers were serving against France, and their bread was baked by foreign nations.

The Marquis de Souday then turned his eyes toward Brittany and La Vendée, where fighting had been going on for the last two years. The state of things in La Vendée was as follows: —

All the first leaders of the great insurrection were dead. Cathélineau was killed at Vannes, Lescure at Tremblay, Bonchamps at Chollet; d'Elbée had been, or was to be, shot at Noirmoutiers; and, finally, what was called the Grand Army had just been annihilated in Le Mans.

This Grand Army had been defeated at Fontenay-le-Comte, at Saumur, Torfou, Laval, and Dol. Nevertheless, it had gained the advantage in sixty fights; it had held its own against all the forces of the Republic, commanded successively by Biron, Rossignol, Kléber, and Westermann. It had seen its homes burned, its children massacred, its old men strangled. Its leaders were Cathélineau, Henri de la Rochejaquelein, Stofflet, Bonchamps, Forestier, d'Elbée, Lescure, Marigny, and Talmont. In spite of all vicissitudes it continued faithful to its king when the rest of France abandoned him; it worshipped its God when Paris proclaimed that there was no God. Thanks to the loyalty and valor of this army, La Vendée won the right to be proclaimed in history throughout all time "the land of giants."

Charette and la Rochejaquelein alone were left. Charette had a few soldiers; la Rochejaquelein had none.

It was while the Grand Army was being slowly destroyed in Le Mans that Charette, appointed commander-in-chief of Lower Poitou and seconded by the Chevalier de Couétu and Jolly, had collected his little army. Charette, at the head of this army, and la Rochejaquelein, followed by ten men only, met near Maulevrier. Charette instantly perceived that la Rochejaquelein came as a general, not as a soldier; he had a strong sense of his own position, and did not choose to share his command with any one. He was therefore cold and haughty in manner, and went to his own breakfast without even asking Rochejaquelein to share it with him.

The same day eight hundred men left Charette's army and placed themselves under the orders of la Rochejaquelein. The next day Charette said to his young rival: —

"I start for Mortagne; you will follow me."

"I am accustomed," replied la Rochejaquelein, "not to follow, but to be followed."

He parted from Charette, and left him to operate his army as he pleased. It is the latter whom we shall now follow, because he is the only Vendéan leader whose last efforts and death are connected with our history.

Louis XVII. was dead, and on the 26th of June, 1795, Louis XVIII. was proclaimed king of France at the headquarters at Belleville. On the 15th of August, 1795, — that is to say, two months after the date of this proclamation, — a young man brought Charette a letter from the new king. This letter, written from Verona, and dated July 8, 1795, conferred on Charette the command of the royalist army.

Charette wished to reply by the same young messenger and thank the king for the honor he had done him; but the young man informed the general that he had re-entered France to stay there and fight there, and asked that the despatch he had brought might serve as a recommendation to the commander-in-chief. Charette immediately attached him to his person.

This young messenger was no other than Monsieur's former page, the Marquis de Souday.

As he withdrew to seek some rest, after doing his last sixty miles on horseback, the marquis came upon a young guard, who was five or six years older than himself, and was now standing, hat in hand, and looking at him with affectionate respect. Souday recognized the son of one of his father's farmers, with whom he had hunted as a lad with huge satisfaction; for no one could head off a boar as well or urge on the hounds after the animal was turned with such vigor.

"Hey! Jean Oullier," he cried; "is that you?"

"Myself in person, and at your service, monsieur le marquis," answered the young peasant.

"Good faith! my friend, and glad enough, too. Are you still as keen a huntsman?"

"Oh, yes, monsieur le marquis; only, just now it is other game than boars we are after."

"Never mind that. If you are willing, we'll hunt this game together as we did the other."

"That's not to be refused, but much the contrary, monsieur le marquis," returned Jean Oullier.

From that moment Jean Oullier was attached to the Marquis de Souday, just as the marquis was attached to Charette, — that is to say, that Jean Oullier was the aide-de-camp of the aide-de-camp of the commander-in-chief. Besides his talents as a huntsman he was a valuable man in other respects. In camping he was good for everything. The marquis never had to think of bed or victuals; in the worst of times he never went without a bit of bread, a glass of water, and a shake-down of straw, which in La Vendée was a luxury the commander-in-chief himself did not always enjoy.

We should be greatly tempted to follow Charette, and consequently our young hero, on one of the many adventurous expeditions undertaken by the royalist general, which won him the reputation of being the greatest partisan leader the world has seen; but history is a seductive siren, and if you imprudently obey the sign she makes you to follow her, there is no knowing where you will be led. We must simplify our tale as much as possible, and therefore we leave to others the opportunity of relating the expedition of the Comte d'Artois to Noirmoutiers and the Île Dieu, the strange conduct of the prince, who remained three weeks within sight of the French coast without landing, and the discouragement of the royalist army when it saw itself abandoned by those for whom it had fought so gallantly for more than two years.

In spite of which discouragement, however, Charette not long after won his terrible victory at Les Quatre Chemins. It was his last; for treachery from that time forth took part in the struggle. De Couëtu, Charette's right arm, his other self after the death of Jolly, was enticed into an ambush, captured, and shot. In the last months of his life Charette could not take a single step without his adversary, whoever he was, Hoche or Travot, being instantly informed of it.

Surrounded by the republican troops, hemmed in on all sides, pursued day and night, tracked from bush to bush, springing from ditch to ditch, knowing that sooner or later he was certain to be killed in some encounter, or, if taken, to be shot on the spot, — without shelter, burnt up with fever, dying of thirst, half famished, not daring to ask at the farmhouses he saw for a little water, a little bread, or a little straw, — he had only thirty-two men remaining with him, among whom were the Marquis de Souday and Jean Oullier, when, on the 25th of March, 1796, the news came that four republican columns were marching simultaneously against him.

"Very good," said he; "then it is here, on this spot, that we must fight to the death and sell our lives dearly."

The spot was La Prélinière, in the parish of Saint-Sulpice. But with thirty-two men Charette did not choose to await the enemy; he went to meet them. At La Guyonnières he met General Valentin with two hundred grenadiers and chasseurs. Charette's position was a good one, and he intrenched it. There, for three hours, he sustained the charges and fire of two hundred republicans. Twelve of his men fell around him. The Army of the Chouannerie, which was twenty-four thousand strong when M. le Comte d'Artois lay off the Île Dieu without landing, was now reduced to twenty men.

These twenty men stood firmly around their general;

not one even thought of escape. To make an end of the business, General Valentin took a musket himself, and at the head of the hundred and eighty men remaining to him, he charged at the point of the bayonet.

Charette was wounded by a ball in his head, and three fingers were taken off by a sabre-cut. He was about to be captured when an Alsatian, named Pfeffer, who felt more than mere devotion to Charette, whom he worshipped, took the general's plumed hat, gave him his, and saying, "Go to the right; they'll follow me," sprang to the left himself. He was right; the republicans rushed after him savagely, while Charette sprang in the opposite direction with his fifteen remaining men.

He had almost reached the wood of La Chabotière when General Travot's column appeared. Another and more desperate fight took place, in which Charette's sole object was to get himself killed. Losing blood from three wounds, he staggered and fell. A Vendéan, named Bossard, took him on his shoulders and carried him toward the wood; but before reaching it, Bossard himself was shot down. Then another man, Laroche-Davo, succeeded him, made fifty steps, and he too fell in the ditch that separates the wood from the plain.

Then the Marquis de Souday lifted Charette in his arms, and while Jean Oullier with two shots killed two republican soldiers who were close at their heels, he carried the general into the wood, followed by the seven men still living. Once fairly within the woods, Charette recovered his senses.

"Souday," he said, "listen to my last orders."

The young man stopped.

"Put me down at the foot of that oak."

Souday hesitated to obey.

"I am still your general," said Charette, imperiously. "Obey me."

The young man, overawed, did as he was told and put down the general at the foot of the oak.

PORTRAIT OF CHARETTE.

CHARETTE'S AIDE-DE-CAMP. 17

"There! now," said Charette, "listen to me. The king who made me general-in-chief must be told how his general died. Return to his Majesty Louis XVIII., and tell him all that you have seen; I demand it."

Charette spoke with such solemnity that the marquis did not dream of disobeying him.

"Go!" said Charette, "you have not a minute to spare; here come the Blues. Fly!"

As he spoke the republicans had reached the edge of the woods. Souday took the hand which Charette held out to him.

"Kiss me," said the latter.

The young man kissed him.

"That will do," said the general; "now go."

Souday cast a look at Jean Oullier.

"Are you coming?" he said.

But his follower shook his head gloomily.

"What have I to do over there, monsieur le marquis?" he said. "Whereas here —"

"Here, what?"

"I'll tell you that if we ever meet again, monsieur le marquis."

So saying, he fired two balls at the nearest republicans. They fell. One of them was an officer of rank; his men pressed round him. Jean Oullier and the marquis profited by that instant to bury themselves in the depths of the woods.

But at the end of some fifty paces Jean Oullier, finding a thick bush at hand, slipped into it like a snake, with a gesture of farewell to the Marquis de Souday.

The marquis continued his way alone.

II.

THE GRATITUDE OF KINGS.

THE Marquis de Souday gained the banks of the Loire and found a fisherman who was willing to take him to Saint-Gildas. A frigate hove in sight, — an English frigate. For a few more louis the fisherman consented to put the marquis aboard of her. Once there, he was safe.

Two or three days later the frigate hailed a three-masted merchantman, which was heading for the Channel. She was Dutch. The marquis asked to be put aboard of her; the English captain consented. The Dutchman landed him at Rotterdam. From Rotterdam he went to Blankenbourg, a little town in the duchy of Brunswick, which Louis XVIII. had chosen for his residence.

The marquis now prepared to execute Charette's last instructions. When he reached the château Louis XVIII. was dining; this was always a sacred hour to him. The ex-page was told to wait. When dinner was over he was introduced into the king's presence.

He related the events he had seen with his own eyes, and, above all, the last catastrophe, with such eloquence that his Majesty, who was not impressionable, was enough impressed to cry out: —

"Enough, enough, marquis! Yes, the Chevalier de Charette was a brave servant; we are grateful to him."

He made the messenger a sign to retire. The marquis obeyed; but as he withdrew he heard the king say, in a sulky tone: —

"That fool of a Souday coming here and telling me such things after dinner! It is enough to upset my digestion!"

THE GRATITUDE OF KINGS. 19

The marquis was touchy; he thought that after exposing his life for six months it was a poor reward to be called a fool by him for whom he had exposed it. One hundred louis were still in his pocket, and he left Blankenbourg that evening, saying to himself: —

"If I had known that I should be received in that way I would n't have taken such pains to come."

He returned to Holland, and from Holland he went to England. There began a new phase in the existence of the Marquis de Souday. He was one of those men who are moulded by circumstances, — men who are strong or weak, brave or pusillanimous, according to the surroundings among which fortune casts them. For six months he had been at the apex of that terrible Vendéan epic; his blood had stained the gorse and the moors of upper and lower Poitou; he had borne with stoical fortitude not only the ill-fortune of battle, but also the privations of that guerilla warfare, bivouacking in snow, wandering without food, without clothes, without shelter, in the boggy forests of La Vendée. Not once had he felt a regret; not a single complaint had passed his lips.

And yet, with all these antecedents, when isolated in the midst of that great city of London, where he wandered sadly regretting the excitements of war, he felt himself without courage in presence of enforced idleness, without resistance under ennui, without energy to overcome the wretchedness of exile. This man, who had bravely borne the attacks and pursuits of the infernal columns of the Blues, could not bear up against the evil suggestions which came of idleness. He sought pleasure everywhere to fill the void in his existence caused by the absence of stirring vicissitudes and the excitements of a deadly struggle.

Now such pleasures as a penniless exile could command were not of a high order; and thus it happened that, little by little, he lost his former elegance and the look and manner of gentleman as his tastes deteriorated. He drank ale and porter instead of champagne, and contented himself with the bedizened women of the Haymarket and Regent Street, — he who had chosen his first loves among the duchesses.

Soon the looseness of his principles and the pressure of his needs drove him into connections from which his reputation suffered. He accepted pleasures when he could not pay for them; his companions in debauchery were of a lower class than himself. After a time his own class of *émigrés* turned away from him, and by the natural drift of things, the more the marquis found himself neglected by his rightful friends, the deeper he plunged into the evil ways he had now entered.

He had been leading this existence for about two years, when by chance he encountered, in an evil resort which he frequented, a young working-girl, whom one of those infamous women who infest London had enticed from her poor home and produced for the first time. In spite of the changes which ill-luck and a reckless life had produced in the marquis, the poor girl perceived the remains of a gentleman still in him. She flung herself at his feet, and implored him to save her from an infamous life, for which she was not meant, having always been good and virtuous till then.

The young girl was pretty, and the marquis offered to take her with him. She threw herself on his neck and promised him all her love and the utmost devotion. Without any thought of doing a good action the marquis defeated the speculation on Eva's beauty, — the girl was named Eva. She kept her word, poor, faithful creature that she was; the marquis was her first and last and only love.

The matter was a fortunate thing for both of them. The marquis was getting very tired of cock-fights and the acrid fumes of beer, not to speak of frays with constables and loves at street-corners. The tenderness of the young girl rested him; the possession of the pure child, white as the swans which are the emblem of Brittany, his own land, satisfied his vanity. Little by little, he changed his course of life, and though he never returned to the habits of his own class, he did adopt a life which was that of a decent man.

He went to live with Eva on the upper floor of a house in Piccadilly. She was a good workwoman, and soon found employment with a milliner. The marquis gave fencing-lessons. From that time they lived on the humble proceeds of their employments, finding great happiness in a love which had now become powerful enough to gild their poverty. Nevertheless, this love, like all things mortal, wore out in the end, though not for a long time. Happily for Eva, the emotions of the Vendéan war and the frantic excitements of London hells had used up her lover's superabundant sap; he was really an old man before his time. The day on which the marquis first perceived that his love for Eva was waning, the day when her kisses were powerless, not to satisfy him but to rouse him, habit had acquired such an influence over him that even had he sought distractions outside his home he no longer had the force or the courage to break a connection in which his selfishness still found the monotonous comforts of daily life.

The former *viveur*, whose ancestors had possessed for three centuries the power of life and death in their province, the ex-*brigand*, the aide-de-camp to the *brigand* Charette, led for a dozen years the dull, precarious, drudging life of a humble clerk, or a mechanic more humble still.

Heaven had long refrained from blessing this illegitimate marriage; but at last the prayers which Eva had never ceased to offer for twelve years were granted. The poor woman became pregnant, and gave birth to twin daughters. But alas! a few hours of the maternal joys she had so longed for were all that were granted to her. She died of puerperal fever.

Eva's tenderness for the Marquis de Souday was as deep and warm at the end of twelve years' devotion as it was in the beginning of their intercourse; yet her love, great as it was, did not prevent her from recognizing that frivolity and selfishness were at the bottom of her lover's character. Therefore she suffered in dying not only the anguish of bidding an eternal farewell to the man she had loved so deeply, but the terror of leaving the future of her children in his hands.

This loss produced impressions upon the marquis which we shall endeavor to reproduce minutely, because they seem to us to give a distinct idea of the nature of the man who is destined to play an important part in the narrative we are now undertaking.

He began by mourning his companion seriously and sincerely. He could not help doing homage to her good qualities and recognizing the happiness which he owed to her affection. Then, after his first grief had passed away, he felt something of the joy of a schoolboy when he gets out of bounds. Sooner or later his name, rank, and birth must have made it necessary for him to break the tie. The marquis felt grateful to Providence for relieving him of a duty which would certainly have distressed him.

This satisfaction, however, was short-lived. Eva's tenderness, the continuity, if we may say so, of the care and attention she had given him, had spoilt the marquis; and those cares and attentions, now that he had suddenly lost them, seemed to him more essential to his happiness than ever. The humble chambers in which they had lived became, now that the Englishwoman's fresh, pure voice no longer enlivened them, what they were in reality, — miserable lodging-rooms; and, in like manner, when his eyes sought involuntarily the silky hair of his companion lying in golden waves upon the pillow, his bed was nothing more than a wretched pallet. Where could he now look for the soft petting, the tender attention to all his wants, with which, for twelve good years, Eva had surrounded him. When he reached this stage of his desolation the marquis admitted to himself that he could never replace them. Consequently, he began to mourn poor Eva more than ever, and when the time came for him to part with his little girls, whom he sent into Yorkshire to be nursed, he put such a rush of tenderness into his grief that the good country-woman, their foster-mother, was sincerely affected.

After thus separating from all that united him with the past, the Marquis de Souday succumbed under the burden of his solitude; he became morose and taciturn. As his religious faith was none too solid, he would probably have ended, under the deep disgust of life which now took possession of him, by jumping into the Thames, if the catastrophe of 1814 had not happened just in time to distract him from his melancholy thoughts. Re-entering France, which he had never hoped to see again, the Marquis de Souday very naturally applied to Louis XVIII., of whom he had asked nothing during his exile in return for the blood he had shed for him. But princes often seek pretexts for ingratitude, and Louis XVIII. was furnished with three against his former page: first, the tempestuous manner in which he had announced to his Majesty Charette's death, — an announcement which had in fact troubled the royal digestion; secondly, his disrespectful departure from Blankenbourg, accompanied by language even more disrespectful than the departure itself; and thirdly (this was the gravest pretext), the irregularity of his life and conduct during the emigration.

Much praise was bestowed upon the bravery and devotion of the former page; but he was, very gently, made to understand that with such scandals attaching to his name he could not expect to fulfil any public functions. The king was no longer an autocrat, they told him; he was now compelled to consider public opinion; after the late period of public immorality it was necessary to introduce a new and more rigid era of morals. How fine a thing it would be if the marquis were willing to sacrifice his own personal ambitions to the necessities of the State.

In short, they persuaded him to be satisfied with the cross of Saint-Louis, the rank and pension of a major of cavalry, and to take himself off to eat the king's bread on his estate at Souday, — the sole fragment recovered by the poor *émigré* from the wreck of the enormous fortune of his ancestors.

What was really fine about all this was that these excuses and hypocrisies did not hinder the Marquis de Souday from doing his duty, — that is, from leaving his poor castle to defend the white flag when Napoleon made his marvellous return from Elba. Napoleon fell again, and for the second time the marquis re-entered Paris with the legitimate princes. But this time, wiser than he was in 1814, he merely asked of the restored monarchy for the place of Master of Wolves to the arrondissement of Machecoul, — an office in the royal gift which, being without salary or emolument, was willingly accorded to him.

Deprived during his youth of a pleasure which in his family was an hereditary passion, the marquis now devoted himself ardently to hunting. Always unhappy in a solitary life, for which he was totally unfitted, yet growing more and more misanthropic as the result of his political disappointments, he found in this active exercise a momentary forgetfulness of his bitter memories. Thus the position of Master of Wolves, which gave him the right to roam the State forests at will, afforded him far more satisfaction than his ribbon of Saint-Louis or his commission as major of cavalry.

So the Marquis de Souday had been living for two years in the mouldy little castle we lately described, beating the woods day and night with his six dogs (the only establishment his slender means permitted), seeing his neighbors just enough to prevent them from considering him an absolute bear, and thinking as little as he could of his past wealth and his past fame, when one morning, as he was starting to explore the north end of the forest of Machecoul, he met on the road a peasant woman carrying a child three or four years old on each arm.

The marquis instantly recognized the woman and blushed as he did so. It was the nurse from Yorkshire, to whom he had regularly for the last thirty-six months neglected to pay the board of her two nurslings. The worthy woman had gone to London, and there made inquiries at the French legation. She had now reached Machecoul with the assistance of the French minister, who of course did not doubt that the Marquis de Souday would be most happy to recover his two children.

The singular part of it is that the ambassador was not entirely mistaken. The little girls reminded the marquis so vividly of his poor Eva that he was seized with genuine emotion; he kissed them with a tenderness that was not assumed, gave his gun to the Englishwoman, took his children in his arms, and returned to the castle with this unlooked-for game, to the utter stupefaction of the cook, who constituted his whole household, and who now overwhelmed him with questions as to the singular accession thus made to the family.

These questions alarmed the marquis. He was only thirty-nine years of age, and vague ideas of marriage still floated in his head; he regarded it as a duty not to let a name and house so illustrious as that of Souday come to an end in his person. Moreover, he would not have been sorry to turn over to a wife the management of his household affairs, which was odious to him. But the realization of that idea would, of course, be impossible if he kept the little girls in his house.

He saw this plainly, paid the Englishwoman handsomely, and the next day despatched her back to her own country.

During the night he had come to a resolution which, he thought, would solve all difficulties. What was that resolution? We shall now see.

III.

THE TWINS.

THE Marquis de Souday went to bed repeating to himself the old proverb, "Night brings counsel." With that hope he fell asleep. When asleep, he dreamed.

He dreamed of his old wars in La Vendée with Charette, — of the days when he was aide-de-camp; and, more especially, he dreamed of Jean Oullier, his attendant, of whom he had never thought since the day when they left Charette dying, and parted in the wood of Chabotière.

As well as he could remember, Jean Oullier before joining Charette's army had lived in the village of La Chevrolière, near the lake of Grand-Lieu. The next morning the Marquis de Souday sent a man of Machecoul, who did his errands, on horseback with a letter, ordering him to go to La Chevrolière and ascertain if a man named Jean Oullier was still living and whether he was in the place. If he was, the messenger was to give him the letter and, if possible, bring him back with him. If he lived at a short distance the messenger was to go there. If the distance was too great he was to obtain every information as to the locality of his abode. If he was dead the messenger was to return at once and say so.

Jean Oullier was not dead; Jean Oullier was not in distant parts; Jean Oullier was in the neighborhood of La Chevrolière; in fact, Jean Oullier was in La Chevrolière itself.

Here is what had happened to him after parting with the marquis on the day of Charette's last defeat. He stayed hidden in the bush, from which he could see all and not be seen himself. He saw General Travot take Charette prisoner and treat him with all the consideration a man like General Travot would show to a man like Charette. But, apparently, that was not all that Jean Oullier expected to see, for after seeing the republicans lay Charette on a litter and carry him away, Jean Oullier still remained hidden in his bush.

It is true that an officer with a picket of twelve men remained in the wood. What were they there for?

About an hour later a Vendéan peasant passed within ten paces of Jean Oullier, having answered the challenge of the sentinel with the word "Friend," — an odd answer in the mouth of a royalist peasant to a republican soldier. The peasant next exchanged the countersign with the sentry and passed on. Then he approached the officer, who, with an expression of disgust which it is quite impossible to represent, gave him a bag that was evidently full of gold. After which the peasant disappeared, and the officer with his picket guard also departed, showing that in all probability they had only been stationed there to await the coming of the peasant.

In all probability, too, Jean Oullier had seen what he wanted to see, for he came out of his bush as he went into it, — that is to say, crawling; and getting on his feet, he tore the white cockade from his hat, and, with the careless indifference of a man who for the last three years had staked his life every day on a turn of the dice, he buried himself still deeper in the forest.

The same night he reached La Chevrolière. He went straight to his own home. On the spot where his house had stood was a blackened ruin, blackened by fire. He sat down upon a stone and wept.

In that house he had left a wife and two children.

Soon he heard a step and raised his head. A peasant passed. Jean Oullier recognized him in the darkness and called: —

"Tinguy!"

The man approached.

"Who is it calls me?" he said.

"I am Jean Oullier," replied the Chouan.

"God help you," replied Tinguy, attempting to pass on; but Jean Oullier stopped him.

"You must answer me," he said.

"Are you a man?"

"Yes."

"Then question me and I will answer."

"My father?"

"Dead."

"My wife?"

"Dead."

"My two children?"

"Dead."

"Thank you."

Jean Oullier sat down again, but he no longer wept. After a few moments he fell on his knees and prayed. It was time he did, for he was about to blaspheme. He prayed for those who were dead.

Then, restored by that deep faith that gave him hope to meet them in a better world, he bivouacked on those sad ruins.

The next day, at dawn, he began to rebuild his house, as calm and resolute as though his father were still at the plough, his wife before the fire, his children at the door. Alone, and asking no help from any one, he rebuilt his cottage.

There he lived, doing the humble work of a day laborer. If any one had counselled Jean Oullier to ask a reward from the Bourbons for doing what he, rightly or wrongly, considered his duty, that adviser ran some risk of insulting the grand simplicity of the poor peasant.

It will be readily understood that with such a nature Jean Oullier, on receiving the letter in which the marquis called him his old comrade and begged him to come to him, he did not delay his going. On the contrary, he locked the door of his house, put the key in his pocket, and then, as he lived alone and had no one to notify, he started instantly. The messenger offered him his horse, or, at any rate, to take him up behind him; but Jean Oullier shook his head.

"Thank God," he said, "my legs are good."

Then resting his hand on the horse's neck, he set the pace for the animal to take, — a gentle trot of six miles an hour. That evening Jean Oullier was at the castle. The marquis received him with visible delight. He had worried all day over the idea that Jean Oullier might be absent, or dead. It is not necessary to say that the idea of that death worried him not for Jean Oullier's sake but for his own. We have already informed our readers that the Marquis de Souday was slightly selfish.

The first thing the marquis did was to take Jean Oullier apart and confide to him the arrival of his children and his consequent embarrassment.

Jean Oullier, who had had his own two children massacred, could not understand that a father should voluntarily wish to part with his children. He nevertheless accepted the proposal made to him by the marquis to bring up the little girls till such a time as they were of age to go to school. He said he would find some good woman at La Chevrolière who would be a mother to them, — if, indeed, any one could take the place of a mother to orphaned children.

Had the twins been sickly, ugly, or disagreeable, Jean Oullier would have taken them all the same; but they were, on the contrary, so prepossessing, so pretty, so graceful, and their smiles so engaging, that the good man instantly loved them as such men do love. He declared that their fair and rosy faces and curling hair were so like those of the cherubs that surrounded the Madonna over the high altar at Grand-Lieu before it was destroyed, that he felt like kneeling to them when he saw them.

It was therefore decided that on the morrow Jean

Oullier should take the children back with him to La Chevrolière.

Now it so happened that, during the time which had elapsed between the departure of the nurse and the arrival of Jean Oullier, the weather had been rainy. The marquis, confined to the castle, felt terribly bored. Feeling bored, he sent for his daughters and began to play with them. Putting one astride his neck, and perching the other on his back, he was soon galloping on all fours round the room, like Henri of Navarre. Only, he improved on the amusement which his Majesty afforded his progeny by imitating with his mouth not only the horn of the hunter, but the barking and yelping of the whole pack of hounds. This domestic sport diverted the Marquis de Souday immensely, and it is safe to say that the little girls had never laughed so much in their lives.

Besides, the little things had been won by the tenderness and the petting their father had lavished upon them during these few hours, to appease, no doubt, the reproaches of his conscience at sending them away from him after so long a separation. The children, on their side, showed him a frantic attachment and a lively gratitude, which were not a little dangerous to the fulfilment of his plan.

In fact, when the carriole came, at eight o'clock in the morning, to the steps of the portico, and the twins perceived that they were about to be taken away, they set up cries of anguish. Bertha flung herself on her father, clasped his knees, clung to the garters of the gentleman who gave her sugar-plums and made himself such a capital horse, and twisted her little hands into them in such a manner that the poor marquis feared to bruise her wrists by trying to unclasp them.

As for Mary, she sat down on the steps and cried; but she cried with such an expression of real sorrow that Jean Oullier felt more touched by her silent grief than by the noisy despair of her sister. The marquis employed all his eloquence to persuade the little girls that by getting into the carriage they would have more pleasure and more dainties than by staying with him; but the more he talked, the more Mary cried and the more Bertha quivered and passionately clung to him.

The marquis began to get impatient. Seeing that persuasion could do nothing, he was about to employ force when, happening to turn his eyes, he caught sight of the look on Jean Oullier's face. Two big tears were rolling down the bronzed cheeks of the peasant into the thick red whiskers which framed his face. Those tears acted both as a prayer to the marquis and as a reproach to the father. Monsieur de Souday made a sign to Jean Oullier to unharness the horse; and while Bertha, understanding the sign, danced with joy on the portico, he whispered in the farmer's ear: —

"You can start to-morrow."

As the day was very fine, the marquis desired to utilize the presence of Jean Oullier by taking him on a hunt; with which intent he carried him off to his own bedroom to help him on with his sporting-clothes. The peasant was much struck by the frightful disorder of the little room; and the marquis continued his confidences with bitter complaints of his female servitor, who, he said, might be good enough among her pots and pans, but was odiously careless as to all other household comforts, particularly those that concerned his clothes. On this occasion it was ten minutes before he could find a waistcoat that was not widowed of its buttons, or a pair of breeches not afflicted with a rent that made them more or less indecent. However, he was dressed at last.

Wolf-master though he was, the marquis, as we have said, was too poor to allow himself the luxury of a huntsman, and he led his little pack himself. Therefore, having the double duty of keeping the hounds from getting at fault, and firing at the game, it was seldom that the poor marquis, passionate sportsman that he was, did not come home at night tired out.

With Jean Oullier it was quite another thing. The vigorous peasant, in the flower of his age, sprang through the forest with the agility of a squirrel; he bounded over bushes when it took too long to go round them, and, thanks to his muscles of steel, he never was behind the dogs by a length. On two or three occasions he supported them with such vigor that the boar they were pursuing, recognizing the fact that flight would not shake off his enemies, ended by turning and standing at bay in a thicket, where the marquis had the happiness of killing him at one blow,— a thing that had never yet happened to him.

The marquis went home light-hearted and joyful, thanking Jean Oullier for the delightful day he owed to him. During dinner he was in fine good-humor, and invented new games to keep the little girls as gay as himself.

At night, when he went to his room, the marquis found Jean Oullier sitting cross-legged in a corner, like a Turk or a tailor. Before him was a mound of garments, and in his hand he held a pair of old velvet breeches which he was darning vigorously.

"What the devil are you doing there?" demanded the marquis.

"The winter is cold in this level country, especially when the wind is from the sea; and after I get home my legs will be cold at the very thought of a norther blowing on yours through these rents," replied Jean Oullier, showing his master a tear which went from knee to belt in the breeches he was mending.

"Ha! so you're a tailor, too, are you?" cried the marquis.

"Alas!" said Jean Oullier, "one has to be a little of everything when one lives alone as I have done these twenty years. Besides, an old soldier is never at a loss."

"I like that!" said the marquis; "pray, am not I a soldier, too?"

"No; you were an officer, and that's not the same thing."

The Marquis de Souday looked at Jean Oullier admiringly. Then he went to bed and to sleep, and snored away, without in the least interrupting the work of his old Chouan. In the middle of the night he woke up. Jean Oullier was still at work. The mound of garments had not perceptibly diminished.

"But you can never finish them, even if you work till daylight, my poor Jean," said the marquis.

"I 'm afraid not."

"Then go to bed now, old comrade; you need n't start till you have mended up all my old rags, and we can have another hunt to-morrow."

IV.

HOW JEAN OULLIER, COMING TO SEE THE MARQUIS FOR AN HOUR, WOULD BE THERE STILL IF THEY HAD NOT BOTH BEEN IN THEIR GRAVE THESE TEN YEARS.

THE next morning, before starting for the hunt, it occurred to the marquis to kiss his children. He therefore went up to their room, and was not a little astonished to find that the indefatigable Jean Oullier had preceded him, and was washing and brushing the little girls with the conscientious determination of a good governess. The poor fellow, to whom the occupation recalled his own lost young ones, seemed to be taking deep satisfaction in the work. The marquis changed his admiration into respect.

For eight days the hunts continued without interruption, each finer and more fruitful than the last. During those eight days Jean Oullier, huntsman by day, steward by night, not only revived and restored his master's wardrobe, but he actually found time to put the house in order from top to bottom.

The marquis, far from urging his departure, now thought with horror of parting from so valuable a servitor. From morning till night, and sometimes from night till morning, he turned over in his mind which of the Chouan's qualities was most serviceable to him. Jean Oullier had the scent of a hound to follow game, and the eye of an Indian to discover its trail by the bend of the reeds or the dew on the grass. He could even tell, on the dry and stony roads about Machecoul, Bourgneuf, and Aigrefeuille, the age and sex of a boar, when the trail was imperceptible to other eyes. No huntsman on horseback had ever followed up the hounds like Jean Oullier on his long and vigorous legs. Moreover, on the days when rest was actually necessary for the little pack of hounds, he was unequalled for discovering the places where snipe abounded, and taking his master to the spot.

"Damn marriage!" cried the marquis to himself, occasionally, when he seemed to be thinking of quite other things. "Why do I want to row in that boat when I have seen so many good fellows come to grief in it? Heavens and earth! I'm not so young a man — almost forty; I have n't any illusions; I don't expect to captivate a woman by my personal attractions. I can't expect to do more than tempt some old dowager with my three thousand francs a year, — half of which dies with me. I should probably get a scolding, fussy, nagging wife, who might interfere with my hunting, which that good Jean manages so well; and I am sure she will never keep the house in such order as he does. Still," he added, straightening himself up, and swaying the upper part of his body, "is this a time to let the old races, the supporters of monarchy, die out? Would n't it be very pleasant to see my son restore the glory of my house? Besides, what would be thought of me, — who am known to have had no wife, no legitimate wife, — what will my neighbors say if I take the two little girls to live with me?"

When these reflections came, which they ordinarily did on rainy days, when he could not be off on his favorite pastime, they cast the Marquis de Souday into painful perplexity, from which he wriggled, as do all undecided temperaments and weak natures, — men, in short, who never know how to adopt a course, — by making a provisional arrangement.

At the time when our story opens, in 1831, Mary and Bertha were seventeen, and the provisional arrangement still lasted; although, strange as it may seem, the Marquis de Souday had not yet positively decided to keep his daughters with him.

Jean Oullier, who had hung the key of his house at La Chevrolière to a nail, had never, in fourteen years, had the least idea of taking it down. He had waited patiently till his master gave him the order to go home. But as, ever since his arrival, the château had been neat and clean; as the marquis had never once missed a button; as the hunting-boots were always properly greased; as the guns were kept with all the care of the best armory at Nantes; as Jean Oullier, by means of certain coercive proceedings, of which he learned the secret from a former comrade of the "brigand army," had, little by little, brought the cook not to vent her ill-humor on her master; as the hounds were always in good condition, shiny of coat, neither fat nor thin, and able to bear a long chase of eight or ten hours, ending mostly in a kill; as the chatter and the pretty ways of his children and their expansive affection varied the monotony of his existence; as his talks and gossip with Jean Oullier on the stirring incidents of the old war, now passed into a tradition (it was thirty-six years distant), enlivened his dull hours and the long evenings and the rainy days, — the marquis, finding once more the good care, the quiet ease, the tranquil happiness he had formerly enjoyed with Eva, with the additional and intoxicating joys of hunting, — the marquis, we say, put off from day to day, from month to month, from year to year, deciding on the separation.

As for Jean Oullier, he had his own reasons for not provoking a decision. He was not only a brave man, but he was a good one. As we have said, he at once took a liking to Bertha and Mary; this liking, in that poor heart deprived of its own children, soon became tender affection, and the tenderness fanaticism. He did not at first perceive very clearly the distinction the marquis seemed to make between their position and that of other children whom he might have by a legitimate marriage to perpetuate his name. In Poitou, when a man gets a worthy girl into trouble he knows of no other reparation than to marry her. Jean Oullier thought it natural, inasmuch as his master could not legitimatize the connection with the mother, that he should at least not conceal the paternity which Eva in dying had bequeathed to him. Therefore, after two months' sojourn at the castle, having made these reflections, weighed them in his mind, and ratified them in his heart, the Chouan would have received an order to take the children away with very ill grace; and his respect for Monsieur de Souday would not have prevented him from expressing himself bluffly on the subject.

Fortunately, the marquis did not betray to his dependant the tergiversations of his mind; so that Jean Oullier did really regard the provisional arrangement as definitive, and he believed that the marquis considered the presence of his daughters at the castle as their right and also as his own bounden duty.

At the moment when we issue from these preliminaries, Bertha and Mary were, as we have said, between seventeen and eighteen years of age. The purity of race in their paternal ancestors had done marvels when strengthened with the vigorous Saxon blood of the plebeian mother. Eva's children were now two splendid young women, with refined and delicate features, slender and elegant shapes, and with great distinction and nobility in their air and manner. They were as much alike as twins are apt to be; only Bertha was dark, like her father, and Mary was fair, like her mother.

Unfortunately, the education of these beautiful young creatures, while developing to the utmost their physical advantages, did not sufficiently concern itself with the needs of their sex. It was impossible that it should be otherwise, living from day to day beside their father, with his natural carelessness and his determination to enjoy the present and let the future take care of itself.

Jean Oullier was the only tutor of Eva's children, as he was formerly their only nurse. The worthy Chouan taught them all he knew himself, — namely, to read. write, cipher, and pray with tender and devout fervor to God and the Virgin; also to roam the woods, scale the rocks, thread the tangle of holly, reeds, and briers without fatigue, without fear or weakness of any kind; to hit a bird on the wing, a squirrel on the leap, and to ride bareback those intractable horses of Mellerault, almost as wild on their plains and moors as the horses of the gauchos on the pampas.

The Marquis de Souday had seen all this without attempting to give any other direction to the education of his daughters, and without having even the idea of counteracting the taste they were forming for these manly exercises. The worthy man was only too delighted to have such valiant comrades in his favorite amusement, uniting, as they did, with their respectful tenderness toward him a gayety, dash, and ardor for the chase, which doubled his own pleasure from the time they were old enough to share it.

And yet, in strict justice, we must say that the marquis added one ingredient of his own to Jean Oullier's instructions. When Bertha and Mary were fourteen years old, which was the period when they first followed their father into the forest, their childish games, which had hitherto made the old castle so lively in the evenings, began to lose attraction. So, to fill the void he was beginning to feel, the Marquis de Souday taught Bertha and Mary how to play whist.

On the other hand, the two children had themselves completed mentally, as far as they could, the education Jean Oullier had so vigorously developed physically. Playing hide-and-seek through the castle, they came upon a room which, in all probability, had not been opened for thirty years. It was the library. There they found a thousand volumes, or something near that number.

Each followed her own bent in the choice of books. Mary, the gentle, sentimental Mary, preferred novels; the turbulent and determined Bertha, history. Then they mingled their reading in a common fund; Mary told Paul and Virginia and Amadis to Bertha, and Bertha told Mèzeray and Velly to Mary. The result of such desultory reading was, of course, that the two young girls grew up with many false notions about real life and the habits and requirements of a world they had never seen, and had, in truth, never heard of.

At the time they made their first communion the vicar of Machecoul, who loved them for their piety and the goodness of their heart, did risk a few remarks to their father on the peculiar existence such a bringing-up must produce; but his friendly remarks made no impression on the selfish indifference of the Marquis de Souday. The education we have described was continued, and such habits and ways were the result that, thanks to their already false position, poor Bertha and her sister acquired a very bad reputation throughout the neighborhood.

The fact was, the Marquis de Souday was surrounded by little newly made nobles, who envied him his truly illustrious name, and asked nothing better than to fling back upon him the contempt with which his ancestors had probably treated theirs. So when they saw him keep in his own house, and call his daughters, the children of an illegitimate union, they began to trumpet forth the evils of his life in London; they exaggerated his wrong-doing and made poor Eva (saved by a miracle from a life of degradation) a common woman of the town. Consequently, little by little, the country squires of Beauvoir, Saint-Leger, Bourgneuf, Saint-Philbert, and Grand-Lieu, avoided the marquis, under pretence that he degraded the nobility, — a matter about which, taking into account the mushroom character of their own rank, they were very good to concern themselves.

But soon it was not the men only who disapproved of the Marquis de Souday's conduct. The beauty of the twin sisters roused the enmity of the mothers and daughters in a circuit of thirty miles, and that was infinitely more alarming. If Bertha and Mary had been ugly the hearts of these charitable ladies and young ladies, naturally inclined to Christian mercy, would perhaps have forgiven the poor devil of a father for his improper paternity; but it was impossible not to be shocked at the sight of two such spurious creatures, crushing by their distinction, their nobility, and their personal charm, the well-born young ladies of the neighborhood. Such insolent superiority deserved neither mercy nor compassion.

The indignation against the poor girls was so general that even if they had never given any cause for gossip or calumny, gossip and calumny would have swept their wings over them. Imagine, therefore, what was likely to happen, and did actually happen, when the masculine and eccentric habits of the sisters were fully known! One universal hue-and-cry of reprobation arose from the department of the Loire-Inférieure and echoed through those of La Vendée and the Maine-et-Loire; and if it had not been for the sea, which bounds the coast of the Loire-Inférieure, that reprobation would, undoubtedly, have spread as far to the west as it did to the south and east. All classes, bourgeois and nobles, city-folk and country-folk, had their say about it. Young men, who had hardly seen Mary and Bertha, and did not know them, spoke of the daughters of the Marquis de Souday with meaning smiles, expressive of hopes, if not of memories. Dowagers crossed themselves on pronouncing their names, and nurses threatened little children when they were naughty with goblin tales of them.

The most indulgent confined themselves to attributing to the twins the three virtues of Harlequin, usually regarded as the attributes of the disciples of Saint-Hubert,—namely, love, gambling, and wine. Others, however, declared that the little castle of Souday was every night the scene of orgies such as chronicles of the regency alone could show. A few imaginative persons went further, and declared that one of its ruined towers — abandoned to the innocent loves of a flock of pigeons — was a repetition of the famous Tour de Nesle, of licentious and homicidal memory.

In short, so much was said about Bertha and Mary that, no matter what had been and then was the purity of their lives and the innocence of their actions, they became an object of horror to the society of the whole region. Through the servants of private houses, through the workmen employed by the bourgeoisie, this hatred and horror of society filtered down among the peasantry, so that the whole population in smocks and wooden shoes (if we except a few old blind men and helpless women to whom the twins had been kind) echoed far and wide the absurd stories invented by the big-wigs. There was not a woodman, not a laborer in Machecoul, not a farmer in Saint-Philbert and Aigrefeuille that did not feel himself degraded in raising his hat to them.

The peasantry at last gave Bertha and Mary a nickname; and this nickname, starting from the lower classes, was adopted by acclamation among the upper, as a just characterization of the lawless habits and appetites attributed to the young girls. They were called the she-wolves (a term, as we all know, equivalent to *sluts*), — the she-wolves of Machecoul.

V

A LITTER OF WOLVES.

THE Marquis de Souday was utterly indifferent to all these signs of public animadversion; in fact, he seemed to ignore their existence. When he observed that his neighbors no longer returned the few visits that from time to time he felt obliged to pay to them, he rubbed his hands with satisfaction at being released from social duties, which he hated and only performed when constrained and forced to do so either by his daughters or by Jean Oullier.

Every now and then some whisper of the calumnies that were circulating about Bertha and Mary reached him; but he was so happy with his factotum, his daughters, and his hounds, that he felt he should be compromising the tranquillity he enjoyed if he took the slightest notice of such absurd reports. Accordingly, he continued to course the hares daily and hunt the boar on grand occasions, and play whist nightly with the two poor calumniated ones.

Jean Oullier was far from being as philosophical as his master; but then it must be said that in his position he heard much more than the marquis did. His affection for the two young girls had now become fanaticism; he spent his life in watching them, whether they sat, softly smiling, in the salon of the château, or whether, bending forward on their horses' necks, with sparkling eyes and animated faces, they galloped at his side, with their long locks floating in the wind from beneath the broad brims of their felt hats and undulating feathers. Seeing them so brave and capable, and at the same time so good and tender to their father and himself, his heart swelled with pride and happiness; he felt himself as having a share in the development of these two admirable creatures, and he wondered why all the world should not be willing to kneel down to them.

Consequently, the first persons who risked telling him of the rumors current in the neighborhood were so sharply rebuked for it that they were frightened and warned others; but Bertha and Mary's true father needed no words to inform him what was secretly believed of the two dear objects of his love. From a smile, a glance, a gesture, a sign, he guessed the malicious thoughts of all with a sagacity that made him miserable. The contempt that poor and rich made no effort to disguise affected him deeply. If he had allowed himself to follow his impulses he would have picked a quarrel with every contemptuous face, and corrected some by knocking them down, and others by a pitched battle. But his good sense told him that Bertha and Mary needed another sort of support, and that blows given or received would prove absolutely nothing in their defence. Besides, he dreaded — and this was, in fact, his greatest fear — that the result of some quarrel, if he provoked it, might be that the young girls would be made aware of the public feeling against them.

Poor Jean Oullier therefore bowed his head before this cruelly unjust condemnation, and tears and fervent prayers to God, the supreme redressor of the cruelties and injustices of men, alone bore testimony to his grief; but in his heart he fell into a state of profound misanthropy. Seeing none about him but the enemies of his two dear children, how could he help hating mankind? And he prepared himself for the day when some future revolution might enable him to return evil for evil.

The revolution of 1830 had just occurred, but it had not given Jean Oullier the opportunity he craved to put these evil designs into execution. Nevertheless, as rioting and disturbances were not yet altogther quelled in the streets of Paris, and might still be communicated to the provinces, he watched and waited.

On a fine morning in September, 1831, the Marquis de Souday, his daughters, Jean Oullier, and the pack — which, though frequently renewed since we made its acquaintance, had not increased in numbers — were hunting in the forest of Machecoul.

It was an occasion impatiently awaited by the marquis, who for the last three months had been expecting grand sport from it, — the object being to capture a litter of young wolves, which Jean Oullier had discovered before their eyes were opened, and which he had, being a faithful and knowing huntsman to a Master of Wolves, watched over and cared for for several months. This last statement may demand some explanations to those of our readers who are not familiar with the noble art of venery.

When the Duc de Biron (beheaded, in 1602, by order of Henri IV.) was a youth, he said to his father at one of the sieges of the religious wars, "Give me fifty cavalry; there's a detachment of two hundred men, sallying out to forage. I can kill every one of them, and the town must surrender." "Suppose it does, what then?" "What then? Why, I say the town will surrender." "Yes; and the king will have no further need of us. We must continue *necessary*, you ninny!" The two hundred foragers were not killed. The town was not taken, and Biron and his son continued "necessary;" that is to say, being necessary they retained the favor and the wages of the king.

Well, it is with wolves as it was with those foragers spared by the Duc de Biron. If there were no longer any wolves how could there be a Wolf-master? Therefore we must forgive Jean Oullier, who was, as we may say, a corporal of wolves, for showing some tender care for the nurslings and not slaying them, them and their mother, with the stern rigor he would have shown to an elderly wolf of the masculine sex.

But that is not all. Hunting an old wolf in the open is

impracticable, and in a battue it is monotonous and tiresome; but to hunt a young wolf six or seven months old is easy, agreeable, and amusing. So, in order to procure this charming sport for his master, Jean Oullier, on finding the litter, had taken good care not to disturb or frighten the mother; he concerned himself not at all for the loss of sundry of the neighbors' sheep, which she would of course inevitably provide for her little ones. He had paid the latter several visits, with touching solicitude, during their infancy, to make sure that no one had laid a disrespectful hand upon them, and he rejoiced with great joy when he one day found the den depopulated and knew that the mother-wolf had taken off her cubs on some excursion.

The day had now come when, as Jean Oullier judged, they were in fit condition for what was wanted of them. He therefore, on this grand occasion, hedged them in to an open part of the forest, and loosed the six dogs upon one of them.

The poor devil of a cub, not knowing what all this trumpeting and barking meant, lost his head and instantly quitted the covert, where he left his mother and brothers and where he still had a chance to save his skin. He took unadvisedly to another open, and there, after running for half an hour in a circuit like a hare, he became very tired from an exertion to which he was not accustomed, and feeling his big paws swelling and stiffening he sat down artlessly on his tail and waited.

He did not have to wait long before he found out what was wanted of him, for Domino, the leading hound, a Vendéan, with a rough gray coat, came up almost immediately and broke his back with one crunch of his jaw.

Jean Oullier called in his dogs, took them back to the starting-point, and ten minutes later a brother of the deceased was afoot, with the hounds at his heels. This one however, with more sense than the other, did not leave the covert, and various sorties and charges, made sometimes by the other cubs and sometimes by the motherwolf, who offered herself voluntarily to the dogs, delayed for a time his killing. But Jean Oullier knew his business too well to let such actions compromise success. As soon as the cub began to head in a straight line with the gait of an old wolf, he called off his dogs, took them to where the cub had broken, and put them on the scent.

Pressed too closely by his pursuers, the poor wolfling tried to double. He returned upon his steps, and left the wood with such innocent ignorance that he came plump upon the marquis and his daughters. Surprised, and losing his head, he tried to slip between the legs of the horses; but M. de Souday, leaning from his saddle, caught him by the tail, and flung him to the dogs, who had followed his doubling.

These successful kills immensely delighted the marquis, who did not choose to end the matter here. He discussed with Jean Oullier whether it was best to call in the dogs and attack at the same place, or whether, as the rest of the cubs were evidently afoot, it would not be best to let the hounds into the wood pell-mell to find as they pleased.

But the mother-wolf, knowing probably that they would soon be after the rest of her progeny, crossed the road not ten steps distant from the dogs, while the marquis and Jean Oullier were arguing. The moment the little pack, who had not been re-coupled, saw the animal, they gave one cry, and, wild with excitement, rushed upon her traces. Calls, shouts, whips, nothing could hold them, nothing stop them. Jean Oullier made play with his legs, and the marquis and his daughters put their horses to a gallop for the same purpose; but the hounds had something else than a timid, ignorant cub to deal with. Before them was a bold, vigorous, enterprising animal, running confidently, as if sure of her haven, in a straight line, indifferent to valleys, rocks, mountains, or water-courses, without fear, without haste, trotting along at an even pace, sometimes surrounded by the dogs, whom she mastered by the power of an oblique look and the snapping of her formidable jaws.

The wolf, after crossing three fourths of the forest, broke out to the plain as though she were making for the forest of Grand'Lande. Jean Oullier had kept up, thanks to the elasticity of his legs, and was now only three or four hundred steps behind the dogs. The marquis and his daughters, forced by the ditches to follow the curve of the paths, were left behind. But when they reached the edge of the woods and had ridden up the slope which overlooks the little village of Marne, they saw, over a mile ahead of them, between Machecoul and La Brillardière, in the midst of the gorse which covers the ground near those villages and La Jacquelerie, Jean Oullier, his dogs, and his wolf, still in the same relative positions, and following a straight line at the same gait.

The success of the first two chases and the rapidity of the ride stirred the blood of the Marquis de Souday.

"Morbleu!" he cried; "I'd give six years of life to be at this moment between Saint-Étienne de Mermorte and La Guimarière and send a ball into that vixen of a wolf."

"She is making for the forest of Grand'Lande," said Mary.

"Yes," said Bertha; "but she will certainly come back to the den, so long as the cubs have not left it. She won't forsake her own wood long."

"I think it would be better to go back to the den," said Mary. "Don't you remember, papa, that last year we followed a wolf which led us a chase of ten hours, and all for nothing; and we had to go home with our horses blown, the dogs lame, and all the mortification of a dead failure?"

"Ta, ta, ta!" cried the marquis; "that wolf wasn't a she-wolf. You can go back, if you like, mademoiselle; as for me, I shall follow the hounds. Corbleu! it shall never be said I wasn't in at the death."

"We shall go where you go, papa," cried both girls together.

"Very good; forward, then!" cried the marquis, vigorously spurring his horse, and galloping down the slope. The way he took was stony and furrowed with the deep ruts of which Lower Poitou keeps up the tradition to this day. The horses stumbled repeatedly, and would soon have been down if they had not been held up firmly; it was evidently impossible to reach the forest of Grand' Lande before the game.

Monsieur de Souday, better mounted than his daughters, and able to spur his beast more vigorously, had gained some rods upon them. Annoyed by the roughness of the road, he turned his horse suddenly into an open field beside it, and made off across the plain, without giving notice to his daughters. Bertha and Mary, thinking that they were still following their father, continued their way along the dangerous road.

In about fifteen minutes from the time they lost sight of their father they came to a place where the road was deeply sunken between two slopes, at the top of which were rows of trees, the branches meeting and interlacing above their heads. There they stopped suddenly, thinking that they heard at a little distance the well-known barking of their dogs. Almost at the same moment a gun went off close beside them, and a large hare, with bloody hanging ears, ran from the hedge and along the road before them, while loud cries of "Follow! follow! tally-ho! tally-ho!" came from the field above the narrow roadway.[1]

The sisters thought they had met the hunt of some of their neighbors, and were about to discreetly disappear, when from the hole in the hedge through which the hare had forced her way, came Rustaud, one of their father's dogs, yelping loudly, and after Rustaud, Faraud, Bellaude, Domino, and Fanfare, one after another, all in pursuit of the wretched hare, as if they had chased that day no higher game.

[1] The English cry "tally-ho" comes from the French cry *taillis au*,— "to the copse," or "covert."

The tail of the last dog was scarcely through the opening before a human face appeared there. This face belonged to a pale, frightened-looking young man, with touzled head and haggard eyes, who made desperate efforts to bring his body after his head through the narrow passage, calling out, as he struggled with the thorns and briars "Tally-ho! tally-ho!" in the same voice Bertha and Mary had heard about five minutes earlier.

VI.

THE WOUNDED HARE.

AMONG the hedges of Lower Poitou (constructed, like the Breton hedges, with bent and twisted branches interlacing each other) it is no reason, because a hare and six hounds have passed through, that the opening they make should be considered in the light of a *porte-cochère;* on the contrary, the luckless young man was held fast as though his neck were in the collar of the guillotine. In vain he pushed and struggled violently, and tore his hands and face till both were bloody; it was impossible for him to advance one inch.

And yet he did not lose courage; he fought on with might and main, until suddenly two peals of girlish laughter arrested his struggles. He looked round, and saw the two riders bending over the pommels of their saddles, and making no effort either to restrain their amusement or conceal the cause of it.

Ashamed of being laughed at by two such pretty girls (he was only twenty), and perceiving how really grotesque his appearance must be, the young man tried to withdraw his head from the hole; but it was written above that that unlucky hedge should be fatal to him either way. The thorns hooked themselves into his clothing and the branches into his game-bag, so that it was literally impossible for him to get back. There he was, caught in the hedge as if in a trap; and this second misfortune only increased the convulsive hilarity of the two spectators.

The luckless youth no longer used mere vigorous energy to free himself from the thicket. His struggles became furious, almost frenzied, and in this last and desperate attempt his face assumed an expression of such pitiable despair that Mary, the gentle one, felt touched.

"We ought not to laugh, Bertha," she said; "don't you see it hurts him?"

"Yes, I see," replied Bertha; "but how can we help it? I can't stop myself."

Then, still laughing, she jumped off her horse and ran to the poor fellow to help him.

"Monsieur," she said, "I think a little assistance may be useful in getting you out of that hedge. Pray accept the help my sister and I are most ready to offer."

But the girl's laughter had pricked the vanity of the youth even more than the thorns had pricked his body; so that no matter how courteously Bertha worded her proposal, it did not make the unfortunate captive forget the hilarity of which he had been the object. So he kept silence; and, with the air of a man resolved to get out of his troubles without the help of any one, he made a last and still more strenuous effort.

He lifted himself by his wrists and endeavored to propel himself forward by the sort of diagonal motion with the lower part of his body that all animals of the snake genus employ. Unluckily, in making this movement his forehead came in contact with the branch of a wild apple-tree, which the shears of the farmer who made the hedge had sharpened like the end of a pike. This branch cut and scraped the skin like a well-tempered razor; and the young man, feeling himself seriously wounded, gave a cry as the blood, spurting freely, covered his whole face.

When the sisters saw the accident, of which they were involuntarily the cause, they ran to the young man, seized him by the shoulders, and uniting their efforts, with a vigor and strength not to be met with among ordinary women, they managed to drag him through the hedge and seat him on the bank. Mary, who could not know that the wound was really a slight one, and only judged by appearances, became very pale and trembling; as for Bertha, less impressionable than her sister, she did not lose her head for a single moment.

"Run to that brook," she said to Mary, "and wet your handkerchief, so that I may wash off the blood that is blinding the poor fellow."

When Mary had done as she was told and had returned with the moistened handkerchief, she asked the young man in her gentle way: —

"Do you suffer much, monsieur?"

"Excuse me, mademoiselle," replied the young man, "but I have so much on my mind at this moment that I do not know whether I suffer most on the inside or the outside of my head." Then suddenly bursting into sobs, with difficulty restrained till then, he cried out, "Ah! the good God has punished me for disobeying mamma!"

Although the youth who spoke was certainly young, — for, as we have said, he was only twenty, — there was something so infantine in his accent and so ludicrously out of keeping with his height and his huntsman's dress in his words, that the sisters, in spite of their compassion for his wound, could not restrain another peal of laughter.

The poor lad cast a look of entreaty and reproach upon them, while two big tears rolled down his cheeks; then he tore from his head, impatiently, the handkerchief wet with water from the brook, which Mary had laid upon his forehead.

"Don't do that!" said Bertha.

"Let me alone!" he cried. "I don't choose to receive attentions I have to pay for in ridicule. I am sorry now I did not follow my first idea and run away, at the risk of getting a worse wound."

"Yes; but as you had the sense not to do so," said Mary, "have sense enough now to let me put that bandage back upon your head."

Picking up the handkerchief she went to him with such

a kindly expression of interest that he, shaking his head, not in sign of refusal but of utter depression, said: —

"Do as you please, mademoiselle."

"Oh! oh!" exclaimed Bertha, who had not lost a single expression on the countenance of the young man; "for a hunter you seem to me rather easily upset, monsieur."

"In the first place, mademoiselle, I am not a hunter, and after what has just happened to me I don't wish ever to become one."

"I beg your pardon," said Bertha, in the same laughing tone which had already provoked the youth, "but judging by the fury with which you assaulted the briers and thorns, and especially by the eagerness with which you urged on our dogs, I think I had every right to at least imagine you a hunter."

"Oh, no, mademoiselle; I am not a hunter. I was carried away by a momentary excitement, which I cannot now at all understand. At present I am perfectly cool, and I know how right my mother was to call the amusement of hunting, which consists in finding pleasure and gratified vanity in the agony and death of a poor, defenceless, dumb animal, ridiculous and degrading."

"Take care, monsieur!" cried Bertha. "To us, who are ridiculous and degraded enough to like that amusement, you seem a good deal like the fox in the fable."

Just then Mary, who had gone a second time to the brook to wet her handkerchief, was about to re-bandage the young man's forehead. But he pushed her away from him angrily.

"In Heaven's name, mademoiselle," he cried, "spare me your attentions! Don't you hear how your sister continues to laugh at me?"

"No, let me tie this on, I beg of you," said Mary.

But he, not allowing himself to be persuaded by the sweetness of her voice, rose to his knees, with the evident intention of escaping altogether. Such obstinacy, which was more that of a child than of a man, exasperated the irascible Bertha; and her irritation, though inspired by the purest feelings of humanity, was none the less expressed in rather too energetic a way for one of her sex.

"Confound it!" she cried, as her father might have done under similar circumstances, "the provoking little fellow won't hear reason! Put on the bandage, Mary; I'll hold his hands, and we'll see if he stirs then."

And Bertha, seizing the young man's wrists with a muscular strength which paralyzed all his efforts to get away, managed to facilitate Mary's task so that she was able to bind the wound and tie the handkerchief, which she did with a nicety that might have done honor to a pupil of Dupuytren or Jobert.

"Now, monsieur," said Bertha, "you are in a fit state to go home, and get away from us, as you are longing to do, without so much as thank you. You can go."

But in spite of this permission and his restored liberty, the youth did not budge. He seemed surprised and also deeply humiliated at having fallen into the hands of two such strong women; his eyes turned from Bertha to Mary and from Mary to Bertha, and still he was unable to find a word to say. At last, seeing no other way out of his embarrassment, he hid his face in his hands.

"Oh!" said Mary, kindly; "do you feel ill?"

The youth made no answer. Bertha gently moved his hands from his face, and finding that he was really weeping, she became as compassionate and gentle as her sister.

"You are more hurt than you seemed to be; is it the pain that makes you cry?" she said. "If so, get on my horse or my sister's, and we will take you home."

But to this the young man eagerly made a sign in the negative.

"Come," said Bertha, "enough of this childish nonsense! We have affronted you; but how could we know that the skin of a girl was under your hunting-jacket. Nevertheless, we were wrong; we admit it, and we beg your pardon.

You may not think we do so in a proper manner; but remember the situation, and say to yourself that sincerity is all you can expect from two girls so neglected by Heaven as to spend their time in the ridiculous amusement which your mother unfortunately disapproves. Now, do you mean to be unforgiving?"

"No, mademoiselle," replied the youth; "it is only with myself that I am annoyed."

"Why so?"

"I can hardly tell you. Perhaps it is that I am ashamed to be weaker than you, — I, a man; perhaps, too, I am all upset at the thought of going home. What can I say to my mother to explain this wound?"

The two girls looked at each other. Women as they were, they would have cared little for such a trifle; but they refrained from laughing, strong as the temptation was, seeing by this time the extreme nervous susceptibility of the young man.

"Well, then," said Bertha, "if you are no longer angry with us, let us shake hands and part friends."

And she held out her hand as a man might have done. The youth was about to reply with a like gesture, when Mary made a sign to call their attention, by lifting her finger in the air.

"Hush!" said Bertha, listening as her sister did, one hand half extended toward that of the young man.

In the distance, but coming rapidly nearer, they heard the sharp, eager, prolonged yelping of hounds, — of hounds that were scenting game. It was the Marquis de Souday's pack, still in pursuit of the wounded hare, which had now doubled on them. Bertha pounced on the young man's gun, the right barrel of which was still loaded. He made a gesture as if to stop a dangerous imprudence, but the young girl only smiled at him. She ran the ramrod hastily down the loaded barrel, as all prudent hunters do when about to use a gun they have not loaded themselves, and finding that the weapon was in proper condition, she advanced a few steps, handling the gun with an ease which showed she was perfectly familiar with the use of it.

Almost at the same moment the hare darted from the hedge, evidently with the intention of returning the way it came; then, perceiving the three persons who stood there, it made a rapid somersault and doubled back. Quick as the movement was Bertha had time to aim; she fired, and the animal, shot dead, rolled down the bank into the middle of the road.

Mary had, meantime, advanced like her sister to shake hands with the young man, and the two stood looking on at what was happening with their hands clasped. Bertha picked up the hare, and returning to the unknown young man who still held Mary's hand, she said, giving him the game: —

"There, monsieur, there's an excuse for you."

"How so?" he asked.

"You can tell your mother that the hare ran between your legs and your gun went off without your knowledge; and you can swear, as you did just now, that it shall never happen again. The hare will plead extenuating circumstances."

The young man shook his head in a hopeless way.

"No," he said, "I should never dare tell my mother I have disobeyed her."

"Has she positively forbidden you to hunt?"

"Oh, dear, yes!"

"Then you are poaching!" said Bertha; "you begin where others finish. Well, you must admit you have a vocation for it."

"Don't joke, mademoiselle. You have been so good to me I don't want to get angry with you; I should only be twice as unhappy then."

"You have but one alternative, monsieur," said Mary; "either tell a lie — which you will not do, neither do we advise it — or acknowledge the whole truth. Believe me, whatever your mother may think of your amusing yourself in defiance of her wishes, your frankness will disarm her. Besides, it is not such a great crime to kill a hare."

"All the same I should never dare to tell her."

"Is she so terrible as all that?" inquired Bertha.

"No, mademoiselle; she is very kind and tender. She indulges all my wishes and foresees my fancies; but on this one matter of guns she is resolute. It is natural she should be," added the young man, sighing; "my father was killed in hunting."

"Then, monsieur," said Bertha, gravely, "our levity has been all the more misplaced, and we regret it extremely. I hope you will forget it and remember only our regrets."

"I shall only remember, mademoiselle, the kind care you have bestowed upon me; and I, in turn, hope you will forget my silly fears and foolish susceptibility."

"No, no, we shall remember them," said Mary, "to prevent ourselves from ever hurting the feelings of others as we hurt yours; for see what the consequences have been!"

While Mary was speaking Bertha had mounted her horse. Again the youth held out his hand, though timidly, to Mary. She touched it with the points of her fingers and sprang into her own saddle. Then, calling in the dogs, who came at the sound of their voices, the sisters gave rein to their horses and rode rapidly away.

The youth stood looking after them, silent and motionless, until they had disappeared round a curve of the road. Then he dropped his head on his breast and continued thoughtful. We will remain a while with this new personage, for we ought to become fully acquainted with him.

VII.

MONSIEUR MICHEL.

WHAT had just happened produced such a powerful impression on the young man's mind that after the girls had disappeared he fancied it must have been a dream.

He was, in fact, at that period of life when even those who are destined to become later the most practical of men pay tribute to the romantic; and this meeting with two young girls, so different from those he was in the habit of seeing, transported him at once into the fantastic world of youth's first dreams, where the imagination wanders as it pleases among the castles built by fairy hands, which topple over beside the path of life as we advance along it.

We do not mean to say, however, that our young man had got as far as falling in love with either of the two amazons, but he felt himself spurred to the keenest curiosity; for this strange mixture of distinction, beauty, elegance of manner, and cavalier virility struck him as extraordinary. He determined to see these girls again, or, at any rate, to find out who they were.

Heaven seemed disposed to satisfy his curiosity at once. He had hardly started on his way home, and was not more than a few hundred steps from the spot where the young girls had left him, when he met an individual in leather gaiters, with a gun and a hunting-horn slung over his blouse and across his shoulders, and a whip in his hand. The man walked fast and seemed much out of temper He was evidently the huntsman who belonged to the young women. Accordingly the youth, assuming his most gracious and smiling manner, accosted him.

"Friend," he said, "you are searching for two young ladies, I think, — one on a brown-bay horse, the other on a roan mare."

"In the first place, I am not your friend, for I don't know you," said the man, gruffly. "I am looking for my dogs, which some fool turned off the scent of a wolf they were after and put on that of a hare, which he missed killing, like the blunderer that he is."

The young man bit his lips. The man in the blouse, whom our readers no doubt recognize as Jean Oullier, went on to say: —

"Yes, I saw it all from the heights of Benaste, which I was coming down when our game doubled, and I'd willingly have given the premium which the Marquis de Souday allows me on the hunt if I could have had that lubber within reach of my whip."

The youth to whom he spoke thought it advisable to make no sign that he was concerned in the affair; he listened, therefore, to Jean Oullier's allocution as if it were absolutely of no interest to him, and said merely: —

"Oh! do you belong to the Marquis de Souday?"

Jean Oullier looked askance at his blundering questioner.

"I belong to myself," said the old Chouan. "I lead the hounds of the Marquis de Souday, as much for my pleasure as for his."

"Dear me!" said the young man, as if speaking to himself, "Mamma never told me the marquis was married."

"Well then," interrupted Oullier, "I tell it you now, my good sir; and if you have anything to say against it, I'll tell you something else, too. Do you hear me?"

Having said these words in a threatening tone, which his hearer seemed not to understand, Jean Oullier, without further concerning himself as to what the other might be thinking, turned on his heel and walked off rapidly in the direction of Machecoul.

Left to himself the young man took a few more steps in the path he had taken when the young girls left him;

then turning to the left he went into a field. In that field was a peasant ploughing. The peasant was a man about forty years of age, who was distinguishable from the peasants of Poitou by a shrewd and sly expression of countenance peculiarly Norman. He was ruddy in complexion, his eyes were keen and piercing; but his constant effort seemed to be to diminish, or rather to conceal, their keenness by perpetually blinking them. He probably thought that proceeding gave a look of stupidity, or at least of good humor, which checked the distrust of others; but his artful mouth, with its corners sharply defined, and curling up like those of an antique Pan, betrayed, in spite of him, that he was one of those wonderful products that usually follow the crossing of Mans and Norman blood.

Although the young man made directly for him, he did not stop his work; he knew the cost of the effort to his horses to start the plough when its motion was arrested in that tough and clayey soil. He therefore continued his way as though he were alone, and it was only at the end of the furrow, when he had turned his team and adjusted his instrument to continue the work, that he showed a willingness to enter into conversation while his horses recovered their wind.

"Well," he said, in a tone that was almost familiar, "have you had good sport, Monsieur Michel?"

The youth, without replying, took the game bag from his shoulder, and dropped it at the peasant's feet. The latter, seeing through the thick netting the yellowish, silky fur of a hare, exclaimed: —

"Ho, ho! pretty good for your first attempt, Monsieur Michel."

So saying, he took the animal from the bag, and examined it knowingly, pressing its belly as if he were not very sure of the precautions so inexperienced a sportsman as Monsieur Michel might have taken.

"Ha! *sapredienne!*" he cried; "the fellow is worth three francs and a half, if he is a farthing. You made a fine shot there, Monsieur Michel; do you know it? You must have found out by this time that it is more amusing to be out with a gun than reading a book, as you are always doing."

"No, upon my word, Courtin, I prefer my books to your gun," said the youth.

"Well, perhaps you are right," replied Courtin, whose face expressed some slight disappointment. "If your late father had thought as you do it might have been better for him, too. But all the same, if I had means and were not a poor devil obliged to work for a living twelve hours out of the twenty-four, I would spend more than my nights in hunting."

"Do you still hunt at night, Courtin?"

"Yes, Monsieur Michel, now and then, for amusement."

"The gendarmes will catch you some night."

"Pooh! they 're do-nothings, those fellows; they don't get up early enough in the morning to catch me." Then, allowing his face to express all its natural cunning, he added, "I know a thing more than they, Monsieur Michel; there are not two Courtins in this part of the country. The only way to prevent me from poaching is to make me a game-keeper like Jean Oullier."

Monsieur Michel made no reply to this indirect proposal, and as he was totally ignorant of who Jean Oullier might be, he did not notice the last part of the sentence any more than the beginning of it.

"Here is your gun, Courtin," he said, holding out the weapon. "Thank you for your idea of lending it to me; you meant well, and it is n't your fault if I don't find as much amusement in hunting as other people do."

"You must try again, Monsieur Michel, and get a liking for it; the best dogs are those that show points last. I 've heard men who will eat thirty dozen oysters at a sitting say they could n't even bear to look at them till they were past twenty. Leave the château with a book, as you did this morning; Madame la baronne won't suspect anything. You'll find me at work about here, and my gun is always at your service. Besides, if I am not too busy, I'll beat the bushes for you. Meantime I'll put the tool in the rack."

Courtin's "rack" was merely the hedge which divided his field from his neighbors. He slipped the gun into it and drew the twigs and briers together, so as to hide the place from a passing eye, and also to keep his piece from rain and moisture, — two things, however, to which a true poacher pays little attention, so long as he still has candle-ends and a bit of linen.

"Courtin," said Monsieur Michel, endeavoring to assume a tone of indifference, "did you know that the Marquis de Souday was married?"

"No, that I didn't," said the peasant.

"And has two daughters?" continued Michel.

Courtin, who was still finishing his work of concealment by twisting a few rebellious branches, raised his head quickly and looked at the young man with such fixedness that although the latter had only asked his question out of vague curiosity he blushed to the very whites of his eyes.

"Have you met the she-wolves?" asked Courtin. "I thought I heard that old Chouan's horn."

"Whom do you call the she-wolves?" said Michel.

"I call those bastard girls of the Marquis de Souday the she-wolves," replied Courtin.

"Do you mean to say you call those two young girls by such a name?"

"Damn it! that's what they're called in all the country round. But you've just come from Paris, and so you don't know. Where did you meet the sluts?"

The coarseness with which Courtin spoke of the young ladies frightened the timid youth so much that, without exactly knowing why, he lied.

"I have not met them," he said.

By the tone of his answer Courtin doubted his words.

"More's the pity for you," he answered. "They are

pretty slips of girls, good to see and pleasant to hug." Then, looking at Michel and blinking as usual, he added, "They say those girls are a little too fond of fun; but that's the kind a jolly fellow wants, does n't he, Monsieur Michel?"

Without understanding the cause of the sensation, Michel felt his heart more and more oppressed as the brutal peasant spoke with insulting approval of the two charming amazons he had just left under a strong impression of gratitude and admiration. His annoyance was reflected in his face.

Courtin no longer doubted that Michel had met the she-wolves, as he called them, and the youth's denial made the man's suspicions as to what the truth might be go far beyond reality. He was certain that the marquis had been within an hour or two close to La Logerie, and it seemed quite probable that Monsieur Michel should have seen Bertha and Mary, who almost always accompanied their father when he hunted. Perhaps the young man might have done more than see them, perhaps he had spoken with them; and, thanks to the estimation in which the sisters were held, a conversation with the Demoiselles de Souday would only mean the beginning of an intrigue.

Going from one deduction to another, Courtin, who was logical in mind, concluded that his young master had reached that point. We say "his young master," because Courtin tilled a farm which belonged to Monsieur Michel. The work of a farmer, however, did not please him; what he coveted was the place of keeper or bailiff to the mother and son. For this reason it was that the artful peasant tried by every possible means to establish a strong relation of some kind between himself and the young man.

He had evidently just failed of his object in persuading Michel to disobey his mother in the matter of hunting. To share the secrets of a love affair now struck him as a part very likely to serve his interests and his low ambitions. The moment he saw the cloud on Monsieur Michel's brow he felt he had made a mistake in echoing the current calumnies, and he looked about him to recover his ground.

"However," he said, with well-assumed kindliness, "there are always plenty of people to find more fault, especially in the matter of girls, than there is any occasion for. Mademoiselle Bertha and Mademoiselle Mary —"

"Mary and Bertha! Are those their names?" asked the young man, eagerly.

"Mary and Bertha, yes. Mademoiselle Bertha is the dark one, and Mademoiselle Mary the fair one."

He looked at Monsieur Michel with all the acuteness of which his eyes were capable, and he thought the young man slightly blushed as he named the fair one.

"Well, as I was saying," resumed the persistent peasant, "Mademoiselle Mary and Mademoiselle Bertha are both fond of hunting and hounds and horses; but that does n't prevent them from being very good girls. Why, the late vicar of Benaste, who was a fine sportsman, did n't say mass any the worse because his dog was in the vestry and his gun behind the altar."

"The fact is," said Monsieur Michel, forgetting that he gave the lie to his own words, — "the fact is, they both look sweet and good, particularly Mademoiselle Mary."

"They are sweet and good, Monsieur Michel. Last year, during that damp, hot weather, when the fever came up from the marshes and so many poor devils died of it, who do you think nursed the sick without shirking, when even some of the doctors and the veterinaries deserted their posts? Why, the she-wolves, as they call them. They did n't do their charity in church, no! They went to the sick people's houses; they sowed alms and reaped blessings. Though the rich hate them, and the nobles are jealous of them, I make bold to say that the poor folk are on their side."

"Why should any one think ill of them?" asked Michel.

"Who knows? Nobody gives any real reason. Men, don't you see, Monsieur Michel, are like birds. When one is sick and in the dumps all the others come about him and pluck out his feathers. What is really true in all this is that people of their own rank fling mud and stones at those poor young ladies. For instance, there's your mamma, who is so good and kind, — is n't she, Monsieur Michel? Well, if you were to ask her she would tell you, like all the rest of the world, 'They are bad girls.'"

But, in spite of this change of front on Courtin's part, Monsieur Michel did not seem disposed to enter into the subject farther. As for Courtin himself, he thought enough had been said to pave the way for future confidences. As Monsieur Michel seemed ready to leave him, he started his horses and accompanied him to the end of the field. He noticed, as they went along, that the young man's eyes were often turned on the sombre masses of the Machecoul forest.

VIII.

THE BARONNE DE LA LOGERIE.

COURTIN was respectfully lowering for his young master the bars which divided his field from the road when a woman's voice, calling Michel, was heard beyond the hedge. The young man stopped short and trembled at the sound.

At the same moment the owner of the voice appeared on the other side of the hedge fence which separated Courtin's field from that of his neighbor. This person, this lady, may have been forty to forty-five years of age. We must try to *explain* her to the reader.

Her face was insignificant, and without other character than an air of haughtiness which contrasted with her otherwise common appearance. She was short and stout; she wore a silk dress much too handsome for the fields, and a gray cambric hat, the floating ends of which fell upon her forehead and neck. The rest of her apparel was so choice that she might have been paying a visit in the Chaussée-d'Antin or the faubourg Saint-Honoré. This was, apparently, the person of whose reproaches the young man stood so much in awe.

"What!" she exclaimed, "you here, Michel? Really, my son, you are very inconsiderate, and you show very little regard for your mother. The bell has been ringing more than an hour to call you in to dinner. You know how I dislike to be kept waiting, and how particular I am that our meals should be regular; and here I find you tranquilly talking to a peasant."

Michel began to stammer an excuse; but, almost at the same instant his mother's eye beheld what Courtin had either not noticed or had not chosen to remark upon, — namely, that the young man's head was bound up with a handkerchief, and that the handkerchief had blood-stains upon it, which his straw hat, although its brim was wide, did not effectually conceal.

"Good God!" she cried, raising a voice, which in its ordinary key was much too high. "You are wounded! What has happened to you? Speak, unfortunate boy! don't you see that I am dying of anxiety?"

Climbing the fence with an impatience, and, above all, an agility which could scarcely have been expected of one of her age and corpulence, the mother of the youth came up to him, and before he could prevent her, took the hat and the handkerchief from his head.

The wound, thus disturbed by the tearing away of the bandage, began to bleed again. Monsieur Michel, as Courtin called him, unprepared for the explanation he so much dreaded, and which was now forced upon him suddenly, stood silent and confused, unable to reply. Courtin came to his aid. The wily peasant saw at once that the youth, fearing to tell his mother that he had disobeyed her, was also unwilling to tell a lie. As he himself had no scruples on that point, he resolutely burdened his conscience with the sin that, in his innocence, Michel dared not commit.

"Oh! Madame la baronne need not be anxious; it is nothing, absolutely nothing."

"But I wish to know how it happened. Answer for him yourself, Courtin, if monsieur is determined to keep silence."

The young man was still dumb.

"It is easily told, Madame la baronne," replied Courtin. "I had a bundle of branches I took off last autumn; it was so heavy I could n't lift it on to my shoulders alone, and Monsieur Michel had the kindness to help me. One branch of the cursed thing got loose and scratched him on the forehead, as you see."

"Scratch! that's more than a scratch! you came near putting his eye out. Another time, Maître Courtin, get your equals to load your fagots; do you hear me? It was a very improper proceeding in itself, besides nearly maiming my son."

Courtin humbly bowed his head, as if recognizing the enormity of his offence; but that did not prevent him from giving the hare, which lay near the game-bag, a vigorous kick, which threw it out of sight under the hedge.

"Come, Monsieur Michel," said the baroness, who seemed appeased by the peasant's submissiveness, "you must go and see the doctor about that wound." Then turning back, after she had taken a few steps, she added, "By the bye, Courtin, you have not paid your mid-summer rent, and yet your lease expires at Easter. Remember that. I am determined not to keep tenants who are not regular in their payments."

Courtin's expression of countenance was more humble than ever; but it changed when the mother, getting over the fence with less agility than before, left the son free to whisper to Courtin: —

"I'll be here to-morrow."

In spite of the threat just made to him, Courtin seized the handle of his plough with more gayety than usually belonged to his disposition, and started upon a new furrow, while his betters returned to the château. For the rest of the day's work he enlivened his horses by singing to them "La Parisienne," a patriotic song then much in vogue.

While Courtin sings the above-mentioned hymn, much to the satisfaction of his steeds, let us say a few words as to the Michel family. You have seen the son, my dear readers, and you have seen the mother. The mother was the widow of one of those government purveyors who had made, at the cost of the State, rapid and considerable fortunes out of the Imperial armies; the soldiers nicknamed them "Rice-bread-salt."

The family name of this purveyor was Michel. He came originally from the department of Mayenne, and was the son of a peasant and the nephew of a village schoolmaster. The latter, by adding a few notions of arithmetic to the reading and writing he imparted to him gratuitously, did actually decide his nephew's future career.

Taken by the first draft, in 1794, Michel the peasant joined the 22d brigade with very little enthusiasm. This man, who later became a distinguished accountant, had already calculated his chances of being killed and of becoming a general. The result of his calculation did not altogether satisfy him, and he therefore, with much adroitness, made the most of his fine handwriting (also due to his uncle, the schoolmaster) to get a place as clerk in the quartermaster's department. He felt as much satisfaction in obtaining that position as another man would have felt at promotion.

It was there, at the base of supplies, that Michel, the father, went through the campaigns of 1792 and 1793. Toward the middle of the latter year General Rossignol, who was sent to either pacify or exterminate La Vendée, having accidentally come across Michel, the clerk, in one of the offices, and hearing from him that he was a native of those regions and that all his friends were in the Vendéan ranks, bethought himself of utilizing this providential circumstance. He gave Michel an indefinite furlough, and sent him home with no other instructions than to take service among the Chouans and do for him, from time to time, what Monsieur de Maurepas did for His Majesty Louis XV., — that is to say, give him the *news of the day*. Michel, who found great pecuniary advantages in this commission, fulfilled it with scrupulous fidelity, not only for General Rossignol but for all his successors.

This anecdotical correspondence was at its height, when

General Travot was sent to La Vendée. We all know the result of his operations; they were the subject of the opening chapters of this book. Here is a recapitulation of them: the Vendéan army defeated, Jolly killed, Couetu enticed into an ambush and taken by a traitor whose name has never been known, Charette made prisoner in the woods of La Chabotière and shot in the market-place of Nantes.

What part did Michel play in the successive vicissitudes of that terrible drama? We may find an answer to that question later; it is certain that soon after the last bloody episodes Michel, still recommended for his beautiful handwriting and his infallible arithmetic, entered, as clerk, the office of a very celebrated army contractor.

There he made rapid progress, for in 1805 we find him contracting on his own account to supply forage to the army of Germany. In 1806 his shoes and gaiters took an active part in the heroic campaign of Prussia. In 1809 he obtained the entire victualling of the army that entered Spain. In 1810 he married the only daughter of another contractor and doubled his fortune with her dowry.

Besides all this, he changed his name, — or rather lengthened it, — which was, for those whose names were too short, the great ambition of that period. This is how the coveted addition was managed.

The father of Monsieur Michel's wife was named Baptiste Durand. He came from the little village of La Logerie, and to distinguish him from another Durand who often crossed his path, he called himself Durand de la Logerie. At any rate, that was the pretext he gave. His daughter was educated at one of the best schools in Paris, where she was registered on her arrival as Stéphanie Durand de la Logerie. Once married to this daughter of his brother contractor, Monsieur Michel thought that his name would look better if his wife's name were added to it. He accordingly became Monsieur Michel de la Logerie.

Finally, at the Restoration, a title of the Holy Roman

Empire, bought for cash, enabled him to call himself the Baron Michel de la Logerie, and to take his place, once for all, in the financial and territorial aristocracy of the day.

A few years after the return of the Bourbons, — that is to say, about 1819 or 1820, — Baron Michel de la Logerie lost his father-in-law, Monsieur Durand de la Logerie. The latter left to his daughter, and consequently to her husband, his estate at La Logerie, standing, as the details given in preceding chapters will have told the reader, about fifteen miles from the forest of Machecoul. The Baron Michel de la Logerie, like the good landlord and seigneur that he was, went to take possession of his estate and show himself to his vassals. He was a man of sense; he wanted to get into the Chamber. He could do that only by election, and his election depended on the popularity he might gain in the department of the Lower Loire.

He was born a peasant; he had lived twenty-five years of his life among peasants (barring the two or three years he was in the quartermaster's office), and he knew exactly how to deal with peasants. In the first place, he had to make them forgive his prosperity. He made himself what is called "the good prince," found a few old comrades of the Vendéan days, shook hands with them, spoke with tears in his eyes of the deaths of poor Monsieur Jolly and dear Monsieur Couetu and the worthy Monsieur Charette. He informed himself about the needs of the village, which he had never before visited, had a bridge built to open important communication between the department of the Lower Loire and that of La Vendée, repaired three county roads and rebuilt a church, endowed an orphan asylum and a home for old men, received so many benedictions, and found such pleasure in playing this patriarchal part that he expressed the intention of living only six months of the year in Paris and the other six at his Château de la Logerie.

Yielding, however, to the entreaties of his wife, who,

being unable to understand the violent passion for country life which seemed to have come over him, wrote letter after letter from Paris to hasten his return, he yielded, we say, to her so far as to promise to return on the following Monday. Sunday was to be devoted to a grand battue of wolves in the woods of La Pauvrière and the forest of Grand'Lande, which were infested by those beasts. It was, in fact, another philanthropic effort on the part of Baron Michel de la Logerie.

At the battue Baron Michel still continued to play his part of a rich, good fellow. He provided refreshments for all, ordered two barrels of wine to be taken on handcarts after the trail, that every one might drink who would; he ordered a positive banquet for the whole party to be ready at an inn on their return, refused the post of honor at the battue, expressed the wish to be treated as the humblest huntsman, and his ill-luck in drawing lots having bestowed upon him the worst place of all, bore his misfortune with a good-humor that delighted everybody.

The battue was splendid. From every covert the beasts came; on all sides guns resounded with such rapidity that the scene resembled a little war. Bodies of wolves and boars were piled up beside the handcarts bearing the wine-barrels, not to speak of contraband game, such as hares and squirrels, which were killed in this battue, as at other battues, under the head of *vermin*, and carefully hidden away, to be fetched during the night.

The intoxication of success was such that the hero of the day was forgotten. It was not until after the last beating-up was over that Baron Michel was missed. Inquiries were made. No one had seen him since the morning; in fact, not since he had drawn the lot which gave him the worst place at the extreme end of the hunt. On making this discovery, it was supposed that finding his chance of amusement very slight, and being solicitous for the entertainment of his guests, he had gone back to the little town of Légé, where the feast was to be given.

But when the huntsmen arrived at Légé they found that the baron was not there. Most of them being tired and hungry sat down to the supper table without him; but a few — five or six — others, feeling uneasy, returned to the woods of La Pauvrière with torches and lanterns and began to search for him.

At the end of two hours' fruitless effort, he was found dead in the ditch of the second covert they had drawn. He was shot through the heart.

This death caused great excitement and many rumors. The police of Nantes investigated it. The huntsman whose place was directly below that of the baron was arrested. He declared that, although he was distant only one hundred and fifty steps from the baron, a corner of the wood concealed them from each other, and he had seen and heard nothing. It was also proved that this man's gun had not been fired that day; moreover, from the place where he stood he could only have hit Baron Michel on the right, whereas the latter had, as a matter of fact, been shot on the left.

The inquiry, therefore, went no farther. The death of the ex-contractor was attributed to accident; it was supposed that a stray ball had struck him (as sometimes happens when game is driven), without evil intention on the part of whoever fired it. And yet, in spite of this explanation, a vague rumor got about of some accomplished revenge. It was said — but said in the lowest whisper, as if each tuft of gorse still concealed the gun of a Chouan — it was said that a former soldier of Jolly or Couetu or Charette had made the unfortunate purveyor expiate the betrayal and death of those illustrious leaders; but there were too many persons interested in the secret to let it ever be openly asserted.

The Baronne Michel de la Logerie was left a widow, with one son. She was one of those women of negative virtues of which the world is full. Of vices she did not possess a spark; of passions she was so far ignorant of their very name. Harnessed at seventeen to the marriage plough, she had plodded along in the conjugal furrow without swerving to the right nor yet to the left, and never so much as asking herself if there were any other road. The idea had never crossed her mind that a woman could revolt against the goad. Relieved of the yoke, she was frightened by her liberty, and instinctively looked about her for new chains. These chains religion gave her; and then, like all narrow minds, she took to vegetating in false, exaggerated, and, at the same time, conscientious devotion.

Madame la Baronne Michel sincerely believed herself a saint; she went regularly to church, kept all the fasts, and was faithful to all the injunctions of the Church. Had any one told her that she sinned seven times a day she would have been greatly astonished. Yet nothing was more true. It is certain that if the humility of Madame la Baronne de la Logerie had been dissected she would have been found at every hour of the day to disobey the precepts of the Saviour of men; for (little ground as she had for it) her pride of rank amounted to mania. We have seen how the sly peasant Courtin, who called the son Monsieur Michel, never failed to give the mother her title of baroness.

Naturally, Madame de la Logerie held the world and the epoch in holy horror; she never read a police report in her newspaper without accusing both (the world and the epoch) of the blackest immorality. To hear her, one would suppose the Iron age dated from 1800. Her utmost care was therefore directed to save her son from the contagion of the ideas of the day by bringing him up at a distance from the world and all its dangers. Never would she listen to the idea of his entering any sort of public school; even those of the Jesuits were dangerous in her eyes, from the readiness of the good fathers to accommodate themselves to the social obligations of the young men confided to their care. Though the heir of all the Michels received some lessons from masters, which, so far as arts and sciences go, were indispensable to the education of a young man, it was always in presence of the mother and on a plan approved by her; for she alone directed the course of ideas and instruction, especially on the moral side, which were given to her son.

A strong infusion of intelligence, which by great good luck nature had placed in the youth's brain, was needed to bring him safe and sound out of the torture to which she had subjected him for over ten years. He did come through it, as we have seen, though feeble and undecided, and with nothing of the strength and resolution which should characterize a man, — the representative of vigor, decision, and intellect.

IX.

GALON-D'OR AND ALLÉGRO.

As Michel had foreseen and feared, his mother scolded him vigorously. She was not duped by Courtin's tale; the wound on her son's forehead was by no means a scratch made by a thorn. Ignorant of what interest her son could have in concealing the matter from her, and quite convinced that even if she questioned him she should not get at the truth, she contented herself by fixing her eyes steadily from time to time on the mysterious wound, and shaking her head with a sigh and a scowl of the maternal forehead.

During the whole dinner Michel was ill at ease, lowering his eyes and scarcely eating; but it must be said that his mother's incessant examination was not the only thing that troubled him. Hovering between his lowered eyelids and his mother's suspecting eyes were two forms, two visions. These visions were the twin shadows of Bertha and of Mary.

Michel thought of Bertha with some slight irritation. Who was this Amazon who handled a gun like a trained huntsman, who bandaged wounds like a surgeon, and who, when she found her patient refractory, twisted his wrists with her white and womanly hands as Jean Oullier might have done with his hard and calloused ones?

But on the other hand, how charming was Mary, with her fine blond hair and her beautiful blue eyes! how sweet her voice, how persuasive its accents! With what gentleness she had touched his wound, washed off the blood, and bound the bandage! Michel scarcely regretted the wound, for without it there was no reason why the young ladies should have spoken to him or, indeed, have taken any notice of him.

It was true that his mother's displeasure and the doubts he had raised in her mind were really the more serious matter; but he persuaded himself that her anger would soon pass off, whereas the thing that would not pass was the impression left on his heart during the few seconds when he held Mary's hand clasped closely in his own. All hearts when they begin to love and yet are not aware of it crave solitude; and for this reason no sooner was dinner over than, profiting by a moment when his mother was discoursing with a servant, he left the room, not hearing or not heeding the words with which she called after him.

And yet those words were important. Madame de la Logerie forbade her son to go near the village of Saint-Christophe-du-Ligneron, where, as she had learned from a servant, a bad fever was raging. She at once put the château under quarantine, and forbade that any one from the infected village should approach it. The order was enforced immediately in the case of a young girl who came to ask assistance of the baroness for her father, just attacked by the fever.

If Michel's mind had not been so pre-occupied he would undoubtedly have paid attention to his mother's words, for the sick man was his foster-father, a farmer named Tinguy, and the girl who had come to ask help was his foster-sister, Rosine, for whom he had the greatest affection. But at this moment his thoughts were all rushing toward Souday, and more especially to that charming creature who bore the name of Mary.

He buried himself in the remotest woodland of the park, taking with him a book as an excuse; but though he read the book attentively till he reached the edge of the forest he would have been puzzled to tell you the name of it had you asked him. Once hidden from his mother's eyes he sat down on a bench and reflected.

What was he reflecting about? Easy to answer. He

was thinking how he could contrive to see Mary and her sister again. Chance had thrown them together once, but chance had taken her time about it, for he had been over six months in the neighborhood. If it pleased chance to be another six months without giving the young baron a second meeting with his new friends the time would be too long for the present state of his heart.

On the other hand, to open communications with the château de Souday himself was hardly feasible. There had never been any sympathy between the Marquis de Souday, an *émigré* of 1790, and the Baron de la Logerie, a noble of the Empire. Besides, Jean Oullier, in the few words he had exchanged with him, had shown plainly there was no disposition to make his acquaintance.

But the young girls, they who had shown him such interest, masterful in Bertha, gentle in Mary, how could he reach the young girls? This indeed was difficult, for though they hunted two or three times a week, they were always in company of their father and Jean Oullier.

Michel resolved to read all the novels in the library of the château, hoping to discover from them some ingenious method which, as he began to fear, his own mind, limited to its own inspirations, could never furnish. At this stage of his reflections a touch was laid upon his shoulder; looking round with a quiver he saw Courtin; the farmer's face expressed a satisfaction he did not take any pains to conceal.

"Beg pardon, excuse me, Monsieur Michel," said the man; "seeing you as still as a milestone, I thought it was your statue instead of yourself."

"Well, you see it is I, Courtin."

"And I'm glad of it, Monsieur Michel; I was anxious to hear what passed between you and Madame la baronne."

"She scolded me a little."

"Oh! I was sure of that. Did you tell her anything about the hare?"

"I took good care not to."

"Or the wolves?"

"What wolves?" asked the young man not ill-pleased to bring the conversation to this point.

"The she-wolves of Machecoul; I told you that was the nickname for the young ladies at Souday."

"Of course I did not tell her; you know that, Courtin. I don't think the Souday hounds and those of La Logerie can hunt together."

"In any case," replied Courtin, in the sneering tone which, in spite of his best efforts, he was sometimes unable to conceal, "if your hounds won't hunt with the Souday pack you, as it seems, can hunt with theirs."

"What do you mean by that?"

"Look!" pulling toward him and, as it were, bringing on the stage two coupled hounds which he held in a leash.

"What are they?" asked the young baron.

"They? Why, Galon-d'Or and Allégro, to be sure."

"I don't know who Galon-d'Or and Allégro are."

"The dogs of that brigand Jean Oullier."

"Why did you take his dogs?"

"I did n't take them; I simply put them in the pound."

"By what right?"

"By two rights: land-owner's rights, and mayor's rights."

Courtin was mayor of the village of La Logerie, which contained about a score of houses, and he was very proud of the title.

"Please explain those rights, Courtin."

"Well, in the first place, Monsieur Michel, I confiscate them as mayor because they hunt at an illegal season."

"I did not know there was an illegal season for hunting wolves; besides as Monsieur de Souday is Master of wolves —"

"That's very true; as Master of wolves he can hunt wolves in the forest of Machecoul, but not on the plain. Besides, as you know yourself," continued Courtin, with a sneering smile, "as you saw yourself, he was not hunting a wolf at all, but a hare — and moreover, that hare was shot by one of his own *cubs*."

The young man was on the point of telling Courtin that the word *cub* applied to the Demoiselles de Souday was offensive to him, and of requesting him not to use it again, but he dared not make so firm a remonstrance.

"It was Mademoiselle Bertha who killed it, Courtin," he said, "but I had previously wounded it; so I am the guilty person."

"Pshaw! what do you mean by that? Would you have fired on the hare if the hounds were not already coursing it? No, of course not. It is the fault of the dogs that you fired, and that Mademoiselle Bertha killed the game; and it is therefore the dogs that I punish as mayor for pursuing hares under pretence of hunting wolves. But that's not all; after punishing them as mayor I punish them as — proprietor. Do you suppose I gave Monsieur le marquis' dogs the right to hunt over my land?"

"Your land, Courtin!" said Michel, laughing; "you are a trifle mistaken; it was over my land, or rather my mother's, that they were trespassing."

"That's no matter, Monsieur le baron, inasmuch as I farm it. You must remember that we are no longer in 1789, when the great lords had a right to ride with their hounds over the harvests of the poor peasants and trample everything down without paying for it; no, no, no, indeed! this is the year 1832, Monsieur Michel; every man is master of the soil he lives on, and game belongs to him who supports it. The hare coursed by the dogs of the marquis is my hare, for it has fed on the wheat in the fields I hire from Madame la baronne, and it is I alone who have the right to eat that hare which you wounded and the she-wolf killed."

Michel made an impatient movement which Courtin detected out of the corner of his eye; but the youth did not dare to further express his displeasure.

"There is one thing that surprises me," he said, "and that is why those dogs that are straining so at the leash ever allowed you to catch them."

"Oh!" said Courtin, "that did not give me any trouble.

After I left you and Madame la baronne at the bars, I came back and found these gentlemen at dinner."

"At dinner?"

"Yes, in the hedge, where I left the hare; they found it and they were dining. It seems they are not properly fed at the château de Souday. Just see the state my hare is in."

So saying, Courtin took from the huge pocket of his jacket the hindquarters of the hare, which formed the incriminating proof of the misdemeanor; the head and shoulders were eaten off.

"And to think," said Courtin, "that they did it in just that minute of time while I was with you and madame! Ah! you scamps, you'll have to help me kill a good many to make me forget that."

"Courtin, let me tell you something," said the young baron.

"Tell away, don't be backward, Monsieur Michel."

"It is that as you are a mayor you ought to respect the laws."

"Laws! I wear them on my heart. Liberty! Public order! Don't you know those words are posted over the door of the mayor's office, Monsieur Michel?"

"Well, so much the more reason why I should tell you that what you are doing is not legal, and threatens liberty and public order."

"What!" exclaimed Courtin. "Shall the hounds of those she-wolves hunt over my land at a prohibited season, and I not be allowed to put them in the pound?"

"They were not disturbing public order, Courtin; they were simply injuring private interests; you have the right to lodge a complaint against them, but not to put them in the pound."

"Oh! that's too round-about a way; if hounds are to be allowed to run where they like and we can only lodge complaints against them, then it isn't men who have liberty, but dogs."

"Courtin," said the youth, with a touch of the assumption observable in men who get a smattering of the Code, "you make the mistake that a great many persons make; you confound liberty with independence; independence is the liberty of men who are not free, my friend."

"Then what is liberty, Monsieur Michel?"

"Liberty, my dear Courtin, is the sacrifice that each man makes of his personal independence for the good of all. It is from the general fund of independence that each man draws his liberty; we are free, Courtin, but not independent."

"Oh, as for me," said Courtin, "I don't know anything about all that. I am a mayor and the holder of land; and I have captured the best hounds of the Marquis de Souday's pack, Galon-d'Or and Allégro, and I shall not give them up. Let him come after them, and when he does I shall ask him what he has been doing in certain meetings at Torfou and Montaigu."

"What do you mean?"

"Oh, I know what I mean."

"Yes, but I don't."

"There is no reason why you should know; you are not a mayor."

"No, but I am an inhabitant of the place and I have an interest in knowing what happens."

"As for that, it is easy to see what is happening; these people are conspiring again."

"What people?"

"Why, the nobles! the — but I'd better hold my tongue, though you are not exactly their style of nobility, you."

Michel reddened to the whites of his eyes.

"You say the nobles are conspiring, Courtin?"

"If not, why do they have these secret meetings at night. If they meet in the day-time, the lazy fellows, to eat and drink, that's all well enough; the law allows it and there's nothing to be said. But when they meet at night it is for no good end, you may be sure. In any case they had better look out; I've got my eye upon them, and I'm the mayor; I may not have the right to put the dogs in the pound, but I have the right to put the men in prison; I know the Code plain enough as to that."

"And you say Monsieur de Souday frequents those meetings?"

"Goodness! do you suppose he does n't? — an old Chouan and a former aide-de-camp of Charette like him! Let him come and claim his dogs; yes, let him come! and I'll send him to Nantes, him and his cubs; they shall be made to explain what they are about, roaming the woods as they do at night."

"But," exclaimed Michel, with an eagerness there was no mistaking, "you told me yourself, Courtin, that if they went about at night it was to help the poor sick people."

Courtin stepped back a pace and pointing his finger at his young master he said with his sneering laugh:—

"Ha! ha! I've caught you."

"Me!" said the young man, coloring, "how have you caught me?"

"Well, they've caught you."

"Caught me!"

"Yes, yes, yes! And I don't blame you either; whatever else these young ladies may be, I must say they are pretty. Come, you need n't blush that way; you are not just out of a seminary; you are neither a priest, nor a deacon, nor a vicar; you are a handsome lad of twenty. Go ahead, Monsieur Michel; they'll have very poor taste if they don't like you when you like them."

"But, my dear Courtin," said Michel, "even supposing what you say were true, which it is not, I don't know these young ladies; I don't know the marquis. I can't go and call there just because I have happened to meet those young girls once on horseback."

"Oh, yes, I understand," said Courtin, in his jeering way; "they have n't a penny, but they've fine manners. You want a pretext, an excuse for going there, don't you?

Well, look about and find one; you, who talk Greek and Latin and have studied the Code, you ought to be able to find one."

Michel shook his head.

"Oh!" said Courtin, "then you have been looking for one?"

"I did not say so," said the young baron, hastily.

"No, but I say so; a man isn't so old at forty that he can't remember what he was at twenty."

Michel was silent and kept his head lowered; the peasant's eye weighed heavily upon him.

"So you couldn't find a way? Well, I've found one for you."

"You!" cried the youth eagerly, looking up. Then, recognizing that he had let his secret thoughts escape him, he added, shrugging his shoulders: "How the devil do you know that I want to go to the castle?"

"Well, the way to do it," said Courtin, seeing that his master made no attempt to deny his wish, "the way is this —"

Michel affected indifference, but he was listening with all his ears.

"You say to me, 'Père Courtin, you are mistaken as to your rights; you cannot, either as mayor or the holder of property put the Marquis de Souday's dogs in the pound; you have a right to an indemnity, but this indemnity must be amicably agreed upon.' To which I, Père Courtin, reply: 'If you are concerned in it, Monsieur Michel, I agree; I know your generosity.' On which you say: 'Courtin, you must give me those dogs; the rest is my affair.' And I reply: 'There are the dogs, Monsieur Michel; as for the indemnity, hang it! a gold piece or two will play the game, and I don't want the death of the sinner.' Then, don't you see? you write a bit of a note to the marquis; you have found the dogs, and you send them back by Rousseau or La Belette, for fear he should be anxious. He can't help thanking you and inviting you to call and see him. Perhaps, however. to make quite sure, you had better take the dogs back yourself."

"That will do, Courtin," said the young baron. "Leave the dogs with me; I'll send them to the marquis, not to make him invite me to the castle, for there's not a word of truth in all you have been supposing, but because, between neighbors, it is a courteous thing to do."

"Very good, — so be it; but, all the same, they are two pretty slips, those girls. As for the indemnity — "

"Ah, yes," said the young baron, laughing, "that's fair; you want the indemnity for the injury the hounds did you by passing over my land and eating up half the hare which Bertha killed."

And he gave the farmer what he happened to have in his pocket, which was three or four louis. It was lucky for him there was no more, for he was so delighted at finding a way to present himself at the château de Souday that he would willingly have given the farmer ten times that sum if by chance it had been in his purse.

Courtin cast an appreciative eye on the golden louis he had just received under the head of "indemnity," and putting the leash in the hand of the young man he went his way.

But after going a few steps he turned round and came back to his master.

"Don't mix yourself up too much with those people, Monsieur Michel," he said. "You know what I told you just now about those *messieurs* at Torfou and Montaigu; it is all true, and mark my words, in less than fifteen days there'll be a fine row."

This time he departed for good, singing "La Parisienne," for the words and tune of which he had a great predilection.

The young man was left alone with the two dogs.

86 THE LAST VENDÉE.

X.

IN WHICH THINGS DO NOT HAPPEN PRECISELY AS BARON
MICHEL DREAMED THEY WOULD.

OUR lover's first idea was to follow Courtin's original advice and send the dogs back to the Marquis de Souday by Rousseau and La Belette, two serving-men belonging partly to the château and partly to the farm, who owed the nicknames by which Courtin has presented them to the reader, one to the ruddy color of his hair, the other to the resemblance of his face to that of a weasel whose obesity La Fontaine has celebrated in one of his prettiest fables.

But after due reflection the young man feared that the Marquis de Souday might content himself with sending a simple letter of thanks and no invitation. If, unfortunately, the marquis should act thus, the occasion was lost; he would have to wait for another; and one so excellent as this could not be expected to happen every day. If, on the contrary, he took the dogs back himself he must infallibly be received; a neighbor would never be allowed to bring back valuable strayed dogs in person, over a distance of ten or a dozen miles, without being invited in to rest, and possibly, if it was late, to pass the night at the castle.

Michel pulled out his watch; it was a little after six. We think we mentioned that Madame la Baronne Michel had preserved, or rather had taken a habit of dining at four o'clock. In her father's house Madame la baronne had dined at mid-day. The young baron had therefore ample time to go to the castle.

But it was a great resolution to take; and decision of character was not, as we have already informed the reader, the predominating feature in Monsieur Michel's character. He lost a quarter of an hour in hesitation. Fortunately, in these May days the sun did not set till eight o'clock. Besides, he could properly present himself as late as nine.

But then — perhaps the young ladies after a hunting-day would go to bed early ? It was not, of course, the marquis whom the baron wanted to see. He would n't have gone a mile for that purpose; whereas to see Mary he felt he could march a hundred. So at last he decided to start at once.

Only, and this was indeed a hindrance, he suddenly perceived that he had no hat. To get it he must return to the château, at the risk of encountering his mother and all her cross-questioning, — whose dogs were those? where was he going ? etc.

But did he really want a hat ? The hat, that is, the lack of it, would be set down to neighborly eagerness; or else the wind had taken it; or else a branch had knocked it down a ravine, and he could not follow it on account of the dogs. At any rate, it was worse to encounter his mother than to go without his hat; accordingly he started, hatless, leading the dogs in the leash.

He had hardly made a dozen steps before he discovered that it would not take him the seventy-five minutes he had calculated to get to Souday. No sooner were the hounds aware of the direction in which their new leader was taking them than it was all he could do to hold them back. They smelt their kennel, and dragged at the leash with all their might; if harnessed to a light carriage they would have made the distance in half an hour. The young man, forced to keep up with them at a trot, would certainly do it in three-quarters.

After twenty minutes of this lively gait Michel reached the forest of Machecoul, intending to make a short cut through it. It was necessary to mount a rather steep slope before entering the wood, and when he reached the top he halted to get his breath. Not so with the dogs, who got their breath while running and wanted to keep on their way. The baron opposed this desire by planting himself firmly on his feet and leaning back while they dragged him forward. Two equal forces neutralize each other, — that is one of the first principles of mechanics. The young baron was the stronger, therefore he neutralized the force of the two dogs.

This done, and quiet resulting, he took out his handkerchief to mop his forehead. While he did so, enjoying the cool freshness of the breeze as it breathed on his face from the invisible lips of evening, he fancied he heard a cry wafted upon that breeze. The dogs heard it too, and they answered it with that long, mournful cry of a lost animal. Then they began to pull at their chain with fresh energy.

The baron was now rested and his forehead was mopped; he was therefore quite as ready as Galon-d'Or and Allégro to continue the way; instead of leaning back he leaned forward, and his little jog-trot was resumed.

He had scarcely gone a few hundred steps before the same cry, or rather call, was repeated, but very much nearer and therefore more distinct than the first. The dogs answered by a long howl and a more determined drag on their collars. The young man now felt certain that the cry proceeded from some one in search of the dogs, and he bawled to them (*hauler*). We beg pardon of our readers for using so unacademic a word, but it is the one our peasants use to represent the peculiar shout of a huntsman calling in his dogs. It has the advantage of being expressive; and besides (for a last and better reason), I know no other.

About six hundred paces farther on the same cry was repeated for the third time by the seeking man and the missing hounds. This time Galon-d'Or and Allégro tore along with such vigor that their conductor was almost carried off his feet, and was forced to make his jog-trot a quick trot and his quick trot a gallop.

He had scarcely kept along at that pace for three minutes before a man appeared among the trees, jumped the ditch beside the road, and barred the baron's way. The man was Jean Oullier.

"Ah, ha!" he cried; "so it's you, my pretty man, who not only turn my dogs off the trail of the wolf I am hunting to that of a hare you're after, but actually couple them, and lead 'em in a leash!"

"Monsieur," said the young man, all out of breath, "if I have coupled them and led them it is to have the honor of returning them to Monsieur le Marquis de Souday myself."

"Ho! yes, that's a likely story, — with no hat on your head! You need n't trouble yourself any further, my good sir. Now you've met me I'll take them back myself."

So saying, and before Monsieur Michel had time to oppose or even guess his intention, Jean Oullier wrenched the chain from his hand and threw it on the necks of the hounds, very much as we throw a bridle on the neck of a horse. Finding themselves at liberty the dogs darted at full speed in the direction of the castle, followed by Jean Oullier, whose pace was equal to theirs as he cracked his whip and shouted: —

"Kennel! kennel, scamps!"

The whole scene was so rapid that dogs and man were nearly out of sight before the young baron recovered himself. He stopped short helplessly in the roadway, and must have been there ten minutes, gazing, with his mouth open, in the direction Jean Oullier and the dogs had taken, when the soft and caressing voice of a young girl said close beside him: —

"Gracious goodness! Monsieur le baron, what are you doing here at this hour, bare-headed?"

What he was doing, the young man would have been rather puzzled to say; in point of fact he was following his hopes, which had flown away in the direction of the castle, whither he dared not follow them. He turned round to see who spoke to him, and recognized his foster-sister, the daughter of the farmer Tinguy.

"Oh, it is you, Rosine, is it?" he said; "what are you doing here yourself?"

"Monsieur le baron," said the girl, in a tearful voice, "I have just come from the château de la Logerie, where Madame la baronne treated me very unkindly."

"Why so, Rosine? You know my mother loves you and takes care of you."

"Yes, as a general thing; but not to-day."

"Why not to-day?"

"She has just had me turned out of the house."

"Why did n't you ask for me?"

"I did ask for you, Monsieur le baron, but they said you were not at home."

"I was at home; I have only just come out, my dear; for fast as you may have come, I'll answer for it I came faster!"

"Maybe; it is likely enough, Monsieur le baron; for when Madame was so cruel to me I thought I would come and ask the wolves to help me, but could n't decide at once to do so."

"What help can the *wolves* give you?"

Michel forced himself to utter the word.

"The help I wanted Madame la baronne to give me, for my poor father who is very ill."

"What is the matter with him?"

"A fever he caught in the marshes."

"A fever?" repeated Michel; "is it a malignant fever, — intermittent or typhoid?"

"I don't know, Monsieur le baron."

"What does the doctor say?"

"Oh, goodness! the doctor lives at Palluau; he won't trouble himself to come here under five francs, and we are not rich enough to pay five francs for a doctor's visit."

"And did n't my mother give you any money?"

"Why, I told you she would n't even see me! 'A fever!' she said; 'and Rosine dares to come to the château when her father has a fever? Send her away.'"

"Oh, impossible!"

"I heard her, Monsieur le baron, she spoke so loud; besides, the proof is that they turned me out of the house."

"Wait, wait!" cried the young man eagerly, "I'll give you the money." He felt in his pockets. Then he remembered that he had given Courtin all he had with him. "Confound it! I have n't a penny on me," he said. "Come back with me to the château, Rosine, and I'll give you all you want."

"No, no!" said the young girl; "I would n't go back for all the gold in the world! No, my resolution is taken: I shall go to the wolves; they are charitable; they won't turn away a poor girl who wants help for a dying father."

"But — but," said the young man, hesitating, "I am told they are not rich."

"Who are not rich?"

"The Demoiselles de Souday."

"Oh! it is n't money people ask of them, — it is n't alms they give; it is something better than that, and God knows it."

"What is it, then?"

"They go themselves when people are sick; and if they can't cure them, they comfort them in dying, and mourn with those who are left."

"Yes," said the young man, "that may be for ordinary illness, but when it is a dangerous fever — "

"They would n't mind that, — not they! There's nothing dangerous to kind hearts. I shall go to them, and you'll see they'll come. If you stay here ten minutes more you'll see me coming back with one or other of the sisters, who will help me nurse my father. Good-bye, Monsieur Michel. I never would have thought Madame la baronne could be so cruel! To drive away like a thief the daughter of the woman who nursed you!"

The girl walked on and the young man made no answer; there was nothing he could say. But Rosine had dropped a word which remained in his mind: "If you stay here ten minutes you will see me coming back with one or other of the sisters." He resolved to stay. The opportunity he had lost in one direction came back to him from another. Oh! if only Mary should be the one to come out with Rosine!

But how could he suppose that a young girl of eighteen, the daughter of the Marquis de Souday, would leave her home at eight o'clock at night and go five miles to nurse a poor peasant ill of a dangerous fever? It was not only improbable, but it was actually impossible. Rosine must have made the sisters better than they were, just as others made them worse.

Besides, was it believable that his mother, noted for her piety and claiming all the virtues, could have acted in this affair just the reverse of two young girls of whom so much evil was said in the neighborhood? But if things should happen as Rosine said, wouldn't that prove that these young girls had souls after God's own heart? Of course, however, it was quite certain that neither of them would come.

The young man was repeating this for the tenth time in as many minutes when he saw, at the angle of the road round which Rosine had disappeared, the shadows of two women. In spite of the coming darkness he saw that one was Rosine; but as for the person with her, it was impossible to recognize her identity, for she was wrapped in a large mantle.

Baron Michel was so perplexed in mind, and his heart above all was so agitated, that his legs failed him, and he stood stock-still till the girls came up to him.

"Well, Monsieur le baron," said Rosine, with much pride, "what did I tell you?"

"What did you tell him?" said the girl in the mantle.

Michel sighed. By the firm and decided tone of voice he knew she was Bertha.

"I told him that I shouldn't be turned away from your house as I was from the château de la Logerie," answered Rosine.

"But," said Michel, "perhaps you have not told Mademoiselle de Souday what is the matter with your father."

"From the symptoms," said Bertha, "I suppose it is typhoid fever. That is why we have not a minute to lose; it is an illness that requires to be taken in time. Are you coming with us, Monsieur Michel?"

"But, mademoiselle," said the young man, "typhoid fever is contagious."

"Some say it is, and others say it is not," replied Bertha, carelessly.

"But," insisted Michel, "it is deadly."

"Yes, in many cases; though it is often cured."

The young man went close up to Bertha.

"Are you really going to expose yourself to such a danger?" he said.

"Of course I am."

"For an unknown man, a stranger to you?"

"Those who are strangers to us," said Bertha, with infinite gentleness, "are fathers, brothers, husbands, to other human beings. There is no such thing as a stranger in this world, Monsieur Michel; even to you this man may be something."

"He was the husband of my nurse," stammered Michel.

"There! you see," said Bertha, "you can't regard him as a stranger."

"I did offer to go back to the château with Rosine and give her the money to get a doctor."

"And she refused, preferring to come to us? Thank you, Rosine," said Bertha.

The young man was dumfounded. He had heard of charity, but he had never seen it; and here it was embodied in the form of Bertha. He followed the young girls thoughtfully, with his head down.

"If you are coming with us, Monsieur Michel," said Bertha, "be so kind as to carry this little box, which contains the medicines."

"No," said Rosine, "Monsieur le baron can't come with

us, for he knows what a dread madame has of contagious diseases."

"You are mistaken, Rosine," said the young man; "I am going with you."

And he took the box from Bertha's hands. An hour later they all three reached the cottage of the sick man.

XI.

THE FOSTER-FATHER.

THE cottage stood, not in the village but on the outskirts of it, a gunshot distant or thereabouts. It was close to a little wood, into which the back-door opened.

The goodman Tinguy — that was the term usually applied to Rosine's father — was a Chouan of the old type. While still a lad, he fought through the first war in La Vendée under Jolly, Couëtu, Charette, La Rochejaquelein, and others. He was afterwards married and had two children. The eldest, a boy, had been drafted, and was now in the army; the youngest was Rosine.

At the birth of each child the mother, like other poor peasant-women, had taken a nursling. The foster-brother of the boy was the last scion of a noble family of Maine, Henri de Bonneville, who will presently appear in this history. The foster-brother of Rosine was, as we have already said, Michel de la Logerie, one of the chief actors in our drama.

Henri de Bonneville was two years older than Michel; the two boys had often played together on the threshold of the door that Michel was about to cross, following Bertha and Rosine. Later on they met in Paris; and Madame de la Logerie had encouraged the intimacy of her son with a young man of large fortune and high rank in the Western provinces.

These foster-children had greatly eased the circumstances of the Tinguy family; but the Vendéan peasant is so constituted that he never admits that he is comfortably off. Tinguy was now making himself out poor at the expense of his life. Ill as he was, nothing would have induced him to send to Palluau for a doctor, whose visit would have cost him five francs. Besides, no peasant, and the Vendéan peasant least of all, believes in a doctor or in medicine. This was why Rosine, when they wanted help, applied first at the château de la Logerie, as foster-sister of the young baron, and then, being driven thence, to the Demoiselles de Souday.

At the noise the young people made on entering the sick man rose on his elbow, with difficulty, but immediately fell back on the bed with a piteous moan. A candle was burning, which lighted the bed only; the rest of the room was in darkness. The light showed, on a species of cot or pallet, a man over fifty years of age, struggling in the grasp of the demon of fever. He was pale to lividness; his eyes were glassy and sunken, and from time to time his body shook from head to foot, as if it had come in contact with a galvanic battery.

Michel shuddered at the sight. He understood at once why his mother, fearing contagion, and knowing that Rosine must come from that bedside impregnated with the miasmas of the disease, which were floating almost visibly in the circle of light around that dying bed, was unwilling to let Rosine enter the château. He wished for camphor, or chloride of lime, or some disinfectant to isolate the sick man from the well man, but having nothing of the kind he stood as near the door as he could to breathe the fresh air.

As for Bertha, she seemed to pay no attention to all that; she went straight to the patient and took his hand. Michel made a motion as if to stop her, and opened his lips to utter a cry; but he was, in a measure, petrified by the boldness of her charity, and he kept his place silently, in admiring terror.

Bertha questioned the sick man. He replied that in the morning, when he rose he had felt so weary that his legs gave way under him when he attempted to walk. This was a warning given by Nature; but the peasantry seldom pay heed to such advice. Instead of getting back into bed and sending for a doctor, Tinguy dressed himself, went down into the cellar for a pot of cider, and cut himself a slice of bread, — to "strengthen him up," as he said. His pot of cider tasted good, but he could not eat the bread. Then he went to his work in the fields.

As he went along, he had terrible pains in his head and a bleeding at the nose; his weariness was excessive, and he was forced to sit down once or twice. When he came to a brook he drank of it; but this did not slake his thirst, which was so great that he even drank the water out of a puddle. When at last he reached his field he had not the strength to put a spade into the furrow he had begun the night before, and he stood for some moments leaning on his tool. Then his head turned, and he lay down, or rather fell down on the ground in a state of utter prostration.

There he remained till seven in the evening, and might have stayed all night if a peasant from the little town of Légé had not happened to come along. Seeing a man lying in the field, he called to him. Tinguy did not answer, but he made a movement. The peasant went nearer and recognized him. With great difficulty he got the sick man home; Tinguy was so feeble that it took him over an hour to go half a mile.

Rosine was watching for him anxiously. When she saw him she was frightened, and wished to go to Palluau and fetch the doctor; but her father positively forbade it, and went to bed, declaring it would be nothing and the next day he should be well. But as his thirst, instead of lessening, continued to increase, he told Rosine to put a pitcher of water by his bedside for the night. He spent the night thus, devoured by thirst, and drinking incessantly without allaying the fever that burned within him. The next morning he tried to rise; but he no sooner sat up in bed than his head, in which he complained of violent shooting pains, became dizzy, and he was seized with a violent pain in the right side.

Rosine insisted on going for M. Roger (that was the name of the doctor at Palluau); but again her father forbade her. The girl then stayed quietly by his bed, ready to obey his wishes and serve his needs. His greatest need was for drink; every ten minutes he asked for water.

Matters went on thus till four in the afternoon. Then the sick man shook his head and said, "I see I have got a bad fever; you must go and get me some help from the good ladies at the castle." We know the results of Rosine's expedition.

After feeling the sick man's pulse and listening to this account of his illness, given with great difficulty, Bertha, who counted above a hundred pulsations, was sure that Tinguy was in a dangerous state. What the exact nature of the fever was she was too ignorant of the science of medicine to decide. But as the sick man was constantly crying for "Drink! drink!" she cut a lemon in slices, boiled it in a potful of water, sweetened it slightly, and let the sick man drink it in place of pure water.

It is to be remarked that when she wanted to sweeten the infusion Rosine told her there was no sugar in the house; sugar, to a Vendéan peasant, is the supreme of luxury. Fortunately, the provident Bertha had put a few lumps into the little box which contained her medicines. She cast her eyes about her in search of the box, and saw it under the arm of the young man, who was still standing near the door.

She made him a sign to come to her; but before he could obey she made him another sign to stay where he was. Then she went up to him herself, laying a finger on her lips, and said in a low voice, so that the patient might not hear her: —

"The man's condition is very serious. I dare not take much upon myself. It is absolutely necessary to have a doctor, and even so, I fear it will be too late. Will you go to Palluau, dear Monsieur Michel, and fetch Doctor Roger? Meantime I will give Tinguy something to quiet him."

"But you — you?" said the young baron, anxiously.

"I shall stay here; you will find me when you get back. I have some important things to say to the patient."

"Important things?" said Michel, astonished.

"Yes."

"But —" insisted the young man.

"I assure you," interrupted the young girl, "that every minute's delay is of consequence. Taken in time these fevers are often fatal; neglected, as this has been, there is little hope. Go at once, — at once, and bring back the doctor."

"But," persisted the young man, "suppose the fever is contagious?"

"What then?"

"Won't you run great risk of taking it?"

"My dear monsieur," said Bertha, "if we stopped to think about such things half the sick peasants would die. Come, go; and trust to God to take care of me."

She held out her hand to him; the young man took it. Carried away by the admiration he felt at seeing in a woman a grand and simple courage of which he, a man, was incapable, he pressed his lips with a sort of passion upon it.

The movement was so rapid and unexpected that Bertha quivered, turned very pale, and sighed as she said: —

"Go, friend; go!"

She did not need, this time, to reiterate her order. Michel sprang from the cottage. A mysterious fire seemed to run through his veins and doubled his vital power; he felt a strange, new force within him. He fancied he was capable of accomplishing miracles; it seemed to him that like the antique Mercury, wings had grown upon his head and heels. If a wall had barred the way he would have scaled it; if a river were flowing across his path, without bridge or ford, he would have swum it, not stopping to fling off his clothes. He only regretted that Bertha had asked him to do so easy a thing; he would fain have had obstacles, some difficult — nay, impossible — quest! How could Bertha be grateful to him for only going a few miles to fetch a doctor? A few miles! when he longed to go to the end of the world for her! Why could n't he give some proof of heroism which might match his courage with Bertha's own?

Of course, in such a state of exaltation the young baron never dreamed of fatigue. The three and a half miles to Palluau were done in less than half an hour. Doctor Roger was a familiar visitor at the château of La Logerie, which is hardly an hour's distance from Palluau. Michel had only to send up his name before the doctor, who had gone to bed called out that he would be ready in five minutes.

At the end of that time he appeared in the salon, and asked the young man what could possibly bring him there at that unusual time of night. In two words Michel told the doctor the state of the case; and as M. Roger seemed a good deal surprised at his taking so lively an interest in a peasant as to come on foot, at night, with an agitated manner and bathed in perspiration, the young baron hastened to explain his interest by the ties of affection which naturally bound him to his foster-father.

Questioned by the doctor as to the symptoms of the illness, Michel repeated faithfully all he had heard, and begged M. Roger to take with him the necessary remedies, — the village of Légé not yet having attained to the civilization of possessing an apothecary. Noticing that the young baron was reeking with perspiration, and finding that he had come on foot, the doctor, who had already ordered his horse to be saddled, changed the order and had him harnessed to his carriole.

Michel was most anxious to prevent this arrangement; he declared that he could go on foot much faster than the doctor could go on horseback. He was, in fact, so powerful, with that valiant vigor of youth and heart, that he probably could have done so as fast, or even faster, than the doctor on his horse. The doctor insisted, Michel refused; and the discussion ended by his darting out of the house and calling back to Monsieur Roger: —

"Come as fast as you can. I'll announce your coming!"

The doctor began to think that Madame de la Logerie's son was mad. He said to himself that he should soon overtake him, and did not change the order for the carriole.

It was the thought of appearing before the eyes of the young girl in a carriole which so exasperated the lover. He fancied Bertha would feel more grateful to him if she saw him arrive all out of breath and open the cottage door, crying out, "Here I am! the doctor is following me!" than if she saw him driving up in a carriole, accompanying the doctor. On horseback, on a fine courser, mane and tail flying in the wind, his arrival announced by snorts and neighs, it would have been another thing; but in a carriole! — ten thousand times better go on foot! A first love teems with poesy, and it feels a bitter hatred to the prosaic. What would Mary think when her sister told her she had sent the young baron to Palluau for Doctor Roger, and that the young baron had returned in the doctor's carriole!

No, no; better a thousand times, as we have said, arrive on foot. The young fellow understood very well that this first appearance on the stage of love with heaving breast and ardent eyes, dust on his clothes, hair streaming in the wind, was good, good, and well done. As for the patient, heavens! he was well-nigh forgotten, we must admit, in the midst of this excitement; at any rate, it was not of him that Michel thought, but of the two sisters. His poor foster-father would not have driven him across the country at the rate of seven miles an hour; it was Bertha, it was Mary. The exciting cause in this grand physiological cataclysm now taking place in our hero had become a mere accessory. Michel, under the name of Hippomenes, struggling for the prize with Atalanta, had no need to drop the golden apples on his way. He laughed to scorn the idea that the doctor and his horse could overtake him; and he felt a sensation of physical delight as the cold night-wind chilled the moisture on his brow. Overtaken by the doctor! Sooner death than that!

It had taken him half an hour to go; it took him twenty-five minutes to return.

As though Bertha had expected or divined this impossible celerity, she had gone to the threshold of the door to await her messenger. She knew that in all probability he could not be back till half an hour later, and yet she went out to listen for him. She thought she heard steps in the far distance. Impossible! it could not be he already; and yet she never doubted that it was he.

In fact, a moment later she saw him looming, appearing, then clearly defined upon the darkness, while at the same time he, with his eyes fixed on the door, all the while doubting them, saw her standing there motionless, her hand on her heart, which, for the first time in her life, was beating violently.

When he reached her the youth, like the Greek of Marathon, was voiceless, breathless, and came near dropping, if not as dead as the Greek, at least in a faint. He had only strength to say: —

"The doctor is following me."

Then, in order not to fall, he leaned with his hand against the wall. If he could have said more he might have cried: —

"You will tell Mademoiselle Mary, won't you? that it was for love of her and of you that I have done seven miles in fifty minutes."

But he could not speak; so that Bertha believed, and had ground for believing, that it was for love of her, and her alone, that the young messenger had performed his feat. She smiled with pleasure. Drawing her handkerchief from her pocket, she said, softly wiping the young man's forehead, and taking great care not to touch his wound: —

"Good heavens! how sorry I am that you took my request to hasten so much to heart! What a state you are in!" Then scolding him like a mother, she added in a tender tone, "What a child you are!"

That word "child" was said in a tone of such indescribable tenderness that it made Michel quiver. He seized Bertha's hand; it was moist and trembling. Just then the sound of wheels was heard on the high-road.

"Ah! here is the doctor," she cried, pushing away the young man's hand.

Michel looked at her in amazement. Why did she push away his hand? He was, of course, unable to give a clear account to himself of what was passing in a girl's mind; but he felt, instinctively, that although she repulsed him it was not from dislike or anger.

Bertha went back into the cottage, no doubt to prepare for the doctor's arrival. Michel stayed at the door to receive him. When he saw him coming along in his wicker vehicle, which shook him grotesquely, the young fellow congratulated himself more than ever for having come on foot. It was true that if Bertha had gone in, as she had just done, when she heard the wheels she would not have seen him in that vulgar trap. But if he had not already returned would she, or would she not, have waited till he came?

Michel told himself that it was more than probable she would have waited, and he felt in his heart, if not the warm satisfactions of love, at any rate the soft ticklings of vanity.

XII.

NOBLESSE OBLIGE.

WHEN the doctor entered the room Bertha was beside the patient. The first thing that met M. Roger's eyes was her graceful form, like those of the angels in German legends bending forward to receive the souls of the dying. He knew her at once, for he was rarely called to the cottages of the poor that he did not find either her or her sister between death and the dying.

"Oh, doctor," she said, "come quick! poor Tinguy is delirious."

The patient was under much excitement. The doctor went to him.

"Come, friend," said he, "be calm."

"Let me alone! let me alone!" cried Tinguy. "I must get up; they want me at Montaigu."

"No, dear Tinguy," said Bertha, "no; they are not expecting you just yet."

"Yes, mademoiselle; yes, they are! It was for to-night. Who will go from house to house and carry the news if I'm not there?"

"Hush, Tinguy, hush!" said Bertha; "remember you are ill, and Doctor Roger is here."

"Doctor Roger is one of us, mademoiselle; we can talk before him. He knows they are waiting for me; he knows I must get up at once. I must go to Montaigu."

Doctor Roger and the young girl looked at each other.

"*Massa*," said the doctor.

"*Marseille*," replied Bertha.

And then, with a spontaneous movement, they shook hands.

Bertha returned to the patient.

"Yes," she said, bending to his ear, "you are right. The doctor is one of us; but there is some one else here who is not." She lowered her voice so that only Tinguy could hear. "And that," she added, "is the young Baron Michel."

"Ah, true," said the goodman. "Don't let him hear anything. Courtin is a traitor. But if I don't go to Montaigu, who will?"

"Jean Oullier. Don't worry, Tinguy."

"Oh! if Jean Oullier will go," said the sick man, — "if Jean Oullier will go I need not. His foot's good, and his eye true; he can fire straight, he can!"

And he burst out laughing; but in that laugh he seemed to expend his last vital strength and fell backward on the bed.

The young baron had listened to this dialogue (of which he could only hear portions) without in the least understanding it. All he distinctly made out was, "Courtin is a traitor," and from the direction of the young girl's eye as she spoke with the peasant he was certain that they were talking of him. His heart contracted; they had some secret in which they would not let him share. He went up to Bertha.

"Mademoiselle," he said, "if I am in your way, or if you have no further need of me, say the word and I retire."

He spoke in a tone of so much pain that Bertha was touched.

"No," she said, "stay. We need you still; you must help Rosine to prepare M. Roger's prescriptions while I talk with him about the case." Then to the doctor she said, in a low voice, "Keep them busy, and you can tell me what you know, and I will tell you what I know." Turning again to Michel she added, in her sweetest voice,

"I know, my dear friend, that you will be willing to help Rosine."

"As long as you wish, mademoiselle; give your orders and I will obey them," said the young man.

"You see, doctor," said Bertha, smiling, "you have two willing helpers."

The doctor went out to his vehicle and returned with a bottle of Sedlitz water and a package of mustard.

"Here," he said to Michel, giving him the bottle, "uncork that and make him drink half a glassful every ten minutes. And you, Rosine," giving her the mustard, "mix that into a paste with hot water; it is to be put on the soles of your father's feet."

The sick man had dropped back into the state of apathetic indifference which preceded the excitement Bertha had calmed by assuring him that Jean Oullier would take his place. The doctor cast a look at him, and seeing that in his present state of quiescence he could safely be left to the care of the young baron, he went eagerly up to Bertha.

"Mademoiselle de Souday," he said, "since it seems that we hold the same opinions, what news have you?"

"Madame left Massa on the 21st of last April, and she ought to have landed at Marseille on the 29th or 30th. This is now the 6th of May. Madame must have disembarked, and the whole South ought by this time to have risen."

"Is that all you know?" asked the doctor.

"Yes, all," replied Bertha.

"You have not read the evening papers of the 3d?"

"We do not get any papers at the château de Souday," she said.

"Well," said the doctor, "the whole thing failed."

"Is it possible! Failed?"

"Yes, Madame was utterly misled."

"Good God! what are you telling me?"

"The exact truth. Madame, after a prosperous voyage in the 'Carlo Alberto,' landed on the coast at some little distance from Marseille. A guide awaited her and took her to a lonely house in the woods. Madame had only six persons with her — "

"Oh! go on; go on!"

"She sent one of those persons to Marseille to inform the leader of the movement that she had landed and was awaiting the result of the promises which had brought her to France — "

"Well?"

"That evening the messenger came back with a note, congratulating the princess on her safe arrival, and saying that Marseille would rise on the following day — "

"Yes; what then?"

"The next day an attempt was made, but Marseille would not rise at all. The people would take no part in the affair, which failed utterly."

"And Madame?"

"It is not known where she is; but they hope she re-embarked on the 'Carlo Alberto.'"

"Cowards!" muttered Bertha. "I am nothing but a woman; but oh! I swear to God that if Madame comes into La Vendée I will set an example to some men. Good-bye, doctor, and thank you."

"Must you go?"

"Yes; it is important that my father should know this news. He is at a meeting to-night at the château de Montaigu. I must get back to Souday. I commit my poor patient to you. Leave exact directions, and I or my sister, unless something unforeseen prevents, will be here to-morrow and watch at night."

"Will you take my carriage? I can get back on foot, and you can return it by Jean Oullier, or any one, to-morrow."

"Thank you, no; I don't know where Jean Oullier may be to-morrow. Besides, I prefer walking; the air will do me good."

Bertha held out her hand to the doctor, pressed his with

almost masculine strength, threw her mantle over her shoulders, and left the cottage. At the door she found Michel, who, although he could not hear the conversation, had kept his eye on the young girl, and, seeing that she was about to depart, got to the door before her.

"Ah! mademoiselle," he exclaimed, "what has happened? What have you just heard?"

"Nothing," said Bertha.

"Nothing! If you had heard nothing you would not be starting off in such a hurry, without a word to me, — without so much as signing to me, or saying good-bye."

"Why should I say good-bye, inasmuch as you are going with me? When we reach the gate of Souday will be time enough to bid you good-bye."

"What! will you allow me?"

"To accompany me? Certainly. After all you have done for me this evening, it is your right, my dear Monsieur Michel, — that is, unless you are too fatigued."

"I, mademoiselle, too fatigued, when it is a matter of accompanying you! With you, or with Mademoiselle Mary, I would go to the end of the world. Fatigued? Heavens, no!"

Bertha smiled, murmuring to herself, "What a pity he is not one of us!" Then she added under her breath, "One could do as one pleased with a nature like his."

"Are you speaking?" said Michel. "I did not quite catch what you say."

"I spoke very low."

"Why do you speak low?"

"Because what I was saying cannot be said out loud, — not yet, at least."

"But later?"

"Ah! later, perhaps — "

The young man in turn moved his lips, and made no sound.

"What does that pantomime mean?" asked Bertha.

"It means that I can speak below my breath as you do, with this difference, that what I say low I am ready to say out loud and instantly, — at this very moment if I dared — "

"I am not a woman like other women," said Bertha, with an almost disdainful smile; "and what is said to me in a low voice may equally well be said aloud."

"Well then, what I was saying below my breath was this; I grieve to see you flinging yourself into danger, — danger as certain as it is useless."

"What danger are you talking about, my dear neighbor?" said the girl, in a slightly mocking tone.

"That about which you were speaking to Doctor Roger just now. An uprising is to take place in La Vendée."

"Really?"

"You will not deny that, I think."

"I? — why should I deny it?"

"Your father and you are taking part in it."

"You forget my sister," said Bertha, laughing.

"No, I forget no one," said Michel, with a sigh.

"Go on."

"Let me tell you — as a tender friend, a devoted friend — that you are wrong."

"And why am I wrong, my tender, my devoted friend," asked Bertha, with the tinge of satire she could never quite eliminate from her nature.

"Because La Vendée is not in 1832 what she was in 1793; or rather, because there is no longer a Vendée."

"So much the worse for La Vendée! But, happily, there is always the Noblesse, — you don't yet know, Monsieur Michel, but your children's children in the sixth generation will know the meaning of the words NOBLESSE OBLIGE."

The young man made a hasty movement.

"Now," said Bertha, "let's talk of something else; for on this topic I will not say another word, inasmuch as you are not — as poor Tinguy says — one of us."

"But," said the young man, hurt by Bertha's tone toward him, "what shall we talk about?"

"Why, anything, — everything. The night is magnificent, talk to me of the night; the moon is brilliant, talk of the moon; the stars are dazzling, tell me about the stars; the heavens are pure, let us talk of the heavens."

She raised her head and let her eyes rest on the clear and starry firmament. Michel sighed; he said nothing, and walked on beside her. What could he say — that man of books and city walls — about the nature that seemed her fitting kingdom? Had he, like Bertha, been in contact from his infancy with the wonders of creation? Had he watched, like her, the gradations through which the dawn ascends and the sun sinks down? Did his ear know, like hers, the mysterious sounds of night? When the lark rang out its reveille did he know what the lark was saying? When the gurgle of the nightingale filled the darkness with harmony could he tell what that throat was uttering? No, no. He knew the things of science, which Bertha did not know; but Bertha knew the things of nature, and of all such things he was ignorant. Oh! if the young girl had only spoken then, how religiously his heart would have listened to her.

But, unfortunately, she was silent. Her heart was full of thoughts which escaped in looks and sighs, and not in sounds and words.

He, too, was dreaming. He walked beside the gentle Mary, not the harsh, firm Bertha; instead of the self-reliant Bertha, he felt the weaker Mary leaning on his arm. Ah! if she were only there words would come; all the thousand things of the night — the moon, the stars, the sky — would have rushed to his lips. With Mary he would have been the teacher and the master; with Bertha he was the scholar and the slave.

The two young people walked silently side by side for more than a quarter of an hour, when suddenly Bertha stopped and made a sign to Michel to stop also. The young man obeyed; with Bertha his place was to obey.

"Do you hear?" said Bertha.

"No," said Michel, shaking his head.

"Well, I hear," she said, her eyes gleaming and her ears alert, as she strained them eagerly.

"What do you hear?"

"My horse's step and that of my sister Mary's horse. They are coming for me. Something must have happened." She listened again. "Mary has come herself."

"How can you tell that?" asked the young man.

"By the way the horses gallop. Let us walk faster, please."

The sounds came nearer, and in less than five minutes a dark group showed in the distance. Soon it was seen to be two horses, — a woman riding one and leading the other.

"I told you it was my sister," said Bertha.

The young man had already recognized her, less by her person, scarcely distinguishable in the darkness, than by the beating of his heart.

Mary, too, had recognized him, and this was plain from the gesture of amazement which escaped her. It was evident that she expected to find her sister alone or with Rosine, — certainly not with the young baron. Michel saw the impression his presence had produced, and he advanced.

"Mademoiselle," he said to Mary, "I met your sister on her way to carry assistance to poor Tinguy, and in order that she might not be alone I have accompanied her."

"You did perfectly right, monsieur," replied Mary.

"You don't understand," said Bertha, laughing. "He thinks he must excuse me or excuse himself. Do forgive him for something; his mamma is going to scold him." Then leaning on Mary's saddle, and speaking close to her ear, "What is it, darling?" she asked.

"The attempt at Marseille has failed."

"I know that; and Madame has re-embarked."

"That's a mistake."

"A mistake?"

"Yes. Madame declares that as she is in France she will stay."

"Can it be true?"

"Yes; and she is now on her way to La Vendée, — in fact, she may actually be here now."

"How did you hear all this?"

"Through a message received from her to-night at the château de Montaigu, just as the meeting was about to break up disheartened."

"Gallant soul!" cried Bertha, enthusiastically.

"Papa returned home at full gallop, and finding where you were, he told me to take the horses and fetch you."

"Well, here I am!" said Bertha, putting her foot into the stirrup.

"Are not you going to bid good-bye to your poor knight?"

"Oh, yes," said Bertha, holding out her hand to the young man, who advanced to take it slowly and sadly.

"Ah! Mademoiselle Bertha," he murmured, taking her hand, "I am very unhappy."

"Why?" she asked.

"Not to be, as you said just now, one of you."

"What prevents it?" said Mary, holding out her hand to him.

The young man darted on that hand and kissed it in a passion of love and gratitude.

"Oh! yes, yes, yes," he murmured, so low that Mary alone could hear him; "for you, mademoiselle, and with you."

Mary's hand was roughly torn from his grasp by a sudden movement of her horse. Bertha, in touching hers, had struck that of her sister on the flank. Horses and riders, starting at a gallop, were soon lost like shadows in the darkness.

The young man stood motionless in the roadway.

"Adieu!" cried Bertha.

"Au revoir!" cried Mary.

"Yes, yes, yes," he said, stretching his arms toward their vanishing figures; "yes, au revoir! au revoir!"

The two girls continued their way without uttering a word, until they reached the castle gate, and there Bertha said, abruptly: —

"Mary, I know you will laugh at me!"

"Why?" asked Mary, trembling.

"I love him!" replied Bertha.

A cry of pain had almost escaped from Mary's lips, but she smothered it.

"And I called to him 'au revoir!'" she whispered to herself. "God grant 1 may never, never see him again."

XIII.

A DISTANT COUSIN.

THE day after the events we have just related, — that is to say, on the 7th of May, 1832, — a great dinner-party was given at the château de Vouillé, to celebrate the birthday of Madame la Comtesse de Vouillé, who had on that day completed her twenty-fourth year.

The company had just sat down to table, and at this table, among twenty-five other guests, was the prefect of Vienne and the mayor of Châtellerault, relations more or less distant of Madame de Vouillé.

The soup was just removed when a servant entered the dining-room, and said a few words in Monsieur de Vouillé's ear. Monsieur de Vouillé made the man repeat them twice. Then addressing his guests, he said: —

"I beg you to excuse me for a few moments. A lady has arrived at the gate in a post-chaise, and she insists on speaking to me personally. Will you allow me to see what this lady wants?"

Permission was, of course, unanimously granted, though Madame de Vouillé's eyes followed her husband to the door with some uneasiness.

Monsieur de Vouillé hastened to the gate. There, sure enough, was a post-chaise, containing two persons, a man and a woman. A servant in sky-blue livery with silver lace, was on the box. When he saw Monsieur de Vouillé, whom he seemed to be expecting impatiently, he jumped lightly down.

"Come, come, slow coach!" he said, as soon as the count was near enough to hear him.

Monsieur de Vouillé stopped short, amazed, — more than amazed, stupefied. What manner of servant was this, who dared to apostrophize him in that style? He went nearer to let the fellow know his mind. Then he stopped, and burst out laughing.

"What! is it you, de Lussac?" he said.

"Yes; undoubtedly, it is I."

"What is all this masquerading about?"

The counterfeit servant opened the carriage door and offered his arm to enable the lady to get out of the chaise. Then he said: —

"My dear count, I have the honor to present you to Madame la Duchesse de Berry." Bowing to the duchess, he continued, "Madame la duchesse, Monsieur le Comte de Vouillé is one of my best friends and one of your most devoted servants."

The count retreated a few steps.

"Madame la Duchesse de Berry!" he exclaimed, stupefied.

"In person, monsieur," said the duchess.

"Are you not proud and happy to receive her Royal Highness?" said de Lussac

"As proud and happy as an ardent royalist can be; but — "

"What! is there a but?" asked the duchess.

"This is my wife's birthday, and we have twenty-five guests now dining with us."

"Well, monsieur, there is a French proverb which says, 'Enough for two is enough for three.' I am sure you will extend the maxim to mean 'Enough for twenty-five is enough for twenty-eight;' for I warn you that Monsieur de Lussac, servant as he is, must dine at table, and he is dying of hunger."

"Yes; but don't be uneasy," said the Baron de Lussac. "I'll take off my livery."

Monsieur de Vouillé seized his head with both hands, as if he meant to tear out his hair.

"What shall I do? what can I do?" he cried.

"Come," said the duchess, "let us talk sense."

"Talk sense!" said the count; "how can I? I am half crazy."

"Evidently not with joy," said the duchess.

"No, with terror, madame."

"Oh! you exaggerate the situation."

"But, madame, you are entering the lion's den. I have the prefect of Vienne and the mayor of Châtellerault at my table."

"Very good; then you will present them to me."

"Good God! and under what title?"

"That of a cousin. You surely have some distant cousin, whose name will answer the purpose."

"What an idea, madame!"

"Come, put it to use."

"I certainly have a cousin in Toulouse, — Madame de la Myre."

"The very thing! I am Madame de la Myre."

Then turning round in the carriage she offered her hand to an old man about sixty-five years of age, who seemed waiting till the discussion ended before he showed himself.

"Come, Monsieur de la Myre," said the duchess, "this is a surprise we are giving our cousin, and we arrive just in time to keep his wife's birthday. Come, cousin!"

So saying she jumped lightly out of the carriage and gayly slipped her arm into that of the Comte de Vouillé.

"Yes, come!" said Monsieur de Vouillé, his mind made up to risk the adventure into which the duchess was so joyously rushing. Come!"

"Wait for me," cried the Baron de Lussac, jumping into the carriage, which he transformed into a dressing-room, and changing his sky-blue livery for a black surtout coat; "don't leave me behind."

"But who the devil are you to be?" asked M. de Vouillé.

"Oh! I'll be the Baron de Lussac, and — if Madame will permit me — the cousin of your cousin."

"Stop! stop! monsieur le baron," said the old gentleman, who had not yet spoken; "it seems to me that you are taking a great liberty."

"Pooh! we are on a campaign," said the duchess; "I permit it."

Monsieur de Vouillé now bravely led the way into the dining-room. The curiosity of the guests and the uneasiness of the mistress of the house were all the more excited by this prolonged absence. So, when the door of the dining-room opened all eyes turned to the new arrivals.

Whatever difficulties there may have been in playing the parts they had thus unexpectedly assumed, none of the actors were at all disconcerted.

"Dear," said the count to his wife, "I have often spoken to you of my cousin in Toulouse — "

"Madame de la Myre?" interrupted the countess, eagerly.

"Yes, — Madame de la Myre. She is on her way to Nantes, and would not pass the château without making your acquaintance. How fortunate that she comes on your birthday! I hope it will bring luck to both."

"Dear cousin!" said the duchess, opening her arms to Madame de Vouillé.

The two women kissed each other. As for the two men M. de Vouillé contented himself with saying aloud, "Monsieur de la Myre," "Monsieur de Lussac."

The company bowed.

"Now," said M. de Vouillé, "we must find seats for these newcomers, who warn me that they are dying of hunger."

Every one moved a little. The table was large, and all the guests had plenty of elbow-room; it was not difficult therefore to place three additional persons.

"Did you not tell me, my dear cousin," said the duchess, "that the prefect of Vienne was dining with you?"

"Yes, madame; and that is he whom you see on the countess's right, with spectacles, a white cravat, and the rosette of an officer of the Legion of honor in his buttonhole."

"Oh! pray present us."

Monsieur de Vouillé boldly carried on the comedy. He felt there was nothing to be done but to play it out. Accordingly, he approached the prefect, who was majestically leaning back in his chair.

"Monsieur le préfet," he said, "this is my cousin, who, with her traditional respect for authority, thinks that a general presentation is not enough, and therefore wishes to be presented to you particularly."

"Generally, particularly, and officially," replied the gallant functionary, "madame is and ever will be welcome."

"I accept the pledge, monsieur," said the duchess.

"Madame is going to Nantes?" asked the prefect, by way of making a remark.

"Yes, monsieur; and thence to Paris, — at least, I hope so."

"It is not, I presume, the first time that Madame visits the capital?"

"No, monsieur; I lived there twelve years."

"And Madame left it — "

"Oh! very unwillingly, I assure you."

"Recently?"

"Two years ago last July."

"I can well understand that having once lived in Paris — "

"I should wish to return there. I am glad you understand that."

"Oh, Paris! Paris!" said the functionary.

"The paradise of the world!" said the duchess.

"Come, take your seats," said Monsieur de Vouillé.

"Oh, my dear cousin," said the duchess, with a glance at the place he intended for her, "leave me beside Monsieur le préfet, I entreat you. He has just expressed himself with so much feeling about the thing I have most at heart that I place him, at once, on my list of friends."

The prefect, delighted with the compliment, drew aside his chair, and Madame was installed in the seat to his left, to the detriment of the person to whom that place of honor had been assigned. The two men accepted without objection the seats given to them, and were soon busy — M. de Lussac especially — in doing justice to the repast. The other guests followed their example, and for a time nothing broke the solemn silence which attends the beginning of a long-delayed and impatiently awaited dinner.

Madame was the first to break that silence. Her adventurous spirit, like the petrel, was more at ease in a gale.

"Well," she remarked, "I think our arrival must have interrupted the conversation. Nothing is so depressing as a silent dinner. I detest such dinners, my dear count; they are like those state functions at the Tuileries, where, they tell me, no one was allowed to speak unless the king had spoken. What were you all talking about before we came in?"

"Dear cousin," said M. de Vouillé, "the prefect was kindly giving us the official details of that blundering affair at Marseille."

"Blundering affair?" said the duchess.

"That's what he called it."

"And the words exactly describe the thing," said the functionary. "Can you conceive of an expedition of that character for which the arrangements were so carelessly made that it only required a sub-lieutenant of the 13th regiment to arrest one of the leaders of the outbreak and knock the whole affair in the head at once?"

"But don't you know, Monsieur le préfet," said the duchess, in a melancholy tone, "in all great events there is a moment, a supreme moment, when the destinies of princes and empires are shaken like leaves in the wind? For example, when Napoleon at La Mure advanced to meet the soldiers who were sent against him, if a sub-lieutenant of any kind had taken him by the collar the return from

Elba would have been nothing more than a *blundering affair.*"

There was silence after that, Madame having said the words in a grieved tone. She herself re-opened the matter.

"And the Duchesse de Berry?" she said; "is it known what became of her?"

"She returned on board of the 'Carlo Alberto.'"

"Ah!"

"It was the only sensible thing she could do, it seems to me," said the prefect.

"You are quite right, monsieur," said the old gentleman, who had accompanied Madame, and who had not before spoken; "and if I had had the honor to be near her Highness and she had granted me some authority, I should have given her that advice."

"No one was addressing you, my good husband," said the duchess. "I am speaking to the prefect, and I want to know if he is quite sure her Royal Highness has re-embarked?"

"Madame," said the prefect, with one of those administrative gestures which admit of no contradiction, "the government is officially informed of it."

"Ah!" exclaimed the duchess, "if the government is officially informed of it, of course there is nothing to be said; but," she added, venturing on still more slippery ground, "I did hear differently."

"Madame!" said the old gentleman, in a tone of slight reproach.

"What did you hear, cousin?" asked M. de Vouillé, who was beginning to take the interest of a gambler in the game that was being played before him.

"Yes, what have you heard, madame?" said the prefect.

"Oh, you understand, Monsieur le préfet, that it is not for me to give you official news," said the duchess. "I am only telling you of rumors, which may be mere nonsense."

"Madame de la Myre!" said the old man.

"Well, Monsieur de la Myre?" said the duchess.

"Do you know, madame," said the prefect, "that I think your husband is very interfering. I will wager it is he who does not want you to go to Paris?"

"That is precisely true. But I hope to go there in spite of him. 'What woman wills, God wills.'"

"Oh, women! women!" cried the public functionary.

"What now?" asked the duchess.

"Nothing," said the prefect. "I am waiting, Madame, to hear the rumors you mentioned just now about the Duchesse de Berry."

"Oh! they are simple enough. I heard, — but pray remember I give them on no authority but common report, — I have heard that the Duchesse de Berry rejected the advice of all her friends, and obstinately refused to re-embark on the 'Carlo Alberto.'"

"Then where is she now?" asked the prefect.

"In France."

"In France! What can she do in France?"

"Why, you know very well, Monsieur le préfet," said the duchess, "that her Royal Highness's chief object is La Vendée."

"No doubt; but having failed so signally at the South — "

"All the more reason why she should try for success at the West."

The prefect smiled disdainfully.

"Then you really think she has re-embarked?" asked the duchess.

"I can positively assure you," said the prefect, "that she is at this moment in the dominions of the king of Sardinia, from whom France is about to ask an explanation."

"Poor king of Sardinia! He will give a very simple one."

"What?"

"He will say, 'I always knew Madame was a crazy creature; but I never thought her craziness would lead her quite as far as this—'"

"Madame! madame!" said the old man.

"Ah, ça! Monsieur de la Myre," said the duchess, "I do hope that although you interfere with my wishes, you will have the grace to respect my opinions, — all the more because I am sure they are those of Monsieur le préfet. Are they not, monsieur?"

"The truth is," said that functionary, laughing, "that her Royal Highness has behaved in this whole affair with the utmost folly."

"There! you see," said the duchess. "What would happen, Monsieur le préfet, if these rumors were true and Madame should really come to La Vendée?"

"How can she get here?" asked the prefect.

"Why, through the neighboring departments, or through yours. They tell me she was seen at Toulouse in an open carriage while changing horses."

"Good heavens!" cried the prefect; "that would be a little too bold."

"So bold that Monsieur le préfet does n't believe it?"

"Not one word of it," said the official emphasizing each monosyllable as he uttered it.

At that moment the door opened, and one of the count's footmen announced that a clerk from the prefecture asked permission to deliver a telegraphic despatch just received from Paris for the prefect.

"Will you permit him to enter?" said the prefect to the count.

"Why, of course," said the latter.

The clerk entered and gave a sealed package to the prefect, who bowed his excuses to the company for opening it.

Absolute silence reigned. All eyes were fixed on the despatch. Madame exchanged signs with M. de Vouillé, who laughed under his breath, with M. de Lussac, who laughed aloud, and with her so-called husband who maintained his imperturbably grave manner.

"Whew!" cried the public functionary suddenly, while his features were indiscreet enough to betray the utmost surprise.

"What is the news?" asked M. de Vouillé.

"The news is," exclaimed the prefect, "that Madame de la Myre was right in what she said about her Royal Highness. Her Royal Highness has not left France; her Royal Highness is on her way to La Vendée, through Toulouse, Libourne, and Poitiers."

So saying, the prefect rose.

"Where are you going, Monsieur le préfet?" asked the duchess.

"To do my duty, madame, painful as it is, and give orders that her Royal Highness be arrested if, as this despatch warns me, she is imprudent enough to pass through my department."

"Do so, Monsieur le préfet; do so," said the duchess. "I can only applaud your zeal and assure you that I shall remember it when occasion offers."

She held out her hand to the prefect, who kissed it gallantly, after having, with a look, asked Monsieur de la Myre's permission to do so.

XIV.

PETIT-PIERRE.

LET us now return to the cottage of the goodman Tinguy, which we left for a time to make that excursion to the château de Vouillé.

Forty-eight hours have gone by. Bertha and Michel are again at the sick man's bedside. Though the regular visits which Doctor Roger now paid rendered the young girl's presence in that fever-stricken place unnecessary, Bertha, in spite of Mary's remonstrances, persisted in her care of the Vendéan peasant. Nevertheless, it is probable that Christian charity was not the only motive which drew her to his cottage.

However that may be, it is certain that, by natural coincidence, Michel, who had got over his terrors, was already installed in the cottage when Bertha got there. Was it Bertha for whom Michel was looking? We dare not answer. Perhaps he thought that Mary, too, might take her turn in these charitable functions. Perhaps, too, he may have hoped that the fair-haired sister would not lose this occasion of meeting him, after the warmth of their last parting. His heart therefore beat violently when he saw the shadow of a woman's form, which he knew by its elegance could belong only to a Demoiselle de Souday, projecting itself upon the cottage door.

When he recognized Bertha the young man felt a measure of disappointed hope; but as, by virtue of his love, he was full of tenderness for the Marquis de Souday, of sympathy for the crabbed Jean Oullier, and of benevolence for even their dogs, how could he fail to love Mary's sister?

The affection shown to one would certainly bring him nearer to the other; besides, what happiness to hear this sister mention the absent sister. Consequently, he was full of attentions and solicitude for Bertha, who accepted all with a satisfaction she took no pains to conceal.

It was difficult, however, to think of other matters than the condition of the sick man, which was hourly growing worse and worse. He had fallen into that state of torpor and insensibility which physicians call coma, and which, in inflammatory diseases, usually characterizes the period preceding death. He no longer noticed what was passing around him, and answered only when distinctly spoken to. The pupils of his eyes, which were frightfully dilated, were fixed and staring. He was almost rigid, though from time to time his hands endeavored to pull the coverlet over his face, or draw to him something that he seemed to see beside his bed.

Bertha, who, in spite of her youth, had more than once been present at such a scene, no longer felt any hope for the poor man's life. She wished to spare Rosine the anguish of witnessing her father's death-struggle, which she knew was beginning, and she told her to go at once and fetch Doctor Roger.

"But I can go, mademoiselle, if you like," said Michel. "I have better legs than Rosine. Besides, it is n't safe for her to go through those roads at night."

"No, Monsieur Michel, there is no danger for Rosine, and I have my own reasons for keeping you here. I hope it is not disagreeable to you to remain?"

"Oh, mademoiselle, how can you think it? Only I am so happy in being able to serve you that I try to let no occasion pass."

"Don't be anxious about that," said Bertha, smiling; "perhaps, before long, I shall have more than one occasion to put your devotion to the proof."

Rosine had hardly been gone ten minutes before the sick man seemed suddenly and extraordinarily better

His eyes lost their fixed stare, his breathing became easier, his rigid fingers relaxed, and he passed them over his forehead to wipe away the sweat which began to pour from it.

"How do you feel, dear Tinguy?" said the girl.

"Better," he answered, in a feeble voice. "The good God does n't mean me to desert before the battle," he added, trying to smile.

"Perhaps not; because it is for him you are going to fight."

The peasant shook his head sadly and sighed.

"Monsieur Michel," said Bertha to the young man, drawing him into a corner of the room, so that her voice should not reach the patient, "go and fetch the vicar and rouse the neighbors."

"Is n't he better? He said so just now."

"Child that you are! Did you never see a lamp go out? The last flame is brightest, and so it is with our miserable bodies. Go at once. There will be no death-struggle. The fever has exhausted him; the soul is going without a struggle, shock, or effort."

"And are you to be left alone with him?"

"Go at once, and don't think about me."

Michel went out, and Bertha returned to Tinguy, who held out his hand.

"Thank you, my brave young lady," said the peasant.

"Thank me for what, père Tinguy?"

"For your care, and also for thinking of sending for the vicar."

"You heard me?"

This time Tinguy smiled outright.

"Yes," he said, "low as you spoke."

"But you must n't think that the presence of the priest means that you are going to die, my good Tinguy. Don't be frightened."

"Frightened!" cried the peasant, trying to sit up in his bed. "Frightened! why? I have respected the old and cared for the young; I have suffered without a murmur; I have toiled without complaining, praising God when the hail beat down my wheat and the harvest failed; never have I turned away the beggar whom Sainte-Anne has sent to my fireside; I have kept the commandments of God and of the Church; when the priests said, 'Rise and take your guns,' I fought the enemies of my faith and my king; I have been humble in victory and hopeful in defeat; I was still ready to give my life for the sacred cause, and shall I be frightened now? Oh, no! mademoiselle; this is the day of days to us poor Christians, — the glorious day of death. Ignorant as I am, I know that this day makes us equals with the great and prosperous of the earth. It has come for me; God calls me to him. I am ready; I go before his judgment-seat in full assurance of his mercy."

Tinguy's face was illuminated as he said the words; but this last religious enthusiasm exhausted the poor man's strength. He fell heavily back upon his pillow, muttering a few unintelligible words, among which could be distinguished "blues," "parish," and the names of God and the Virgin.

The vicar entered at this moment. Bertha showed him the sick man, and the priest, understanding what she wanted of him, began at once the prayer for the dying.

Michel begged Bertha to leave the room, and the young girl consenting, they both went out after saying a last prayer at Tinguy's bedside.

One after the other, the neighbors came in; each knelt down and repeated after the priest the litanies of death. Two slender candles of yellow wax, placed on either side of a brass crucifix, lighted the gloomy scene.

Suddenly, at the moment when the priest and the assistants were reciting mentally the "Ave Maria!" an owl's cry, sounding not far distant from the cottage, rose above the dull hum of their mutterings. The peasants trembled.

At the sound the dying man, whose eyes were already glazing and his breath hissing, raised his head.

"I'm here!" he cried; "I'm ready! I am the guide."

Then he tried to imitate the owl's cry in reply to the one he had heard, but he could not. The lingering breath gave a sob, his head fell back, his eyes opened widely. He was dead.

A stranger stood on the threshold of the door. He was a young Breton peasant, wearing a broad-brimmed hat, a red waistcoat and silver buttons, a blue jacket embroidered with red, and high leather gaiters. He carried in his hand one of those sticks with iron points, which the country people use when they make a journey.

He seemed surprised at the scene before his eyes; but he asked no question of any one. He quietly knelt down and prayed; then he approached the bed, looked earnestly at the pale, discolored face of the poor peasant. Two heavy tears rolled down his cheeks; he wiped them away, and went out as he had come, silently.

The peasants, used to the religious custom which expects all those who pass the house of death to enter and say a prayer for the soul of the dying and a blessing on the body, were not surprised at the presence of a stranger, and paid no heed to his departure. The latter, on leaving the cottage, met another peasant, younger and smaller than himself, who seemed to be his brother; this one was riding a horse saddled and bridled in peasant fashion.

"Well, Rameau-d'or," said the younger, "what is it?"

"This," replied the other: "there is no place for us in that house. A guest is there whose presence fills it."

"Who is he?"

"Death."

"Who is dead?"

"He whose hospitality we came to ask. I would suggest to you to make a shield of his death and stay here; but I heard some one say that Tinguy died of typhoid fever, and though doctors deny the contagion, I cannot consent to expose you to it."

"You are not afraid that you were seen and recognized?"

"No, impossible. There were eight or ten persons, men

and women, praying round the bed. I went in and knelt down and prayed with them. That is what all Breton and Vendéan peasants do in such cases."

"Well, what can we do now?" asked the younger of the two.

"I have already told you. We had to decide between the château of my former comrade or the cottage of the poor fellow who was to have been our guide, — between luxury and a princely house with poor security, and a narrow cottage, bad beds, buckwheat bread, and absolute safety. God himself has decided the matter. We have no choice; we must take the insecure comfort."

"But you think the château is not safe?"

"The château belongs to a friend of my childhood, whose father was made a baron by the Restoration. The father is dead, and the widow and son are now living in the château. If the son were alone, I should have no anxiety. He is rather weak, but his heart is sound. It is his mother I fear; she is selfish and ambitious, and I could not trust her."

"Oh, pooh! just for one night! You are not adventurous, Rameau-d'or."

"Yes I am, on my own account; but I am answerable to France, or at any rate, to my party for the life of Ma—"

"For Petit-Pierre. Ah, Rameau-d'or, that is the tenth forfeit you owe me since we started."

"It shall be the last, Ma — Petit-Pierre, I should say. In future I will think of you by no other name, and in no other relation than that of my brother."

"Come, then; let us go to the château. I am so weary that I would ask shelter of an ogress, — if there were' any."

"We'll take a crossroad, which will carry us there in ten minutes," said the young man. "Seat yourself more comfortably in the saddle; I will walk before you, and you must follow me; otherwise we might miss the path, which is very faint."

"Wait a moment," said Petit-Pierre, slipping from his horse.

"Where are you going?" asked Rameau-d'or, anxiously.

"You said your prayer beside that poor peasant, and I want to say mine."

"Don't think of it!"

"Yes, yes; he was a brave and honest man," persisted Petit-Pierre. "He would have risked his life for us; I may well offer a little prayer beside his body."

Rameau-d'or raised his hat and stood aside to let his young companion pass.

The lad, like Rameau-d'or, entered the cottage, took a branch of holly, dipped it in holy water, and sprinkled the body with it. Then he knelt down and prayed at the foot of the bed, after which he left the cottage; without exciting more attention than his companion had done.

The elder helped Petit-Pierre to mount, and together, one in the saddle, the other on foot, they took their way silently across the fields and along an almost invisible path which led, as we have said, in a straight line to the château de la Logerie. They had hardly gone a hundred steps into the grounds when Rameau-d'or stopped short and laid his hand on the bridle of the horse.

"What is it now?" asked Petit-Pierre.

"I hear steps," said the young man. "Draw in behind those bushes; I will stand against this tree. They'll probably pass without seeing us."

The manœuvre was made with the rapidity of a military evolution, and none too soon; for the new-comer was seen to emerge from the darkness as the pair reached their posts. Rameau-d'or, whose eyes were by this time accustomed to the dim light, saw at once that he was a young man about twenty years of age, running, rather than walking, in the same direction as themselves. He had his hat in his hand, which made him the more easily recognized, and his hair, blown back by the wind, left his face entirely exposed.

An exclamation of surprise burst from Rameau-d'or, as the young man came close to him; then he hesitated a minute, still in doubt, and allowed the other to pass him by three or four steps, before he cried out: —

"Michel!"

The new-comer, who did not expect to hear his name called in that lonely place, jumped to one side, and said in a voice that quivered with emotion: —

"Who called me?"

"I," said Rameau-d'or, taking off his hat and a wig he had been wearing, and advancing to his friend with no other disguise than his Breton clothes.

"Henri de Bonneville!" exclaimed Baron Michel, in amazement.

"Myself. But don't say my name so loud. We are in a land where every bush and ditch and tree shares with the walls the privilege of having ears."

"True!" said Michel, alarmed; "and besides — "

"Besides what?" asked M. de Bonneville.

"You must have come for the uprising they talk of?"

"Precisely. And now, in two words, on which side are you?"

"I?"

"Yes, you."

"My good friend," said the young baron, "I have no fixed opinions; though I will admit in a whisper — "

"Whisper as much as you like; admit what? Make haste."

"Well, I will admit that I incline toward Henri V."

"My dear Michel," cried the count, gayly, "if you incline toward Henri V. that's enough for me."

"Stop; I don't say that I am positively decided."

"So much the better. I shall finish your conversion; and, in order that I may do so at once, I shall ask you to take me in for the night at your château, and also a friend who accompanies me."

"Where is your friend?" asked Michel.

"Here he is," said Petit-Pierre, riding forward, and bowing to the young baron, with an ease and grace that contrasted curiously with the dress he wore. Michel looked at the little peasant for a moment, and then approaching Bonneville, he said: —

"Henri, what is your friend's name?"

"Michel, you are lacking in all the traditions of hospitality. You forget the 'Odyssey,' my dear fellow, and I am distressed at you. Why do you want to know my friend's name? Isn't it enough if I tell you he is a man of good birth?"

"Are you sure he is a man at all?"

The count and Petit-Pierre burst out laughing.

"So you insist on knowing the names of those you receive in your house?"

"Not for my sake, my dear Henri, — not for mine, I swear to you; but in the château de la Logerie — "

"Well? — in the château de la Logerie?"

"I am not master."

"Oh! then the Baronne Michel is mistress. I had already told my little friend Petit-Pierre that she might be. But it is only for one night. You could take us to your own room, and I can forage in the cellar and larder. I know the way. My young friend could get a night's rest on your bed, and early in the morning I'll find a better place and relieve you of our presence."

"Impossible, Henri. Do not think that it is for myself, I fear; but it will compromise your safety to let you even enter the château."

"How so?"

"My mother is still awake; I am sure of it. She is watching for me; she would see us enter. Your disguise we might find some reason for; but that of your companion, which has not escaped me, how could we explain it to her?"

"He is right," said Petit-Pierre.

"But what else can we do?"

"And," continued Michel, "it is not only my mother that I fear, but—"

"What else?"

"Wait!" said the baron, looking uneasily about him; "let us get away from these bushes."

"The devil!"

"I mean Courtin."

"Courtin? Who is he?"

"Don't you remember Courtin the farmer?"

"Oh! yes, to be sure,— a good sort of fellow, who was always on your side, even against your mother."

"Yes. Well, Courtin is now mayor of the village and a violent Philippist. If he found you wandering about at night in disguise he would arrest you without a warrant."

"This is serious," said Henri de Bonneville, gravely. "What does Petit-Pierre think of it?"

"I think nothing, my dear Rameau-d'or; I leave you to think for me."

"The result is that you close your doors to us?" said Bonneville.

"That won't signify to you," said Baron Michel, whose eyes suddenly lighted up with a personal hope, — "it won't signify, for I will get you admitted to another house, where you will be in far greater safety than at La Logerie."

"Not signify! but it does signify. What says my companion?"

"I say that provided some door opens, I don't care where it is. I am ready to drop with fatigue, I am so tired."

"Then follow me," said the baron.

"Is it far?"

"An hour's walk, — about three miles."

"Has Petit-Pierre the strength for it?" asked Henri.

"Petit-Pierre will find strength for it," said the little peasant, laughing.

"Then let us follow Baron Michel," said Bonneville. "Forward, baron!"

And the little group, which had been at a standstill for the last ten minutes, moved away. But they had hardly gone a few hundred steps before Bonneville laid a hand on Michel's shoulder.

"Where are you taking us?" he said.

"Don't be uneasy."

"I will follow you, provided you can promise me a good bed and a good supper for Petit-Pierre, who, as you see, is rather delicate."

"He shall have all and more than I could give him at La Logerie, — the best food in the larder, the best wine in the cellar, the best bed in the castle."

On they went. At the end of some little time Michel said suddenly: —

"I'll go forward now, so that you may not have to wait."

"One moment," said Henri. "Where are we going?"

"To the château de Souday."

"The château de Souday!"

"Yes; you know it very well, with its pointed towers roofed with slate, on the left of the road opposite to the forest of Machecoul."

"The wolves' castle?"

"Yes, the wolves' castle, if you choose to call it so."

"Is that where we are to stay?"

"Yes."

"Have you sufficiently reflected, Michel?"

"Yes, yes; I will answer for everything."

The baron waited to say no more, but set off instantly for the castle, with that velocity of which he had given such unmistakable proof on the night when he went to fetch the doctor to the dying Tinguy.

"Well," asked Petit-Pierre, "what shall we do?"

"There is no choice now but to follow him."

"To the wolves' castle?"

"Yes, to the wolves' castle."

"So be it; but to enliven the way," said the little

peasant, "will you be good enough to tell me, my dear Rameau-d'or, who the wolves are?"

"I will tell you what I have heard of them."

"I can't expect more."

Resting his hand on the pommel of the saddle, the Comte de Bonneville related to Petit-Pierre the sort of legend attaching, throughout the department of the Lower Loire, to the daughters of the Marquis de Souday. But presently, stopping short in his tale, he announced to his companion that they had reached their destination.

Petit-Pierre, convinced that he was about to see beings analogous to the witches in "Macbeth," was calling up all his courage to enter the dreaded castle, when, at a turn of the road, he saw before him an open gate, and before the gate two white figures, who seemed to be waiting there, lighted by a torch carried behind them by a man of rugged features and rustic clothes. Mary and Bertha — for it was they — informed by Baron Michel, had come to meet their uninvited guests. Petit-Pierre eyed them curiously. He saw two charming young girls, — one fair, with blue eyes and an almost angelic face; the other, with black hair and eyes, a proud and resolute bearing, a frank and loyal countenance. Both were smiling.

Rameau-d'or's young companion slid from his horse, and the two advanced together toward the ladies.

"My friend Baron Michel encouraged me to hope, mesdemoiselles, that your father, the Marquis de Souday, would grant us hospitality," said the Comte de Bonneville, bowing to the two girls.

"My father is absent, monsieur," replied Bertha. "He will regret having lost this occasion to exercise a virtue which in these days we cannot often practise."

"I do not know if Michel told you, mademoiselle, that this hospitality may possibly involve some danger. My young companion and I are almost proscribed persons. Persecution may be the cost of your granting us an asylum."

"You come here in the name of a cause which is ours,

monsieur. Were you merely strangers, you would be hospitably received. Being, as you are, royalists and proscribed, you are heartily welcome, even if death and ruin enter this poor household with you. If my father were here he would say the same."

"Monsieur le Baron Michel has, no doubt, told you my name; it remains for me to tell you that of my young companion."

"We do not ask to know it, monsieur; your situation is more to us than your names, whatever they may be. You are royalists, proscribed for a cause to which, women as we are, we would gladly give every drop of our blood. Enter this house; it is neither rich nor sumptuous, but at least you will find it faithful and discreet."

With a gesture of great dignity, Bertha pointed to the gate, and signed to the two young men to enter it.

"May Saint-Julien be ever blessed!" said Petit-Pierre in Bonneville's ear. "Here is the château and the cottage between which you wanted me to choose, united in this night's lodging. They please me through and through, your wolves."

So saying, he entered the postern, with a graceful inclination of the head to the two young girls. The Comte de Bonneville followed. Mary and Bertha made an amicable gesture of farewell to Michel, and the latter held out her hand to him. But Jean Oullier closed the gate so roughly that the luckless young man had no time to grasp it.

He looked for a few moments at the towers of the castle, which stood out blackly against the dark background of the sky. He watched the lights appearing, one by one, in the windows; and then, at last, he turned and went away.

When he had fairly disappeared the bushes moved, and gave passage to an individual who had witnessed this scene, with a purpose very different from that of the actors in it. That individual was Courtin, who, after satisfying himself that no one was near, took the same path his young master had taken to return to La Logerie.

XV.

AN UNSEASONABLE HOUR.

It was about two in the morning, perhaps, when the young Baron Michel again reached the end of the avenue, which leads to the château de la Logerie. The atmosphere was calm; the majestic silence of the night, which was broken only by the rustling of the leaves, led him into reverie. It is not necessary to say that the two sisters were the objects of his thought, and that the one whose image the baron followed with as much respect and love as Tobit followed the angel in the Bible, was Mary.

But when he saw before him, at the farther end of the dark arcade of trees beneath which he was walking, the windows of the château, which were sparkling in the moonlight, all his charming visions vanished, and his ideas took a far more practical direction. In place of the ravishing figures of girlhood so lately beside him, he saw the stern and threatening outline of his mother.

We know the terror with which she inspired him. He stopped short. If in all the neighborhood there were any shelter, even a tavern, in which he could spend the night, he would not have returned to the house till the next day, so great were his apprehensions. It was the first time he had ever been late in getting home, and he felt instinctively that his mother was on the watch for him. What should he answer to the dreadful inquiry, "Where have you been?"

Courtin could give him a night's lodging; but if he went to Courtin he should have to tell him all, and the young baron fully understood the danger there was in taking a man like Courtin into his confidence. He decided, therefore, to brave the maternal wrath, — very much as the criminal decides to brave the scaffold, simply because he cannot do otherwise, — and continued his way home.

Nevertheless, the nearer he got to the château the more his resolution faltered. When he reached the end of the avenue where he had to cross the lawn, and when he saw his mother's window, the only lighted window in the building, his heart failed him. No, his forebodings had not misled him; his mother was on the watch. His resolution vanished entirely, and fear, developing the resources of his imagination, put into his head the idea of a trick which, if it did not avert his mother's anger, would at any rate delay the explosion of it.

He turned to the right, glided along in the shadow of a buckthorn hedge, reached the wall of the kitchen garden, over which he climbed, and passed through the gate leading from the kitchen-garden to the park.

Up to this moment all was well; but now came the most difficult, or rather the most hazardous part of his enterprise. He had to find some window left unfastened by a careless servant, by which he could enter the house and slip back to his own apartment unperceived.

The château de la Logerie consists of a large, square building, flanked at the corners with four towers of the same shape. The kitchens and offices were underground, the reception-rooms on the ground-floor, those of the baroness on the next floor, those of her son above her. Michel examined the house on three sides, trying gently but persistently every door and window, keeping close to the walls, stepping with precaution, and even holding his breath. Neither doors nor windows yielded.

There was still the front of the house to be examined. This was much the most dangerous side, for the windows of the baroness commanded it, and there were no shrubs to cast a protecting shadow. Here he found a window open. True, it was that of his mother's bedroom: but Michel.

CASTLE SOUDAY

now desperate, reflected that if he had to be scolded he would rather it were without than within the house, and he resolved on making the attempt.

He was cautiously advancing round the corner tower when he saw a shadow moving on the lawn. A shadow of course meant a body. Michel stopped and gave all his attention to the new arrival. He saw it was a man, and the man was following the path he himself would have taken had he gone, in the first instance, straight to the house. The young baron now made a few steps backward and crouched in the heavy shadow projected by the tower.

The man came nearer. He was not more than fifty yards from the house when Michel heard the harsh voice of his mother speaking from her window. He congratulated himself on not having crossed the lawn and taken the path the man was on.

"Is that you, Michel?" asked the baroness.

"No, madame, no," replied a voice, which the young baron recognized, with amazement not unmingled with fear, as that of Courtin, "you do me too much honor in taking me for Monsieur le baron."

"Good heavens!" cried the baroness, "what brings you here at this hour?"

"Ah! you may well suppose it is something important, Madame la baronne."

"Has any harm happened to my son?"

The tone of agony in which his mother said these words touched the young man so deeply that he was about to rush out and reassure her when Courtin's answer, which came immediately, paralyzed this good intention.

"Oh! no, no, madame; I have just seen the young *gars*, if I may so call Monsieur le baron, and he is quite well, — up to the present moment at least."

"Present moment!" said the baroness. "Is he in any danger?"

"Well, yes," said Courtin; "he may get into trouble if he persists in running after those female Satans, — and may hell clutch them! It is to prevent such a misfortune that I've taken the liberty to come to you at this time of night, feeling sure that as Monsieur Michel is so late in getting home you would surely be sitting up for him."

"You did right, Courtin. Where is he now, — do you know?"

Courtin looked about him.

"I am surprised he has not come in. I took the county road so as to leave him the wood-path clear, and that's a good half-mile shorter than the road."

"But tell me at once, where has he been; where is he coming from; what has he done; why is he roaming the country at two in the morning, without considering my anxiety or reflecting that he is injuring my health as well as his own?"

"Madame la baronne, I cannot answer those questions in the open air." Then, lowering his voice, he added, "What I have to tell madame is so important that she had better hear it in her own room. Besides, as the young master is not yet in, he may be here at any moment," said the farmer, looking uneasily about him, "and I would n't for all the world have him suspect that I keep a watch upon him, though it is for his own good, and to do you a service."

"Come in, then; you are right," said the baroness. "Come in, at once."

"Beg pardon, madame, but how, if you please?"

"True," said the baroness, "the door is locked."

"If madame will throw me the key — "

"It is inside the door."

"Oh, bother it!"

"I sent the servants to bed, not wishing them to know of my son's misconduct. Wait; I will ring for my maid."

"Oh, madame, no!" exclaimed Courtin, "it is better not to let any one into our secrets; it seems to me the matter is so important that madame might disregard appearances. I know madame was not born to open the door to a poor farmer like me; but once in a way it wouldn't signify. If everybody is asleep in the château, so much the better; we shall be safe from curiosity."

"Really, Courtin, you alarm me," said the baroness, who was in fact prevented from opening the door by a petty pride, which had not escaped the farmer's observation. "I will hesitate no longer."

The baroness withdrew from the window, and a moment later Michel heard the grinding of the key and the bolts of the front door. He listened at first in an agony of apprehension; then he became aware that the door, which opened with difficulty, had not been relocked or bolted, — no doubt because his mother and Courtin were so pre-occupied in mind. He waited a few seconds till he was sure they had reached the upper floor. Then, gliding along the wall, he mounted the portico, pushed open the door, which turned noiselessly on its hinges, and entered the vestibule.

His original intention had been, of course, to regain his room and await events, while pretending to be asleep. In that case the exact hour of his return home would not be known, and he might still have a chance to get out of the scrape by a fib. But matters were much changed since he formed that intention. Courtin had followed him; Courtin had seen him. Courtin must know that the Comte de Bonneville and his companion had taken refuge in the château de Souday. For a moment Michel forgot himself to think of his friend, whom the farmer, with his violent political opinions, might greatly injure.

Instead of going up to his own floor, he slipped, like a wolf, along his mother's corridor. Just as he reached her door he heard her say: —

"So you really think, Courtin, that my son has been enticed by one of those miserable women?"

"Yes, madame, I am sure of it; and they've got him so fast that I am afraid you'll have a deal of trouble to get him away from them."

"Girls without a penny!"

"As for that, they come of the oldest blood in the country, madame," said Courtin, wishing to sound his way; "and for nobles like you that's something, at any rate."

"Faugh!" exclaimed the baroness; "bastards!"

"But pretty; one is like an angel, the other like a demon."

"Michel may amuse himself with them, as so many others, they say, have done; that's possible; but you can't suppose that he ever dreamed of marrying one of them? Nonsense! he knows me too well to think that I would ever consent to such a marriage."

"Barring the respect I owe to him, Madame la baronne, my opinion is that Monsieur Michel has never reflected at all about it, and does n't yet know what he feels for the wolves; but one thing I'm sure of, and that is he is getting himself into another kind of trouble, which may compromise him seriously."

"What do you mean, Courtin?"

"Well, confound it!" exclaimed the farmer, seeming to hesitate, "do you know, madame, that it would be very painful to me, who love and respect you, if my duty compelled me to arrest my young master?"

Michel trembled where he stood; and yet it was the baroness to whom the shock was most severe.

"Arrest Michel!" she exclaimed, drawing herself up; "I think you forget yourself, Courtin."

"No, madame, I do not."

"But —"

"I am your farmer, it is true," continued Courtin, making the baroness a sign with his hand to control herself. "I am bound to give you an exact account of the harvests, on which you have half the profits, and to pay you promptly on the day and hour what is due, — which I do to the best of my ability, in spite of the hard times; but before being your farmer I am a citizen, and I am, moreover, mayor, and in those capacities I have duties, Madame la baronne, which I must fulfil, whether my poor heart suffers or not."

"What nonsense are you talking to me, Maître Courtin? Pray, what has my son to do with your duties as a citizen and your station as mayor?"

"He has this to do with it, Madame la baronne: your son has intimate acquaintance with the enemies of the State."

"I know very well," said the baroness, "that Monsieur le Marquis de Souday holds exaggerated opinions; but any love-affairs that Michel may have with one of his daughters cannot, it seems to me, be turned into a political misdemeanor."

"That love-affair is carrying Monsieur Michel much farther than you think for, Madame la baronne, and I tell you so now. I dare say he has so far only poked the end of his nose into the troubled waters about him; but that's enough for a beginning."

"Come, enough of such metaphors! Explain what you mean, Courtin."

"Well, Madame la baronne, here's the truth. This evening, after being present at the death-bed of that old Chouan Tinguy, and running the risk of bringing a malignant fever home with him, and after accompanying one of the wolves to the château de Souday, Monsieur le baron served as guide to two peasants who were no more peasants than I'm a gentleman; and he took them to the château de Souday."

"Who told you so, Courtin?"

"My own two eyes, Madame la baronne; they are good, and I trust them."

"Did you get an idea who those peasants were?"

"The two false peasants?"

"Yes, of course."

"One, I'd take my oath of it, was the Comte de Bonneville, — a violent Chouan, he! No one can fool me about him; he has been long in the country, and I know him. As for the other —"

Courtin paused.

"Go on," said the baroness, impatiently.

"As for the other, if I 'm not mistaken, that 's a better discovery still —"

"But who is it? Come, Courtin, tell me at once."

"No, Madame la baronne. I shall tell the name — I shall probably be obliged to do so — to the authorities."

"The authorities! Do you mean to tell me you are going to denounce my son?" cried the baroness, amazed and stupefied at the tone her farmer, hitherto so humble, was assuming.

"Assuredly I do, Madame la baronne," said Courtin, composedly.

"Nonsense! you would not think of it."

"I do think it, Madame la baronne, and I should be now on the road to Montaigu or even to Nantes, if I had not wished to warn you, so that you may put Monsieur Michel out of harm's way."

"But, supposing that Michel is concerned in this affair," said the baroness, vehemently; "you will compromise me with all my neighbors, and — who knows? — you may draw down horrible reprisals on La Logerie."

"Then we must defend the château, that 's all, Madame la baronne."

"Courtin!"

"I saw the great war, Madame la baronne. I was a little fellow then, but I remember it, and on my word of honor I don't want to see the like again. I don't want to see my twenty acres of land a battlefield for both parties, my harvests eaten by one or burned by the other; still less do I want to see the Whites lay hands on the National domain, which they will do if they get the chance. Out of my twenty acres, five belonged to *émigrés*. I bought 'em and paid for 'em; that 's one quarter of all I own. Besides, here 's another thing: the government relies upon me, and I wish to justify the confidence of the government."

"But, Courtin," said the baroness, almost ready to come

down to entreaty, "matters can't be as serious as you imagine, I am sure."

"Beg pardon, Madame la baronne, they are very serious indeed. I am only a peasant, but that does n't prevent me from knowing as much as others know, being blessed with a good ear and a gift for listening. The Retz district is all but at the boiling-point; another fagot and the pot will boil over."

"Courtin, you must be mistaken."

"No, Madame la baronne, I am not mistaken. I know what I know. God bless me! the nobles have met three times, — once at the Marquis de Souday's, once at the house of the man they call Louis Renaud, and once at the Comte de Saint-Amand's. All those meetings smelt of powder, Madame la baronne. *À propos* of powder, there's two hundred weight of it and sacks of cartridges in the Vicar of Montbert's house. Moreover, — and this is the most serious thing of all, — they are expecting Madame la Duchesse de Berry, and from something I have just seen, it is my opinion they won't have long to wait for her."

"Why so?"

"I think she is here already."

"Good God! where?"

"Well, at the château de Souday, where Monsieur Michel took her this evening."

"Michel! oh, the unfortunate boy! But you won't say a word about it, will you, Courtin? Besides, the government must have made its plans. If the duchess attempts to return to La Vendée, she will be arrested before she can get here."

"Nevertheless, she is here," persisted Courtin.

"All the more reason why you should hold your tongue."

"I like that! And what becomes of the profits and the glory of such a prize, not counting that before the capture is made by somebody else the whole country will be in blood and arms? No, Madame la baronne; no, I cannot hold my tongue."

"Then what is to be done? Good God! what can I do?"

"I'll tell you, Madame la baronne; listen to me —"

"Go on."

"Well, as I want to remain your zealous and faithful servant, all the while being a good citizen, — and because I hope that in gratitude for what I am doing for you, you will let me keep my farm on terms that I am able to pay, — I will agree to say nothing about Monsieur Michel. But you must try to keep him out of this wasps' nest in future. He is in it now, that's true; but there's still time to get him out."

"You need not trouble yourself about that, Courtin."

"But if I might say a word, Madame la baronne —"

"Well, what?"

"I don't quite dare to give advice to Madame la baronne; it is not my place, but—"

"Go on, Courtin; go on."

"Well, in order to get Monsieur Michel completely out of this hornets' nest, I think you'll have — by some means or other, prayers or threats — to make him leave la Logerie and go to Paris."

"Yes, you are right, Courtin."

"Only, I am afraid he won't consent."

"If I decide it, Courtin, he must consent."

"He will be twenty-one in eleven months; he is very nearly his own master."

"I tell you he shall go, Courtin. What are you listening for?"

Courtin had turned his head to the door, as if he heard something.

"I thought some one was in the corridor," he said.

"Look and see."

Courtin took a light and rushed into the passage.

"There was no one," he said, "though I certainly thought I heard a step."

"Where do you suppose he can be, the wretched boy, at this time of night?" said the baroness.

"Perhaps he has gone to my house," said Courtin. "He has confidence in me, and it would n't be the first time he has come to tell me of his little troubles."

"Possibly. You had better go home now; and remember your promise."

"And do you remember yours, Madame la baronne. If he comes in lock him up. Don't let him communicate with the wolves, for if he sees them —"

"What then?"

"I should n't be surprised to hear some day that he was firing behind the gorse."

"God forbid! Oh! he 'll kill me with anxiety. What a luckless idea it was of my husband ever to come to this cursed place!"

"Luckless, indeed, madame, — especially for him."

The baroness bowed her head sadly under the recollections thus evoked. Courtin now left her, looking about him carefully to see that no one was stirring in the château de la Logerie.

XVI.

COURTIN'S DIPLOMACY.

COURTIN had hardly taken a hundred steps on the path that led to his farmhouse before he heard a rustling in the bushes near which he passed.

"Who's there?" he said, standing in the middle of the path, and putting himself on guard with the heavy stick he carried.

"Friend," replied a youthful voice.

And the owner of the voice came through the bushes.

"Why, it is Monsieur le baron!" cried the farmer.

"I, myself, Courtin," replied Michel.

"Where are you going at this time of night? Good God! if Madame la baronne knew you were roaming about in the darkness, what do you suppose she would say?" said the farmer, pretending surprise.

"That's just it, Courtin."

"Hang it! I suppose Monsieur le baron has his reasons," said the farmer, in his jeering tone.

"Yes; and you shall hear them as soon as we get to your house."

"My house! Are you going to my house?" said Courtin, surprised.

"You don't refuse to take me in, do you?" asked Michel.

"Good heavens, no! Refuse to take you into a house which, after all, is yours?"

"Then don't let us lose time, it is so late. You walk first. I'll follow."

Courtin, rather uneasy at the imperative tone of his young master, obeyed. A few steps farther on he climbed a bank, crossed an orchard, and reached the door of his farmhouse. As soon as he entered the lower room, which served him as kitchen and living-room, he drew a few scattered brands together on the hearth and blew up a blaze; then he lighted a candle of yellow wax and stuck it on the chimney-piece. By the light of this candle he saw what he could not see by the light of the moon, — namely, that Michel was as pale as death.

"My God! what's the matter with you, Monsieur le baron?" he exclaimed.

"Courtin," said the young man, frowning, "I heard every word of your conversation with my mother."

"Confound it! were you listening?" said the farmer, a good deal surprised. But, recovering instantly, he added, "Well, what of it?"

"You want your lease renewed next year?"

"I, Monsieur le baron?"

"You, Courtin; and you want it much more than you choose to own."

"Of course I shouldn't be sorry to have it renewed, Monsieur le baron; but if there's any objection it wouldn't be the death of me."

"Courtin, I am the person who will renew your lease, because I shall be of age by that time."

"Yes, that's so, Monsieur le baron."

"But you will understand," continued the young man, to whom the desire of saving the Comte de Bonneville and staying near Mary gave a firmness and resolution quite foreign to his character, "you understand, don't you, that if you do as you said to-night, — that is, if you denounce my friends, — I shall most certainly not renew the lease of an informer?"

"Oh! oh!" exclaimed Courtin.

"That is certain. Once out of this farm you may say good-bye to it, Courtin; you shall never return to it."

"But my duty to the government and Madame la baronne?"

"All that is nothing to me. I am Baron Michel de la Logerie; the estate and château de la Logerie belong to me; my mother resigns them when I come of age; I shall be of age in eleven months, and your lease falls in eight weeks later."

"But suppose I renounce my intention, Monsieur le baron?"

"If you renounce your intention, your lease shall be renewed."

"On the same conditions as before?"

"On the same conditions as before."

"Oh, Monsieur le baron, if I were not afraid of compromising you," said Courtin, fetching pen, ink, and paper from the drawer of a desk.

"What does all this mean?" demanded Michel.

"Oh, hang it! if Monsieur le baron would only have the kindness to write down what he has just said, — who knows which of us will die first? For my part, I am ready to swear, — here's a crucifix, — well, I swear by Christ — "

"I don't want your oaths, Courtin, for I shall go from here to Souday and warn Jean Oullier to be on his guard, and Bonneville to get another resting-place."

"So much the more reason," said Courtin, offering a pen to his young master.

Michel took the pen and wrote as follows on the paper which the farmer laid before him: —

"I, the undersigned, Auguste-François Michel, Baron de la Logerie, agree to renew the lease of farmer Courtin on the same conditions as the present lease."

Then, as he was about to date it, Courtin stopped him.

"Don't put the date, if you please, my young master," he said. "We will date it the day after you come of age."

"So be it," said Michel.

He then merely signed it, and left, between the pledge and the signature, a line to receive the future date.

"If Monsieur le baron would like to be more comfortable for the night than on that stool," said Courtin, "I will take the liberty to mention that there is, at his service upstairs, a bed that is not so bad."

"No," replied Michel; "did you not hear me say I was going to Souday?"

"What for? Monsieur le baron has my promise, I pledge him my word to say nothing. He has time enough."

"What you saw, Courtin, another may have seen. You may keep silence because you have promised it; but the other, who did not promise, will speak. Good-bye to you."

"Monsieur le baron will do as he likes," said Courtin; "but he makes a mistake, yes, a great mistake, in going back into that mouse-trap."

"Pooh! I thank you for your advice; but I am not sorry to let you know I am of an age now to do as I choose."

Rising as he said the words, with a firmness of which the farmer had supposed him incapable, he went to the door and left the house. Courtin followed him with his eyes till the door was closed; after which, snatching up the written promise, he read it over, folded it carefully in four, and put it away in his pocket-book. Then, fancying he heard voices at a little distance, he went to the window and, drawing back the curtain, saw the young baron face to face with his mother.

"Ha, ha, my young cockerel!" he said; "you crowed pretty loud with me, but there's an old hen who'll make you lower your comb."

The baroness, finding that her son did not return, thought that Courtin might be right when he suggested that Michel was possibly at the farmhouse. She hesitated a moment, partly from pride, partly from fear of going out alone at night; but, finally, her maternal uneasiness got the better of her reluctance, and wrapping herself in a large shawl, she set out for the farmhouse. As she approached the door her son came out of it. Then, relieved of her fears for his safety, and seeing him sound and well, her imperious nature reasserted itself.

Michel, for his part, on catching sight of his mother, made a step backward in terror.

"Follow me, sir," said the baroness. "It is not too early, I think, to return home."

The poor lad never once thought of arguing or resisting; he followed his mother passively and obediently as a child. Not a word was exchanged between mother and son the whole way. For that matter, Michel much preferred this silence to a discussion in which his filial obedience, or rather, let us say, his weak nature, would have had the worst of it.

When they reached the château day was breaking. The baroness, still silent, conducted the young man to his room. There he found a table prepared with food.

"You must be hungry and very tired," said the baroness. "There you have food, and here you can rest," she added, waving her hand to the table and the bed, after which she retired, closing the door after her.

The young man trembled as he heard the key turned twice in the lock. He was a prisoner! He fell helplessly into an arm-chair. Events were rushing on like an avalanche, and a more vigorous organization than that of Baron Michel might have given way under them. As it was, he had only a certain small amount of energy, and that was all expended in his interview with Courtin.

Perhaps he had presumed too much upon his strength when he told Courtin he should go to the château de Souday; at any rate, he was, as his mother said, tired out and very hungry. At Michel's age Nature is a mother, too, who will have her rights. Besides, a certain ease of mind had stolen over him. His mother's words, as she pointed to the table and the bed, seemed to imply that she did not mean to return until he had eaten and slept. It gave him some hours of calm before the storm of explanation.

Michel ate hastily, and then, after trying the door to make sure that he was really a prisoner, he went to bed and to sleep.

At ten o'clock he awoke. The beams of a splendid May sun were coming joyously through his windows. He opened the windows. The birds were singing in the branches, which were just then covered with their young and tender leafage. The roses were budding; the first butterflies were circling in the air. On such a day it seemed as though misfortune were imprisoned and could not come to any one. The young man found a sort of strength in this revival of Nature, and awaited the dreaded interview with his mother with more composure.

But the hours went by. Mid-day struck, and still the baroness did not appear. Michel then noticed, with a certain uneasiness, that the table had been amply supplied, not only for his supper of the night before, but also for the breakfast and dinner of the following day. He began to fear that his captivity might last much longer than he expected. This fear grew deeper as two and then three o'clock struck. He listened for every sound, and after a time he fancied he heard shots in the direction of Montaigu. These sounds had all the regularity of platoon firing, and yet it was impossible to say whether they came actually from a fusillade. Montaigu was six miles from La Logerie, and a distant thunder-storm might produce somewhat the same sounds.

But no! the sky was cloudless; there was no storm. The sounds lasted over an hour; then all was silent. The baron's uneasiness now became so great that he forgot to eat the food prepared for him. He resolved on one thing, — namely, as soon as night came and the people of the house were in bed he would cut out the lock of the door with his knife and leave the château, not by the front entrance, but by some window on the lower floor.

This possibility of flight restored the prisoner's appetite. He dined like a man who thinks he has a toilsome night before him, and who gathers strength to make head against it.

He finished his dinner about seven in the evening. It would be dusk in another hour. He flung himself on his bed and waited. He would fain have slept, for sleep would have shortened the time of waiting, but his mind was too uneasy. He closed his eyes, to be sure, but his ears, constantly alert, heard every sound. One thing surprised him much; he had seen nothing of his mother. She would certainly, he thought, expect him to do what he could to escape as soon as it was dark. No doubt she was planning something; but what could it be?

Suddenly Michel thought he heard the tinkling of bells which are usually fastened to the collars of post-horses. He ran to the window. He seemed to see, coming along the road from Montaigu, an indistinct group moving rapidly in the gathering darkness toward the château de la Logerie. The sound of horses' hoofs now mingled with the tinkling of the bells. Presently the postilion cracked his whip, probably to announce his coming. No doubt remained; it certainly was a postilion with post-horses on his way to the château.

Instinctively the young man looked toward the stables, and there he saw the servants dragging his mother's travelling-carriage from the coach-house. A flash of light came into his mind. These post-horses from Montaigu, the postilion cracking his whip, the travelling-carriage making ready for use, — no doubt, no doubt at all remained; his mother meant to leave La Logerie and take him with her. That was why she had locked him up and kept him a prisoner. She meant to come for him at the last moment, force him to get into the carriage with her, and away, away from everything he would be forced to go. She knew her ascendency over her son sufficiently well to be certain he would not venture to resist her.

The consciousness that his mother had this conviction exasperated the young man all the more because he knew it was a true one. It was evident to his own mind that if the baroness once came face to face with him he would not dare to oppose her.

But to leave Mary, renounce that life of emotion to which the sisters had introduced him, to take no part in the drama which the Comte de Bonneville and his mysterious companion had come into La Vendée to play, seemed to him impossible and dishonoring. What would those young girls think of him?

Michel resolved to run all risks rather than endure the humiliation of their contempt.

He went to the window and measured with his eye the height from the ground; it was thirty feet. The young baron stood in thought for a moment. Evidently some great struggle was going on within him. At last it was decided. He went to his desk and took out a large sum of money in gold, with which he filled his pockets. Just then he thought he heard steps in the corridor. He hastily closed his desk and threw himself on his bed, expectant. An observer would have seen by the unusual firmness of the muscles of his face that his resolution was taken.

What was that resolution? In all probability we shall sooner or later discover what it was.

XVII.

THE TAVERN OF AUBIN COURTE-JOIE.

IT was plain, — even to the authorities, who are usually the last to be informed as to the state of public opinion in the countries they are called upon to govern, — it was plain, we say, that an uprising was contemplated in Brittany and in La Vendée.

We have heard Courtin tell Madame de la Logerie of the meetings of the legitimist leaders. Those meetings were a secret to no one. The names of the new Bonchamps and Elbées, who were to put themselves at the head of this last Vendéan struggle, were well-known and noted; the organizations of the former period into "parishes," "captaincies," and "divisions," were renewed; the priests refused to chant the *Domine salvum fac regem Philippum*, commending to the prayers of their people Henri V., king of France, and Marie-Caroline, regent. In short, in all the departments bordering on the Loire, particularly those of the Lower Loire and of the Maine-et-Loire, the air was filled with that smell of powder which precedes, as a general thing, all great political convulsions.

In spite of this wide-spread fermentation, — perhaps in consequence of it, — the fair at Montaigu promised to be very brilliant. Although it was usually of small importance, the influx of peasants on this occasion was considerable. The men from the high lands of Mauges and Retz rubbed shoulders with those from the Bocage and the plain; and the warlike inclination of all these country-folk was manifested by the prevalence of broad-brimmed hats and long-haired heads, and the absence of caps. In fact, the women, who were usually the majority in these commercial assemblies, did not come, on this occasion, to the Montaigu fair.

Moreover, — and this alone would have sufficed to show the incipient state of things to the least observing person, — though customers were plentiful at the fair of Montaigu, horses, cows, sheep, butter, and corn, which constituted the ordinary traffic, were conspicuously absent. The peasants, whether they came from Beaupréau, Mortagne, Bressuire, Saint-Fulgent, or Machecoul, carried in place of their usual marketable produce nothing but stout cudgels of dogwood tipped with iron, and by the way they grasped them it was plain enough that they meant to do business of that kind.

The market-place and the main (and only) street in Montaigu, which were used as the fair-ground, had a serious, almost threatening, and certainly solemn aspect, which is not usual in such assemblages. A few jugglers, a few vendors of quack medicines, a few teeth-pullers tapped their boxes, blew their bugles, clanged their gongs, and vaunted their trades facetiously to no purpose; frowns continued on the anxious faces that passed them by without deigning to listen to their music or their chatter.

The people of La Vendée, like their neighbors of the North, the Bretons, talk but little. On this occasion they talked less than ever. Most of them stood with their backs against the houses or the garden walls or the wooden bars that inclosed the market-place, and there they stood, motionless, their legs crossed, their heads under their broad hats inclining forward, and their hands leaning on their sticks, like so many statues. Some were gathered in little groups, and these groups, which seemed to be awaiting something, were, strange to say, as silent as the solitary individuals.

The crowds were great in the drinking-shops. Cider, brandy, and coffee were dispensed there in vast quantities; but the constitution of the Vendéan peasant is so robust that the enormous quantities of liquor absorbed had no visible influence on the faces and conduct of any of them. Their color might be a little higher, their eyes more brilliant, but the men were masters of themselves, and all the more so because they distrusted those who kept the wine-shops, and the village folk whom they met there. In the towns and villages along the great high-roads of La Vendée and Brittany the minds of the inhabitants were, as a general thing, awakened to ideas of progress and liberty; but these sentiments, which cooled at a little distance, disappeared altogether when the interior country districts were reached.

Consequently, all the inhabitants of the chief centres of population, unless they had given unequivocal proofs of devotion to the royal cause, were classed as "patriots" by the peasantry; and patriots were to the peasants enemies, to whom they attributed all the evils resulting from the great insurrection, hating them with that deep, undying hatred which characterizes civil and religious warfare.

In coming to the fair at Montaigu — a centre of population, and occupied at this time by a company of some hundred or so of Mobile guards — the inhabitants of the country districts had penetrated to the very centre of their enemies. They understood this thoroughly, and that is why they maintained under a pacific demeanor the reserve and vigilance of soldiers under arms.

Only one of the numerous drinking-shops of Montaigu was kept by a man on whom the Vendéans could rely, and before whom, consequently, they discarded all constraint. His tavern was in the centre of the town, on the fair-ground itself, at the corner of the market-place and a side alley leading, not to another street nor to the fields, but to the river Maine, which skirts the town to the southeast.

The tavern had no sign. A branch of dry holly, stuck horizontally into a crack of the wall, and a few apples, seen through window-panes so covered with dust that no curtain was needed, informed all strangers of the nature of the establishment. As for its regular customers, they needed no indications.

The proprietor of this tavern was named Aubin Courte-Joie. Aubin was his family name; Courte-Joie was a nickname, which he owed to the jeering propensities of his friends. He came by it in this way. The part, insignificant as it is, which Aubin Courte-Joie plays in this history obliges us to say a word on his antecedents.

At twenty years of age Aubin was so frail, debilitated, and sickly, that even the conscription, which did not look very closely into such matters, rejected him as unfit for the favors which his Imperial and Royal Majesty bestowed upon his conscripts. But in 1814 this same conscription, having then aged by two years, was less fastidious, and came to the conclusion that what it had so far considered an abortion was at any rate a numerical figure, somewhere between a one and a nought, and could, if only on paper, contribute to the terrifying of the kings of Europe. Consequently, the conscription laid hands on Aubin.

But Aubin, whom the original disdain manifested by the authorities toward his person had alienated from all desire for military glory, resolved to desert the government, and taking to flight he connected himself with one of those bands of refractories (as recalcitrant conscripts were then called) who roamed the interior of the country. The less plentiful recruits became, the more pitiless grew the agents of imperial authority.

Aubin, whom Nature had not endowed with excessive conceit, would never have thought himself so necessary to the government if he had not seen with his own eyes the trouble that the government took to hunt for him through the forests of Brittany and the bogs of La Vendée. The *gendarmes* were active in their pursuit of refractories.

In one of the encounters that resulted from this pursuit, Aubin had used his gun with a courage and tenacity which proved that the conscription of 1814 was not altogether wrong in wishing to lay hands on him as one of its elect,

— in one of these encounters, we were about to say, Aubin was hit by a ball and left for dead in the roadway.

On that day a bourgeoise of Ancenis took the road by the river bank, which leads from Ancenis to Nantes. She was in her carriole, and it might be about eight or nine o'clock at night; at any rate, it was dusk. When she came to the body the horse shuddered in the shafts and refused to go on. She whipped him, he reared. On further whipping, the animal tried to turn short round and go back to Ancenis. His mistress, who had never known him to behave in that way before, got out of her carriole. All was then explained. Aubin's body lay across the road.

Such encounters were not infrequent in those days. The bourgeoise was only slightly alarmed. She fastened her horse to a tree, and began to drag Aubin's body into the ditch, to make room for her vehicle and others that might pass that way. But she had no sooner touched the body than she found it warm. The motion she gave to it, perhaps the pain of the motion, brought Aubin to his senses; he gave a sigh and moved his arms.

The end of it was that, instead of putting him into the ditch, the bourgeoise put him into her carriole; and instead of continuing her way to Nantes she returned to Ancenis. The good dame was pious and a royalist. The cause for which Aubin was wounded, the scapulary she found on his breast, interested her deeply. She sent for a surgeon. The luckless Aubin had both legs fractured by one shot; it was necessary to amputate them. The worthy woman nursed him and took care of him with all the devotion of a sister of charity. Her good deed, as often happens, attached her to the object of it, and when Aubin was once more well in health it was with the utmost astonishment that he received an offer of her heart and hand. Needless to say that Aubin accepted.

Thenceforth Aubin became, to the stupefaction of all the country round one of the small proprietors of the canton.

But, alas! his joy was of short duration. His wife died within a year. She had taken the precaution to make a will, leaving him all her property; but her natural heirs attacked it for some error of form, and the court at Nantes having decided in their favor, the poor ex-recruit was no better off than before his luck happened to him. It was in reference to the short duration of his opulence that the inhabitants of Montaigu, who were not, as will be imagined, without envy at his rise or rejoicing at his fall, bestowed upon him the significant addition of Courte-Joie (Short-Joy) to his proper name.

Now, the heirs who had managed to set aside the will belonged to the liberal party. Aubin could not, therefore, do less than vent upon that party in general the anger that the loss of his property excited in him. He did so, and he did it conscientiously. Soured by his infirmities, embittered by what seemed to him a horrible injustice, Aubin Courte-Joie felt to all those whom he blamed for his misfortunes — judges, patriots, and adversaries — a savage hatred. Public events had encouraged this hatred, and it was now awaiting a favorable moment to convert itself into deeds which the sullen and vindictive nature of the man would undoubtedly render terrible.

With his twofold infirmity it was impossible for Aubin to go back to his old life and become a farmer and tiller of the ground like his father and grandfather before him. He was compelled, therefore, much against his will, to live in a town. Gathering up the fragments of his lost opulence he came to live in the midst of those he hated most, at Montaigu itself, where he kept the tavern in which we find him eighteen years after the events we have just recorded.

In 1832 there was not in all La Vendée a more enthusiastic adherent to royalist opinions than Aubin Courte-Joie. In serving that cause was he not fulfilling a personal vengeance? Aubin Courte-Joie was, therefore, in spite of his two wooden legs, the most active and intelligent agent in the uprising which was now being organized. Standing sentinel in the midst of the enemy's camp, he kept the Vendéan leaders informed of all the government preparations for defence, not only in the canton of Montaigu, but also throughout the adjoining districts.

The tramps who roamed the country — those customers of a day, whom other tavern-keepers considered of no profit and paid no heed to — were in his hands marvellous auxiliaries, whom he kept employed in a circuit of thirty miles. He used them as spies, and also as messengers to and from the inhabitants of the country districts. His tavern was the rendezvous of all those who were distinctively called Chouans. It was the only one, as we have said, where they were not obliged to repress their royalist sentiments.

On the day of the fair at Montaigu Aubin Courte-Joie's drinking-shop did not at first sight seem so full of customers as might have been expected from the great influx of country people. In the first of the two rooms, a dark and gloomy apartment, furnished with an unpolished wooden counter and a few benches and stools, not more than a dozen peasants were assembled. By the cleanliness, we might say the nicety of their clothes, it was plain that these peasants belonged to the upper class of farmers.

This first room was separated from the second by a glass partition, behind which was a cotton curtain with large red and white squares. The second room served as kitchen, dining-room, bedroom, and office, becoming also, on great occasions an annex to the common hall; it was where Aubin Courte-Joie received his special friends.

The furniture of this room showed its quintuple service. At the farther end was a very low bed, with a tester and curtains of green serge; this was evidently the couch of the legless proprietor. It was flanked by two huge hogsheads, from which brandy and cider were drawn on demand of customers. To right, on entering, was the fireplace, with a wide, high chimney-piece like those of cottages.

In the middle of the room was an oak table with wooden benches on each side of it. Opposite to the fireplace stood a dresser with crockery and tin utensils. A crucifix surmounted by a branch of consecrated holly, a few wax figurines of a devotional character coarsely colored, constituted the decoration of the apartment.

On this occasion Aubin Courte-Joie had admitted to this sanctuary a number of his numerous friends. In the outer room there were, as we have said, not more than a dozen; but at least a score were in the second. Most of these were sitting round the table drinking and talking with great animation. Three or four were emptying great bags piled up in one corner of the room and containing large, round sea-biscuits; these they counted and put in baskets, giving the baskets to tramps or women who stood by an outer door in the corner of the room behind the cider cask. This door opened upon a little courtyard, which itself opened into the alley-way leading to the river, which we have already mentioned.

Aubin Courte-Joie was seated in a sort of arm-chair under the mantel-shelf of the chimney. Beside him was a man wearing a goatskin garment and a black woollen cap, in whom we may recognize our old friend Jean Oullier, with his dog lying at his feet between his legs. Behind them Courte-Joie's niece, a young and handsome peasant girl, whom the tavern-keeper had taken to do the serving of his business, was stirring the fire and watching some dozen brown cups in which was gently simmering in the heat from the hearth what the peasants call "a roast of cider."

Aubin Courte-Joie was talking eagerly in a low voice to Jean Oullier, when a slight whistle, like the frightened cry of a partridge, came from the outer room.

"Who came in?" said Courte-Joie, looking through a peephole he had made in the curtain. "The man from La Logerie. Attention!"

Even before this order was given to those whom it concerned, all was still and orderly in Courte-Joie's sanctum. The outer door was gently closed; the women and the tramps disappeared; the men who were counting the biscuits had closed and turned over their sacks, and were sitting on them, and smoking their pipes in an easy attitude.

As for the men drinking at the table, three or four had suddenly gone to sleep as if by enchantment. Jean Oullier turned round toward the hearth, thus concealing his face from the first glance of any one entering the apartment.

XVIII.

THE MAN FROM LA LOGERIE.

COURTIN, — for it was he whom Courte-Joie designated as the man from La Logerie, — Courtin had entered the outer room. Except for the little cry of warning, so well imitated that it was really like the cry of a frightened partridge, no one appeared to take any notice of his presence. The men who were drinking continued their talk, although, serious as their manner was when Courtin entered, it now became suddenly very gay and noisy.

The farmer looked about him, but evidently did not find in the first room the person he wanted, for he resolutely opened the door of the glass partition and showed his sneaking face on the threshold of the inner room. There again, no one seemed to notice him. Mariette alone, Aubin Courte-Joie's niece, who was waiting on the customers, withdrew her attention from the cider cups, and looking at Courtin said, as she would have done to any of her uncle's guests: —

"What shall I bring you, Monsieur Courtin?"

"Coffee," replied Courtin, inspecting the faces that were round the table and in the corners of the room.

"Very good; sit down," said Mariette. "I'll bring it to your seat presently."

"That's not worth while," replied Courtin, good-humoredly; "pour it out now. I'll drink it here in the chimney-corner with the friends."

No one seemed to object to this qualification; but neither did any one stir to make room for him. Courtin was therefore obliged to make further advances.

"Are you well, *gars* Aubin?" he asked, addressing the tavern-keeper.

"As you see," replied the latter, without turning his head.

It was obvious to Courtin that he was not received with much good-will; but he was not a man to disconcert himself for a trifle like that.

"Here, Mariette," said he, "give me a stool, that I may sit down near your uncle."

"There are no stools left, Maître Courtin," replied the girl. "I should think your eyes were good enough to see that."

"Well, then, your uncle will give me his," continued Courtin, with audacious familiarity, though at heart he felt little encouraged by the behavior of the landlord and his customers.

"If you will have it," grumbled Aubin Courte-Joie, "you must, being as how I am master of the house, and it shall never be said that any man was refused a seat at the Holly Branch when he wanted to sit down."

"Then give me your stool, as you say, smooth-tongue, for there's the very man I'm after, right next to you."

"Who's that?" said Aubin, rising; and instantly a dozen other stools were offered.

"Jean Oullier," replied Courtin; "and it's my belief that here he is."

Hearing his name, Jean Oullier rose and said, in a tone that was almost menacing: —

"What do you want with me?"

"Well, well! you need n't eat me up because I want to see you," replied the mayor of la Logerie. "What I have to say is of more importance to you than it is to me."

"Maître Courtin," said Jean Oullier, in a grave tone, "whatever you may choose to pretend, we are not friends; and what's more, you know it so well that you have not come here with any good intentions."

"Well, you are mistaken, *gars* Oullier."

"Maître Courtin," continued Jean Oullier, paying no attention to the signs which Aubin Courte-Joie made, exhorting him to prudence, "Maître Courtin, ever since we have known each other you have been a Blue, and you bought bad property."

"Bad property!" exclaimed Courtin, with his jeering smile.

"Oh! I know what I mean, and so do you. I mean illgotten property. You 've been hand and glove with the curs of the towns; you have persecuted the peasantry and the villagers, — those who have kept their faith in God and the king. What is there in common between you, who have done all that, and me, who have done just the reverse?"

"True," replied Courtin, "true, *gars* Oullier, I have not navigated in your waters; but, for all that, I say that neighbors ought not to wish the death of each other. I have come in search of you to do you a service; I 'll swear to that."

"I don't want your services, Maître Courtin," replied Jean Oullier.

"Why not?" persisted the farmer.

"Because I am certain they hide some treachery."

"So you refuse to listen to me?"

"I refuse," replied the huntsman, roughly.

"You are wrong," said Aubin Courte-Joie, in a low voice; for he thought the frank, outspoken rudeness of his friend a mistaken manœuvre.

"Very good," said Courtin; "then remember this. If harm comes to the inhabitants of the château de Souday, you have nobody to thank but yourself, *gars* Oullier."

There was evidently some special meaning in Courtin's manner of saying the word "inhabitants;" "inhabitants" of course included guests. Jean Oullier could not mistake this meaning, and in spite of his habitual self-command he turned pale. He regretted he had been so decided, but it was dangerous now to retrace his steps. If Courtin had suspicions, such a retreat would confirm them. He therefore did his best to master his emotion, and sat down again, turning his back on Courtin with an indifferent air; in fact, his manner was so careless that Courtin, sly dog as he was, was taken in by it. He did not leave the tavern as hastily as might have been expected after delivering his warning threat; on the contrary, he searched his pockets a long time to find enough change to pay for his coffee. Aubin Courte-Joie understood the meaning of this by-play, and profited by Courtin's lingering to put in a word himself.

"My good Jean," he said, addressing Jean Oullier in a hearty way, "we have long been friends, and have followed the same road for many years, I hope — here are two wooden legs that prove it. Well, I am not afraid to say to you, before Monsieur Courtin, that you are wrong, don't you see, wrong! So long as a hand is closed none but a fool will say, 'I know what is in it.' It is true that Monsieur Courtin" (Aubin Courte-Joie punctiliously gave that title to the mayor of la Logerie) "has never been one of us; but neither has he been against us. He has been for himself, and that is all the blame we can put upon him. But nowadays, when quarrels are over and there are neither Blues nor Chouans any more, to-day when, thank God, there's peace in the land, what does the color of his cockade signify to you? Faith! if Monsieur Courtin has, as he says, something useful to tell you it seems to me a pity not to hear it."

Jean Oullier shrugged his shoulders impatiently.

"Old fox!" thought Courtin, who was far too well informed as to the real state of things to be taken in by the pacific flowers of rhetoric with which Aubin Courte-Joie thought proper to wreathe his remarks. But aloud he said, "All the more because what I have to say has nothing to do with politics."

"There! you see," said Courte-Joie, "there is no reason why you should not talk with the mayor. Come, come, sit down here and have a talk with him at your ease."

All this made no difference in Jean Oullier, who was neither mollified toward Courtin, nor did he even turn his head; only, when the mayor sat down beside him he did not get up and walk away, as might have been expected.

"*Gars* Oullier," said Courtin, by way of preamble, "I think talks are all the better for being moistened. 'Wine is the honey of words,' as our vicar says, — not in his sermons, but that don't make it less true. If we drink a bottle together perhaps that will sweeten our ideas."

"As you please," replied Jean Oullier, who, while feeling the strongest repugnance to hob-nob with Courtin, regarded the sacrifice as necessary to the cause he had at heart.

"Have you any wine?" said Courtin to Mariette.

"What a question!" she exclaimed. "Have we any wine, indeed! I should think so!"

"Good wine, I mean; sealed bottles."

"Sealed bottles, yes," said Mariette, proudly; "but they cost forty sous each."

"Pooh!" said Aubin, who had seated himself in the other chimney-corner to catch, if he could, some scraps of the promised communication, "the mayor is a man who has got the wherewithal, my girl, and forty sous won't prevent his paying his rent to Madame la Baronne Michel."

Courtin regretted his show of liberality; if the days of the old war were really coming back it might be dangerous to pass for rich.

"Wherewithal!" he exclaimed; "how you talk, *gars* Aubin! Yes, certainly, I have enough to pay my rent, but that paid I consider myself a lucky man if I can make both ends meet; that's my wealth!"

"Whether you are rich or poor is none of our business," remarked Jean Oullier. "Come, what have you to say to me? Make haste."

Courtin took the bottle which Mariette now brought him, wiped the neck of it carefully with his sleeve, poured a few drops into his own glass, filled that of Jean Oullier, then his own, touched glasses, and slowly emptied his.

"No one is to be pitied," he said, smacking his lips, "if they can drink such wine as that every day."

"Especially if they drink it with a clear conscience," added Jean Oullier. "In my opinion that's what makes wine taste good."

"Jean Oullier," said Courtin, without noticing the philosophical reflection of his companion, "you bear me ill-will, and you are wrong. On my word of honor, you are wrong."

"Prove it, and I'll believe you. That's all the confidence I have in you."

"I don't wish you harm; I wish good for myself, as Aubin Courte-Joie, who is a man of judgment, said just now; but you don't call that a crime, I hope. I mind my own little matters without meddling much in other people's business, because, as I say to myself, 'My good fellow, if at Easter or Christmas you haven't got your money ready in your pouch the king, be he Henri V. or Louis Philippe, will send the Treasury after you, and you'll get a paper in his name, which may be an honor, but it will cost you dear.' You reason differently; that's your affair. I don't blame you, — at the most I only pity you."

"Keep your pity for others, Maître Courtin," replied Jean Oullier, haughtily; "I don't want it any more than I want your confidences."

"When I say I pity you, *gars* Oullier, I mean your master as well as yourself. Monsieur le marquis is a man I respect. He fought through the great war. Well, what did he gain by it?"

"Maître Courtin, you said you were not going to talk politics, and you are breaking your word."

"Yes, I did say so, that's true; but it is not my fault if in this devilish country politics are so twisted in with everybody's business that the one can't be separated from the other. As I was saying, *gars* Oullier, Monsieur le marquis is a man I respect, and I am very sorry, very sorry indeed, to see him ridden over by a lot of common rich folks, — he who used to be the first in the province."

"If he is satisfied with his lot why need you care?" replied Jean Oullier. "You never heard him complain; he has never borrowed money of you."

"What would you say to a man who offered to restore to the château de Souday all the wealth and consideration it has lost? Come," continued Courtin, not hindered by the coldness of the Chouan, "do you think that a man who is ready to do *that* can be your enemy? Don't you think, on the contrary, that Monsieur le marquis would owe him a debt of gratitude? There, now, answer that question squarely and honestly, as I have spoken to you."

"Of course he would, if the man you speak of did what you say by honest means; but I doubt it."

"Honest means! Would any one dare propose to you any that were not honest?" See here, my *gars!* I'll out with it at once, and not take all day and many words to say it. I can, — yes, I, who speak to you, — I can make the money flow into the château de Souday, as it hasn't done of late years; only — "

"Only — yes, that's it; only what? Ha! that's where the collar galls."

"Only, I was going to say, I must get my profit out of it."

"If the matter is an honest one, that's only fair; you will certainly get your part."

"That's all I want to know to set the wheel in motion, — and it's little enough, too."

"Yes; but what is it you are after? What is it you ask?" returned Jean Oullier, now very curious to know what was in Courtin's head.

"Oh! it is just as simple as nothing. In the first place, I want it so arranged that I need n't renew my lease or have any rent to pay for twelve years to come on the farm I occupy."

"In other words, you want a present?"

"If Monsieur de Souday offers it I shall not refuse, you understand. Of course I shouldn't be such a fool as to stand in my own light."

"But how can it be arranged? Your farm belongs to young Michel or his mother. I have not heard that they want to sell it. How can any man give you that which he doesn't possess?"

"Oh!" said Courtin, "if I interfere in the matter I speak of perhaps that farm may soon belong to some of you, and then it would be easy enough. What do you say?"

"I say I don't understand what you are talking about, Maître Courtin."

"Nonsense! Ha, ha! but it isn't a bad match for our young man. Don't you know that besides La Logerie he owns the estate of la Coudraie, the mills at La Ferronnerie, the woods of Gervaise, all of which bring in, one year with another, a pretty sum of money? And I can tell you this, the old baroness has laid by as much more, which he will get at her death."

"What has that Michel youth to do with the Marquis de Souday? they have nothing in common," said Jean Oullier. "And why should the property of your master be of any interest to mine?"

"Come, come, let's play above-board, *gars* Oullier. Damn it! you must have seen that our young man is sweet upon one of your young ladies, very sweet, indeed! Which of them it is, I can't tell you; but let Monsieur le marquis just say the word and sign me a paper about that farm, and the minute the girl, whichever it is, is married, — they are as smart as flies, those two, — she can manage her husband as she likes and get all she wants. He'll never refuse her a few acres of ground, especially when she wants to give them to a man to whom he'll be grateful, too. In this way I kill two birds with one stone, do your business and my own too. There is but one obstacle, and that's the mother. Well," added Courtin, leaning close to Oullier's ear, "I'll undertake to get rid of that."

Jean Oullier made no answer; but he looked fixedly at his companion.

"Yes," continued the latter, "if everybody wishes it, Madame la baronne won't be able to refuse it. I'll tell you this, Oullier," added Courtin, striking the other familiarly on the knee, "I know the whole story of Monsieur Michel."

"Why should you want our help, then? What hinders you from getting all you want out of her without delay?"

"What hinders me is this: I want to add to the word of a youth who, while keeping his sheep, heard a treacherous bargain made, — I want to add to his word the testimony of the man who was in the woods of La Chabotière some forty years ago, and saw the price of that bloody and treacherous bargain paid. You know best who saw that sight and who can give that testimony, *gars* Oullier. If you and I make common cause, the baroness will be as supple as a handful of flax. She is miserly, but she is also proud; the fear of public dishonor and the gossip of the neighborhood will make her docile enough. She'll see that, after all, Mademoiselle de Souday, poor and illegitimate as she is, is more than a match for the son of Baron Michel, whose grandfather was a peasant like ourselves, and whose father the baron was — you know what. Enough! Your young lady will be rich, our young man will be happy, and I shall be very glad. What objection can be offered to all that? — not to speak of our becoming friends, *gars* Oullier; and I think my friendship is worth something to you, I must say."

"Your friendship?" replied Jean Oullier, who had repressed with great difficulty the indignation he felt at the singular proposal that Courtin had just made to him.

"Yes, my friendship," returned the latter. "You need n't shake your head like that. I have told you that I know more than any man about the life of Baron Michel;

I will add that I know more than any man but one about his death. I was one of the beaters of the drive at which he was killed, and my post placed me just opposite to him. I was young, and even then I had a habit (which God preserve to me) of not gabbling unless it were my interest to do so. Now, then, do you think my services to your party of no account if my interests take me over to your side?"

"Maître Courtin," replied Jean Oullier, frowning, "I have no influence on the plans and determinations of the Marquis de Souday, but if I had any at all, even the smallest, never should that farm of yours come into the family; and if it did come in, never should it serve as the price of treachery."

"Fine words, all that!" exclaimed Courtin.

"No; poor as the Demoiselles de Souday may be, never do I want either of them to marry the young man you speak of. Rich as he may be, and even if he bore another name than he does, no Demoiselle de Souday could buy her marriage by a base act."

"You call that a base act, do you? I call it a good stroke of business."

"It may be so for you; but for those I serve, a marriage with Monsieur Michel, bought through you, would be more than a base act; it would be an infamy."

"Take care, Jean Oullier. I want to act a kind part, and I won't let myself quarrel with the label you choose to stick upon my acts. I came here with good intentions; it is for you not to let me leave this place with bad ones."

"I care as little for your threats as I do for your proposals, Courtin; remember that. But if you force me to repeat it I shall say it to the end of time."

"Once more, Jean Oullier, listen to me. I will admit to you that I want to be rich. That is my whim, just as it is yours to be faithful as a dog to folks who don't care more for you than you do for your terrier. I thought I could be useful to your master, and I hoped he would not let my services go without reward. You say it is impossible. Then we'll say no more about it. But if the nobles whom you serve wished to show their gratitude to me in the way I ask I would rather do a service to them than to others; and I desire to tell you so once more."

"Because you think that nobles would pay more for it than others. Is n't that it?"

"Undoubtedly, *gars* Oullier. I don't conceal anything from you, and I'll repeat that, as you say, to the end of time."

"I shall not make myself the go-between in any such bargain, Maître Courtin. Besides, I have no power in the matter, and anything I could do for you is so small it is n't worth talking about."

"Hey, how do you know that? You did n't know, my *gars*, that I knew all about what happened in the wood at Chabotière. Perhaps I could astonish you if I told you all I know."

Jean Oullier was afraid of appearing afraid.

"Come," said he, "enough of this. If you want to sell yourself apply to others. Such bargains are hateful to me, even if I had any means of making them. They don't concern me, God be thanked."

"Is that your last word, Jean Oullier?"

"My first and my last. Go your ways, Maître Courtin, and leave me to mine."

"So much the worse for you," said Courtin, rising; "but, on my word, I would gladly have gone your way."

So saying, he nodded to Jean Oullier and went out. He had hardly crossed the threshold before Aubin Courte-Joie, stumping along on his wooden legs, came close to Jean Oullier.

"You have done a foolish thing," he whispered.

"What ought I to have done?"

"Taken him to Louis Renaud or to Gaspard; they would have bought him."

"Him, — that wicked traitor?"

"My good Jean, in 1815, when I was mayor, I went to Nantes, and there I saw a man named ——, who was, or had been, a minister; and I heard him say two things I have always remembered. One was that traitors make and unmake empires; the other was that treachery is the only thing in this world that is not to be measured by the size of him who makes it."

"What do you advise me to do now?"

"Follow and watch him."

Jean Oullier reflected a moment. Then he rose.

"I think you are right," he said.

And he went out anxiously.

XIX.

THE FAIR AT MONTAIGU.

THE effervescent state of minds in the west of France did not take the government unawares. Political faith had grown too lukewarm to allow a probable uprising, covering so large an extent of territory and involving so many conspirators, to remain long a secret.

Some time before Madame's arrival off the coast of Provence the authorities in Paris knew of the projected scheme, and repressive measures both prompt and vigorous had been arranged. No sooner was it evident that the princess was making her way to the western provinces than it was only a question of carrying out those measures and of putting the execution of them into safe and able hands.

The departments whose uprising was expected were divided into as many military districts as there were sub-prefectures. Each of these arrondissements, commanded by a chief of battalion, was the centre of several secondary cantonments commanded by captains, around which several minor detachments were encamped under command of lieutenants and sub-lieutenants, serving as guards and outposts into the interior districts as far as the safety of communications would permit.

Montaigu, in the arrondissement of Clisson, had its garrison, which consisted of a company of the 32d regiment of the line. The day on which the events we have now related occurred this garrison had been reinforced by two brigades of gendarmerie, which had reached Nantes that morning, and about a score of mounted chasseurs. The chasseurs were serving as escort to a general officer from the garrison at Nantes, who was on a tour of inspection of the various detachments. This was General Dermoncourt.

The inspection of the Montaigu garrison was over. Dermoncourt, a veteran as intelligent as he was energetic, thought it would not be out of place to inspect those whom he called his old Vendéan friends, now swarming into the streets and market-place of the town. He accordingly took off his uniform, put on citizen's clothes, and mingled with the crowds, accompanied by a member of the civil administration who happened to be at Montaigu at that moment.

The general bearing of the population though lowering was calm. The crowd opened to allow passage to the two gentlemen, and, although the martial carriage of the general, his heavy moustache, black, in spite of his sixty years, his scarred face, and the self-sufficient air of his companion, excited the inquisitive curiosity of the multitude, no hostile demonstration was made to them.

"Well, well," said the general, "my old friends the Vendéans are not much changed. I find them as uncommunicative as I left them thirty-eight years ago."

"To me such indifference seems a favorable sign," said the civil administrator, in a pompous tone. "The two months I have just passed in Paris, where there was a riot every day, gave me an experience in such matters, and I think I may safely assert that these people here show no signs of insurrection. Remark, general, that there are no knots of talkers, no orators in full blast, no animation, no mutterings; all is perfectly quiet. Come, come! these people are here for their business only, and have no thought of anything else, I'll answer for it."

"You are quite right, my dear sir; I am wholly of your mind. These worthy people, as you say, are thinking of absolutely nothing but their business; but that business is to distribute to the best advantage the leaden balls and the sabre-blades they keep hidden away out of sight, which they intend to bestow upon us as soon as possible."

"Do you really think so?"

"I don't think so, I am sure of it. If the religious element were not, fortunately for us, absent from this new uprising, a fact which makes me think it may not be general, I should confidently assure you that there is not one of those fellows you see over there in serge jackets and linen breeches and wooden shoes but has his post and rank and number in battalions raised by Messieurs the nobles."

"What! those tramps and beggars too?"

"Yes, those tramps and beggars especially. What characterizes this warfare, my good sir, is the fact that we have to do with an enemy who is everywhere and nowhere. You know he is there; you seek for him, and you find only a peasant like those about us, who bows to you, a beggar who holds out his hand, a pedler who offers his merchandise, a musician who rasps your ears with his hurdy-gurdy, a quack who vaunts his medicine, a little shepherd who smiles at you, a woman suckling her child on the threshold of her cottage, a harmless furze-bush growing beside the road. You pass them all without the slightest feeling of distrust, and yet, peasant, shepherd, beggar, musician, pedler, quack, and woman are the enemy. Even the furze-bush is in league with them. Some, creeping through the gorse, will follow you like your shadow, — indefatigable spies that they are! — and at the first alarming manœuvre on your part, those you are tracking are warned long before you are able to surprise them. Others will have picked up from the hedges and ditches and furrows their rusty guns concealed among the reeds or the long grass, and if you are worth the trouble, they will follow you, as the others did, from bush to bush and cover to cover, till they find some favorable opportunity for a sure aim. They are saving with their powder. The furze-bush will send you a shot, and if by chance it misses you, and you are able to examine the covert, you'll find nothing there but a tangle of branches, thorns, and leaves. That's what it is to be inoffensive in these regions, my good sir."

"Are not you exaggerating, general?" said the civil officer, with a doubting air.

"Heavens and earth, Monsieur le sous-préfet! perhaps you'll come to know it by experience. Here we are in the midst of an apparently pacific crowd. We have, you say, nothing but friends about us, Frenchmen, compatriots; well, just arrest one of those fellows —"

"What would happen if I arrested him?"

"It would happen that some one of the rest, — perhaps that young *gars* in a white smock, perhaps this beggar who is eating with such an appetite on the sill of that doorway, who may be, for all we know, Diot Jambe-d'Argent, or Bras-de-fer, or any other leader of the band, — will rise and make a sign. At that sign a dozen or more sticks, now peacefully carried about, will be down on our heads, and before my escort could get to our assistance we should be as flat as wheat beneath the sickle. You are not convinced? Then suppose you make the attempt."

"No, no; I believe you, general," cried the sub-prefect, eagerly. "The devil! all this is no joke. Ever since you have been enlightening me I fancy I see the scowls on their faces; they look like scoundrels."

"Not a bit of it! They are worthy people, very worthy fellows; only, you must know how to take them; and, unluckily, that is not always the case with those who are sent to manage them," said the general, with a sarcastic smile. "Do you want a specimen of their conversation? You are, or you have been, or you ought to have been a lawyer; but I'll bet you never met in all your experience of the profession fellows as clever at talking without saying anything as these Vendéan peasants. Hey, *gars!*" continued the general, addressing a peasant between thirty-five and forty years old, who was hovering about them, and examining, apparently with curiosity, a biscuit which he held in his hand, — "Hey, *gars*, show me where those good biscuits are sold; they look to me very tempting."

"They are not sold, monsieur; they are given away."

"Bless me! Well, I want one."

"It is curious," said the peasant, "very curious that good white wheat biscuits should be given away, when they might so easily be sold."

"Yes, very singular; but what is still more singular is that the first individual I happen to address not only answers my question, but anticipates those I might ask him. Show me that biscuit, my good man."

The general examined the article which the peasant handed to him. It was a plain biscuit made of flour and milk, on which, before it was baked, a cross and four parallel bars had been marked with a knife.

"The devil! Well! a present that is amusing as well as useful is good to get. There must be a riddle of some kind in those marks. Who gave you that biscuit, my good friend?"

"No one; they don't trust me."

"Ah! then you are a patriot?"

"I am mayor of my district, and I hold by the government. I saw a woman giving a lot of these biscuit to men from Machecoul, without their asking for them and without their giving her anything in return. So then I offered to buy one, and she dared not refuse. I bought two. I ate one before her, and the other, this one, I slipped into my pocket."

"Will you let me have it? I am making a collection of rebuses, and this one seems interesting."

"I will give it or sell it, as you please."

"Ah, ha!" exclaimed Dermoncourt, looking at the man with more attention than he had paid to him hitherto, "I think I understand you. You can explain these hieroglyphics?"

"Perhaps; at any rate, I can give you other information that is not to be despised."

"And you wish to be paid for it?"

"Of course I do," replied the peasant, boldly.

"That is how you serve the government which made you mayor?"

"The devil! Has the government put a tiled roof on my house? No! Has it changed the mud walls to stone? No! My house is thatched with straw and built of wood and mud. The Chouans could set fire to it in a minute, and it would burn to ashes. Whoso risks much ought to earn much; for, as you see, I might lose my all in a single night."

"You are right. Come, Monsieur le sous-préfet, this belongs to your department. Thank God, I'm only a soldier, and my supplies are paid for before delivery. Pay this man and hand his information over to me."

"And do it quickly," said the farmer, "for we are watched on all sides."

The peasants had, in fact, drawn nearer and nearer to the little group. Without, apparently, any other motive than the curiosity which all strangers in a country place naturally excite, they had formed a tolerably compact circle round the three speakers. The general took notice of it.

"My dear fellow," he said aloud, addressing the sub-prefect, "I wouldn't rely on that man's word, if I were you. He offers to sell you two hundred sacks of oats at nineteen francs the sack, but it remains to be seen when he will deliver them. Give him a small sum down and make him sign a promise of delivery."

"But I have neither paper nor pencil," said the sub-prefect, understanding the general's meaning.

"Go to the hotel, hang it! Come," said the general, looking about him, "are there any others here who have oats to sell? We have horses to feed."

One peasant answered in the affirmative, and while the general was discussing the price with him the sub-prefect and the man with the biscuit slipped away, almost un-

THE FAIR AT MONTAIGU. 183

noticed. The man, as our readers are of course aware, was no other than Courtin. Let us now try to explain the manœuvres which Courtin had executed since morning. After his interview with Michel, Courtin had reflected long. It seemed to him that a plain and simple denunciation of the visitors at the château de Souday was not the course most profitable to his interests. It might very well be that the government would leave its subordinate agents without reward, in which case the act was dangerous and without profit; for, of course, Courtin would draw down upon him the enmity of the royalists, who were the majority of the canton. It was then that he thought of the little scheme we heard him propound to Jean Oullier. He hoped by assisting the loves of the young baron to draw a pretty penny to himself, to win the good will of the marquis, whose ambition must be, as he thought, to obtain such a marriage for his daughter, and, finally, to sell at a great price his silence as to the presence of a personage whose safety, if he were not mistaken, was of the utmost consequence to the royalist party.

We have seen how Jean Oullier received his advances. It was then that Courtin, considering himself to have failed in what he regarded as an excellent scheme, decided on contenting himself with a lesser, and made the move we have now related toward the government.

XX.

THE OUTBREAK.

HALF an hour after the conference of the sub-prefect and Courtin a *gendarme* was making his way among the groups, looking for the general, whom he found talking very amicably with a respectable old beggar in rags. The *gendarme* said a word in the general's ear, and the latter at once made his way to the little inn of the Cheval Blanc. The sub-prefect stood in the doorway.

"Well?" asked the general, noticing the highly satisfied look on the face of the public functionary.

"Ah, general! great news and good news!" replied the sub-prefect.

"Let's hear it."

"The man I've had to deal with is really very clever."

"Fine news, indeed! they are all very clever. The greatest fool among them could give points to Monsieur de Talleyrand. What has he told you, this clever man?"

"He saw the Comte de Bonneville, disguised as a peasant, enter the château de Souday last night, and with the count was another little peasant, whom he thinks was a woman —"

"What next?"

"Next! why there's no doubt, general."

"Go on, monsieur; I am all impatience," said the general, in the calmest tone.

"I mean to say that in my opinion the woman is no other than the one we have been told to look out for, — namely, the princess."

"There may be no doubt for you; there are a dozen doubts for me."

"Why so, general?"

"Because I, too, have had some confidences."

"Voluntary or involuntary?"

"Who knows, with these people?"

"Pooh! But what did they tell you?"

"They told me nothing."

"Well, what then?"

"Then, after you left me I went on bargaining for oats."

"Yes. What next?"

"Next, the peasant who spoke to me asked for earnest-money; that was fair. I asked him for a receipt; that was fair, too. He wanted to go to a shop and write it. 'No,' I said. 'Here's a pencil; have n't you a scrap of paper about you? My hat will do for a table.' He tore off the back of a letter and gave me a receipt. There it is. Read it."

The sub-prefect took the paper, and read: —

"Received, of M. Jean-Louis Robier, the sum of fifty francs, on account, for thirty sacks of flour, which I engage to deliver to him May 28.

May 14, 1832.
F. TERRIEN.

"Well," said the sub-prefect, "I don't see any information there."

"Turn over the paper."

"Ah, ha!" exclaimed the functionary.

The paper which he held was one half of a page of letter paper torn through the middle. On the other side from that on which the receipt was written were these words: —

arquis
ceived this instant the news
her whom we are expecting.
Beaufays, evening of 26th
send officers of your division
presented to Madame.

your people in hand.
respectfully,
OUX.

"The devil!" cried the sub-prefect; "that is nothing more nor less than a call to arms. It is easy enough to make out the rest."

"Nothing easier," said the general. Then he added, in a low voice, "Too easy, perhaps."

"Ah, ça! did n't you tell me these people were sly and cautious? I call this, on the contrary, a bit of innocent carelessness which is amazing."

"Wait," said Dermoncourt; "that's not all."

"Ah, ha!"

"After parting with my seller of oats I met a beggar, half an idiot. I talked to him about the good God and the saints and the Virgin, about the buckwheat and the apple year (you observe that the apple-trees are in bloom), and I ended by asking him if he could not act as guide for us to Loroux, where, as you know, I am to make an inspection. 'I can't,' said my idiot, with a mischievous look. 'Why not?' I asked in the stupidest way I could. 'Because I am ordered to guide a lady and two gentlemen from Puy-Laurens to La Flocelière.'"

"The devil! here's a complication."

"On the contrary, enlightenment."

"Explain."

"Confidences which are given when not extorted, in a region where it is so difficult to get them, seem to me such clumsy traps that an old fox like myself ought to be ashamed to be caught by them. The Duchesse de Berry, if she is really in La Vendée, cannot be at Souday and Beaufays and Puy-Laurens at the same time. What do you think, my dear sub-prefect?"

"Confound it all!" replied the public functionary, scratching his head, "I think she may have been, or still may be, in all those places, one after another; but if I were you, instead of chasing her round from place to place, where she may or may not have been, I should go straight to La Flocelière, where your idiot is to take her to-day."

"Then you would make a very poor bloodhound, my dear fellow. The only reliable information we have so far received is that given by the scamp who had the biscuit, and whom you examined here—"

"But the others?"

"I'll bet my general's epaulets against those of a sub-lieutenant that the others were put in my way by some shrewd fellows who saw and suspected our talk with the man about his biscuit. Let us begin the hunt, my dear sub-prefect, and confine our attention to Souday, if we don't want to make an utter failure of it."

"Bravo!" cried the sub-prefect. "I feared I had committed a blunder; but what you say reassures me."

"What have you done?"

"Well, I have got the name of this mayor. He is called Courtin, and is mayor of the village of la Logerie."

"I know that. It is close by the spot where we came near capturing Charette thirty-seven years ago."

"Well, this man has pointed out to me an individual who could serve us as guide, and whom it would be well to arrest so that he may not go back to the château and give the alarm."

"Who is the man?"

"The marquis's steward. Here is a description of him."

The general took the paper and read: —

"Short gray hair, low forehead, keen black eyes, bushy eyebrows, wart on his nose, hair in the nostrils, whiskers round the face, round hat, velveteen jacket, waistcoat and breeches the same, leathern belt and gaiters. Special points: a brown retriever, and the second incisor on the left side broken."

"Good!" said the general; "that's my oat-seller to a tee. Terrien! His name is no more Terrien than mine's Barabbas."

"Well, general, you can soon make sure of that."

"How so?"

"He'll be here in a minute."

"Here?"

"Yes."

"Is he coming here?"

"He is coming here."

"Of his own will?"

"His own will, or by force."

"Force?"

"Yes; I have just given the order to arrest him. It is done by this time."

"Ten thousand thunders!" cried the general, letting his fist fall upon the table with such a thud that the public functionary bounded in his chair. "Ten thousand thunders!" he cried again; "what have you done?"

"He seems to me, general, a dangerous man from all I hear of him, and there was but one thing to do, — namely, arrest him."

"Dangerous! dangerous! He is much more dangerous now than he was ten minutes ago."

"But if he is in custody he can't do harm."

"No matter how quick your men are they won't prevent his giving warning. The princess will be warned before we have gone a couple of miles. It will be lucky for us if you have n't roused the whole population so that I cannot take a single man from the garrison."

"Perhaps there's yet time," said the sub-prefect, rushing to the door.

"Yes, make haste. Ah! thunder! it's too late!"

A dull roar was heard without, deepening every second until it reached the volume of that dreadful concert of sounds made by a multitude as the prelude to a battle.

The general opened the window. He saw, at a short distance from the inn, Jean Oullier, bound and in the grasp of *gendarmes* who were bringing him along. The crowd surrounded them, howling and threatening. The *gendarmes* came on slowly and with difficulty. They had not as yet made use of their arms. There was not a moment to lose.

"Well, the wine is drawn; we have got to drink it," said the general, pulling off his civilian clothes, and hastily getting into his regimentals. Then he called to his secretary.

"Rusconi, my horse! my horse!" he shouted. "As for you, Monsieur le sous-préfet, call out your militia, if you have any; but not a gun is to be fired without my orders."

A captain, sent by the secretary, entered the room.

"Captain," said the general, "bring your men into the courtyard. Order my chasseurs to mount; two days' rations, and twenty-five cartridges to each man; and hold yourself ready to follow me at the first signal I give you."

The old general, recovering all the fire of his youth, went down into the courtyard, where, sending the civilians to the right-about, he ordered the gates into the street to be opened.

"What!" cried the sub-prefect, "you are surely not going to present yourself to that furious crowd all alone?"

"That's precisely what I am going to do. Damn it! your men must be supported. This is no time for sentiment. Open that gate."

The two sides of the gate were no sooner opened than the general, setting spurs to his horse, was instantly in the middle of the street and the thick of the mêlée. This sudden apparition of an old soldier, with a determined face and martial bearing, in full uniform, and glittering with decorations, together with the bold promptitude of his action, produced an electric effect upon the crowd. The clamoring ceased as if by magic. Cudgels were lowered; the peasants who were nearest to the general actually touched their hats; the crowd made way, and the soldier of Rivoli and the Pyramids rode on some twenty paces in the direction of the *gendarmes*.

"Why, what's the matter with you, my *gars*?" he cried, in so stentorian a voice that he was heard even to the neighboring streets.

"They've arrested Jean Oullier; that's what's the matter with us," replied a voice.

"And Jean Oullier is a good man," shouted another.

"They ought to arrest bad men, and not good ones," said a third.

"And that's why we are not going to let them take Jean Oullier," cried a fourth.

"Silence!" said the general, in so imperious a tone that every voice was hushed. "If Jean Oullier is a good man, a worthy man, — which I do not doubt, — Jean Oullier will be released. If he is one who is trying to deceive you and take advantage of your good and loyal feelings, Jean Oullier will be punished. Do you think it unjust to punish those who try to plunge the country back into those horrors of civil war of which the old now tell the young with tears?"

"Jean Oullier is a peaceable man, and does n't do harm to any one," said a voice.

"What are you wanting now?" continued the general, without noticing the interruption. "Your priests are respected; your religion is ours. Have we killed the king, as in 1793? Have we abolished God, as in 1794? Is your property in danger? No; you and your property are safe under the common law. Never were your trades and your commerce so flourishing."

"That is true," said a young peasant.

"Don't listen to bad Frenchmen who, to satisfy their selfish passions, do not shrink from calling down upon their country all the horrors of civil war. Can't you remember what those horrors were? Must I remind you of them? Must I bring to mind your old men, your mothers, your wives, your children massacred before your eyes, your harvests trampled under foot, your cottages in flames, death and ruin at every hearth!"

"It was the Blues who did it all," cried a voice.

"No, it was not the Blues," continued the general. "It was those who drove you to that senseless struggle, senseless then, but wicked now, — a struggle which had at least a pretext then, but has none whatever in these days."

While speaking the general pushed his horse in the direction of the *gendarmes*, who, on their side, made every effort to reach the general. This was all the more possible because his address, soldierly as it was, made an evident impression on some of the peasants. Many lowered their heads and were silent; others made remarks to their neighbors, which seemed from their manner to imply approval.

Nevertheless, the farther the general advanced into the crowd, the less favorable grew the expression of the faces. In fact, the nearest to him were altogether menacing; and the owners of these faces were evidently the promoters and the leaders of the uproar, — probably the chiefs of the various bands and what were called the captains of parishes.

For such men as these it was useless to be eloquent; their determination was fixed not to listen and not to let others listen. They did not shout nor cry; they roared and howled. The general understood the situation. He resolved to impress the minds of these men by one of those acts of personal vigor which have such enormous influence on the multitude.

Aubin Courte-Joie was in the front rank of the rioters. This may seem strange in view of his crippled condition. But Aubin Courte-Joie had, for the time being, added to his useless wooden legs two good and powerful legs of flesh and blood. In other words, he was mounted on the shoulders of a colossal tramp; and the said tramp, by means of straps attached to the wooden legs of his rider, was able to hold the cripple as firmly in his seat as the general was in his saddle.

Thus perched, Aubin Courte-Joie's head was on the

level of the general's epaulet, where he kept up a series of frantic vociferations and threatening gestures. The general stretched out his hand, took the tavern-keeper by the collar of his jacket, and then, by sheer force of wrist, raised him, held him a moment suspended above the crowd, and then handed him over to a *gendarme*, saying: —

"Lock up that mountebank; he is enough to give one a headache."

The tramp, relieved of his rider, raised his head, and the general recognized the idiot he had talked with an hour earlier; only, by this time the idiot looked as shrewd and clever as any of them.

The general's action had raised a laugh from the crowd, but this hilarity did not last long. Aubin Courte-Joie happened to be held by the *gendarme* who was placed to the left of Jean Oullier. He gently drew from his pocket an open knife, and plunged it to the hilt in the breast of the *gendarme*, crying out: —

"Vive Henri V.! Fly, *gars* Oullier!"

At the same instant the tramp, inspired perhaps by a legitimate sentiment of emulation, and wishing to make a worthy rejoinder to the athletic action of the general, glided under his horse, caught the general by the boot, and with a sudden and vigorous movement, pitched him over on the other side.

The general and the *gendarme* fell at the same instant, and they might have been thought dead; but the general was up immediately and into his saddle with as much strength as adroitness. As he sprang to his seat he gave such a powerful blow with his fist on the bare head of the late idiot that the latter, without uttering a cry, fell to the ground as if his skull were broken. Neither tramp nor *gendarme* rose again. The tramp had fainted; the *gendarme* was dead.

Jean Oullier, on his part, though his hands were bound, gave such a vigorous blow with his shoulder to the *gendarme* on his right that the latter staggered. Jean Oullier jumped over the dead body of the *gendarme* on the left, and darted into the crowd.

But the general's eye was everywhere, even behind him.

Instantly he turned his horse. The animal bounded into the centre of the living whirlpool, and the old soldier caught Jean Oullier as he had caught Aubin Courte-Joie, and threw him across the pommel of his own saddle. Then the stones began to rain, and the cudgels rose. The *gendarmes* held firm, presenting their bayonets to the crowd, which dared not attack them at close quarters and was forced to content itself by flinging projectiles.

They advanced in this way to about sixty feet from the inn. Here the position of the general and his men became critical. The peasants, who seemed determined that Jean Oullier should not be left in the enemy's power, grew more and more aggressive. Already the bayonets were stained with blood, and the fury of the rioters was evidently increasing. Fortunately the general was now near enough to the courtyard of the inn for his voice to reach it.

"Here! grenadiers of the 32d!" he shouted.

At the same instant the gates opened, and the soldiers poured forth with fixed bayonets and drove back the crowd. The general and the *gendarmes* entered the yard. Here the general encountered the sub-prefect, who was awaiting him.

"There's your man," he said, flinging Jean Oullier to him, as if the Chouan were a bale of goods; "and trouble enough he has cost us! God grant he is worth his price."

Just then a brisk firing was heard from the farther end of the market-place.

"What's that?" cried the general, listening with all his ears, and his nostrils open.

"The National Guard, no doubt," replied the sub-prefect. "I ordered them out, and they must have met the rioters."

"Who ordered them to fire?"

"I did, general. I was bound to go to your rescue."

"Ten thousand thunders! Can't you see that I rescued

myself?" said the old soldier. Then, shaking his head, he added, "Monsieur, remember this: to shed blood in civil war is worse than a crime; it is a blunder."

An officer galloped into the courtyard.

"General," he said, "the rioters are flying in all directions. The chasseurs are here. Shall we pursue them?"

"Not a man is to stir," said the general. "Leave the National Guard to manage the affair. They are friends; they'll settle it."

A second discharge of musketry proved that the militia and the peasantry were indeed settling it. This was the firing heard at La Logerie by Baron Michel.

"Ah!" said the general, "now we must see what profit we can get out of this melancholy business." Pointing to Jean Oullier, he added, "We have but one chance, and that is that no one but this man is in the secret. Did he have any communication with any one after you arrested him, *gendarmes?*"

"No, general, not even by signs, for his hands were bound."

"Did n't he make any gestures with his head, or say a word to anybody? You know very well that a nod or a single word is enough with these fellows."

"No, general, not one."

"Well then, we may as well run the chance. Let your men eat their rations, captain; in half an hour we start. The *gendarmes* and the National Guard are enough to guard the town. I shall take my escort of chasseurs to clear the way."

So saying, the general retired into the inn. The soldiers made their preparations for departure.

During this time Jean Oullier sat stolidly on a stone in the middle of the courtyard, kept in sight by the two *gendarmes* who were guarding him. His face retained its habitual impassibility. With his two bound hands he stroked his dog, which had followed him, and was now resting its head on his knees and licking his hand, as if to remind the prisoner in his misfortune that a friend was near him.

Jean Oullier was gently stroking the faithful creature's head with the feather of a wild duck he might have picked up in the courtyard. Suddenly, profiting by a moment when his two guards were speaking to each other and not observing him, he slipped the feather between the teeth of the animal, made it a sign of intelligence, and rose, saying, in a low voice: —

"Go, Pataud!"

The dog gently moved away, looking back at his master from time to time. Then, when he reached the gate, he bounded out, unobserved by any one, and disappeared.

"Good!" said Jean Oullier to himself. "He'll get there before we do."

Unfortunately, the *gendarmes* were not the only ones who were watching the prisoner.

XXI.

JEAN OULLIER'S RESOURCES.

EVEN in these days there are few good roads in La Vendée, and those few have been made since 1832, that is, since the period of which we are now writing. This lack of roads was the principal strength of the insurgents in the great war. Let us say a word on those that then existed, concerning ourselves only with those on the left bank of the Loire.

They were two in number. The first went from Nantes to Rochelle, through Montaigu; the second from Nantes to Paimbœuf by the Pélerin, following almost continuously the banks of the river.

Besides these two main highways, there were other secondary or cross roads; these went from Nantes to Beaupréau through Vallet, from Nantes to Mortagne, Chollet, and Bressuire by Clisson, from Nantes to Sables-d'Olonne by Légé, and from Nantes to Challans by Machecoul. To reach Machecoul by either of these roads it was necessary to make a long detour, in fact, as far round as Légé; thence along the road from Nantes to Sables-d'Olonne, following that until it was crossed by the road to Challans, by which the traveller retraced his way to Machecoul.

The general knew too well that the whole success of his expedition depended on the rapidity with which it was conducted to be willing to resign himself to so long a march. Besides, none of these roads were favorable for military operations. They were bordered by deep ditches, gorse, bushes of all kinds, and trees; in many places they were sunken between high banks with hedges at the top. Such roads, under any of these conditions, were favorable for ambuscades; the little advantage they offered in no way counterbalanced their risks. The general therefore determined to follow a cross-country road which led to Machecoul by Vieille-Vigne and shortened the way by over four miles.

The system of encampments the general had adopted since coming to La Vendée had familiarized his soldiers with the nature of the land and given them a good eye for dangerous places. The captain in command of the infantry knew the way as far as the Boulogne river; but from that point it was necessary to have a guide. It was plain that Jean Oullier would not be willing to show the way, and another man was therefore obtained on whose fidelity they could rely.

The general in deciding on the cross-road took every precaution against a surprise. Two chasseurs, pistol in hand, went first to reconnoitre the way for the column; while a dozen men on each side of the road examined the gorse and the bushes which lined it everywhere and sometimes overtopped it. The general marched at the head of his little troop, in the midst of which he had placed Jean Oullier.

The old Vendéan, with his wrists bound, was mounted behind a chasseur; for greater security a girth had been passed around his body and buckled across the breast of the soldier before him; so that Jean Oullier if he could even have freed his hands could not escape his bonds to the rider before him. Two other chasseurs rode to the left and right with special orders to watch him carefully.

It was about six in the evening when the detachment left Montaigu; they had fifteen miles to do, and, supposing that those fifteen miles took five hours, they ought to be at the château de Souday by eleven. The hour seemed favorable to the general for his plans. If Courtin's report was correct, if he had not been misled in his conclusions, the leaders of the last Vendéan movement were now assembled at Souday to confer with the princess, and it was likely that they would not have left the château before his arrival. If this were so, nothing could prevent him from capturing them all by one throw of the net.

After marching for half an hour, that is, to a distance of about a mile and a half from Montaigu, just as the little column was passing the crossway of Saint-Corentin they came upon an old woman in rags, who was praying on her knees before a wayside crucifix. At the noise the column made she turned her head, and then, as if impelled by curiosity, she rose and stood beside the road to see it pass. The gold-laced coat of the general seemed to give her the idea of begging, and she muttered the sort of prayer with which beggars ask for alms.

Officers and soldiers, preoccupied with other matters, and growing surly as the twilight deepened, passed on without attending to her.

"Your general took no notice of that poor woman who asked for bread," said Jean Oullier to the chasseur who was on his right.

"Why do you think so?" said the soldier.

"Because he did not give her anything. Let him beware. Whoso repulses the open palm must fear the closed fist, says the proverb. Harm will happen to us."

"If you take that prediction to yourself, my good man, you are not mistaken, inasmuch as you are already in peril."

"Yes, and that is why I would like to conjure it away."

"How can you?"

"Feel in my pocket for me and take out a piece of money."

"What for?"

"To give to that old woman, and then she'll share her prayers between me who give the alms and you who enable her to get them."

The chasseur shrugged his shoulders; but superstitions are singularly contagious, and those attached to ideas of charity are more so than others. The soldier, while pretending to be above such nonsense, thought he ought not to refuse to do the kindness Jean Oullier asked of him, which might, moreover, bring down the blessing of Heaven on both of them.

The troop was at this moment wheeling to the right into the sunken road which leads to Vieille-Vigne. The general stopped his horse to watch the men file past him, and see with his own eyes that all the arrangements he had ordered were carried out; it thus happened that he saw Jean Oullier speaking to the chasseur, and he also saw the soldier's action.

"What do you mean by letting the prisoner speak to strangers on the road?" he said sharply.

The chasseur related what had happened.

"Halt!" cried the general; "arrest that woman, and search her."

The order was instantly obeyed, but nothing was found on the old beggar-woman but a few pieces of copper money, which the general examined with the utmost care. In vain did he turn and re-turn the coins; nothing could he find in the least suspicious about them. He put the coins in his pocket, however, giving to the old woman a five-franc piece in exchange. Jean Oullier watched the general's actions with a sarcastic smile.

"Well, you see," he said in a low voice but loud enough for the beggar-woman to hear him without losing a single word, "you see the poor alms of a *prisoner*" (he emphasized the word) "have brought you luck, old mother; and that's another reason still why you should remember me in your prayers. A dozen *Ave Marias* said for him will greatly help the salvation of a poor devil."

Jean Oullier raised his voice as he said the last words.

"My good man," said the general to Jean Oullier when the column had resumed its march, "in future you must address yourself to me when you have any charity to do; I'll recommend you to the prayers of those you want to succor; my mediation won't do you any harm up above, and it may spare you many an annoyance here below. As for you, men," continued the general, speaking gruffly to his cavalry, "don't forget my orders in future; for the harm will fall upon yourselves, and I tell you so!"

At Vieille-Vigne they halted fifteen minutes to rest the infantry. The Chouan was placed in the centre of the square, so as to isolate him completely from the population which flocked inquisitively about the troop. The horse on which Jean Oullier was mounted had cast a shoe, and was, moreover, tired with its double burden. The general picked out the strongest animal in the squadron to take its place. This horse belonged to one of the troopers in the front rank, who, in spite of the greater exposure to danger where he was, seemed very reluctant to change places with his comrade.

The man was short, stocky, vigorous, with a gentle but intelligent face; and was quite devoid of the cavalier manner which characterized his comrades. During the preparations for this change, which was made by the light of a lantern (by that time the night was very dark) Jean Oullier caught sight of the face of the man behind whom he was to continue his way; his eyes met those of the soldier, and he noticed that the latter lowered his.

Again the column started, taking every precaution; for the farther they advanced, the thicker grew the bushes and the coverts beside the road; consequently the easier it became to attack them. The prospect of danger to be met and weariness to be endured, on roads which were little better in many places than beds of water-courses strewn with rocks and stones, did not lessen the gayety of the soldiers, who now began, after recovering from their first surliness at nightfall, to find amusement in the idea of danger, and to talk among themselves with that liveliness which seldom deserts a French soldier for any length of time. The chasseur behind whom Jean Oullier was mounted alone took no part in the talk, but was thoughtful and gloomy.

"Confound you, Thomas," said the trooper on the right, addressing him, "you never have much to say for yourself, but to-day, I will declare, one would think you were burying the devil."

"At any rate," said the one to the left, "he has got him

on his back. You ought to like that, Thomas, for you are half a Chouan yourself."

"He's a whole Chouan, I'm thinking; does n't he go to mass every Sunday?"

The chasseur named Thomas had no time to answer these twittings, for the general's voice now ordered the men to break ranks and advance single file, the way having become so narrow and the bank on each side so steep that it was impossible for two horsemen to ride abreast.

During the momentary confusion caused by this manœuvre Jean Oullier began to whistle in a low key the Breton air "The Chouans are men of heart."

At the first note the rider quivered. Then, as the other troopers were now before and behind them, Jean Oullier, safe from observation, put his mouth close to the ear of the one behind whom he was mounted.

"Ha! you may be as silent as you like, Thomas Tinguy," he whispered; "I knew you at once, and you knew me."

The soldier sighed and made a motion with his shoulders which seem to mean that he was acting against his will. But he made no answer.

"Thomas Tinguy," said Jean Oullier, "do you know where you are going? Do you know where you are taking your father's old friend? To the pillage and destruction of the château de Souday, whose masters have been for years and years the benefactors of your family."

Thomas Tinguy sighed again.

"Your father is dead," continued Jean Oullier.

Thomas made no reply, but he shuddered in his saddle; a single word escaped his lips and reached the ears of Jean Oullier: —

"Dead!"

"Yes, dead," replied the Chouan; "and who watched beside his dying bed with your sister Rosine and received his last sigh? The two young ladies from Souday whom you know well, Mademoiselle Bertha and Mademoiselle Mary; and that at the risk of their lives, for your father died of a malignant fever. Not being able to save his life, angels that they are they stayed beside him to ease his death. Where is your sister now, having no home? At the château de Souday. Ah! Thomas Tinguy, I'd rather be poor Jean Oullier, whom they'll shoot against a wall, than he who takes him bound to execution."

"Hush! Jean, hush!" said Thomas Tinguy, with a sob in his voice; "we are not there yet — wait and see."

While this little colloquy was passing between Jean Oullier and the son of the older Tinguy, the ravine through which the little column was moving began to slope downward rapidly. They were nearing one of the fords of the Boulogne river.

It was a dark night without a star in the sky; and such a night, while it might favor the ultimate success of the expedition, might also, on the other hand, hinder its march and even imperil it in this wild and unknown country.

When they reached the ford they found the two chasseurs who had been sent in advance, awaiting them, pistol in hand. They were evidently uneasy. The ford, instead of being a clear, shallow stream rippling over pebbles, was a dark and stagnant body of water, washing softly against a rocky bank.

They looked on all sides for the guide whom Courtin had agreed should meet them at this point. The general gave a loud call. A voice answered on the opposite shore, —

"Qui vive?"

"Souday!" replied the general.

"Then you are the ones I am waiting for," said the guide.

"Is this the ford of the Boulogne?" asked the general.

"Yes."

"Why is the water so high?"

"There's a flood since the last rains."

"Is the crossing possible in spite of it?"

"Damn it! I don't know. I have never seen the river as high as this. I think it would be more prudent —"

The guide's voice suddenly stopped, or rather seemed to turn into a moan. Then the sound of a struggle was plainly heard, as if the feet of several men were tussling on the pebbles.

"A thousand thunders!" cried the general, "our guide is being murdered!"

A cry of agony replied to the general's exclamation and confirmed it.

"A grenadier up behind every trooper!" cried the general. "The captain behind me! The two lieutenants stay here with the rest of the troop, the prisoner, and his three guards. Come on, and quickly too!"

In a moment the seventeen chasseurs had each a grenadier behind him. Eighty grenadiers, the two lieutenants, the prisoner and his three guards, including Tinguy, remained on the right bank of the river. The order was executed with the rapidity of thought, and the general, followed by his chasseurs and the seventeen grenadiers behind them, plunged into the bed of the river.

Twenty feet from the shore the horses lost foothold, but they swam for a few moments and reached, without accident, the opposite bank. They had hardly landed when the grenadiers dismounted.

"Can you see anything?" said the general, trying himself to pierce the darkness that surrounded the little troop.

"No, general," said the men with one voice.

"Yet it was certainly from here," said the general, as if speaking to himself, "that the man answered me. Look behind the bushes, but without scattering; you may find his body."

The soldiers obeyed, searching round a radius of some hundred and fifty feet. But they returned in about fifteen minutes and reported that they could see nothing, and had found no traces of the body.

"You saw absolutely nothing?" asked the general.

One grenadier alone came forward, holding in his hand a cotton cap.

"I found this," he said.

"Where?"

"Hooked to a bush."

"That's our guide's cap," said the general.

"How do you know?" asked the captain.

"Because the men who attacked him would have worn hats," replied the general, without the slightest hesitation.

The captain was silent, not daring to ask further; but it was evident that the general's explanation had explained nothing to his mind.

Dermoncourt understood the captain's silence.

"It is very simple," he said; "the men who have just murdered our guide have followed us ever since we left Montaigu for the purpose of rescuing the prisoner. The arrest must be a more important matter than I thought it was. These men who have followed us were at the fair, and wore hats, as they always do when they go to the towns; whereas our guide was called from his bed suddenly by the man who sent him to us, and he would of course put on the cap he was in the habit of wearing; it may even have been on his head as he slept."

"Do you really think, general," said the captain, "that those Chouans would dare to come so near our line of march?"

"They have come step by step with us from Montaigu; they have not let us out of their sight one single instant. Heavens and earth! people complain of our inhumanity in this war, and yet at every step we are made to feel, to our cost, that we have not been inhuman enough. Fool and simpleton that I have been!"

"I understand you less and less, general," said the captain, laughing.

"Do you remember that beggar-woman who spoke to us just after we left Montaigu?"

"Yes, general."

"Well, it was that old hag who put up this attack. I wanted to send her back into the town; I did wrong not to follow my own instinct; I should have saved the life of this poor devil. Ah! I see now how it was done. The *Ave Marias* for which the prisoner asked have been answered here."

"Do you think they will dare to attack us?"

"If they were in force it would have been done before now. But there are only six or eight of them at the most."

"Shall I bring over the men on the other bank, general?"

"No, wait; the horses lost foothold and the infantry would drown. There must be some better ford near by."

"You think so, general?"

"Damn it! I'm sure."

"Then you know the river?"

"Never saw it before."

"Then why — ?"

"Ah! captain, it is easy to see that you didn't go through the great war, as I did, — that war of savages, in which we had to go by induction. These Vendéan fellows were not posted here on this side of the river in ambuscade at the moment when we came up on the other; that is clear."

"For you, general."

"Hey! bless my soul, — clear to anybody! If they had been posted there, they would have heard the guide and killed him or captured him before we came; consequently the band were on our flank as we came along."

"That is probably so, general."

"And they must have reached the bank of the river just before us. Now the interval between the time we arrived and halted and the moment our guide was attacked was too short to allow of their making a long detour to another ford — no, they must have forded close by."

"Why couldn't they have crossed here?"

"Because a peasant, especially in these interior regions, hardly ever knows how to swim. The ford is close at hand, that is certain. Send four men up the river and four men down. Quick! We don't want to die here, especially in wet clothes."

At the end of ten minutes the officer returned.

"You are right, general," he said; "three hundred yards from here there's a small island; the trunk of a tree joins it with the other bank, and another trunk with this side."

"Good!" said the general; "then they can get across without wetting a cartridge."

Calling to the officer on the opposite bank, —

"Ohé! lieutenant," he said, "go up the river till you come to a tree, cross there, and be sure you watch the prisoner."

XXII.

FETCH! PATAUD, FETCH!

For the next five minutes the two troops advanced slowly up the river, one on each bank. When they reached the place discovered by the captain the general called a halt.

"One lieutenant and forty men across!" he cried.

Forty men and one lieutenant came over with the water up to their shoulders, though they were able to lift their guns and their cartridge-boxes above the surface. On landing, they ranged in line of battle.

"Now," said the general, "bring over the prisoner."

Thomas Tinguy entered the water with a chasseur on each side of him.

"Thomas," said Jean Oullier, in a low but penetrating voice, "If I were in your place I should be afraid of one thing; I should expect to see the ghost of my father rising before me and asking why I shed the blood of his best friend rather than just unbuckle a miserable girth."

The chasseur passed his hand over his forehead, which was bathed in sweat, and made the sign of the cross. At this moment the three riders were in the middle of the river, but the current had slightly separated them.

Suddenly, a loud sound accompanied by the splashing of water proved that Jean Oullier had not in vain evoked before the poor superstitious Breton soldier the revered image of his father.

The general knew at once what the sound meant.

"The prisoner is escaping!" he cried in a voice of thunder. "Light torches, spread yourselves along the bank, fire upon him if he shows himself. As for you," he added addressing Thomas Tinguy, who came ashore close to him without attempting to escape, — "as for you, you go no farther."

Taking a pistol from his belt he fired.

"Thus die all traitors!" he cried.

And Thomas Tinguy, shot through the breast, fell dead.

The soldiers, obeying orders with a rapidity which showed they felt the gravity of their situation, rushed along the river in the direction of the current. A dozen torches lighted on each bank threw their ruddy glare upon the water.

Jean Oullier, released from his chief bond when Thomas Tinguy unbuckled the girth, slid from the horse and plunged into the river, passing between the legs of the horse on the right. We may now inquire how it is possible for a man to swim with his hands bound in front of him.

Jean Oullier had relied so confidently on his appeal to the son of his old friend that as soon as the darkness fell he began to gnaw the rope that bound his wrists with his teeth. He had good teeth, so that by the time they reached the river the rope held only by a single strand; once in the water a vigorous jerk parted it altogether.

At the end of a few seconds the Chouan was forced to come to the surface and breathe; instantly a dozen shots were fired at him, and as many balls set the water foaming about him. By a miracle none touched him; but he felt the wind of their passage across his face.

It was not prudent to tempt such luck a second time, for then it would be tempting God, not luck. He plunged again, and finding foothold turned to go up the river instead of keeping down with the current; in short, he made what is called in the hunting-field a double; it often succeeds with a hare, why not with a man? thought he.

Jean Oullier therefore doubled, went up the river under water, holding his breath till his chest came near to bursting, and not reappearing on the surface till he was beyond the line of light thrown by the torches on the river.

This manœuvre deceived his enemies. Little supposing that he would voluntarily add another danger to his flight, the soldiers continued to look for him down instead of up the river, holding their guns like hunters watching for game, and ready to fire the instant that he showed himself. Their interest in the sport was all the greater because the game was a man.

Half a dozen grenadiers alone beat up the river, and they carried but one torch among them.

Stifling as best he could the heavy sound of his breathing, Jean Oullier managed to reach a willow the branches of which stretched over the river, their tips even touching the water. The swimmer seized a branch, put it between his teeth, and held himself thus with his head thrown back so that his mouth and nostrils were out of water and able to breathe the air.

He had hardly recovered his breath before he heard a plaintive howl from the spot where the column had halted and where he himself had dropped into the river. He knew the sound.

"Pataud!" he murmured; "Pataud here, when I sent him to Souday! Something has happened to him! Oh, my God! my God!" he cried with inexpressible fervor and deep faith, "now, *now* it is all-important to save me from being recaptured."

The soldiers had seen Jean Oullier's dog in the courtyard and they recognized him.

"There's his dog! there's his dog!" they cried.

"Bravo!" cried a sergeant; "he'll help us to catch his master."

And he tried to lay a hand on him. But although the poor animal seemed stiff and tired, he eluded the man's grasp, and sniffing the air in the direction of the current he jumped into the river.

"This way, comrades, this way!" cried the sergeant, stretching his arm in the direction taken by the dog. "He's after his master."

The moment Jean Oullier heard Pataud's cry he put his head out of water, regardless of the consequences to himself. He saw the dog cutting diagonally across the river, swimming directly for him; he knew he was lost if he did not make some mighty effort. To sacrifice his dog was to Jean Oullier a supreme effort. If his own life alone had been in the balance Jean Oullier would have taken his risks and been lost or saved with Pataud; at any rate he would have hesitated before he saved himself at the cost of the dog's life.

He quickly took off the goatskin cape he wore over his jacket and let it float on the surface of the water, giving it a strong push into the middle of the current. Pataud was then not twenty feet from him.

"Seek! fetch!" he said in a low voice showing the direction to the dog. Then, as the poor animal, feeling no doubt that his strength was leaving him, hesitated to obey,

"Fetch, Pataud, fetch!" cried Jean Oullier, imperatively.

Pataud turned and swam in the direction of the goatskin, which was now about fifty feet away from him. Jean Oullier, seeing that his trick had succeeded, dived again at the moment when the soldiers on the bank were alongside the willow. One of them carrying the torch scrambled quickly up the tree and lit the whole bed of the river. The goatskin was plainly seen floating rapidly down the current, and Pataud was swimming after it, moaning and whining as if distressed that his failing strength prevented him from accomplishing his master's order.

The soldiers, following the dog's lead, redescended the river, going farther and farther away from Jean Oullier. As soon as one of them caught sight of the goatskin he shouted to his comrades: —

"Here, friends! here he is! here he is, the brigand!" and he fired at the goatskin.

Grenadiers and chasseurs ran pell-mell along both banks, getting farther and farther from Jean Oullier, and riddling the goatskin, after which Pataud was still swimming, with their balls. For some minutes the firing was so continuous that there was no need of torches; the flashes of burning sulphur from the muskets lit up the wild ravine through which the Boulogne flows, while the rocks, echoing back the volleys, redoubled the noise.

The general was the first to discover the blunder of his men.

"Stop the firing!" he said to the captain who was still beside him; "those fools have dropped the prey for the shadow."

Just then a brilliant light shone from the crest of the rocky ridge overhanging the river; a sharp hiss sounded above the heads of the two officers, and a ball buried itself in the trunk of a tree beyond them.

"Ah ha!" exclaimed the general, coolly; "that rascal only asked for a dozen *Ave Marias*, but his friends are inclined to be liberal!"

Three or four more shots were now fired, and the balls ricochetted along the shore. One man cried out. Then, in a voice that overpowered the tumult, the general shouted:

"Bugles, sound the recall! and you, there, put out the torches!"

Then in a low voice to the captain, —

"Bring the other forty over at once; we shall need every man here in a minute."

The soldiers, startled by this night attack, clustered round their general. Five or six flashes, at rather long distances apart, shone from the crest of the ravine, and lit up momentarily the dark dome of the sky. A grenadier fell dead; the horse of a chasseur reared and fell over on his rider with a ball through his chest.

"Forward! a thousand thunders! forward!" cried the general, "and let's see if those night-hawks will dare to wait for us."

Putting himself at the head of his men he began to climb the slope of the ravine with such vigor that, in spite of the darkness which made the ascension difficult, and in spite of the balls which met them and brought down two more of his men, the little troop soon scaled the height. The enemy's fire stopped instantly, and though a few shaking furze-bushes still showed the recent presence of Chouans, it might be thought that the earth had opened and swallowed them up.

"Sad war! sad war!" muttered the general. "And now, of course, our whole expedition is a failure. No matter! better attempt it. Besides, Souday is on the road to Machecoul, and we can't rest our men short of Machecoul."

"But we want a guide, general," said the captain.

"Guide! Don't you see that light, a thousand feet off, over there?"

"A light?"

"Damn it, yes! — a light."

"No, I don't, general."

"Well, I see it. That light means a hut; a hut means a peasant; and whether that peasant be man, woman, or child, he or she shall be made to guide us through the forest."

Then, in a tone which augured ill for the inhabitant of the hut, the general gave orders to resume the march, after carefully extending his line of scouts and guards as far as he dared expose the individual safety of his men.

The general, followed by his little column, had hardly passed out of sight beyond the ridge before a man came out of the water, stopped an instant behind a willow to listen attentively, and then glided from bush to bush along the shore, with the evident intention of following the path the troop had taken.

As he grasped a tuft of heather to begin the ascent he heard a feeble moan at a little distance. Jean Oullier — for of course it was he — turned instantly in the direction of the moans. The nearer he approached them, the more distressing they became. The man stooped down with his hands stretched out and felt them licked with a warm, soft tongue.

"Pataud! my poor Pataud!" murmured the Vendéan.

It was, indeed, poor Pataud, who had spent the last of his strength in dragging ashore the goatskin his master had sent him for, on which he had now lain down to die.

Jean Oullier took the garment from under him, and called him by name. Pataud gave one long moan, but did not move. Jean Oullier lifted him in his arms to carry him; but the dog no longer stirred. The Vendéan felt the hand with which he held him wet with a warm and viscous fluid. He raised it to his face and smelt the fetid odor of blood. He tried to open the jaws of the poor creature, but they were clenched. Pataud had died in saving his master, whom chance had brought back to him for a last caress.

Had the dog been wounded by a ball aimed by the soldiers at the goatskin, or was he already wounded when he jumped into the water to follow Jean Oullier?

The Vendéan leaned to the last opinion. Pataud's halt beside the river, the feebleness with which he swam, — all induced Jean Oullier to think that the poor animal had been previously wounded.

"Well," he said sadly, "to-morrow I'll clear it up, and sorrow to him who killed you, my poor dog!"

So saying, he laid Pataud's body beneath a shrubby bush, and springing up the hillside was lost to sight among the gorse.

XXIII.

TO WHOM THE COTTAGE BELONGED.

THE cottage, where the general had seen the light his captain could not see, was occupied by two families. The heads of these families were brothers. The elder was named Joseph, the younger Pascal Picaut. The father of these Picauts had taken part, in 1792, in the first uprising of the Retz district, and followed the fortunes of the sanguinary Souchu, as the pilot-fish follows the shark, as the jackal follows the lion; and he had taken part in the horrible massacres which signalized the outbreak of the insurrection on the left bank of the Loire.

When Charette did justice on that Carrier of the white cockade Souchu, Picaut, whose sanguinary appetites were developed, sulked at the new leader, who, to his mind, made the serious mistake of not desiring blood except upon the battlefield. He therefore left the division under Charette, and joined that commanded by the terrible Jolly, an old surgeon of Machecoul. He, at least, was on a level with Picaut's enthusiasm. But Jolly, recognizing the need of unity, and instinctively foreseeing the military genius of the leader of the Lower Vendée, placed himself under Charette's banner; and Picaut, who had not been consulted, dispensed with consulting his commander, and once more abandoned his comrades. Tired out with these perpetual changes, profoundly convinced that time would never lessen the savage hatred he felt for the murderers of Souchu, he sought a general who was not likely to be seduced by the splendor of Charette's exploits, and found him in Stofflet, whose antagonism against the hero of the Retz region was already revealed in numberless instances.

On the 25th of February, 1796, Stofflet was made prisoner at the farm of Poitevinière, with two aides-de-camp and two chasseurs who accompanied him. The Vendéan leader and his aides were shot, and the peasants were sent back to their cottages. Picaut was one of them. It was then two years since he had seen his home.

Arriving there, he found two fine young men, vigorous and well-grown, who threw themselves upon his neck and embraced him. They were his sons. The eldest was seventeen years old, the youngest sixteen. Picaut accepted their caresses with a good grace and looked them well over. He examined their structure, their athletic frames, and felt their muscles with evident satisfaction. He had left two children behind him; he found two soldiers. Only, like himself, these soldiers were unarmed.

The Republic had, in fact, taken from Picaut the carbine and sabre he had obtained through English gold. But Picaut resolved that the Republic should be generous enough to return them and to arm his two sons in compensation for the harm she had done him. It is true that he did not intend to consult the Republic on this point.

The next day he ordered his sons to take their cudgels of wild apple-wood and set out with him for Torfou. At Torfou there was a demi-brigade of infantry. When Picaut, who marched by night and scorned all regular roads, saw, as he crossed the fields, an agglomeration of lights before him, which revealed the town and showed him he had almost reached the end of his journey, he ordered his sons to continue to follow him, but to imitate all his movements and to stop short, motionless, the instant they heard the cry made by a blackbird when suddenly awakened. There is no hunter but knows that the blackbird, suddenly roused, utters three or four rapid notes which are quite peculiar and unmistakable.

Then, instead of walking forward as before, Picaut began

to crawl around the outskirts of the town, in the shadow of the hedges, listening every twenty steps or so, with the utmost attention.

At last he heard a step, — the slow, measured, monotonous step of one man. Picaut went flat on his stomach, and continued to crawl toward the sound on his knees and elbows. His sons imitated him. When he came to the end of the field he was in, Picaut made an opening in the hedge and looked through it. Being satisfied with what he saw he enlarged the hole, and, without much regard to the thorns he encountered, he slipped like an adder through the branches. When he reached the other side he gave the cry of the blackbird. His sons stopped at the given signal; but they stood up, and looking over the top of the hedge they watched their father's proceedings.

The field into which Picaut had now passed was one of tall and very thick grass, which was swaying in the wind. At the farther end of this field, about fifty yards off, was the high-road. On this road a sentry was pacing up and down, about three hundred feet from a building which was used as barracks, before the door of which another sentry was placed. The two young men took all this in with a single glance, and then their eyes returned to their father, who continued to crawl through the grass in the direction of the sentinel.

When Picaut was not more than six feet from the road he stopped behind a bush. The sentinel was pacing up and down, and each time that he turned his back toward the town, as he paced along, his clothes or his musket touched the bush behind which Picaut was crouching. The lads trembled for their father every time that this happened.

Suddenly, and at a moment when the wind seemed to rise, a stifled cry came to them on the breeze. Then, with that acuteness of vision which men accustomed to use their faculties at night soon acquire, they saw on the white line of road a struggling black mass. It was Picaut and the sentinel. After stabbing the sentinel with a knife, Picaut was strangling him.

A moment later the Vendéan was on his way back to his sons; and presently, like the she-wolf after slaughter dividing her booty among her cubs, he bestowed the musket, sabre, and cartridges on the youths. With this first equipment for service it was very much easier to obtain a second.

But weapons were not all that Picaut wanted; his object was to obtain the occasion to use them. He looked about him. In Messieurs d'Autichamp, de Scepeaux, de Puisaye, and de Bourmont, who still kept the field, he found only what he called rose-water royalists, who did not make war in a way to suit him, none of them resembling Souchu, the type of all that Picaut wanted in a leader.

It resulted that Picaut, rather than be, as he thought, ill-commanded, resolved to make himself an independent leader and command others. He recruited a few malcontents like himself, and became the leader of a band which, though numerically small, never wearied in giving proofs of its hatred to the Republic.

Picaut's tactics were of the simplest. He lived in the forests. During the day he and his men rested. At night he left the sheltering woods, and ambushed his little troop behind the hedges. If a government convoy or a diligence came along, he attacked and robbed it. When convoys were rare and diligences too strongly escorted, Picaut found his compensation with the pickets whom he shot, and the farmhouses and buildings of the patriots, which he burned. After one or two expeditions his followers gave him the name of "Sans-Quartier," and Picaut, who resolved, conscientiously, to deserve that title, never failed, after its bestowal, to hang, shoot, or disembowel all republicans — male and female, citizens or soldiers, old men and children — who fell into his hands.

He continued his operations till 1800. At that period, Europe, leaving the First Consul some respite (or the First

Consul leaving Europe a respite), Bonaparte, who had no doubt heard of the fame of Picaut Sans-Quartier's exploits, resolved to consecrate his leisure to that warrior, and sent against him, not a *corps d'armée*, but two Chouans, recruited in the rue de Jérusalem, and two brigades of gendarmerie.

Picaut, not distrustful, admitted his two false compatriots into his band. A few days later he fell into a snare. He was caught, together with most of his men, and he paid with his head for the bloody renown he had acquired. It was as a highwayman and a robber of diligences, and not as a soldier, that he was condemned to the guillotine instead of being shot. He went boldly to the scaffold, asking no more quarter for himself than he had given to others.

Joseph, his eldest son, was sent to the galleys with those of the band who were captured. Pascal, the younger, escaped the trap laid for his father, and took to the forests, where he continued to "Chouanize" with the remnants of the band. But this savage life soon became intolerable to him, and one fine day he went to Beaupréau, gave his sabre and musket to the first soldier he met, and asked to be taken to the commandant of the town, to whom he related his history.

This commandant, a major of dragoons, took an interest in the poor devil, and, in consideration of his youth and the singular confidence with which he had come to him, he offered young Picaut to enlist him in his regiment. In case of refusal, he should, he said, be obliged to hand him over to the legal authorities. Before such an alternative Pascal Picaut (who had now heard of the fate of his father and brother, and had no desire to return to his own neighborhood) did not hesitate. He donned the Republican uniform.

Fourteen years later the two sons of Sans-Quartier met again and returned to their former home, to claim possession of their father's little property. The return of the

Bourbons had opened the gates of the galleys for Joseph and released Pascal, who, from being a brigand of La Vendée, was then a brigand of the Loire.

Joseph, issuing from the galleys, returned to the family cottage more violent in feeling than ever his father had been. He burned to avenge in the blood of patriots the death of his father, and his own tortures.

Pascal, on the contrary, returned home with ideas quite changed from his earlier ones, changed by the different world he had seen, and changed, above all, by contact with men to whom hatred of the Bourbons was a duty, the fall of Napoleon a sorrow, the entrance of the Allies a disgrace, — feelings which were kept alive in his heart by the cross that he wore on his breast.

Nevertheless, in spite of these differences of opinion, which led, of course, to frequent discussion, and in spite of the chronic misunderstanding between them, the two brothers did not separate, but continued to live on in the house their father had left them, and to cultivate on shares the fields belonging to it. Both were married, — Joseph, to the daughter of a poor peasant; Pascal, to whom his cross and his little pension gave a certain consideration in the neighborhood, to the daughter of a bourgeois of Saint-Philbert, a patriot like himself.

The presence of two wives in one house, each of whom — one from envy, the other from rancor — exaggerated the sentiments of their husbands, added not a little to the household discord. Nevertheless, the two brothers and their families continued to live together till 1830. The revolution of July, which Pascal approved, roused all the fanatical wrath of Joseph. Pascal's father-in-law became mayor of Saint-Philbert, and then the Chouan and his wife launched forth into such invectives and insults against "those clumsy villains" that Madame Pascal told her husband she would not live any longer with galley-slaves, for she did not feel her life was safe among them.

The old soldier had no children, and he was singularly

attached to those of his brother. In particular there was a little fair-haired boy, with cheeks as round and as rosy as a pigeon-apple, whom he felt he could not part with. his chief pleasure in life being to dandle the fellow on his knee for hours together. Pascal felt his heart wrung at the very thought of losing his adopted son. In spite of the wrongs done him by his elder brother, he was strongly attached to him. He knew he was impoverished by the costs of his large family; he feared that the separation might cast him into utter poverty, and he therefore refused his wife's request. But he so far regarded it that the two families ceased to take their meals together. The house had three rooms, and Pascal retired into one, leaving two for his brother's family and walling up the door of communication.

The evening of the day on which Jean Oullier was made prisoner, the wife of Pascal Picaut was very uneasy. Her husband had left home at four in the afternoon, — about the time when General Dermoncourt and his detachment started from Montaigu. Pascal had to go, he said, and settle some accounts with Courtin at la Logerie; and now, although it was nearly eight o'clock, he had not returned. The poor woman's uneasiness became agony when she heard the shots in the direction of the river. From time to time she left her wheel, on which she was spinning beside the fire, and went to listen at the door. After the firing ceased she heard nothing except the wind in the tree-tops and the plaintive whine of a dog in the distance.

Little Louis, the child whom Pascal loved so much, came to ask if his uncle had returned; but hardly had he put his rosy little face into the room before his mother, calling him harshly back, obliged him to disappear.

For several days Joseph Picaut had shown himself more surly, more threatening than ever; and that very morning, before starting for the fair at Montaigu, he had had a scene with his brother, which if Pascal's patience had not held good, might have ended in a scuffle. The latter's wife dared not say a word to her sister-in-law about her uneasiness.

Suddenly she heard voices muttering in mysterious, low tones in the orchard before the cottage. She rose so hastily that she knocked over her spinning-wheel. At the same instant the door opened, and Joseph Picaut appeared on the threshold.

XXIV.

HOW MARIANNE PICAUT MOURNED HER HUSBAND.

THE presence of her brother-in-law, whom Marianne Picaut did not expect at that time, and a vague presentiment of misfortune which came over her at the sight of him, produced such a painful impression on the poor woman that she fell back into her chair, half dead with terror.

Joseph advanced slowly, without uttering a word to his brother's wife, who stared at him as though she saw a ghost. When he reached the fireplace Joseph Picaut, still silent, took a chair, sat down, and began to stir the embers on the hearth with a stick which he carried in his hand. In the circle of light thrown by the fire Marianne could see that he was very pale.

"In the name of the good God, Joseph," she said, "tell me what is the matter?"

"Who were those villains who came here to-night, Marianne?" asked the Chouan, answering one question by asking another.

"No one came here," she replied, shaking her head to give force to her denial. Then she added, "Joseph, have you seen your brother?"

"Who persuaded him away from home?" continued the Chouan, still questioning, and making no reply.

"No one, I tell you. He left home about four o'clock to go to La Logerie and pay the mayor for that buckwheat he bought for you last week."

"The mayor of La Logerie?" said Joseph Picaut, frowning. "Yes, yes! Maître Courtin. A bold villain, he!

Many's the time I've told Pascal, — and this very morning I repeated it, — 'Don't tempt the God you deny, or some harm will happen to you.'"

"Joseph! Joseph!" cried Marianne; "how dare you mingle the name of God with words of hatred against your brother who loves you so, you and yours, that he'd take the bread out of his own mouth to give it to your children! If an evil fate brings civil war into the land that's no reason why you should bring it into our home. Good God! Keep your own opinions and let Pascal keep his. His are inoffensive, but yours are not. His gun stays hooked over the fireplace, he meddles with no intrigues, and threatens no party; whereas, for the last six months there has not been a day you haven't gone out armed to the teeth, and sworn evil to the townspeople, of whom my father is one, and even to my family itself."

"Better go out with a musket and face the villains than betray those among whom you live, like a coward, and guide another army of Blues into the midst of us, that they may pillage the château of those who have kept the faith."

"Who has guided the Blues?"

"Pascal."

"When? where?"

"To-night; at the ford of Pont-Farcy."

"Good God! It was from there the shots came!" cried Marianne.

Suddenly the eyes of the poor woman became fixed and haggard. They lighted on Joseph's hands.

"You have blood on your hands!" she cried. "Whose blood is it? Joseph, tell me that! Whose blood is it?"

The Chouan's first movement was to hide his hands, but he thought better of it, and brazened the matter out.

"That blood," he answered, his face, which had been pale, becoming purple, is the blood of a traitor to his God, his country, and his king. It is the blood of a man who forgot that the Blues had sent his father to the scaffold and his brother to the galleys, — a man who did not shrink from taking service with the Blues."

"You have killed my husband! you have murdered your brother!" cried Marianne, facing Joseph with savage violence.

"No, I did not."

"You lie."

"I swear I did not."

"Then if you swear you did not, swear also that you will help me to avenge him."

"Help you to avenge him! I, Joseph Picaut? Never!" said the Chouan, in a determined voice. "For though I did not kill him, I approved of those who did; and if I had been in their place, though he were my brother, I swear by our Lord that I would have done as they did."

"Repeat that," said Marianne; "for I hope I did not hear you right."

The Chouan repeated his speech, word for word.

"Then I curse you, as I curse them!" cried Marianne, raising her hand with a terrible gesture above her brother-in-law's head. "That vengeance which you refuse to take, in which I now include you, — you, your brother's murderer in heart, if not in deed, — God and I will accomplish together; and if God fails me, then I alone! And now," she added, with an energy which completely subdued the Chouan, "where is he? What have they done with his body? Speak! You intend to return me his body, don't you?"

"When I got to the place, after hearing the guns," said Joseph, "he was still alive. I took him in my arms to bring him here, but he died on the way."

"And then you threw him into the ditch like a dog, you Cain! Oh! I would n't believe that story when I read it in the Bible!"

"No, I did not," said Joseph; "I have laid him in the orchard."

"My God! my God!" cried the poor woman, whose whole body was shaken with a convulsive movement. "Perhaps you are mistaken, Joseph; perhaps he still breathes, and we may save him. Come, Joseph, come! If we find him living I'll forgive you for being friends with your brother's murderers."

She unhooked the lamp, and sprang toward the door. But instead of following her, Joseph Picaut, who for the last few moments had been listening to a noise without, hearing that the sounds — evidently those of a body of marching men — were approaching the cottage, darted from the door, ran round the buildings, jumped the hedge between them and the fields, and took the direction of the forest of Machecoul, the black masses of which loomed up in the distance.

Poor Marianne, left alone, ran hither and thither in the orchard. Bewildered and almost maddened, she swung her lamp about her, forgetting to look in the circle of light it threw, and fancying that her eyes must pierce the darkness to find her husband. Suddenly, passing a spot she had passed already once or twice, she stumbled and nearly fell. Her hand, stretched out to save herself from the ground, came in contact with a human body.

She gave a great cry and threw herself on the corpse, clasping it tightly. Then, lifting it in her arms, as she might, under other circumstances, have lifted a child, she carried her husband's body into the cottage and laid it on the bed.

In spite of the jarring relations of the two families, Joseph's wife came into Pascal's room. Seeing the body of her brother-in-law, she fell upon her knees beside the bed and sobbed.

Marianne took the light her sister-in-law brought with her — for hers was left in the orchard — and turned it full upon her husband's face. His mouth and eyes were open, as though he still lived. His wife put her hand eagerly upon his heart, but it did not beat. Then, turning to her sister-in-law, who was weeping and praying beside her, the widow of Pascal Picaut, with blood-shot eyes flaming like firebrands, cried out: —

"Behold what the Chouans have done to my husband, — what Joseph has done to his brother! Well, here upon this body, I swear to have no peace nor rest until those murderers have paid the price of blood."

"You shall not wait long, poor woman, or I'll lose my name," said a man's voice behind her.

Both women turned round and saw an officer wrapped in a cloak, who had entered without their hearing him. Bayonets were glittering in the darkness outside the door, and they now heard the snorting of horses who snuffed the blood.

"Who are you?" asked Marianne.

"An old soldier, like your husband, — one who has seen battlefields enough to have the right to tell you not to lament the death of one who dies for his country, but to avenge him."

"I do not lament, monsieur," replied the widow, raising her head, and shaking back her fallen hair. "What brings you to this cottage at the same time as death?"

"Your husband was to serve as guide to an expedition that is important for the peace and safety of your unhappy country. This expedition may prevent the flow of blood and the destruction of many lives for a lost cause. Can you give me another guide to replace him?"

"Shall you meet the Chouans on your expedition?" asked Marianne.

"Probably we shall," replied the officer.

"Then I will guide you," said the widow, unhooking her husband's gun, which was hanging above the mantel. "Where do you wish to go? I will take you. You can pay me in cartridges."

"We wish to go to the château de Souday."

"Very good; I can guide you. I know the way."

Casting a last look at her husband's body, the widow of Pascal Picaut left the house, followed by the general. The wife of Joseph Picaut remained on her knees, praying, beside the corpse of her brother-in-law.

XXV.

IN WHICH LOVE LENDS POLITICAL OPINIONS TO THOSE WHO HAVE NONE.

WE left the young Baron Michel on the verge of coming to a great resolution. Only, just as he was about to act upon it, he heard steps outside his room. Instantly he threw himself on his bed and closed his eyes, keeping his ears open.

The steps passed; then a few moments later they repassed his door, but without pausing. They were not those of his mother, nor were they in quest of him. He opened his eyes, sat up on the bed, and began to think. His reflections were serious.

Either he must break away from his mother, whose slightest word was law to him, renounce all the ambitious ideas she centred on him, — ideas which had hitherto been most attractive to his vacillating mind, — he must bid farewell to the honors the dynasty of July was pledged to bestow on the millionnaire youth, and plunge into a struggle which would undoubtedly be a bloody one, leading to confiscation, exile, and death, while his own good sense and judgment told him it was futile; or else he must resign himself and give up Mary.

Let us say at once that Michel, although he reflected, did not hesitate. Obstinacy is the first outcome of weakness, which is capable of being obstinate even to ferocity. Besides, too many other good reasons spurred the young baron to allow him to succumb.

In the first place, duty and honor both required him to warn the Comte de Bonneville of the dangers that might threaten him and the person who was with him. Michel already reproached himself for his delay in doing so.

Accordingly, after a few moments' careful reflection, Michel decided on his course. In spite of his mother's watchfulness, he had read novels enough to know that if occasion came, a simple pair of sheets could make an all-sufficient ladder. Naturally enough, this was the first thought that came into his mind. Unfortunately, the windows of his bedroom were directly over those of the kitchen, where he would infallibly be seen when he fluttered down through mid-air, although, as we have said, darkness was just beginning. Moreover, the height was really so great from his windows to the ground that in spite of his resolution to conquer, at the cost of a thousand dangers, the heart of her whom he loved, he felt cold chills running down his back at the mere idea of being suspended by such a fragile hold above an abyss.

In front of his windows was a tall Canadian poplar, the branches of which were about six feet from his balcony. To climb down that poplar, inexperienced though he was in all athletic exercises, seemed to him easy enough, but how to reach its branches was a problem; for the young man dared not trust to the elasticity of his limbs and take a spring.

Necessity made him ingenious. He had in his room a quantity of fishing-tackle, which he had lately been using against the carp and roach in the lake of Grand-Lieu, — an innocent pleasure, which maternal solicitude had authorized. He selected a rod, fastened a hook at the end of the line, and put the whole beside the window. Then he went to his bed and took a sheet. At one end of the sheet he tied a candlestick, — he wanted an article with some weight; a candlestick came in his way, and he took a candlestick. He flung this candlestick in such a way that it fell on the other side of the stoutest limb of the poplar. Then with his hook and line he fished in the end of the sheet, and brought it back to him.

After this he tied both ends firmly to the railing of his balcony, and he thus had a sort of suspension-bridge, solid beyond all misadventure, between his window and the poplar. The young man got astride of it, like a sailor on a yard-arm, and gently propelling himself along, he was soon in the tree, and next on the ground. Then, without caring whether he was seen or not, he crossed the lawn at a run and went toward Souday, the road to which he now knew better than any other.

When he reached the heights of Servière he heard musketry, which seemed to come from somewhere between Montaigu and the lake of Grand-Lieu. His emotion was great. The echo of every volley that came to him on the breeze produced a painful commotion in his mind, which reacted on his heart. The sounds evidently indicated danger, perhaps even death to her he loved, and this thought paralyzed him with terror. Then when he reflected that Mary might blame him for the troubles he had not averted from her head and from those of her father and sister and friends, the tears filled his eyes.

Consequently, instead of slackening speed when he heard the firing, he only thought of quickening it. From a rapid walk he broke into a run, and soon reached the first trees of the forest of Machecoul. There, instead of following the road, which would have delayed him several minutes, he flung himself into a wood-path that he had taken more than once for the very purpose of shortening the way.

Hurrying beneath the dark, overhanging dome of trees, falling sometimes into ditches, stumbling over stones, catching on thorny briers, — so dense was the darkness, so narrow the way, — he presently reached what was called the Devil's Vale. There he was in the act of jumping a brook which runs in the depths of it, when a man, springing abruptly from a clump of gorse, seized him so roughly that he knocked him down into the slimy bed of the brook, pressing the cold muzzle of a pistol to his forehead.

"Not a cry, not a word, or you are a dead man!" said the assailant.

The position was a frightful one for the young baron. The man put a knee on his chest, and held him down, remaining motionless himself, as though he were expecting some one. At last, finding that no one came, he gave the cry of the screch-owl, which was instantly answered from the interior of the wood, and the rapid steps of a man were heard approaching.

"Is that you, Picaut?" said the man whose knee was on Michel's breast.

"No, not Picaut; it is I," said the new-comer.

"Who is 'I'?"

"Jean Oullier."

"Jean Oullier!" cried the other, with such joy that he raised himself partially, and thus relieved, to some extent, his prisoner. "Really and truly you? Did you actually get away from the red-breeches?"

"Yes, thanks to all of you, my friends. But we have not a minute to lose if we want to escape a great disaster."

"What's to be done? Now that you are free and here with us, all will go well."

"How many men have you?"

"Eight on leaving Montaigu; but the *gars* of Vieille-Vigne joined us. We must be sixteen or eighteen by this time."

"How many guns?"

"Each man has one."

"Good. Where are they stationed?"

"Along the edge of the forest."

"Bring them together."

"Yes."

"You know the crossway at the Ragots?"

"Like my pocket."

"Wait for the soldiers there, not in ambush but openly. Order fire when they are within twenty paces. Kill all you can, — so much vermin the less."

"Yes. And then?"

"As soon as your guns are discharged separate in two bodies, — one to escape by the path to La Cloutière, the other by the road to Bourgnieux. Fire as you run, and coax them to follow you."

"To get them off their track, hey?"

"Precisely, Guérin; that's it."

"Yes; but — you?"

"I must get to Souday. I ought to be there now."

"Oh, oh, Jean Oullier!" exclaimed the peasant, doubtfully.

"Well, what?" asked Jean Oullier. "Does any one dare to distrust me?"

"No one says they distrust you; they only say they don't trust any one else."

"I tell you I must be at Souday in ten minutes, and when Jean Oullier says 'I must,' it is because it *must* be done. If you can delay the soldiers half an hour that's all I want."

"Jean Oullier! Jean Oullier!"

"What?"

"Suppose I can't make the *gars* wait for the soldiers in the open?"

"Order them in the name of the good God."

"If it were you who ordered them they would obey; but me — Besides, there's Joseph Picaut among them, and you know Joseph Picaut will only do as he chooses."

"But if I don't go to Souday I have no one to send."

"Let me go, Monsieur Jean Oullier," said a voice from the earth.

"Who spoke?" said the wolf-keeper.

"A prisoner I have just made," said Guérin.

"What's his name?"

"I did not ask his name."

"I am the Baron de la Logerie," said the young man, managing to sit up; for the Chouan's grip was loosened and he had more freedom to move and breathe.

"Ah! Michel's son! You here!" muttered Jean Oullier, in a savage voice.

"Yes. When Monsieur Guérin stopped me I was on my way to Souday to warn my friend Bonneville and Petit-Pierre that their presence in the château was known."

"How came you to know that?"

"I heard it last evening. I overheard a conversation between my mother and Courtin."

"Then why, as you had such fine intentions, did n't you go sooner to warn your friend?" retorted Jean Oullier, in a tone of doubt and also of sarcasm.

"Because the baroness locked me into my room, and that room is on the second floor, and I could not get out till to-night through the window, and then at the risk of my life."

Jean Oullier reflected a moment. His prejudice against all that came from la Logerie was so intense, his hatred against all that bore the name of Michel so deep, that he could not endure to accept a service from the young man. In fact, in spite of the latter's ingenuous frankness, the distrustful Vendéan suspected that such a show of goodwill meant treachery. He knew, however, that Guérin was right, and that he alone in a crucial moment could give the Chouans confidence enough in themselves to let the enemy come openly up to them, and therefore that he alone could delay their march to Souday. On the other hand, he felt that Michel could explain to the Comte de Bonneville better than any peasant the danger that threatened him, and so he resigned himself, though sulkily, to be under an obligation to one of the Michel family.

"Ah, wolf-cub!" he muttered, "I can't help myself." Then aloud, "Very well, so be it. Go!" he said; "but have you the legs to do it?"

"Steel legs."

"Hum!" grunted Jean Oullier.

"If Mademoiselle Bertha were here she would certify to them."

"Mademoiselle Bertha!" exclaimed Jean Oullier, frowning.

"Yes; I fetched the doctor for old Tinguy, and I took only fifty minutes to go seven miles and a half there and back."

Jean Oullier shook his head like a man who is far from being satisfied.

"Do you look after your enemies," said Michel, "and rely on me. If it takes you ten minutes to get to Souday it will take me five, I'll answer for that."

And the young man shook from his clothes the mud and slime with which he was covered, and prepared to depart.

"Do you know the way?" asked Jean Oullier.

"Know the way! As well as I do the paths at la Logerie." And darting off in the direction of Souday, he called back, "Good luck to you, Monsieur Jean Oullier!"

Jean Oullier stood thoughtful a moment. The knowledge the young baron declared he possessed of the neighborhood of the château greatly annoyed him.

"Well, well," he growled at last, "we'll put that in order when we get time." Then addressing Guérin, "Come," said he, "call up the *gars*."

The Chouan took off one of his wooden shoes and putting it to his mouth he blew into it in a way that exactly represented the howling of wolves.

"Do you think they'll hear that?" asked Jean Oullier.

"Of course they will. I chose the farthest place to windward to make sure of it."

"Then we had better not wait for them here. Let us get to the Ragot crossways. Keep on calling as you go along; we shall gain time that way."

"How much time have we in advance of the soldiers?" asked Guérin, following Jean Oullier rapidly through the brake.

"A good half-hour and more. They have halted at the farm of Pichardière."

"Pichardière!" exclaimed Guèrin.

"Yes. They have probably waked up Pascal Picaut, who will guide them. He is a man to do that, is n't he?"

"Pascal Picaut won't serve as guide to any one. He 'll never wake up again," said Guérin, gloomily.

"Ah!" exclaimed Jean Oullier; "then it was he just now, was it?"

"Yes, it was he."

"Did you kill him?"

"He struggled and called for help. The soldiers were within gunshot of us; we had to kill him."

"Poor Pascal!" said Jean Oullier.

"Yes," said Guérin, "though he belonged to the scoundrels, he was a fine man."

"And his brother?" asked Jean Oullier.

"His brother?"

"Yes, Joseph."

"He stood looking on."

Jean Oullier shook himself like a wolf who receives a charge of buckshot in the flank. That powerful nature accepted all the consequences of the terrible struggle which is the natural outcome of civil wars, but he had not foreseen this horror, and he shuddered at the thought of it. To conceal his emotion from Guérin he hurried his steps and bounded through the undergrowth as rapidly as though following his hounds.

Guérin, who stopped from time to time to howl in his shoe, had some trouble in following. Suddenly he heard Jean Oullier give a low whistle warning him to halt.

They were then at a part of the forest called the springs of Baugé, only a short distance from the crossways.

XXVI.

THE SPRINGS OF BAUGÉ.

THE springs of Baugé are really marshes, or rather a marsh, above which the road leading to Souday rises steeply. It is one of the most abrupt ascents of this mountain forest.

The column of the "red-breeches," as Guérin called the soldiers, was obliged to first cross the marsh and then ascend the steep incline. Jean Oullier had reached the part of the road where it crosses this bog on piles before the ascent begins. From there he had whistled to Guérin, who found him apparently reflecting.

"What are you thinking of?" asked Guérin.

"I am thinking that perhaps this is a better place than the crossways," replied Jean Oullier.

"Yes," said Guérin; "for here's a wagon behind which we can ambush."

Jean Oullier, who had not before noticed it, now examined the object his companion pointed out to him. It was a heavy cart loaded with wood, which the driver had left for the night beside the marsh, fearing, no doubt, to cross the narrow causeway after dusk.

"I have an idea," said Jean Oullier, looking alternately at the cart and at the hill, which rose like a dark rampart on the other side of the bog. "Only, they must — "

He looked all about him.

"Who must? What?"

"The *gars* must be here."

"They are here," said Guérin. "See, here's Patry, the two Gambier brothers, and there are the Vieille-Vigne men and Joseph Picaut."

Jean Oullier turned his back so as not to see the latter.

It was true enough; the Chouans were flocking up on all sides. First one and then another came from behind each bush and hedge. Soon they were all collected.

"*Gars!*" said Jean Oullier, addressing them, "Ever since La Vendée was La Vendée, — that is, ever since she has fought for her principles, — her children have never been called upon to show their courage and their faith more than they are to-day. If we cannot now stop the march of Louis Philippe's soldiers great misfortunes will happen; I tell you, my sons, that all the glory which covers the name of La Vendée will be wiped out. As for me, I am resolved to leave my bones in the bog of Baugé sooner than allow that infernal column of troops to go beyond it."

"So are we, Jean Oullier!" cried many voices.

"Good!" that is what I expected from men who followed us from Montaigu to deliver me, and who succeeded. Come, to begin with, help me to drag this cart to the top of the hill."

"We'll try," said the Vendéans.

Jean Oullier put himself at their head, and the heavy vehicle, pushed from behind or by the wheels by some, while eight or ten pulled it by the shafts, crossed the narrow causeway, and was hoisted rather than dragged to the summit of the steep embankment. There Jean Oullier wedged the wheels with stones to prevent it from running backward by its own weight down the steep rise it had gone up with so much difficulty.

"Now," he said, "put yourselves in ambush each side of the marsh, half to the right, half to the left, and when the time comes, — that's to say, when I shout 'Fire!' — fire instantly. If the soldiers turn to pursue you, as I hope they may, retreat toward Grand-Lieu, striving to lead them on as best you can away from Souday, which they are aiming for. If, on the contrary, they continue their way we will all wait for them at the Ragot crossways. There we must stand firm and die at our posts."

The Chouans instantly disappeared into their hiding-places on either side the marsh, and Jean Oullier was left alone with Guérin. Thereupon, he flung himself flat on his stomach with his ear to the ground and listened.

"They are coming," he said. "They are following the road to Souday as if they knew it. Who the devil can be guiding them, now that Pascal Picaut is dead?"

"They must have found some peasant and compelled him."

"Then that's another we shall have to get rid of. If they once get into the depths of the forest of Machecoul without a guide, not one of them will ever return to Montaigu."

"Ah, ça, Jean Oullier!" exclaimed Guérin, suddenly. "You have n't any weapon!"

"I!" said the old Vendéan, laughing between his teeth. "I've a weapon that can bring down more men than your carbine; and in ten minutes, if everything goes as I hope it will, there'll be plenty of guns to pick up beside the marsh."

So saying, Jean Oullier again went up the ascent, which he had partly descended to explain to the men his plan of battle, and reached the cart. It was high time. As he gained the summit he heard on the opposite hillside, which led down to the marsh, the sound of stones rolling from the feet of horses, and he saw two or three flashes of light from their iron shoes. The air was quivering, as it does in the night-time, with the approach of a body of armed men.

"Come, go down and join the rest," he said to Guérin.
"I stay here."

"What are you going to do?"

"You'll see presently."

Guérin obeyed. Jean Oullier crept under the cart and waited. Guérin had hardly taken his place among his comrades when the two leading chasseurs of the advanced-guard came upon the edge of the marsh. Seeing the difficulties before them, they stopped and hesitated.

"Straight on!" cried a firm voice, although it had a feminine ring. "Straight on!"

The two chasseurs advanced, and seeing the narrow causeway built on piles they crossed it and began the ascent, coming nearer and nearer to the cart, and, consequently, to Jean Oullier.

When they were twenty steps away from him, Jean Oullier, still beneath the cart, hung himself by his hands to the axletree, and resting his feet on the front bars of the wagon, remained quite motionless. The chasseurs were presently beside the cart. They examined it carefully from their saddles, and seeing, of course, nothing of the man beneath it or anything else to excite distrust, they continued their way.

The main column was by this time at the edge of the marsh. The widow Picaut passed first, then the general, then the chasseurs. The marsh was crossed in that order.

But just as they reached the foot of the slope a thundering sound was heard from the summit of the rise they were about to ascend; the ground shook under their feet, and a sort of avalanche came tearing down the hill with the rapidity of a thunder-bolt.

"Stand aside!" cried Dermoncourt, in a voice which rose above that horrible uproar.

Seizing the widow by the arm, he spurred his horse into the bushes. The general's first thought was for his guide, who was, for the moment, the most precious thing he had. The guide and he were safe.

But the soldiers for the most part did not have time to obey their leader. Paralyzed by the strange noise they heard and not knowing what enemy to look for, blinded by the darkness, and feeling danger everywhere about them, they held to the road, where the cart (for of course it was the cart, violently impelled by Jean Oullier from the top of the steep embankment) cut its way through them like a monstrous cannon-ball, killing those the wheels ran over, and wounding others with its logs and splinters.

A moment of stupefaction followed this catastrophe, but it could not check Dermoncourt.

"Forward, men!" he cried, "and let's get out of this cut-throat place!"

At the same moment a voice, not less powerful than his own, called out: —

"Fire, my *gars!*"

A flash issued from every bush on either side of the marsh and a rain of balls came pelting down among the little troop. The voice that ordered the volley resounded from its front, but the shots came from its rear. The general, an old war-wolf, as sly and wary as Jean Oullier himself, saw through the manœuvre.

"Forward!" he cried; "don't lose time answering them. Forward! forward!"

The column continued to advance, and in spite of the volleys which followed it, reached the top of the hill.

While the general and his men were making the ascent Jean Oullier, hiding among the underbrush, went rapidly down the hill and joined his companions.

"Bravo!" said Guérin. "Ah! if we had only ten arms like yours and a few such wood-carts as that we could get rid of this cursed army in a very short time."

"Hum!" growled Jean Oullier, "I'm not as satisfied as you. I hoped to turn them back, but we have not done it. It looks to me as if they were keeping on their way. To the crossroads, now, and as fast as our legs will take us!"

"Who says the red-breeches are keeping on their way?" asked a voice.

Jean Oullier went to the boggy path whence the voice had come, and recognized Joseph Picaut. The Vendéan, kneeling on the ground, with his gun beside him, was conscientiously emptying the pockets of three soldiers whom Jean Oullier's mighty projectile had knocked over and crushed to death. The wolf-keeper turned away with an expression of disgust.

"Listen to Joseph," said Guérin, in a low voice to Jean Oullier. "You had better listen to him, for he sees by night like the cats, and his advice is not to be despised."

"Well, I say," said Joseph Picaut, putting his plunder into a canvas bag he always carried with him, — "I say that since the Blues reached the top of the embankment they have n't budged. You have n't any ears, you fellows, or you would hear them stamping up there like sheep in a fold. If you don't hear them, I do."

"Let us make sure of that," said Jean Oullier to Guérin, thus avoiding a reply to Joseph.

"You are right, Jean Oullier, and I'll go myself," replied Guérin.

The Vendéan crossed the marsh, crept through the reeds, and went half way up the ascent, crawling on his stomach like a snake among the rocks, and gliding so gently under the bushes that they scarcely stirred as he passed. When he was only about thirty paces from the summit he stood up, put his hat on the end of a long stick, and waved it above his head. Instantly a shot from the summit sent it spinning a hundred feet below its owner.

"He was right," said Jean Oullier, who heard the shot. "But what is hindering them? Is their guide killed?"

"Their guide is not killed," said Joseph Picaut, in a savage voice.

"Did you see him?" asked another voice, for Jean Oullier seemed determined not to speak to Joseph Picaut.

"Yes," replied the Chouan.

"Did you recognize him?"

"Yes."

"Then it must be," said Jean Oullier, as if speaking to himself, "that they wanted to get away from the marsh and bivouac behind those rocks, where they are safe from our guns. No doubt they will stay there till morning."

THE SPRINGS OF BAUGÉ. 241

Presently a few lights were seen flickering on the height. Little by little they increased in number and in size, until four or five camp fires lit up with a ruddy glow the sparse vegetation which grew among the rocks.

"This is very strange if their guide is still with them, said Jean Oullier. "However, as they are certain to go by the Ragot crossways in any case, take your men there, Guérin," he said to the Chouan, who by this time had returned to his side.

"Very good," said the latter.

"If they continue their way, you know what you have to do; if, on the contrary, they have really bivouacked up there, you can let them take their ease beside their fires. It is useless to attack them."

"Why so?" asked Joseph Picaut.

Thus directly questioned as to his own order, Jean Oullier was forced to reply.

"Because," he said, "it is a crime to uselessly expose the lives of brave men."

"Say rather — "

"What?" demanded the old keeper, violently.

'Say 'Because my masters, the nobles whose servant I am, no longer want the lives of those brave men.' Say that, and you 'll tell the truth, Jean Oullier."

"Who dares to say that Jean Oullier lies?" asked the wolf-keeper, frowning.

"I!" said Joseph Picaut.

Jean Oullier set his teeth, but contained himself. He seemed resolved to have neither friendship nor quarrel with the man.

"I!" repeated Picaut, — "I say that it is not out of love for our bodies that you want to prevent us from profiting by our victory, but because all you have made us fight for is to keep the red-breeches from pillaging the castle of Souday."

"Joseph Picaut," replied Jean Oullier, calmly "though we both wear the white cockade we do not follow the same paths nor work for the same ends. I have always thought that no matter how their opinions may differ, brothers are brothers, and it grieves me to see the blood of my brethren uselessly shed. As for my relation to my masters I have always regarded humility as the first duty of a Christian, above all when that Christian is a poor peasant, as I am, and as you are. Also I consider obedience the most imperative duty of a soldier. I know that you don't think as I do, — so much the worse for you! Under other circumstances I might have made you repent for what you have just said; but at this moment I do not belong to myself. You may thank God for that."

"Well," said Joseph Picaut, sneering, "when you return into possession of yourself you'll know where to find me, Jean Oullier; you won't have far to look." Then, turning to the little troop of men, he went on: "Now, if there are any among you who think it is folly to course the hare when you can take it in its form, follow me."

He started as if to go. No one stirred; no one even answered him. Joseph Picaut, seeing that total silence followed his proposal, made an angry gesture and disappeared into the thicket.

Jean Oullier, taking Picaut's words for mere boastfulness, shrugged his shoulders.

"Come, you fellows," he said to the Chouans, "be off to the Ragot crossways, and quickly, too. Follow the bed of the brook to the clearing at Quatre-Vents; from there it will take you fifteen minutes to get to the crossways."

"Where are you going, Jean Oullier?" said Guérin.

"To Souday," said the wolf-keeper. "I must make sure that Michel did his errand."

The little band departed obediently, following, as Jean Oullier told them, the course of the rivulet. The old keeper was left alone. He listened for a few moments to the sound of the water which the Chouans splashed as they marched; but that noise soon mingled with the rippling and dash of the little rapids, and Jean Oullier turned his head in the direction of the soldiers.

THE SPRINGS OF BAUGÉ.

The rocks on which the column had halted formed a chain, running from east to west in the direction of Souday. On the east this chain ended in a gentle slope, which came down to the rivulet up which the Chouans had just passed in order to turn the encampment of the troops. On the west it stretched for a mile and a half or more, and the nearer it came to Souday the higher and more jagged grew the rocks, the steeper and more denuded of vegetation were the slopes. On this side the miniature mountain ended in an actual precipice formed by enormous perpendicular rocks, which overhung the rivulet that washed their base. Once or twice in his life Jean Oullier had risked the descent of this precipice to gain upon a boar his dogs were pursuing. It was done by a path scarcely a foot wide, hidden among the gorse and called the Viette des Biques, meaning "the goat-path." The way was known to a few hunters only. Jean Oullier himself had been exposed to such danger in descending it that he considered it impossible that the troops should attempt it in the darkness.

If the enemy's column intended to continue its aggressive movement on Souday it must either take this goat-path, or meet the Chouans at the Ragot crossways, or return upon its steps and follow the brook up which the Chouans had just gone. All this seemed to throw the enemy into his hands, and yet Jean Oullier, by a sort of presentiment, was uneasy.

It seemed to him extraordinary that Dermoncourt had yielded to the first attack and resigned so quickly and readily his evident intention of advancing to Souday. Instead of continuing his own way to Souday, as he had told Guérin he should, he remained where he was, watching the heights, when suddenly he observed that the fires were going down and the light they threw upon the rocks was growing fainter and fainter.

Jean Oullier's decision was made in a moment. He darted along the same path Guérin had taken to observe the enemy, and used the same tactics; only, he did not stop, as Guérin had stopped, half-way up the ascent. He continued to crawl up until he was at the foot of the blocks of stone which surrounded the flat summit.

There he listened; he heard no noise. Then, rising cautiously to his feet in a space between two large rocks, he looked before him and saw nothing. The place was solitary. The fires were deserted; the furze with which they were built was crackling and going out. Jean Oullier climbed the rocks and dropped into the space where he had supposed the soldiers were. Not a man was there.

He gave a terrible cry of rage and disappointment, and shouted to his companions below to return and follow him. Then, with the swiftness of a hunted deer, straining his iron muscles to the utmost, he rushed along the summit of the rocks in the direction of Souday. No doubt remained in his mind. Some unknown guide, unknown except to Joseph Picaut, had led the soldiers to the Viette des Biques.

Notwithstanding the difficulties of the way, Jean Oullier, slipping on the flat rocks covered with mosses, striking against the granite blocks which rose in his path like sentinels, catching his feet in the briers which tore his flesh as he rushed through them, — Jean Oullier, we say, was not ten minutes in getting over the whole length of the little chain. When he reached its extremity he climbed the last line of rocks which overlooked the valley, and saw the soldiers.

They were just descending the slope of the hill, having risked the path of the Viette des Biques. The line of their torches could be seen filing cautiously along by the edge of the abyss. Jean Oullier clung to the enormous stone on which he stood and shook it, hoping to detach it and send it rolling on their heads. But all such efforts of mad anger were powerless, and only a mocking laugh replied to his imprecations. He turned round and looked behind him, thinking that Satan himself could alone laugh thus. The laugher was Joseph Picaut.

"Well, Jean Oullier," he said, coming out of a clump of gorse, "my scent was better than yours; you ought to have followed me. As it was, you made me lose my time. I got here too late; and your friends will be cooked in spite of me."

"My God! my God!" cried Jean Oullier, grasping his hair with both hands. "Who could have guided them down that path?"

"Whoever did guide them down shall never come up again, either by this path or any other," said Joseph Picaut. "Look at that guide now, Jean Oullier, if you want to see her living."

Jean Oullier leaned forward once more. The soldiers had crossed the rivulet and were gathered round the general. In the midst of them, not a hundred paces from the two men, though separated from them by the precipice, they saw a woman with dishevelled hair, who was pointing out to the general with her finger the path he must now take.

"Marianne Picaut!" exclaimed Jean Oullier.

The Chouan made no answer, but he raised his gun to his shoulder and slowly aimed it. Jean Oullier turned round when he heard the click of the trigger, and as the Chouan fired he threw up the muzzle of the gun.

"Wretch!" he cried; "give her time to bury your brother!"

The ball was fired into space.

"Damn you!" cried Joseph Picaut, furiously, seizing his gun by the barrel, and giving a terrible blow with the stock on Jean Oullier's head. "I treat Whites like you as I would Blues!"

In spite of his Herculean strength the blow was so violent that it brought the old Vendéan to his knees; then, not able to maintain himself in that position, he rolled over the edge of the precipice. As he fell he caught instinctively at a tuft of gorze; but he soon felt it yielding under the weight of his body.

Bewildered as he was, he did not altogether lose consciousness, and, expecting every moment to feel the slender shoots which alone supported him above the abyss give way, he commended his soul to God. At that instant he heard shots from the gorse and saw through his half-closed eyelids the flash of arms. Hoping that the Chouans had returned, led by Guérin, he tried to call out, but his voice felt imprisoned in his chest, and he could not raise the leaden hand which seemed to hold the breath from his lips. He was like a man in a frightful nightmare; and the pain the effort cost him was so violent that he fancied — forgetting the blow he had received — that his forehead was sweating blood.

Little by little his strength abandoned him. His fingers weakened, his muscles relaxed, and the agony he endured became so terrible that he believed he must voluntarily let go the branches which alone held him above the void. Soon he felt himself attracted to the abyss below him by an irresistible impulse. His fingers loosened their last hold; but at the very moment when he imagined he should hear the air whistling and whirling as he fell through it, and feel the jagged points of rocks tearing his body as he passed, a pair of vigorous arms caught him and bore him to a narrow platform which overhung the precipice at a little distance.

He was saved! But he knew at once that the arms that were brutally handling him were not those of friends.

XXVII.

THE GUESTS AT SOUDAY.

THE day after the arrival of the Comte de Bonneville and his companion at the château de Souday, the marquis returned from his expedition, or rather, his conference. As he got off his horse it was quite evident that the worthy gentleman was in a savage ill-humor.

He growled at his daughters, who had not come even so far as the door to meet him; he swore at Jean Oullier, who had taken the liberty to go off to the fair at Montaigu without his permission; he quarrelled with the cook, who, in the absence of the major-domo, came forward to hold his stirrup, and instead of grasping the one to the right, pulled with all her strength on the one to the left, thus obliging the marquis to get off on the wrong side of his horse and away from the portico.

When he reached the salon M. de Souday's wrath was still exhaling itself in monosyllables of such vehemence that Bertha and Mary, accustomed as their ears were to the freedom of language the old *émigré* allowed himself, did not, on this occasion, know which way to look.

In vain they attempted to coax him and smooth his angry brow. Nothing did any good; and the marquis, as he warmed his feet before the fire and switched his topboots with his riding-whip, seemed to regret bitterly that Messieurs Blank and Blank were not the top-boots themselves, to whom he addressed, as he flourished his whip, some very offensive epithets indeed.

The fact is, the marquis was furious. For some time past he had been sadly conscious that the pleasures of the chase were beginning to pall upon him; also he had found himself yawning over the whist which regularly concluded his evenings. The joys of trumps and odd tricks were beginning to be insipid, and life at Souday threatened to become distasteful to him. Besides, for the last ten years his legs had never felt as elastic as they did now. Never had his lungs breathed freer, or his brain been so active and enterprising. He was just entering that Saint-Martin's summer for old men, — the period when their faculties sparkle with a brighter gleam before paling, and their bodies gather strength as if to prepare for the final struggle. The marquis, feeling himself more lively, more fit than he had been for many a year, growing restless in the little circle of his daily avocations, now insufficient to occupy him, and conscious, alas! that ennui was creeping over him, took it into his head that a new Vendée would be admirably suited to his renewed youth, and did not doubt that he should find in the adventurous life of a partisan those earlier enjoyments the very memory of which was the charm of his old age.

He had therefore hailed with enthusiasm the prospect of a new uprising and call to arms. A political commotion of that kind, coming as it did, proved to him once more what he had often in his placid and naive egotism believed, — that the world was created and managed for the satisfaction and benefit of so worthy a gentleman as M. le Marquis de Souday.

But he had found among his co-royalists a lukewarmness and a disposition to procrastinate which fairly exasperated him. Some declared that the public mind was not yet ripe for any movement; others that it was imprudent to attempt anything unless assured that the army would side with legitimacy; others, again, insisted that religious and political enthusiasm was dying out among the peasantry, and that it would be difficult to rouse them to a new war. The heroic marquis, who could not comprehend why all France should not be ready when a small

campaign would be so very agreeable to him, — when Jean
Oullier had burnished up his best carbine, and his daughters had embroidered for him a scarf and a bloody heart,
— the marquis, we say, had just quarrelled vehemently
with his friends the Vendéan leaders, and leaving the
meeting abruptly, had returned to the château without
listening to reason.

Mary, who knew to what excess her father respected the
duty of hospitality, profited by a lull in his ill-humor to
tell him gently of the arrival of the Comte de Bonneville
at the château, hoping in this way to create a diversion
for his mind.

"Bonneville! Bonneville! And who may that be?"
growled the irascible old fellow. "Bonneville? Some
cabbage-planter or lawyer or civilian who has jumped into
epaulets, some talker who can't fire anything but words,
a dilettante who 'll tell me we ought to wait and let
Philippe waste his popularity! Popularity, indeed! As
if the thing to do were not to turn that popularity on our
own king!"

"I see that Monsieur le marquis is for taking arms
immediately," said a soft and flute-like voice beside him.

The marquis turned round hastily and beheld a very
young man, dressed as a peasant, who was leaning, like
himself, against the chimney-piece, and warming his feet
before the fire. The stranger had entered the room by a
side door, and the marquis, whose back was toward him
as he entered, being carried away by the heat of his wrath
and his imprecations, paid no heed to the signs his daughters made to warn him of the presence of a guest.

Petit-Pierre, for it was he, seemed to be about sixteen
or eighteen years old; but he was very slender and frail
for his years. His face was pale, and the long black hair
which framed it made it seem whiter still; his large blue
eyes beamed with courage and intellect; his mouth, which
was delicate and curled slightly upward at the corners,
was now smiling with a mischievous expression; the chin,

250   THE LAST VENDÉE.

strongly defined and prominent, indicated unusual strength of will; while a slightly aquiline nose completed a cast of countenance, the distinction of which contrasted strangely with the clothes he wore.

"Monsieur Petit-Pierre," said Bertha, taking the hand of the new-comer, and presenting him to her father.

The marquis made a profound bow, to which the young man replied with a graceful salutation. The old *émigré* was not very much deceived by the dress and name of Petit-Pierre. The great war had long accustomed him to the use of nicknames and aliases by which men of high birth concealed their rank, and the disguises under which they hid their natural bearing; but what did puzzle him was the extreme youth of his unexpected guest.

"I am happy, monsieur," he said, "if my daughters have been able to be of service to you and Monsieur de Bonneville; but all the same I regret that I was absent from home at the time of your arrival. If it were not for an extremely unpleasant interview with some gentlemen of my political opinions, I should have had the honor to put my poor castle at your service myself. However, I hope my little chatterers have been good substitutes, and that nothing our limited means can procure has been spared to make your stay as comfortable as it can be."

"Your hospitality, Monsieur le marquis, can only gain in the hands of such charming substitutes," said Petit-Pierre, gallantly.

"Humph!" said the marquis, pushing out his lower lip; "in other times than these we are in, my daughters ought to be able to procure for their guests some amusement. Bertha, here, knows how to follow a trail, and can turn a boar as well as any one. Mary, on the other hand, has n't her equal for knowing the corner of the marsh where the snipe are. But except for a sound knowledge of whist, which they get from me, I regard them as altogether unfit to do the honors of a salon; and here we are, for the present, shut up with nothing to do but poke the fire." So saying, Monsieur de Souday gave a vigorous kick to the logs on the hearth, proving that his anger was not yet over.

"I think few women at court possess more grace and distinction than these young ladies; and I assure you that none unite with those qualities such nobility of heart and feeling as your daughters, Monsieur le marquis, have shown to us."

"Court?" said the marquis, interrogatively, looking with some surprise at Petit-Pierre.

Petit-Pierre colored and smiled deprecatingly, like an actor who blunders before a friendly audience.

"I spoke, of course, on presumption, Monsieur le marquis," he said, with an embarrassment that was obviously factitious. "I said the court, because that is the sphere where your daughters' name would naturally place them, and also, because it is there I should like to see them."

The marquis colored because he had made his guest color. He had just involuntarily meddled with the incognito the latter seemed anxious to preserve, and the exquisite politeness of the old gentleman reproached him bitterly for such a fault.

Petit-Pierre hastened to add: —

"I was saying to you, Monsieur le marquis, when these young ladies did me the honor to introduce us, that you seem to be one of those who desire an immediate call to arms."

"I should think so! parbleu! and I am willing to say so to you, monsieur, who, as I see, are one of us — "

Petit-Pierre nodded in affirmation.

"Yes, that is my desire," continued the marquis; "but no matter what I say and do, I can't get any one to believe an old man who scorched his skin in the terrible fire which laid waste the country from 1793 to 1797. No! they listen to a pack of gabblers, lawyers without a brief, fine dandies who dare not sleep in the open air for fear of spoiling their clothes, milk-sops, fellows," added the marquis, kicking at the logs, which revenged themselves by showering his boots with sparks, — "fellows who —"

"Papa!" said Mary, gently, observing a furtive smile on Petit-Pierre's face. "Papa, do be calm!"

"No, I shall not be calm," continued the fiery old gentleman. "Everything was ready. Jean Oullier assured me that my division was boiling over with enthusiasm; and now the affair is adjourned over from the 14th of May to the Greek Calends!"

"Patience, Monsieur le marquis," said Petit-Pierre, "the time will soon be here."

"Patience! patience! that's easy for you to say," replied the marquis, sighing. "You are young, and you have time enough to wait; but I — Who knows if God will grant me days enough to unfurl the good old flag I fought under so gayly once upon a time?"

Petit-Pierre was touched by the old man's regret.

"But have you not heard, Monsieur le marquis, for I have," he said, "that the call to arms was only postponed because of the uncertainty that exists as to the arrival of the princess?"

This speech seemed to increase the marquis's ill-humor.

"Let me alone, young man," he said, in an angry tone. "Don't I know the meaning of that old joke? During the five years that I fought to the death in La Vendée were not they always telling us that a royal personage would draw his sword and rally all ambitions round him? Didn't I myself, with many others, wait for the Comte d'Artois to land on the shores of the Île Dieu on the 2d of October? We shall no more see the Duchesse de Berry in 1832 than we saw the Comte d'Artois in 1796. That, however, will not prevent me from getting myself killed on their behalf, as becomes a loyal gentleman."

"Monsieur le Marquis de Souday," said Petit-Pierre, in a voice of strange emotion, "I swear to you, myself, that if the Duchesse de Berry had nothing more than a nutshell at her command she would cross the seas and place herself under Charette's banner, borne by a hand so valiant and so noble. I swear to you that she will come now, if not to conquer, at least to die with those who have risen to defend the rights of her son."

There was such energy and determination in the tone with which he spoke, and it seemed so extraordinary that such words should issue from the lips of a little lad of sixteen, that the marquis looked him in the face with extreme surprise.

"Who are you?" he said, giving way to his astonishment. "By what right do you speak thus of the intentions of her Royal Highness, and pledge your word for her, young man — or rather, child?"

"I think, Monsieur le marquis, that Mademoiselle de Souday did me the honor to mention my name when she presented me to you."

"True, Monsieur Petit-Pierre," replied the marquis, confused at his outburst. "I beg your pardon. But," he added conjecturing the youth to be the son of some great personage, "is it indiscreet to ask your opinion as to the present likelihood of a call to arms? Young as you are, you speak with such excellent sense that I do not conceal from you my desire for your opinion."

"My opinion, Monsieur le marquis, can be all the more readily given because I see plainly that it is much the same as yours."

"Really?"

"My opinion — if I may permit myself to give one —"

"Heavens! after the pitiful creatures I heard talk tonight you seem to me as wise as the seven sages of Greece."

"You are too kind. It is my opinion, Monsieur le marquis, that it was most unfortunate we could not rise, as agreed upon, on the night of the 13th and 14th of May."

"That's just what I told them. May I ask your reasons, monsieur?"

"My reasons are these: The soldiers were at that time quartered in the villages, among the inhabitants, scattered here and there, without object and without a flag. Nothing was easier than to surprise and disarm them in a sudden attack."

"Most true; whereas now —"

"Now the order has been given to break up the small encampments and draw into a focus all the scattered military forces and bodies, — not of mere companies and detachments, but of battalions and regiments. We shall now need a pitched battle to reach the results we might have gained by the cost of that one night's sleep."

"That's conclusive!" cried the marquis, enthusiastically, "and I am dreadfully distressed that out of the forty and one reasons I gave my opponents to-night I never thought of that. But," he continued, "that order which you say has been sent to the troops, are you quite sure it has been actually issued?"

"Quite sure," said Petit-Pierre, with the most modest and deferential look he could put upon his face.

The marquis looked at him in stupefaction.

"It is a pity," he went on, "a great pity! However, as you say, my young friend, — you will permit me to give you that title, — it is better to have patience and wait till our new Maria Theresa comes into the midst of her new Hungarians, and meantime to drink to the health of her royal son and his spotless banner. That reminds me that these young ladies must deign to get our breakfast ready, for Jean Oullier has gone off, as some one," he added, with a half-angry look at his daughters, "has taken upon herself to allow him to go to Montaigu without my orders."

"That some one was I, Monsieur le marquis," said Petit-Pierre, whose courteous tone was not quite free from command. "I beg your pardon for having thus employed one of your men; but you were absent, and it was most urgent that we should judge exactly what we had to expect from the temper of the peasantry assembled at Montaigu for the fair."

There was a tone of such easy and natural assurance in that soft, sweet voice, such a consciousness of authority in the person who spoke, that the marquis was speechless. He ran over in his mind the various great personages he could think of who might have a son of this age, and all he managed to say in reply were a few stammered words of acquiescence.

The Comte de Bonneville entered the room at this moment. Petit-Pierre, as the older acquaintance of the two, presented him to the marquis.

The open countenance and frank, joyous manner of the count immediately won upon the old gentleman, already delighted with Petit-Pierre. He dismissed his ill-humor, and vowed not to think any more of the cold hearts and backwardness of his late companions; and he inwardly resolved, as he led his guests to the dining-room, to use all his wit to extract from the Comte de Bonneville the real name of the youth who now chose to pass under the incognito of Petit-Pierre.

XXVIII.

IN WHICH THE MARQUIS DE SOUDAY BITTERLY REGRETS THAT PETIT-PIERRE IS NOT A GENTLEMAN.

THE two young men, whom the Marquis de Souday pushed before him, stopped on the threshold of the dining-room door. The aspect of the table was literally formidable.

In the centre rose, like an ancient citadel commanding a town, an enormous pasty of boar's meat and venison, A pike weighing fifteen pounds, three or four chickens in a stew, and a regular tower of Babel in cutlets flanked this citadel to the north, south, east, and west; and for outposts or picket-guards M. de Souday's cook had surrounded these heavy works with a cordon of dishes, all touching one another, and containing aliments of many kinds, — hors-d'œuvres, entrées, entremets, vegetables, salads, fruits, and marmalades, — all huddled together and heaped in a confusion that was certainly not picturesque, though full of charm for appetites sharpened by the cutting air of the forests of the Mauge region.

"Heavens!" cried Petit-Pierre, drawing back, as we have said, at the sight of such victualling. "You treat poor peasants too royally, Monsieur de Souday."

"Oh, as for that, I have nothing to do with it, my young friend, and you must neither blame me nor thank me. I leave all that to these young ladies. But it is, I hope, unnecessary to say how happy I am that you honor the board of a poor country gentleman."

So saying, the marquis gently impelled Petit-Pierre, who still seemed to hesitate, to approach the table. He yielded to the pressure with some reserve.

"I know I cannot worthily respond to what you expect of me, Monsieur le marquis," he said; "for I must humbly admit to you that I am a very poor eater."

"I understand," said the marquis; "you are accustomed to delicate dishes. As for me, I am a regular peasant, and I prefer good, solid, succulent food, which repairs the waste of the system, to all the dainties of a fine table."

"That's a point I have often heard King Louis XVIII. and the Marquis d'Avaray discuss," said Petit-Pierre.

The Comte de Bonneville touched the youth's arm.

"Then you knew King Louis XVIII. and the Marquis d'Avaray?" said the old gentleman, in much amazement, looking at Petit-Pierre, as if to make sure that the youth was not laughing at him.

"Yes, I knew them well, in my youth," replied Petit-Pierre, simply.

"Hum!" said the marquis, shortly.

They had now taken their places round the table, Mary and Bertha with them, and the formidable breakfast began. But in vain did the marquis offer dish after dish to his younger guest. Petit-Pierre refused all, and said if his host were willing he would like a cup of tea and two fresh eggs from the fowls he heard clucking so cheerfully in the poultry-yard.

"As for fresh eggs," said the marquis, "that's an easy matter. Mary shall get you some warm from the nest; but as for tea, the devil! I doubt if there is such a thing in the house."

Mary did not wait to be sent on this errand. She was already leaving the room when her father's remark about the tea stopped her, and she seemed as embarrassed as he. Evidently tea was lacking. Petit-Pierre noticed the quandary of his hosts.

"Oh!" he said, "don't give yourself any uneasiness. Monsieur de Bonneville will have the kindness to take a few spoonfuls from my dressing-case."

"Your dressing-case!"

"Yes," said Petit-Pierre. "As I have contracted the bad habit of drinking tea, I always carry it with me in travelling."

And he gave the Comte de Bonneville a little key, selecting it from a bunch that was hanging to a gold chain. The Comte de Bonneville hastened away by one door as Mary went out by the other.

"Upon my soul!" cried the marquis, engulfing an enormous mouthful of venison, "you are something of a girl, my young friend; and if it were not for the opinions I heard you express just now, which I consider too profound for the female mind, I should almost doubt your sex."

Petit-Pierre smiled.

"Wait till you see me at work, Monsieur le marquis, when we meet Philippe's troops. You'll soon resign the poor opinion you are forming of me now."

"What? Do you mean to belong to any of our bands?" cried the marquis, more and more puzzled.

"I hope so," said the youth.

"And I'll answer for it," said Bonneville, returning and giving Petit-Pierre the little key he had received from him, "I'll answer for it you'll always find him in the front rank."

"I am glad of it, my young friend," said the marquis; "but I am not surprised. God has not measured courage by the bodies to which he gives it, and I saw in the old war one of the ladies who followed M. de Charette fire her pistols valiantly."

Just then Mary returned, bringing in one hand a teapot, and in the other a plate with two boiled eggs on it.

"Thank you, my beautiful child," said Petit-Pierre, in a tone of gallant protection, which reminded M. de Souday of the seigneurs of the old court. "A thousand excuses for the trouble I have given you."

"You spoke just now of his Majesty Louis XVIII.," said

the Marquis de Souday, "and his culinary opinions. I have heard it said that he was extremely fastidious about his meals and his way of eating them."

"That is true," said Petit-Pierre; "he had a fashion of eating ortolans and cutlets which was his alone."

"And yet," said the Marquis de Souday, setting his handsome teeth into a cutlet and gnawing off the whole lean of it with one bite, "it seems to me there is only one way of eating a cutlet."

"Your way, I suppose, Monsieur le marquis," said Bonneville, laughing.

"Yes, faith! and as for ortolans, when by chance Mary and Bertha condescend to gunning, and bring home, not ortolans, but larks and fig-peckers, I take them by the beak, salt and pepper them nicely, put them whole into my mouth, and crunch them off at the neck. They are excellent eaten that way; only, it requires two or three dozen for each person."

Petit-Pierre laughed. It reminded him of the story of the Swiss guard who wagered he would eat a calf in six weeks for his dinner.

"I was wrong in saying that Louis XVIII. had a peculiar way of eating ortolans and cutlets; I should have said a peculiar way of having them cooked."

"Bless me!" exclaimed the marquis; "it seems to me there are no two ways for that either. You roast ortolans on a spit, and you broil cutlets on a gridiron."

"True," said Petit-Pierre, who evidently took pleasure in all these recollections; "but his Majesty Louis XVIII. refined upon the process. As for cutlets, the *chef* at the Tuileries was careful to cook the ones which 'had the honor,' as he said, to be eaten by the king between two other cutlets, so that the middle cutlet got the juices of the other two. He did something the same thing with the ortolans. Those that were eaten by the king were put inside a thrush, and the thrush inside a woodcock, so that by the time the ortolan was cooked the woodcock

PORTRAIT OF LOUIS XVIII.

was uneatable, but the thrush was excellent, and the ortolan superlative."

"But really, young man," said the marquis, throwing himself back in his chair, and looking at Petit-Pierre with extreme astonishment, "one would think you had seen the good King Louis XVIII. performing all these gastronomic feats."

"I have seen him," replied Petit-Pierre.

"Did you have a place at court?" asked the marquis, laughing.

"I was page," replied Petit-Pierre.

"Ah! that explains it all," said the marquis. "Upon my soul! you have seen a good deal for one of your age."

"Yes," replied Petit-Pierre, with a sigh. "Too much, in fact."

The two young girls glanced sympathetically at the young man. The face which looked so youthful at first sight showed, on closer examination, that a certain number of years had passed over it, and that troubles had left their mark there.

The marquis made two or three attempts to continue the conversation; but Petit-Pierre, buried in thought, seemed to have said all he meant to say, and whether he did not hear the various theories the marquis advanced on dark meats and white meats, and on the difference of flavor between the wild game of the forest and the domesticated game of the poultry-yard, or whether he did not think it worth while to approve or to confute, he maintained an absolute silence.

Nevertheless, in spite of this non-responsiveness, the marquis, now in high good-humor after the generous satisfaction of his appetite, was enchanted with his young friend. They returned to the salon; but there, Petit-Pierre, instead of remaining with the two young girls and the count and marquis near the fireplace, — where a fire which testified to an abundance of wood from the neighboring forest was blazing, — Petit-Pierre, thoughtful or dreamy as the reader chooses, went straight to the window and rested his forehead against the glass.

An instant later, as the marquis was making sundry compliments to the count on his young companion, the latter's name, pronounced in a curt, imperious tone, made him start with astonishment.

Petit-Pierre called to Bonneville, who turned hastily and ran rather than walked in the direction of the young peasant. The latter spoke for some moments and seemed to be giving orders. At each sentence uttered by the youth Bonneville bowed in token of assent, and as soon as Petit-Pierre had ended what he had to say the count took his hat, saluted every one present, and left the room.

Petit-Pierre then approached the marquis.

"Monsieur de Souday," he said, "I have just assured the Comte de Bonneville that you will not object. to his taking one of your horses to make a trip to all the châteaus in the neighborhood and call a meeting here at Souday, this evening, of those very men whom you quarrelled with this morning. They are no doubt still assembled at Saint-Philbert. I have therefore enjoined him to make haste."

"But," said the marquis, "some of those gentlemen must be affronted with me for the manner in which I spoke to them this morning; they will probably refuse to come to my house."

"An order shall be given to those who resist an invitation."

"An order! from whom?" asked the marquis, in surprise.

"Why, from Madame la Duchesse de Berry, from whom M. de Bonneville has full powers. But," said Petit-Pierre, with a certain hesitation, "perhaps you fear that such a meeting at the château de Souday may have some fatal result for you or for your family. In that case, marquis, say so at once. The Comte de Bonneville has not yet started."

"God bless me!" cried the marquis, "let him go, and take my best horse, and founder him if he chooses!"

The words had scarcely left his lips before the Comte de Bonneville, as though he had heard them and meant to profit by the permission, rode at full speed past the windows and through the great gates to the main-road, which led to Saint-Philbert.

The marquis went to the window to follow the rider with his eyes, and did not leave it until he was lost to sight. Then he turned to speak to Petit-Pierre; but Petit-Pierre had disappeared, and when the marquis asked his daughters where he was they answered that the young man had gone to his room, remarking that he had letters to write.

"Queer little fellow!" muttered the marquis to himself.

XXIX.

THE VENDÉANS OF 1832.

THE same day, about five in the afternoon the Comte de Bonneville returned. He had seen five of the principal leaders and they agreed to be at Souday that night between eight and nine o'clock.

The marquis, always hospitable, ordered his cook to tax the poultry-yard and the larder to the utmost, and to get ready the most plentiful supper she could possibly manage.

The five leaders who agreed to assemble that evening were Louis Renaud, Pascal, Cœur-de-Lion, Gaspard, and Achille. Those of our readers who are somewhat familiar with the events of 1832 will easily recognize the personages who concealed their identity under these *noms de guerre* for the purpose of throwing the authorities off the scent in case of intercepted despatches.

By eight o'clock Jean Oullier, to the marquis's deep regret, had not returned. Consequently, the care of the entrance gates was intrusted to Mary, who was not to open them unless in reply to a knock given in a peculiar manner.

The salon, with shutters closed and curtains drawn, was the place selected for the conference. By seven o'clock four persons were ready and waiting in this room, — namely, the Marquis de Souday, the Comte de Bonneville, Petit-Pierre, and Bertha. Mary, as we have said, was stationed at the gates, in a sort of little lodge, which had an iron-barred window toward the road, through which it was possible to see whoever rapped, and so admit none until assured of the visitor's identity.

Of all those in the salon the most impatient was Petit-Pierre, whose dominant characteristic did not seem to be calmness. Though the clock said barely half-past seven, and the meeting was fixed for eight, he went restlessly to the door again and again to hear if any sounds along the road announced the expected gentlemen. At last, precisely at eight o'clock, a knock was heard at the gate, or rather three knocks separated in a certain manner, which indicated the arrival of a leader.

"Ah!" exclaimed Petit-Pierre, going eagerly to the door.

But the Comte de Bonneville stopped him with a respectful smile and gesture.

"You are right," said the young man, and he went back and seated himself in the darkest corner of the salon. Almost at the same moment one of the expected leaders appeared in the doorway.

"M. Louis Renaud," said the Comte de Bonneville, loud enough for Petit-Pierre to hear him, and to recognize the man under the disguise of the assumed name.

The Marquis de Souday went forward to meet the newcomer, with all the more eagerness because this young man was one of the few at the conference of the morning who had favored an immediate call to arms.

"Ah, my dear count," said the marquis, "come in. You are the first to arrive, and that's a good omen."

"If I am the first, my dear marquis," replied Louis Renaud, "I assure you it is not that others are less eager; but my home being nearer to the château I have not so far to come, you know."

So saying, the personage who called himself Louis Renaud, and who was dressed in the ordinary simple clothes of a Breton peasant, advanced into the room with such perfect juvenile grace and bowed to Bertha with an ease so essentially aristocratic, that it was quite evident he would have found it difficult to assume, even momentarily, the manners and language of the social caste whose clothes he borrowed.

These social duties duly paid to the marquis and Bertha, the new-comer turned his attention to the Comte de Bonneville; but the latter, knowing the impatience of Petit-Pierre, who, though he remained in his corner, was making his presence known by movements the count alone could interpret, at once proceeded to open the question.

"My dear count," he said to the so-called Louis Renaud, "you know the extent of my powers, you have read the letter of her Royal Highness Madame, and you know that, momentarily at least, I am her intermediary to you. What is your opinion on the situation?"

"My opinion, my dear count, I may not give precisely as I gave it this morning. Here, where I know I am among the ardent supporters of Madame, I shall risk telling the plain truth."

"Yes, the plain truth," said Bonneville; "that is what Madame desires to know. And whatever you tell me, my dear count, she will know exactly as if she heard it."

"Well, my opinion is that nothing ought to be done until the arrival of the maréchal."

"The maréchal!" exclaimed Petit-Pierre. "Is he not at Nantes?"

Louis Renaud, who had not before noticed the young man in his corner, turned his eyes to him on hearing this question. Then he bowed, and replied: —

"On reaching home this morning I heard for the first time that the maréchal had left Nantes as soon as he heard of the failure at Marseille, and no one knows either the road he has taken or the purpose that carried him away."

Petit-Pierre stamped his foot with impatience.

"But," he cried, "the maréchal is the soul of the enterprise. His absence will check the uprising and diminish the confidence of our men. Unless he commands, all the leaders will be of equal rank, and we shall see the same rivalries among them that were so fatal to the royalist party in the old wars of La Vendée."

Seeing that Petit-Pierre assumed the conversation, Bonneville stepped backward, giving place to the youth, who now advanced into the circle of light cast by the lamps and candles. Louis Renaud looked with amazement at a young man, apparently almost a child, who spoke with such assurance and decision.

"It is a delay, monsieur," he said; "that is all. You may be sure that as soon as the maréchal knows of the arrival of Madame in La Vendée, he will instantly return to his post."

"Did not M. de Bonneville tell you that Madame was on the way and would be speedily among her friends?"

"Yes, he did tell me so; and the news has given me the keenest satisfaction."

"Delay! delay!" murmured Petit-Pierre. "I have always heard it said that any uprising in your part of the country ought to take place during the first two weeks in May. After that the inhabitants are busy with their agriculture and are not so easily aroused. Here it is the 14th, and we are already late. As for the leaders, they are convoked, are they not?"

"Yes, monsieur," said Louis Renaud, with a certain sad gravity, "they are; and I ought to add that you can hardly count on any but the leaders." Then he added, with a sigh, "And not all of them either, as M. le Marquis de Souday discovered this morning."

"You surely do not mean to say that, monsieur!" cried Petit-Pierre. "Lukewarmness in La Vendée! and that too, when our friends in Marseille — and I can speak confidently, for I have just arrived from there — are so furious at their failure that they are longing to take revenge!"

A pale smile crossed the lips of the young leader.

"You are from the South, monsieur," he said, "though you have not the accent of it."

PORTRAIT OF DERMONCOURT

"You are right; I am," answered Petit-Pierre. "What of it?"

"You must not confound the South with the West, the Marseillais with the Vendéans. A proclamation may rouse the South, and a check rebuff it. Not so in La Vendée. When you have been here some time you will appreciate the truth of what I say. La Vendée is grave, cold, silent. All projects are discussed slowly, deliberately; the chances of success and defeat are each considered. Then, if La Vendée sees a prospect of success she holds out her hand, says *yes*, and dies, if need be, to fulfil her promise. But as she knows that *yes* and *no* are words of life and death to her, she is slow in uttering them."

"You forget enthusiasm, monsieur," said Petit-Pierre.

"Ah, enthusiasm!" he replied; "I heard that talked of in my boyhood. It is a divinity of a past age which has stepped from its pedestal since the days when so many pledges were made to our fathers only to be forgotten. Do you know what passed this morning at Saint-Philbert?"

"In part, yes; the marquis told me."

"But after the marquis left?"

"No; I know nothing."

"Well, out of the twelve leaders present who were appointed to command the twelve divisions, seven protested in the name of their men, and they have by this time sent those men back to their homes, all the while declaring, every one of them, that personally and under all circumstances, they would shed their blood for Madame; only they would not, they added, take before God the terrible responsibility of dragging their peasantry into an enterprise which promised to be nothing more, so it seemed to them, than a bloody skirmish."

"Then it comes to this," said Petit-Pierre. "Must we renounce all hope, all effort?"

The same sad smile crossed the lips of the young leader.

"All *hope*, yes, perhaps; all effort, *no*. Madame has written that she is urged forward by the committee in

Paris; Madame assures us that she has ramifications in the army. Let us therefore make the attempt! Possibly a riot in Paris, combined with a defection in the army, may prove her judgment to have been better than ours. If we make no attempt on her behalf, Madame will always be convinced that had it been made it would have been successful; and no doubt ought to be left in Madame's mind."

"But if the attempt fails?" cried Petit-Perre.

"Five or six hundred men will have been uselessly killed, that is all. It is well that from time to time a party, even if it fails, should give such examples, not only to its own country but to neighboring nations."

"You are not of those who have sent back their men, then?" asked Petit-Pierre.

"No, monsieur; but I am of those who have sworn to die for her Royal Highness. Besides," he added, "perhaps the affair has already begun, and there may be no choice but to follow the movement."

"How so?" asked Petit-Pierre, Bonneville, and the marquis, in one breath.

"Shots were fired to-day at the fair at Montaigu —"

"And firing is going on now at the fords of the Boulogne," said an unknown voice from the doorway, on the threshold of which a new personage now appeared.

XXX.

THE WARNING.

THE person we now introduce, or rather the person who now introduced himself into the salon of the Marquis de Souday, was the commissary-general of the future Vendéan army, who had changed his name, well-known at the bar of Nantes, for that of Pascal.

He had gone several times into foreign lands to confer with Madame, and knew her personally. It was scarcely two months since he had last seen her, on which occasion after delivering to her Royal Highness the news from France, he had received her last instructions in return. It was he who had come into La Vendée to tell the adherents to hold themselves in readiness.

"Aha!" exclaimed the Marquis de Souday, with a motion of the lips which meant that he did not hold lawyers in cherished admiration, "M. le Commissaire-général Pascal."

"Who brings news, apparently," said Petit-Pierre, with the evident intention of drawing upon himself the attention of the new-comer. The latter, when he heard the voice, turned immediately to the young man, who made him an almost imperceptible sign with lips and eyes, which, however, sufficed to let him know what was expected of him.

"News? Yes," he said.

"Good or bad?" asked Louis Renaud.

"Mixed. But we'll begin with the good."

"Go on."

"Her Royal Highness has crossed the South successfully, and is now safe and sound in La Vendée."

"Are you sure of that?" asked the Marquis de Souday and Louis Renaud in one breath.

"As sure as that I see you all five here in good health," replied Pascal. "Now let us go to the other news."

"Have you heard anything from Montaigu?" asked Louis Renaud.

"They fought there yesterday," said Pascal; "that is, a few shots were fired by the National Guard and some peasants were killed and wounded."

"What occasioned it?" asked Petit-Pierre.

"A dispute at the fair, which became a riot."

"Who commands at Montaigu?" again asked Petit-Pierre.

"A mere captain usually," replied Pascal; "but yesterday, in consequence of the fair, the sub-prefect and the general commanding the military sub-division were both there."

"Do you know the general's name?"

"Dermoncourt."

"And pray, who is General Dermoncourt?"

"Under what head do you desire to know of him, monsieur, — man, opinions, or character?"

"All three heads."

"As a man, he is from sixty to sixty-two years old, and he belongs to that iron race which fought the wars of the Revolution and the Empire. He will be night and day in the saddle, and not leave us an instant's rest."

"Very good," said Louis Renaud, laughing. "Then we'll try to tire him out; and as we are, none of us, half his age we shall be very unlucky or very stupid if we fail."

"His opinions?" asked Petit-Pierre.

"At heart I believe him to be a republican."

"In spite of twelve years' service under the Empire! He must have been dyed in the wool."

"There are many like him. You remember what Henri

IV. said of the Leaguers, — 'The barrel smells of the herring.'"

"His character?"

"Oh, as for that, loyalty itself! He is neither an Amadis nor a Galahad. He's a Ferragus, and if ever Madame had the misfortune to fall into his hands —"

"What are you talking about, Monsieur Pascal?" exclaimed Petit-Pierre.

"I am a lawyer, monsieur," replied the civil commissary, "and in that capacity I foresee all the chances of a case. I repeat, therefore, that if Madame were unfortunately to fall into the hands of General Dermoncourt she would have full opportunity to recognize his courtesy."

"Then," said Petit-Pierre, "that is the sort of enemy Madame would choose for herself, — brave, vigorous, and loyal. Monsieur, we are fortunate — But you spoke of shots at the fords of the river?"

"I presume that those I heard on my way came from there."

"Perhaps," said the marquis, "Bertha had better go and reconnoitre. She will soon let us know what is happening."

Bertha rose.

"What!" exclaimed Petit-Pierre, "do you send mademoiselle?"

"Why not?" asked the marquis.

"I think it is a man's duty, not a woman's."

"My young friend," said the old gentleman, "in such matters I rely first upon myself, next upon Jean Oullier, and after Jean Oullier on Bertha and on Mary. I desire the honor of staying here with you; my fellow, Jean Oullier, is off amusing himself. Consequently, Bertha must go."

Bertha went toward the door; but on the threshold she met her sister and exchanged a few words with her in a low voice.

"Here is Mary," she said, turning back.

"Ah!" exclaimed the marquis; "did you hear the firing, my girl?"

"Yes, father," said Mary; "they are fighting."

"Where?"

"At the springs of Baugé."

"You are sure?"

"Yes; the shots came from the marsh."

"You see," said the marquis; "the news is precise. Who keeps the gate in your absence?"

"Rose Tinguy."

"Listen!" said Petit-Pierre.

Loud raps were heard upon the gate.

"The devil!" cried the marquis; "that's not one of us."

They all listened attentively.

"Open! open!" cried a voice. "There's not an instant to lose!"

"It is his voice!" exclaimed Mary, eagerly.

"His voice? — whose voice?" said the marquis.

"Yes, I recognize it," said Bertha, — "the voice of young Baron Michel."

"What does that cabbage-grower want here?" said the marquis, making a step toward the door as if to prevent his entrance.

"Let him come, let him come, marquis!" cried Bonneville. "I'll answer for him; there's nothing to fear."

He had hardly said the words before the sound of a rapid step was heard, and the young baron rushed into the salon, pale, breathless, covered with mud, dripping with perspiration, and with scarcely breath enough to say: —

"Not a moment to lose! Fly! Escape! They are coming!"

He dropped on one knee, resting one hand on the ground, for his breath failed him, his strength was exhausted. He had done, as he promised Jean Oullier, nearly a mile and a half in six minutes.

There was a moment of trouble and confusion in the salon.

"To arms!" cried the marquis. Springing to his own gun, he pointed to a rack at the corner of the room, where three or four carbines and fowling-pieces were hanging.

The Comte de Bonneville and Pascal, with one and the same movement, threw themselves before Petit-Pierre as if to defend him.

Mary sprang to the young baron to raise him and give him what help he needed, while Bertha ran to a window looking toward the forest and opened it.

Shots were then heard, evidently coming nearer, though still at some distance.

"They are on the Viette des Biques," said Bertha.

"Nonsense!" said the marquis; "impossible they should attempt such a dangerous path!"

"They are there, father," said Bertha.

"Yes, yes," gasped Michel. "I saw them there; they have torches. A woman is guiding them, marching at their head; the general is second."

"Oh, that cursèd Jean Oullier! Why is n't he here?" said the marquis.

"He is fighting, Monsieur le marquis," said Michel. "He sent me; he could n't come himself."

"He!" exclaimed the marquis.

"But I was coming, mademoiselle; I was coming myself. I knew yesterday the château was to be attacked, but I was a prisoner; I got down from a second-story window."

"Good God!" cried Mary, turning pale.

"Bravo!" exclaimed Bertha.

"Gentlemen," said Petit-Pierre, tranquilly, "I think we must decide on a course. Shall we fight? If we do, we must arm ourselves at once, bar the gates, and take our posts. Shall we escape? If so, there is even less time to lose."

"Let us fight!" said the marquis.

"No, escape!" cried Bonneville. "When Petit-Pierre is safe we will fight."

"What is that you say, count?" exclaimed Petit-Pierre.

"I say that nothing is ready; we are not prepared to fight. Are we, gentlemen?"

"Oh, yes, we can always fight," said the youthful, light-hearted voice of a new-comer, addressing himself partly to those in the salon, and partly to two other young men who were following him, and whom, no doubt, he had met at the gate.

"Ah, Gaspard! Gaspard!" cried Bonneville.

Springing to meet the new arrival, he whispered something in his ear.

"Gentlemen," said Gaspard, turning to the others, "the Comte de Bonneville is perfectly right; we must retreat." Then addressing the marquis, he added, "Have n't you some secret door or issue to the castle, marquis? We have no time to lose; the last shots we heard at the gate — Achille, Cœur-de-Lion, and I — were not half a mile distant."

"Gentlemen," said the Marquis de Souday, "you are in my house, and it is for me to assume the responsibility. Silence! listen to me and obey me to-night; I will obey you to-morrow."

All were silent.

"Mary," said the marquis, "close the gates, but do not barricade them; leave them so that they can be opened at the first rap. Bertha, to the underground passage instantly, and don't lose a moment. My daughters and I will receive the general and do the honors of the château to him. To-morrow, wherever you are, we will join you; only, let us know where that will be."

Mary sprang from the room to execute her father's order, while Bertha, signing to Petit-Pierre to follow her, went out by the opposite door, crossed the inner courtyard, entered the chapel, took two wax tapers from the altar, lighted them, gave one to Bonneville, one to Pascal, and then, pushing a spring which made the front of the altar turn of itself, she pointed to a stairway, leading to the vaults in which the lords of Souday were formerly buried.

"You can't lose your way," she said; "you will find a door at the farther end, and the key is in it. That door leads into the open country. These gentlemen all know how to find their way there."

Petit-Pierre took Bertha's hand and pressed it warmly. Then he sprang down the steps to the vault behind Bonneville and Pascal, who lighted the way.

Louis Renaud, Achille, Cœur-de-Lion, and Gaspard followed Petit-Pierre.

Bertha closed the aperture behind them. She noticed that Michel was not among the fugitives.

XXXI.

MY OLD CRONY LORIOT.

THE Marquis de Souday, after watching the fugitives with his eyes until they entered the chapel, gave one of those deep exclamations which mean that the breast is relieved of a heavy weight; then he returned to the vestibule. But instead of proceeding from the vestibule to the salon, he went from the vestibule to the kitchen.

Contrary to all his habits and to the great astonishment of his cook, he walked to the fire, raised the covers of the saucepans anxiously, made sure that no ragout was sticking to the bottom of them, and put back the spits a trifle so that no unexpected flame should dishonor the roasts; having done this he returned to the vestibule, thence to the dining-room, where he inspected the bottles, doubled their number, looked to see if the table was properly set, and then, satisfied with the inspection, returned to the salon.

There he found his daughters, the castle gate being intrusted to Rosine, whose only duty was to open it on the first rap.

The girls were seated beside the fire when their father entered. Mary was anxious, Bertha dreamy. Both were thinking of Michel. Bertha was intoxicated with that pungent joy which follows the revelation of love in the heart of the one we love; she fancied she read in the glances of the young baron the assurance that it was for her the poor lad, so timid, so hesitating, had conquered his weakness and braved real perils. She measured the greatness of the love she supposed him to feel by the revolution that love had evidently made in his nature. She built her castles in the air, and blamed herself bitterly for not having urged him to return to the châteauwhen she noticed that he did not follow those whom his devotion had saved. Then she smiled; for suddenly a thought crossed her mind: if he had remained behind he must be hidden in some corner of the château, and was it not for the pleasure of meeting her privately ? Perhaps if she went into the shrubbery of the park he would start up beside her and say : " See what I have done to obtain a word with you ! "

The marquis had scarcely seated himself in his accustomed easy-chair, and had not had time to notice the preoccupation of his daughters, which he would, of course, attribute to another cause than the true one, when a single rap was heard on the gate. The marquis started, — not because he did not expect the rap, but because this rap was not the one he expected. It was timid, almost obsequious, and, consequently, there was nothing military about it.

"Oh! oh !" exclaimed the marquis; " whom have we here, I 'd like to know."

" Some one knocked," said Bertha, coming out of her revery.

" One rap," said Mary.

The marquis shook his head as if to say, "That's not the point," and then, deciding to see for himself what the matter was, he left the salon, crossed the vestibule, and advanced as far as the top step of the portico.

There, instead of the bayonets and sabres he was expecting to see glitter in the darkness, instead of the soldierly figures and moustaches with which he proposed to make acquaintance, the Marquis de Souday saw nothing but the enormous dome of a blue cotton umbrella, which approached him, point forward, up the steps of the portico.

As this umbrella, steadily advancing like a turtle's carapace, threatened to put out his eye with its point, which stuck forth like the central spot of an ancient shield, the marquis raised the orb of this buckler and came face to face with a weasel's muzzle, surmounted by two little, glittering eyes, like carbuncles, and topped with a very tall hat, extremely narrow in the brim and so much brushed and rebrushed that it shone in the dusky light as though it were varnished.

"By all the devils of hell!" cried the marquis, "if it isn't my old crony Loriot!"

"Ready to offer you his little services if you think him worthy," replied a falsetto voice which its owner endeavored to make ingratiating.

"You are very welcome indeed to Souday, Maître Loriot," said the marquis, in a tone of good-humor and as if he expected some genuine pleasure from the presence of the person he welcomed so cordially. "I expect quite a numerous party this evening, and you shall help me do the honors. Come in, and see the young ladies."

Thereupon the old gentleman, with an easy air that showed how convinced he was of the distance between a Marquis de Souday and a village notary, preceded his guest into the salon. It is true that Maître Loriot took so much time to wipe his boots on the mat which lay at the door of that sanctuary that the politeness of the marquis, had he exercised it in remaining behind his visitor, would have been sorely tried and lessened.

Let us profit by the moment when the legal functionary shuts his umbrella and dries his feet to sketch his portrait, if indeed the undertaking is not beyond our powers.

Maître Loriot, the notary of Machecoul, was a little old fellow, thin and slim and seeming smaller than he really was from his habit of never speaking except half double in an attitude of the profoundest respect. A long, sharp nose was the whole of his face; nature, in developing beyond all reason that feature of his countenance, had economized on the rest with such extraordinary parsimony that it was necessary to look at him for some time before perceiving that Maître Loriot had a mouth and chin and eyes like other men; but when that knowledge was once attained it was observable that the eyes were vivacious and the mouth not by any means devoid of shrewdness.

Maître Loriot fulfilled the promises of his physiognomical prospectus; and he was clever enough to wring some thirty thousand francs out of a country practice in which his predecessors had hardly managed to make both ends meet. To attain this result, supposed until he came to be impossible, M. Loriot had studied, not the Code, but men; he had learned from that study that vanity and pride were the dominant instincts of mankind; and he had, in consequence, endeavored to make himself agreeable to those two vices, in which effort he succeeded so well that he soon became absolutely necessary to those who possessed them.

By reason of this system of behavior, politeness in Maître Loriot had become servility; he did not bow, he prostrated himself; and, like the fakirs of India, he had so trained his body to certain submissive motions that this attitude was now habitual with him. Never would he have addressed a titled person, were that person only a baron or even a chevalier, in any other than the third person. He showed a gratitude both humble and overflowing for all affability bestowed upon him; and as, at the same time, he manifested an exaggerated devotion to the interests confided to him, he had finally, little by little, obtained a very considerable *clientèle* among the nobility of the neighborhood.

But the thing above all others which contributed to the success of Maître Loriot in the department of the Loire-Inférieure and even in the adjoining departments, was the ardor of his political opinions. He was one of those who might well be called "more royalist than the king himself." His little gray eye flamed when he heard the name of a Jacobin, and to his mind all who had ever belonged to the liberal side, from M. de Chateaubriand to M. de la Fayette were Jacobins. Never would he have recognized the monarchy of July, and he always called the King Louis-Philippe

"Monsieur le Duc d'Orléans," not even allowing him the title of Royal Highness which Charles X. did grant him.

Maître Loriot was a frequent visitor to the Marquis de Souday. It was part of his policy to parade an extreme respect for this illustrious relic of the former social order, — a social order he deeply regretted; and his respect had gone so far that he had made various loans to the marquis, who, being very careless, as we have said, in the matter of money, neglected as a matter of course to pay the interest on them.

The Marquis de Souday always welcomed Maître Loriot, partly on account of the said loans; also because the old gentleman's fibre was not less sensitive than that of others to agreeable flattery; and, lastly, because the coolness which existed between the owner of Souday and the other proprietors of the neighborhood made him rather lonely, and he was glad of any distraction to the monotony of his life.

When the little notary thought his boots were cleaned of every vestige of mud he entered the salon. There he again bowed to the marquis, who had returned to his usual easy chair, and then he began to compliment the two young girls. But the marquis did not leave him time to do much of that.

"Loriot," he said, "I am always glad to see you."

The notary bowed to the ground.

"Only," continued the marquis, "you will permit me to ask, won't you? what brings you here into our desert at half-past nine o'clock of a rainy night. I know that when a man has such an umbrella as yours the sky above him is always blue, but — "

The notary judged it proper not to allow such a joke to be made by a marquis without laughing, and murmuring "Ah, good! very good!" Then, making a direct answer, he said: —

"I was at the château de la Logerie very late, having been there to carry some money to Madame la baronne on an order I did not receive till two in the afternoon. I was coming back on foot, as I usually do, when I heard noises of evil portent in the forest, which confirmed what I already knew of a riot at Montaigu. I feared, if I went any farther, that I might meet the soldiers of the Duc d'Orléans; and to avoid that unpleasantness I thought that M. le marquis would deign to let me lodge here for the night."

At the mention of la Logerie Mary and Bertha raised their heads like two horses who hear from afar and suddenly the sound of the bugle.

"Oh! you have come from la Logerie, have you?" said the marquis.

"Yes, as I have just had the honor of mentioning to Monsieur le marquis," replied Maître Loriot.

"Well! well! well! We have had another visitor from la Logerie this evening."

"The young baron, perhaps?" suggested the notary.

"Yes."

"I am looking for him."

"Loriot," said the marquis, "I am astonished to hear you — a man whose principles I have always considered sound — to hear you prostituting a title which you habitually respect by attaching it to the name of those Michels."

As the marquis uttered this remark with an air of superb disdain Bertha turned crimson and Mary turned pale. The impression produced by his words was lost upon the old gentleman, but it did not escape the little gray eye of the notary. He was about to speak when Monsieur de Souday made a sign with his hand that he had not finished his remarks.

"And I wish to know why you, my old crony," he continued, "whom we have always treated well and kindly, why you think it necessary to put forward a subterfuge in order to enter my house."

"Monsieur le marquis!" stammered Loriot.

"You came here to look for young Michel, did n't you? That's all very well, but why lie about it?"

"I beg Monsieur le marquis to accept my most humble

excuses. The mother of the young man, whom I have been obliged to accept as a client, being a legacy with the practice of my predecessor, is very anxious. Her son got out of a window on the second story at the risk of breaking his neck, and in defiance of her maternal wishes he has run away; consequently Madame Michel requests me — "

"Ha! ha!" cried the marquis, "did he really do that?"

"Literally, Monsieur le marquis."

"Well, that reconciles me to him, — not perhaps altogether, but somewhat."

"If Monsieur le marquis would indicate to me where I am likely to find the young man," said Loriot, "I could take him back to his mother."

"As for that, the devil knows where he has taken himself, I don't! Do you know, girls?" asked the marquis, turning to his daughters.

Bertha and Mary both made signs in the negative.

"You see, my dear crony, that we can't be of the least use to you," said the marquis. "But do tell me why mother Michel locked up her son."

"It seems," replied the notary, "that young Michel, hitherto so gentle, and docile, and obedient, has fallen suddenly in love."

"Ah, ha! taken the bit in his teeth? I know what that is! Well, Maître Loriot, if you are called in counsel, do you tell mother Michel to give him his head and keep a light rein on him; that's better than a martingale. He strikes me as a pretty good little devil, what I have seen of him."

"An excellent heart, Monsieur le marquis; and then, an only son! — more than a hundred thousand francs a year!" said the notary.

"Hum!" exclaimed the marquis, "if that's all he has, it is little enough to cover the villanies of the name he bears."

"Father!" said Bertha, while Mary only sighed, "You forget the service he did us to-night."

"Hey! hey!" thought Loriot, looking at Bertha, "can the baroness be right after all ? It would be a fine contract to draw."

And he began to add up the fees he might expect from a marriage contract between Baron Michel de la Logerie and the daughter of the Marquis de Souday.

"You are right, my child," said the marquis; "we 'll leave Loriot to hunt up mother Michel's lost lamb, and say no more about them." Then, turning to Loriot, he added: "Are you going any further on your quest, Mr. Notary ?"

"If Monsieur le marquis will deign to permit, I would prefer —"

"Just now, you gave me, as a pretext for staying here, your dread of encountering the soldiers," interrupted the marquis. "Are you really afraid of them ? Heavens and earth, what's the meaning of that ? You, one of us, afraid of soldiers!"

"I am not afraid," replied Loriot; "Monsieur le marquis may believe me. But those cursèd Blues turn my stomach; I feel such an aversion for them that after I have seen even one of their uniforms I can't eat anything for twenty-four hours."

"That explains your leanness; but the saddest part of it is that this aversion of yours obliges me to turn you out of my house."

"Monsieur le marquis is making fun of his humble servant."

"Indeed I am not; I don't wish your death, that's all."

"My death ?"

"Yes, if the sight of one soldier gives you twenty-four hours of inanition, you'll certainly die of starvation outright if you pass a whole night under the same roof as a regiment."

"A regiment ?"

"Yes, a regiment. I have invited a regiment to sup at Souday to-night; and the regard I have for you obliges me to send you off, hot foot, at once. Only, be careful which way you go because those scamps the soldiers if they catch you in the fields, or rather in the woods, at this time of night may take you for what you are not — I mean to say, for what you are."

"What then?"

"What then! why, they'd honor you with a shot or two, and the muskets of M. le Duc d'Orléans are loaded with ball, you know."

The notary turned pale and stammered a few unintelligible words.

"Decide; you have the choice, — death by hunger, or by guns. You've no time to lose; I hear the tramp of men — and there! precisely! — that's the general knocking at the gate."

Sure enough, the knocker resounded; this time it was vigorously handled, as became the guest whose arrival it announced.

"In company with Monsieur le marquis," said Loriot, "I will conquer my aversion, invincible as it is."

"Good! then take that torch and go with me to meet my guests."

"Your guests? Why, really, Monsieur le marquis, I can't believe — "

"Come, come, *Thomas* Loriot, you shall see first, and believe afterwards."

And the Marquis de Souday, taking a torch himself, advanced to the portico. Bertha and Mary followed him; Mary thoughtful, Bertha anxious, — both looking earnestly into the shadows of the courtyard to see if they could discover any sign of the presence of him they were both thinking of.

XXXII.

THE GENERAL EATS A SUPPER WHICH HAD NOT BEEN PREPARED FOR HIM.

ACCORDING to the instructions of the marquis transmitted by Mary to Rosine, the gate was opened to the soldiers at the first rap. No sooner was this done than they filed into the courtyard and hastened to surround the house.

Just as the old general was about to dismount he saw the two torchbearers on the portico, and beside them, partly in shadow, partly in the light, the two young girls. They all came toward him with a gracious, hospitable manner which greatly amazed him.

"Faith! general," said the marquis, coming down the last step, as if to go as far as possible to meet the general. "I began to despair of seeing you, this evening at least."

"You despaired of seeing me, Monsieur le marquis!" exclaimed the general, astonished at this exordium.

"Yes, I despaired of seeing you. At what hour did you leave Montaigu, — at seven?"

"At seven precisely?"

"Well, that's just it! I calculated that it would take you about two hours to march here, and I expected you at nine or half-past, and here it is half-past ten. I was just wondering if some accident could have happened to deprive me of the honor of receiving so brave and gallant a soldier."

"Then you expected me, monsieur?"

"Why, of course, I did. I'll bet it was that cursed ford at Pont-Farcy which detained you. What an abominable country it is, general! — brooks that become impassible torrents from the slightest rain; roads — call them roads indeed! I call them bogs! How did you get over those dreadful springs of Baugé? — a sea of mud in which you are sure to flounder to the waist, and are lucky enough if it does n't come over your head. But even that is nothing to the Viette des Biques. When I was a young fellow and a frantic hunter I used to think twice before risking myself over it. Really, general, I feel very grateful for this visit when I think what trouble and fatigue it has caused you."

The general saw that, for the moment, he had to do with as shrewd a player as himself; and he resolved to eat with a good grace the dish that the marquis served to him.

"I beg you to believe, Monsieur le marquis," he replied, "that I regret having kept you waiting, and that the fault of the delay is none of mine. In any case, I will try to profit by the lesson you give me, and the next time I come I will set out in time to defy fords, bogs, and precipices from hindering my arrival politely in season."

At this moment an officer came up to the general to take his orders about the search to be made of the château.

"It is useless, my dear captain," replied the general; "the marquis tells me we have come too late; in other words, we have nothing to do here, — the château is all in order."

"But, my dear general!" said the marquis, "in order or not, my house is at your disposal; pray do exactly as you like with it."

"You offer it with such good grace I cannot refuse."

"Well, young ladies, what are you about," exclaimed the marquis, "that you let me keep these gentlemen talking here in the rain? Pray come in, general, come in, gentlemen; there's an excellent fire in the salon which will dry your clothes — which that cursed ford must have soaked thoroughly."

"How shall I thank you for all your considerateness?"

said the general, biting his moustache and secretly his lips.

"Oh! you are a man I am glad to serve, general," replied the marquis, preceding the officers whom he was lighting, the little notary modestly bringing up the rear with the other torch. "But permit me," he added, "to present to you my daughters, Mesdemoiselles Bertha and Mary de Souday."

"Faith, marquis," said the general, gallantly, "the sight of two such charming faces is worth the risks of taking cold at the fords, or getting muddy in the bog, or even breaking one's neck on the Viette des Biques."

"Well, young ladies," said the marquis, "make use of your pretty eyes to see if supper, which has long been waiting for these gentlemen, intends to keep us waiting now."

"Really, marquis," said Dermoncourt, turning to his officers, "we are quite confounded by such kindness; and our gratitude — "

"Is amply relieved by the pleasure your visit affords us. You can easily believe, general, that having grown accustomed to the two pretty faces you compliment so charmingly, and being moreover their father, I should sometimes find life in my little castle a trifle insipid and monotonous. You can understand, therefore, that when an imp of my acquaintance came and whispered in my ear, 'General Dermoncourt started from Montaigu at seven o'clock, with his staff, to pay you a visit,' I was delighted."

"Ah! it was an imp who told you?"

"Yes; there is always such a being in every cottage and every castle in this region of country. So the prospect of the pleasant evening I should owe to your coming, general, gave me something of my old elasticity, which, alas! I am losing. I hurried my people and put my hen-house and larder under contribution, set my daughters in motion, and kept my old crony Loriot, the Machecoul notary, to do you honor; and I have even, God damn me! put my own hand in the pie, and we have managed, among us, to prepare a supper which is ready for you, and also for your soldiers — for I don't forget I was once a soldier myself."

"Ah! you have served in the army, Monsieur le marquis?" said Dermoncourt.

"Perhaps in the same wars as yourself; though, instead of saying that I served, I ought only say that I fought."

"In this region?"

"Yes, under the orders of Charette."

"Ah ha!"

"I was his aide-de-camp."

"Then this is not the first time we have met, marquis."

"Is that really so?"

"Yes, I made the campaigns of 1795 and 1796 in La Vendée."

"Ah! bravo! that delights me," cried the marquis; "then we can talk at dessert of our youthful prowess — Ah, general," said the old gentleman, with a certain melancholy, "it is getting to be a rare thing on either side to find those who can talk of the old campaigns. But here come the young ladies to tell us that supper is ready. General, will you give your arm to one of them? the captain will take the other." Then, addressing the rest of the officers, he said, "Gentlemen, will you follow the general into the dining-room?"

They sat down to table, — the general between Mary and Bertha, the marquis between two officers. Maître Loriot took the seat next to Bertha, intending, in the course of the meal, to get in a word about Michel. He had made up his mind that, so far as he was concerned, the marriage contract should be drawn in his office.

For some minutes nothing was heard but the clatter of plates and glasses; all present were silent. The officers, following the example of their general, accepted complacently this unexpected termination of their intended attack. The marquis, who usually dined at five o'clock, and was therefore nearly six hours late in getting anything to eat, was making up to his stomach for its lost time. Mary and Bertha, both of them pensive, were not sorry to have an excuse for their silent reflections in the aversion they felt to the tricolor cockade.

The general was evidently reflecting on some means of getting even with the marquis. He understood perfectly well that Monsieur de Souday had received warning of his approach. Practised in Vendéan warfare, he well knew the facility and rapidity with which news is communicated from one village to another. Surprised at first by the heartiness of the Marquis de Souday's welcome, he had gradually recovered his coolness and returned to his habits of minute observation. All he saw, whether it was his host's extreme attentions, or the profusion of the repast, far too sumptuous to have been prepared for enemies, only confirmed his suspicions; but, patient as all good hunters of men and game should be, and certain that if his illustrious prey had taken flight (as he believed she had) it would be useless to pursue her in the darkness, he resolved to postpone his more serious investigations and to let no indication of what was below the surface escape him.

It was the general who first broke silence.

"Monsieur le marquis," he said, raising his glass, "the choice of a toast may be as difficult for you as for us; but there is one that cannot be embarrassing, and has, indeed, the right to precede all others. Permit me to drink to the health of the Demoiselles de Souday, thanking them for their share in the courteous reception with which you have honored us."

"My sister and I thank you, monsieur," said Bertha; "and we are very glad to have pleased you in accordance with our father's wishes."

"Which means," said the general, smiling, "that you are only gracious to us under orders, and that our gratitude for your attentions is really due to Monsieur le marquis. Well, that's all right; I like such military frankness, which would induce me to leave the camp of your admirers and enter that of your friends, if I thought I could be received there wearing, as I do, the tricolor cockade."

"The praises you give to my frankness, monsieur," replied Bertha, "induce me to say honestly that the colors you wear are not those I like to see upon my friends; but, if you really wish for that title I will grant it, hoping that the day may come when you will wear mine."

"General," said the marquis, scratching his ear, "your remark is perfectly true; what toast can I give in return for your graceful compliment to my daughters without compromising either of us? Have you a wife?"

The general was determined to nonplus the marquis.

"No," he said.

"A sister?"

"No."

"A mother, perhaps?"

"Yes," said the general, issuing from the ambush in which he seemed to have been awaiting the marquis, "France, our common mother."

"Ah, bravo! then I drink to France! and may the glory and the grandeur that her kings have given her for the last eight centuries long continue."

"And, permit me to add, the half-century of liberty which she owes to her sons."

"That is not only an addition, but a modification," said the marquis. Then, after an instant's silence, he added, "Faith! I'll accept that toast! White or tricolor, France is always France!"

All the guests touched glasses, and Loriot himself, carried off his balance by the enthusiasm of the marquis, emptied his glass.

Once launched in this direction, and moistened abundantly, the conversation became so lively and even vagabond that after the supper was two thirds through, Mary and Bertha, thinking they had better not wait till the end of it, rose from table and passed without remark into the salon.

Maître Loriot, who seemed to have come there as much for the daughters as for their father, rose a few moments later and followed them.

XXXIII.

IN WHICH MAÎTRE LORIOT'S CURIOSITY IS NOT EXACTLY SATISFIED.

MAÎTRE LORIOT profited, as we have said, by the example of the young ladies, and left the marquis and his guests to evoke at ease their memories of the "war of giants." He rose from table and followed the Demoiselles de Souday into the salon. There he advanced toward them, bending almost double, and rubbing his hands.

"Ah!" said Bertha; "you seem to be pleased about something, Monsieur le notaire."

"Mesdemoiselles," replied Maître Loriot, in a low voice, "I have done my best to second your father's trick. I hope that if need be you will not refuse to certify to the coolness and self-possession I have shown under the circumstances."

"What trick do you mean, dear Monsieur Loriot," said Mary, laughing. "Neither Bertha nor I know what you mean."

"Good heavens!" said the notary; "I don't know any more than you know, but it seems to me that Monsieur le marquis must have some serious and powerful reasons to treat as old friends, and even better than some old friends are treated, those hateful bullies whom he has admitted to his table. The attentions he is paying to those hirelings of the usurper strike me as very strange, and I fancy they have a purpose."

"What purpose?" asked Bertha.

"Well, that of filling those fellows' minds with such a sense of security that they will neglect to look after their own safety, and then — taking advantage of their carelessness, to make them share the fate — "

"The fate?"

"The fate of — " repeated the notary.

"The fate of whom?"

The notary passed his hand across his throat.

"Holofernes, perhaps?" cried Bertha, laughing.

"Exactly," said Maître Loriot.

Mary joined her sister in the peals of laughter this assurance called forth. The little notary's supposition delighted the sisters beyond measure.

"So you assign us the part of Judith!" cried Bertha, endeavoring to check her laughter.

"But, mesdemoiselles — "

"If my father were here, Monsieur Loriot, he might be angry that you suppose him capable of such proceedings, which would be in my opinion, a little too Biblical. But don't be uneasy; we will tell neither papa nor the general, who certainly would not be flattered at the meaning you put upon our attentions."

"Young ladies," entreated Loriot, "forgive me if my political fervor, my horror for all the partisans of the present unfortunate doctrines, carried me rather too far."

"I forgive you, Monsieur Loriot," replied Bertha, who, having been, in consequence of her frank, decided nature, the most suspicious, felt that she had the most to pardon, — "I forgive you; and in order that you may not make such mistakes in future I shall give you the key-note of the situation. You must know that General Dermoncourt, whom you regard as Antichrist, has merely come to Souday to make exactly the same search that is made in all the neighboring châteaus."

"If that's the case," said the little notary, who was getting himself deeper and deeper into trouble, "why treat him with, — yes, I will say the word, — with such luxury and splendor? The law is precise."

"The law! How so?"

"Yes; it forbids all magistrates and civil and military officers charged with the execution of judicial authority to seize, carry away, or appropriate any articles other than those named in the warrant. What are these men now doing with the viands and wines of all sorts which are on the table of the Marquis de Souday? They are ap-pro-priating them!"

"It seems to me, my dear Monsieur Loriot," said Mary, "that my father has the right to invite whom he chooses to his table."

"Even those who come to execute — to bring into his home — an odious and tyrannical power? Certainly he has the right, mademoiselle; but you will allow me to regard it as a most unnatural thing, and to suppose it has some secret cause or object."

"In other words, Monsieur Loriot, you see a secret which you want to penetrate."

"Oh, mademoiselle — "

"Well, I'll confide it to you, as well as I can, my dear Monsieur Loriot. I am willing to trust you, if you, on your side, will tell me how it happened that having to look for Monsieur Michel de la Logerie, you came straight to the château de Souday."

Bertha said the words in a firm, incisive way, and the notary, to whom they were addressed, heard them with more embarrassment than was felt by the lady who uttered them.

As for Mary, she came up to her sister, slipped her arm within Bertha's, and resting her head upon the latter's shoulder, awaited, with a curiosity she did not seek to disguise, the answer of Maître Loriot.

"Well, if you really wish to know why, young ladies — "

The notary made a pause, as though expecting to be encouraged; and Bertha did encourage him with a nod.

"I came," continued Maître Loriot, "because Madame la Baronne de la Logerie informed me that the château de Souday was probably the place to which her son went on taking flight from his home."

"And on what did Madame la Baronne de la Logerie base that supposition?" asked Bertha, with the same questioning look and the same firm, incisive voice.

"Mademoiselle," replied the notary, more and more embarrassed, "after what I said to your father, really I do not know whether, in spite of the reward you promise to my frankness, I have the courage to say more."

"Why not?" said Bertha, with the same coolness. "Shall I help you? It is because she thinks, I believe you said, that the object of Monsieur Michel's love is at Souday."

"Yes, mademoiselle, that is just it."

"Very good; but what I desire to know, and what I shall insist on knowing, is Madame de la Logerie's opinion of that love."

"Her opinion is not exactly favorable, mademoiselle," returned the notary; "that I must admit."

"That's a point on which my father and the baroness will agree," said Bertha, laughing.

"But," continued the notary, pointedly, "Monsieur Michel will be of age in a few months, — consequently, free as to his actions, and the master of an immense fortune."

"As to his actions," said Bertha, "so much the better for him."

"In what way, mademoiselle?" asked the notary, maliciously.

"Why to rehabilitate the name he bears and efface the evil memories his father left behind him. As to the fortune, if I were the woman Monsieur Michel honored with his affection, I should advise him to make such use of it that there would soon be no name in the whole province more honored than his."

"What use would you advise him to make of it?" exclaimed the notary, much astonished.

"To return that money to those from whom they say his father got it, and to make restitution to the former proprietors of the national domain which M. Michel bought."

"But in that case, mademoiselle, you would ruin the man who had the honor to be in love with you," said the little notary, quite bewildered.

"What would that matter if he obtained the respect of all, and the regard of her who advised the sacrifice?"

Just then Rosine appeared at the door of the salon.

"Mademoiselle," she said, not addressing herself particularly to either Mary or Bertha, "will you please come here?"

Bertha wanted to continue her conversation with the notary. She was eager for information as to the feelings Madame de la Logerie had against her; and, moreover, she enjoyed talking, however vaguely, of projects which for some time past had been the theme of her meditations. So she told Mary to go and see what was wanted.

But Mary, on her side, was rather unwilling to leave the salon. She was frightened to see to what lengths Bertha's love had developed within the last few days; every word her sister said echoed painfully in her soul. She felt sure that Michel's love was wholly her own, and she thought with actual terror of Bertha's despair when she should discover how strangely she had deceived herself. Besides, in spite of Mary's immense affection for her sister, love had already poured into her heart the little dose of selfishness which always accompanies that emotion, and she was quite joyful, from another point of view, at what she was now hearing. The part which Bertha was tracing out for the wife of Michel she felt should be her own. So it happened that Bertha was obliged to ask her for the second time to see what Rosine wanted.

"Go, dearest," she said, kissing Mary's forehead, "go; and while you are there please give orders about preparing Monsieur Loriot's room; for I fear, in all this turmoil, it has been forgotten."

Mary was accustomed to obey, and she obeyed. Of the two sisters, she was by far the most docile and gentle. She found Rosine at the door.

"What do you want of us?" she asked.

Rosine did not reply. Then, as if she feared to be overheard from the dining-room, where the marquis was narrating the last day of Charette's life, she took Mary by the arm and drew her under the staircase at the farther end of the vestibule.

"Mademoiselle," she said, "he is hungry."

"He is hungry?" repeated Mary.

"Yes; he has just told me so."

"Who is it you are talking of? Who is hungry?"

"He, the poor lad."

"Who is he?"

"Why, Monsieur Michel."

"Monsieur Michel here!"

"Did n't you know it?"

"No."

"Two hours ago — after Mademoiselle Bertha returned from the chapel, just before the soldiers arrived — he came to the kitchen."

"Did n't he go away with Petit-Pierre?"

"No."

"And you say he went to the kitchen?"

"Yes; and he was so tired, it was quite pitiful. 'Monsieur Michel,' I said like that, 'why don't you go into the salon?' 'My dear Rosine,' said he, in his gentle way, 'they did n't ask me.' Then he wanted to go and sleep at Machecoul, for he said he would n't go back to La Logerie for all the world. It seems his mother meant to take him to Paris. So I would n't let him leave the house."

"You did quite right, Rosine. Where is he now?"

"I put him in the tower chamber; but as the soldiers have taken the ground-floor, we can't get in there now except through the passage at the end of the hay-loft, and I came to ask you for the key."

Mary's first thought (it was her good thought) was to tell her sister; but a second thought succeeded the first, and that, it must be owned, was less generous. It was no other than to see Michel first and alone. Rosine gave her the opportunity.

"I'll tell you where the key is," said Mary.

"Oh, mademoiselle," replied Rosine, "do come with me. There are so many men about that I don't like to be alone, and I should die of fright to go up there by myself; whereas if you, the marquis's daughter, were with me they would all respect us."

"But the provisions?"

"Here they are."

"Where?"

"In this basket."

"Oh, very good; then come."

And Mary sprang up the stairs with the agility of the kids she sometimes hunted among the rocks in the forest of Machecoul.

XXXIV.

THE TOWER CHAMBER.

WHEN Mary reached the second floor she stopped before the room occupied by Jean Oullier. The key she wanted was kept in that room.

Then she opened a door which gave entrance from this floor on a winding stairway which led to the upper portion of the tower, where, preceding Rosine whose basket hindered her, she continued her ascension, which was somewhat dangerous, for the stairs of the half-abandoned tower had fallen into a state of dilapidation and decay. It was at the top of this tower, in a little chamber under the roof, that Rosine and the cook, forming themselves into a committee of deliberation, had shut up the young Baron Michel de la Logerie.

The intention of these honest girls was excellent; the result was in no sense equal to their good-will. It would be impossible to imagine a more miserable refuge, or one where it would be less possible to obtain even a slight repose. The room was, in fact, used by Jean Oullier to store the seeds, tools, and other necessary articles for his various avocations as Jack-at-all-trades. The walls were literally palisaded with branches of beans, cabbages, lettuce, onions, of diverse varieties, all gone to seed and exposed to the air for the purpose of ripening and drying them. Unfortunately, these botanic specimens had acquired such a coating of dust, while awaiting the period of their return to earth, that the least movement made in the narrow chamber sent up a cloud of leguminous atoms which affected the atmosphere disagreeably.

The sole furniture of this room was a wooden bench, which was not a very comfortable seat, certainly; and Michel, unable to endure it, had betaken himself to a pile of oats of a rare species, which obtained, on account of their rarity, a place in this collection of precious germs. He seated himself in the midst of the mound, and there, in spite of some inconveniencies, he found enough elasticity to rest his limbs, which were cramped with fatigue.

But after a time Michel grew weary of lying on this movable and prickly sofa. When Guérin threw him down into the brook a goodly quantity of mud became attached to his garments, and the dampness soon penetrated to his skin. His stay before the kitchen fire had been short, so short that the dampness now returned, more penetrating than ever. He began, therefore, to walk up and down in the turret-room, cursing the foolish timidity to which he owed not only the cold, stiffness, and hunger he began to feel, but also — more dismal still — the loss of Mary's presence. He scolded himself for not securing his own profit out of the valiant enterprise he had undertaken, and for losing courage to end successfully an affair he had so well begun.

Let us hasten to say here, in order that we may not misrepresent our hero's character, that the consciousness of his mistake did not make him a whit more courageous, and it never for an instant occurred to him to go frankly to the marquis and ask for hospitality, — a desire for which had been one of the determining motives of his flight.

Meantime the soldiers had arrived, and Michel, attracted by the noise to the narrow casement of his turret-chamber, saw the Demoiselles de Souday, their father, the general, and his officers, passing and repassing before the brilliantly lighted windows of the main building. It was then that, seeing Rosine in the courtyard beneath, he asked, with all the modesty of his character, for a bit of bread, and declared himself hungry.

Hearing, soon after, a light step apparently approaching his room, he began to feel a lively satisfaction under two heads: first, he was likely to get something to eat; and next, he should probably hear news of Mary.

"Is that you, Rosine?" he asked, when he heard a hand endeavoring to open the door.

"No, it is not Rosine; it is I, Monsieur Michel," said a voice.

Michel recognized it as Mary's voice; but he could not believe his ears. The voice continued: —

"Yes, I, — I, who am very angry with you!"

As the tone of the voice was not in keeping with the words, Michel was less alarmed than he might have been.

"Mademoiselle Mary!" he cried; "Mademoiselle Mary! Good heavens!"

He leaned against the wall to keep himself from falling. Meanwhile the young girl had opened the door.

"You!" cried Michel, — "you, Mademoiselle Mary! Oh, how happy I am!"

"Not so happy as you say."

"Why not?"

"Because, as you must admit, in the midst of your happiness you are dying of hunger."

"Ah, mademoiselle! who told you that?" stammered Michel, coloring to the whites of his eyes.

"Rosine. Come, Rosine, quick!" continued Mary. "Here, put your lantern on this bench, and open the basket at once; don't you see that Monsieur Michel is devouring it with his eyes?"

These laughing words made the young baron rather ashamed of the vulgar need of food he had expressed to his foster-sister. It came into his head that to seize the basket, fling it out of the window, at the risk of braining a soldier, fall upon his knees, and say to the young girl pathetically, with both hands pressed to his heart, "Can I think of my stomach when my heart is satisfied?" would be a rather gallant declaration to make. But Michel might have had such ideas in his head for a number of consecutive years without ever bringing himself to act in so cavalier a manner. He therefore allowed Mary to treat him exactly like a foster-brother. At her invitation he went back to his seat on the oats, and found it a very enjoyable thing to eat the food cut for him by the delicate hand of the young girl.

"Oh, what a child you are!" said Mary. "Why, after doing so gallant an act and rendering us a service of such importance, at the risk, too, of breaking your neck, — why did n't you come to my father, and say to him, as it was so natural to do, 'Monsieur, I cannot go home to my mother to-night; will you keep me till to-morrow morning?'"

"Oh, I never should have dared!" cried Michel, letting his arms drop on each side of him, like a man to whom an impossible proposal was made.

"Why not?" asked Mary.

"Because your father awes me."

"My father! Why, he is the kindest man in the world. Besides, are you not our friend?"

"Oh, how good of you, mademoiselle, to give me that title." Then, venturing to go a step farther, he added, "Have I really won it?"

Mary colored slightly. A few days earlier she would not have hesitated to reply that Michel was indeed her friend, and that she was constantly thinking of him. But during those few days Love had strangely modified her feelings and produced an instinctive reticence which she was far from comprehending. The more she was revealed to herself as a woman, by sensations hitherto unknown to her, the more she perceived that the manners, habits, and language resulting from the education she had received were unusual; and with that faculty of intuition peculiar to women she saw what she lacked on the score of reserve, and she resolved to acquire it for the sake of the emotion that filled her soul and made her feel the necessity of dignity.

Consequently, Mary, who up to this time had never concealed a single thought, began to see that a young girl must sometimes, if not lie, at least evade the truth; and she now put in practice this new discovery in her answer to Michel's question.

"I think," she replied, "that you have done quite enough to earn the name of friend." Then without giving him time to return to a subject on hazardous ground, she continued, "Come, give me proof of the appetite you were boasting of just now by eating this other wing of the chicken."

"Oh, mademoiselle, no!" said Michel, artlessly, "I am choking as it is."

"Then you must be a very poor eater. Come, obey; if not, as I am only here to serve you, I shall go."

"Mademoiselle," said Michel, stretching out both his hands, in one of which was a fork, in the other a piece of bread, — "mademoiselle, you cannot be so cruel. Oh! if you only knew how sad and dismal I have been here for the last two hours in this utter solitude — "

"You were hungry; that explains it," said Mary, laughing.

"No, no, no; that was not it! I could see you from here, going and coming with all those officers."

"That was your own fault. Instead of taking refuge like an owl in this old turret, you ought to have come into the salon and gone with us to the dining-room and eaten your supper sitting, like a Christian, on a proper chair. You would have heard my father and General Dermoncourt relating adventures to make your flesh creep, and you would have seen the old weasel Loriot — as my father calls him — eating his supper, which was scarcely less alarming."

"Good God!" cried Michel.

"What?" asked Mary, surprised by the sudden exclamation.

"Maître Loriot, of Machecoul?"

THE TOWER CHAMBER. 303

"Maître Loriot, of Machecoul," repeated Mary.

"My mother's notary?"

"Ah, yes, that's true; so he is!" said Mary.

"Is he here?" asked Michel.

"Yes, of course he is here; and what do you think he came for?" continued Mary, laughing.

"What?"

"To look for you."

"For me?"

"Exactly; sent by the baroness."

"But, mademoiselle," cried Michel, much alarmed, "I don't wish to go back to La Logerie."

"Why not?"

"Because, — well, because they lock me up, they detain me; they want to keep me at a distance from — from my friends."

"Nonsense! La Logerie is not so very far from Souday."

"No; but Paris is far from Souday, and the baroness wants to take me to Paris. Did you tell that notary I was here?"

"No, indeed."

"Oh! I thank you, mademoiselle."

"You need not thank me, for I did not know it myself."

"But now that you do know it — "

Michel hesitated.

"Well, what?"

"You must not tell him, Mademoiselle Mary," said Michel, ashamed of his weakness.

"Upon my word, Monsieur Michel," replied Mary, "you must allow me to say one thing."

"Say it, mademoiselle; say it!"

"Well, it seems to me if I were a man Maître Loriot should not disturb me under any circumstances."

Michel seemed to gather all his strength in order to take a resolution.

"You are right," he said; "and I will go and tell him that I will not return to La Logerie."

At this moment they were startled by loud cries from the cook, calling to Rosine.

"Good heavens!" they both cried, one as frightened as the other.

"Do you hear that, mademoiselle?" said Rosine.

"Yes."

"They want me."

"Oh!" said Mary, rising, and all ready to flee away, "can they know we are here?"

"Suppose they do," said Rosine; "what does it matter?"

"Nothing," said Mary; "but —"

"Listen!" exclaimed Rosine.

They were silent, and the cook was heard to go away. Presently her voice was heard in the garden.

"Dear me!" said Rosine; "there she is, calling me outside."

And Rosine was for running down at once.

"Heavens!" cried Mary; "don't leave me here alone."

"Why, you are not alone," said Rosine, naïvely. "Monsieur Michel is here."

"Yes, but to get back to the house," stammered Mary.

"Why, mademoiselle," cried Rosine, astonished, "have you suddenly turned coward, — you so brave, who are in the woods by night as much as by day! It is n't a bit like you."

"Never mind; stay, Rosine."

"Well, for all the help I have been to you for the last half-hour I might as well go."

"Very true; but that's not what I want of you."

"What do you want?"

"Well, don't you see?"

"What?"

"Why, that this unfortunate boy can't pass the night here, in this room."

"Then where can he pass it?" asked Rosine.

"I don't know; but we must find him another room."

"Without telling the marquis?"

"Oh, true! my father does n't know he is here. Good heavens! what's to be done? Ah, Monsieur Michel, it is all your fault!"

"Mademoiselle, I am ready to leave the house if you demand it."

"What makes you say that?" cried Mary, quickly. "No; on the contrary, stay."

"Mademoiselle Mary, an idea!" interrupted Rosine.

"What is it?"

"Suppose I go and ask Mademoiselle Bertha what we had better do?"

"No," replied Mary, with an eagerness which surprised herself; "no, that's useless! I will ask her myself presently when I go down, after Monsieur Michel has finished his wretched little supper."

"Very good; then I'll go now," said Rosine.

Mary dared not keep her longer. Rosine disappeared, leaving the two young people entirely alone.

XXXV.

WHICH ENDS QUITE OTHERWISE THAN AS MARY EXPECTED.

THE little room was lighted only by the lantern, the rays of which were concentrated on the door, leaving in darkness, or at any rate in obscurity, the rest of the room, — if, indeed, the word "room" can be applied to the sort of pigeon-loft in which the two young people were now alone.

Michel was still sitting on the heap of oats. Mary was kneeling on the ground, looking into the basket with more embarrassment than interest, ostensibly in search of some dainty which might still be forthcoming to conclude the repast.

But so many things had now happened that Michel was no longer hungry. His head was resting on his hand and his elbow on his knee. He was watching with a lover's eye the soft, sweet face before him, now foreshortened by the girl's attitude in a way to double the charm of her delicate features. He breathed in with delight the waves of perfumed air that came to him from the long fair curls, which the breeze entering through the window gently raised and wafted to his lips. At that contact, that perfume, that sight, his blood circulated more rapidly in his veins. He heard the arteries of his temples beating; he felt a quiver running through every limb until it reached his brain. Under the influence of sensations so new to him the young man felt his soul animated by unknown aspirations; he learned to *will*.

What he willed he felt to the depths of his soul; he willed to find some way of telling Mary that he loved her.

He sought the best; but with all his seeking he found no better way than the simple means of taking her hand and carrying it to his lips. Suddenly he did it, without really knowing what he did.

"Monsieur Michel! Monsieur Michel!" cried Mary, more astonished than angry; "what are you doing?"

The young girl rose quickly. Michel saw that he had gone too far and must now go farther still and say all. It was he who now took Mary's posture; that is, he fell upon his knees and again took the hand which had escaped him. It is true that hand made no effort to avoid his clasp.

"Oh! can I have offended you?" he cried. "If that were so I should be most unhappy, and ask pardon of you on my knees."

"Monsieur Michel!" began the young girl, without knowing what she meant to say.

But the baron, afraid that the little hand might be snatched away from him, folded it in both his own; and as, on his side, he did not very well know what he was saying, he continued: —

"If I have abused your goodness, mademoiselle, tell me, — I implore you, — tell me that you are not angry with me."

"I will say so, monsieur, when you rise," said Mary, making a feeble effort to withdraw her hand. But the effort was so feeble it had no other result than to show Michel its captivity was not altogether forced upon her.

"No," said the young baron, under the influence of a growing ardor caused by the change from hope into something that was almost certainty, — "no, leave me at your feet. Oh! if you only knew how many times, since I have known you, I have dreamed of the moment when I should kneel thus at your feet; if you knew how that dream, mere dream as it was, gave me the sweetest sensations, the most delightful agony, you would let me enjoy the happiness which is at this moment a reality."

"But, Monsieur Michel," replied Mary, in a voice of increasing emotion as she spoke, for she felt she had reached the moment when she could have no further doubt as to the nature of his affection for her, — "Monsieur Michel, we should not kneel except to God and to the saints."

"I know not to whom we ought to kneel, nor why I kneel to you," said the young man. "What I feel is far beyond all that I ever felt before,— greater than my affection for my mother, so great that I do not know where to place or what to call the sentiment that leads me to adore you. It is something which belongs to the reverence you speak of, which we offer to God and to the saints. For me you are the whole creation; in adoring you it seems to me that I adore the universe itself."

"Oh, monsieur, cease to say such things! Michel! my friend!"

"No, no, leave me as I am; suffer me to consecrate myself to you with an absolute devotion. Alas! I feel, — believe me, I am not mistaken, — I feel, since I have seen men who are truly men, that the devotion of a timid, feeble child, which, alas! I am, is but a paltry thing at best; and yet it seems to me that the joy of suffering, of shedding my blood, of dying, if need be, for you, must be so infinite that the hope of winning it would give me the strength and courage that I lack."

"Why talk of suffering and of death?" said Mary, in her gentle voice. "Do you think death and suffering absolutely necessary to prove an affection true?"

"Why do I speak of them, Mademoiselle Mary? Why do 1 call them to my aid? Because I dare not hope for another happiness; because to live happy, calm, and peaceful beside you, to enjoy your tenderness, in short, to make you my wife, seems to me a dream beyond all human hope. I cannot picture to my mind that such a dream should ever be reality for me."

"Poor child!" said Mary, in a voice of at least as much compassion as tenderness; "then you do indeed love me truly?"

"Oh, Mademoiselle Mary, why must I tell you? Why should I repeat it? Do you not see it with your eyes and with your heart? Pass your hand across my forehead bathed in sweat, place it on my heart that is beating wildly; see how my body trembles, and can you doubt I love you?"

The feverish excitement, which suddenly transformed the young man into another being, was communicated to Mary; she was no less agitated, no less trembling than himself. She forgot all, — the hatred of her father for all that bore the name of Michel, the repugnance of Madame de la Logerie toward her family, even the delusions Bertha cherished of Michel's love to herself, delusions which Mary had so many times determined to respect. The native warmth and ardor of her vigorous and primitive nature gained an ascendency over the reserve she had for some time thought it proper to assume. She was on the point of yielding wholly to the tenderness of her heart and of replying to that passionate love by a love even, perhaps, more passionate, when a slight noise at the door caused her to turn her head.

There stood Bertha, erect and motionless, on the threshold. The eye of the lantern, as we have said, was turned toward the door, so that the light was concentrated on Bertha's face. Mary could therefore see plainly how white her sister was, and also how pain and anger were gathering upon that frowning brow and behind those lips so violently contracted. She was so terrified by the unexpected and almost menacing apparition that she pushed away the young man, whose hand had not left hers, and went up to her sister.

But Bertha, who had now entered the turret, did not stop to meet Mary. Pushing her aside with her hand as though she were an inert object, she went straight to Michel.

"Monsieur," she said, in a ringing voice, "has my sister not told you that Monsieur Loriot, your mother's notary, is in the salon and wishes to speak to you?"

Michel muttered a few words.

"You will find him in the salon," continued Bertha, in the tone of voice she would have used in giving an order.

Michel, cast suddenly back into his usual timidity and all his terrors, stood up in a confused and vacillating manner without saying a word, and turned to leave the room, like a child detected in a fault who obeys without having the courage to excuse himself.

Mary took the lantern to light him down, but Bertha snatched it from her hand and put it into that of the young man, making him a sign to go.

"But you, mademoiselle?" he ventured to say.

"We know the house," replied Bertha. Then stamping her foot impatiently, as she noticed that Michel's eyes were seeking those of Mary, "Go, go! I tell you; go!" she exclaimed.

The young man disappeared, leaving the two young girls without other light than the pale gleam of a half-veiled moon, which entered the turret through the narrow casement.

Left alone with her sister, Mary expected to be severely blamed for the impropriety of her conduct in permitting such a *tête-à-tête*, — an impropriety of which she herself was now fully aware. In this she was mistaken. As soon as Michel had disappeared down the spiral stairway, and Bertha, with her ears strained to the door, had heard him leave the tower, she seized her sister's hand, and pressing it with a force which proved the violence of her feelings, asked in a choking voice: —

"What was he saying to you on his knees?"

For all answer Mary threw herself on her sister's neck, and in spite of Bertha's efforts to repulse her she wound her arms about her and kissed her, moistening Bertha's face with the tears that flowed from her own eyes.

"Why are you angry with me, dear sister?" she said.

"It is not being angry with you, Mary, to ask what a

young man whom I find kneeling at your feet was saying to you."

"But this is not the way you usually speak to me."

"What matters it how I usually speak to you? What I wish and what I exact is that you answer my question."

"Bertha! Bertha!"

"Come, answer me; speak! What was he saying? I ask you what he said?" cried the girl, harshly, shaking her sister so violently by the arm that Mary gave a cry and sank to the floor as if about to faint.

The cry recalled Bertha to her natural feeling. This impetuous and violent nature, fundamentally kind, softened at the expression of the pain and distress she had wrung from her sister. She did not let her fall to the ground, but took her in her arms, raised her as though she were a child, and laid her on the bench, holding her all the while tightly embraced. Then she covered her with kisses, and a few tears, gushing from her eyes like sparks from a brazier, dropped upon Mary's cheek. Bertha wept as Maria Theresa wept, — her tears, instead of flowing, burst forth like lightning.

"Poor little thing! poor little thing!" she said, speaking to her sister as if to a child she had chanced to injure; "forgive me! I have hurt you, and, worse still, I have grieved you; oh, forgive me!" Then, gathering herself together, she repeated, "Forgive me! It is my fault. I ought to have opened my heart to you before letting you see that the strange love I feel for that man — that child," she added with a touch of scorn — "has such power over me that it makes me jealous of one whom I love better than all the world, better than life itself, better than I love him, — jealous of you! Ah! if you only knew, my poor Mary, the misery this senseless love, which I know to be beneath me, has already brought upon me! If you knew the struggles I have gone through to subdue it! how bitterly I deplore my weakness! There is nothing in him of all I respect, nothing of what I love, — neither distinction of race, nor religious faith, nor ardor, nor vigor, nor strength, nor courage; and yet, in spite of all, I love him! I loved him the first moment that I saw him. I love him so much that sometimes, breathless, frantic, bathed in perspiration, and suffering almost unspeakable anguish, I have cried aloud like one possessed, 'My God! make me die, but let him love me!' For the last few months — ever since, to my misfortune, we met him — the thought of this man has never left me for an instant. I feel for him some strange emotion, which must be that a woman feels to a lover, but which is really far more like the affection of a mother for her child. Each day that passes, my life is more bound up in him; I put not only my thoughts, but all my dreams, my hopes on him. Ah, Mary! Mary! just now I was asking you to pardon me; but now I say to you, pity me, sister! Oh, my sister, have pity upon me!"

And Bertha, quite beside herself, clasped her sister frantically in her arms.

Poor Mary had listened, trembling, to this explosion of an almost savage passion, such as the powerful and self-willed nature of Bertha alone could feel. Each cry, each word, each sentence tore to shreds the rosy vapors which a few moments earlier she had seen on the horizon. Her sister's impetuous voice swept those fragments from her sight, as the gust of a rising tempest sweeps the light, fleecy clouds before it. Her grief and bewilderment was such during Bertha's last words that the latter's silence alone warned her she was expected to reply. She made a great effort over herself, striving to check her sobs.

"Oh, sister," she said, "my heart is breaking; my grief is all the greater because what has happened to-night is partly my fault."

"No, no!" cried Bertha, with her accustomed violence. "It was I who ought to have looked to see what became of him when we left the chapel. But," she continued, with that pertinacity of ideas which characterizes persons who are violently in love, "what was he saying to you? Why was he kneeling at your feet?"

Mary felt that Bertha shuddered as she asked the question; she herself trembled violently at the thought of what she had to answer. It seemed to her that each word by which she was forced to explain the truth to Bertha would scorch her lips as they left her heart.

"Come, come!" said Bertha, weeping, her tears having more effect on Mary than her anger, — "Come, tell me, dear sister; have pity on me! The suspense is worse a hundred-fold than any pain. Tell me, tell me; did he speak to you of love?"

Mary could not lie; or rather, self-devotion had not yet taught her to do so.

"Yes," she said.

"Oh, my God! my God!" cried Bertha, tearing herself from her sister's breast and falling, with outstretched arms, her face against the wall.

There was such a tone of absolute despair in the cry that Mary was terrified. She forgot Michel, she forgot her love; she forgot all except her sister. The sacrifice before which her heart had quailed at the moment when she first heard that Bertha loved Michel, she now made valiantly, with sublime self-abnegation; for she smiled, with a breaking heart.

"Foolish girl that you are!" she cried, springing to Bertha's neck; "let me finish what I have to say."

"Did you not tell me that he spoke of love?" replied the suffering creature.

"Yes; but I did not tell you whom he loves."

"Mary! Mary! have pity on my heart!"

"Bertha! dear Bertha!"

"Was it of me he spoke?"

Mary had not the strength to reply in words; she made a sign of acquiescence with her head.

Bertha breathed heavily, passed her hand several times over her burning forehead. The shock had been too violent to allow her to recover instantly her normal condition.

"Mary," she said, "what you have just told me seems so unlikely, so impossible, that you must swear it. Swear to me —" She hesitated.

"I will swear what you will, sister," said Mary, who was eager herself to put some insurmountable barrier between her heart and her love.

"Swear to me that Michel does not love you, and that you do not love him." She laid her hand on her sister's shoulder. "Swear it by our mother's grave."

"I swear, by the grave of our mother," said Mary, resolutely, "that I will never marry Michel."

She threw herself into her sister's arms, seeking compensation for her sacrifice in the caresses the latter gave her. If the room had been less dark Bertha might have seen on Mary's features the anguish that oath had cost her. As it was, it restored all Bertha's calmness. She sighed gently, as though her heart were lightened of a heavy weight.

"Thank you!" she said; "oh, thank you! thank you! Now let us return to the salon."

But, half-way down, Mary made an excuse to go to her room. There she locked herself in to pray and weep.

The company had not yet left the supper-table. As Bertha crossed the vestibule to reach the salon she heard bursts of laughter from the guests.

When she entered the salon Monsieur Loriot was arguing with the young baron, endeavoring to persuade him that it was his interest as well as his duty to return to La Logerie. But the negative silence of the young man was so eloquent that the notary presently found himself at the end of his arguments. It is true, however, that he had been talking for half an hour.

Michel was probably not less embarrassed than the notary himself, and he welcomed Bertha as a battalion formed in a hollow square and attacked on all sides welcomes an auxiliary who will strengthen its defence. He sprang to meet her with an eagerness which owed as much to his present difficulty as to the closing scene of his interview with Mary.

To his great surprise, Bertha, incapable of concealing for a moment what she was feeling, stretched out her hand and pressed his with effusion. She mistook the meaning of the young man's eager advance, and from being content she became radiant.

Michel, who expected quite another reception, did not feel at his ease. However, he immediately recovered himself so far as to say to Loriot: —

"You will tell my mother, monsieur, that a man of principle finds actual duties in his political opinions, and that I decide to die, if need be, in accomplishing mine."

Poor boy! he was confounding love with duty.

XXXVI.

BLUE AND WHITE.

IT was almost two in the morning when the Marquis de Souday proposed to his guests to return to the salon. They left the table in that satisfied condition which always follows a plenteous repast if the master of the house is in good-humor, the guests hungry, and the topics of conversation interesting enough to fill the spare moments of the chief occupation.

In proposing to adjourn to the salon the marquis had probably no other idea than change of atmosphere; for as he rose he ordered Rosine and the cook to follow him with the liqueurs, and to array the bottles with a sufficient number of glasses on a table in the salon.

Then, humming the great air in "Richard, Cœur-de-Lion," and paying no heed to the fact that the general replied by a verse from the "Marseillaise," which the noble panels of the castle of Souday heard, no doubt, for the first time, the old gentleman, having filled all glasses, was preparing to resume a very interesting controversy as to the treaty of Jaunaye, which the general insisted had only sixteen articles, when the latter, pointing to the clock, called his attention to the time of night.

Dermoncourt said, laughing, that he suspected the marquis of intending to paralyze his enemies by the delights of a new Capua; and the marquis, accepting the joke with infinite tact and good-will, hastened to yield to his guests' wishes and took them at once to the bedrooms assigned to them, after which he betook himself to his own.

The Marquis de Souday, excited by the warlike inclinations of his mind and by the conversation which enlivened the evening, dreamed of combats. He was fighting a battle, compared to which those of Torfou, Laval, and Saumur were child's play; he was in the act of advancing under a shower of shot and shell, leading his division to the assault of a redoubt, and planting the white flag in the midst of the enemy's intrenchments, when a rapping at his door interrupted his exploits.

In the dozing condition which preceded his full awakening, the dream continued, and the noise at his door was the roar of cannon. Then, little by little, the clouds rolled away from his brain, the worthy old gentleman opened his eyes, and, instead of a battlefield covered with broken gun-carriages, gasping horses, and dead bodies, over which he thought he was leaping, he found himself lying on his narrow camp bed of painted wood draped with modest white curtains edged with red.

The knocking was renewed.

"Come in!" cried the marquis, rubbing his eyes. "Ha! bless me, general, you've come just in time," he cried; "two minutes more, and you were dead."

"How so?"

"Yes, by a sword-thrust I was just putting through you."

"By way of retaliation, my good friend," said the general, holding out his hand.

"That's how I take it. But I see you are looking rather puzzled by my poor room; its shabbiness surprises you. Yes, there is some difference between this bare, forlorn place, with its horsehair chairs and carpetless floor, and the fine apartments of your Parisian lords. But I can't help it. I spent one third of my life in camps and another third in penury, and this little cot with its thin mattress seems to me luxury enough for my old age. But what in the world brings you here at this early hour, general? It is hardly light yet."

"I came to bid you good-bye, my kind host," replied the general.

"Already? Ah, see what life is! I must tell you now that only yesterday I had all sorts of prejudices against you before your arrival."

"Had you? And yet you welcomed me most cordially."

"Bah!" said the marquis, laughing; "you've been in Egypt. Did you never receive a few shots from the midst of a cool and pleasant oasis?"

"Bless me, yes! The Arabs regard an oasis as the best of ambuscades."

"Well, I was something of an Arab last night; and I say my *mea culpa*, regretting it all the more because I am really and truly sorry you leave me so soon."

"Is it because there is still an unexplored corner of your oasis you want me to see?"

"No; it is because your frankness, loyalty, and the community of dangers we have shared (in opposite camps) inspired me — I scarcely know why, but instantly — with a sincere and deep regard for you."

"On your word as a gentleman?"

"On my word as a gentleman and a soldier."

"Well, then, I offer you my friendship in return, my dear enemy," replied Dermoncourt. "I expected to find an old *émigré*, powdered like a white frost, stiff and haughty, and larded with antediluvian prejudices — "

"And you've found out that a man may wear powder and have no prejudices, — is that it, general?"

"I found a frank and loyal heart and an amiable, — bah! let's say the word openly, — jovial nature, and this with exquisite manners, which might seem to exclude all that; in short, you've seduced an old veteran, who is heartily yours."

"Well, it gives me a great deal of pleasure to hear you say so. Come, stay one more day with me!"

"Impossible!"

"Well, I have nothing to say against that decisive word;

but make me a promise that you will pay me a visit after the peace, if we are both of us still living."

"After the peace!" cried the general, laughing. "Are we at war?"

"We are between peace and war."

"Yes, the happy medium."

"Well, let us say after the happy medium. Promise you will come and see me then?"

"Yes, I give you my word."

"And I shall hold you to it."

"But come, let us talk seriously," said the general, taking a chair and sitting down at the foot of the old *émigré's* bed.

"I am willing," replied the latter, "for once in a way."

"You love hunting?"

"Passionately."

"What kind?"

"All kinds."

"But there must be one kind you prefer?"

"Yes, boar-hunting. That reminds me most of hunting the Blues."

"Thanks."

"Boars and Blues, — they both charge alike."

"What do you say to fox-hunting?"

"Peuh!" exclaimed the marquis, sticking out his under-lip like a prince of the House of Austria.

"Well, it is a fine sport," said the general.

"I leave that to Jean Oullier, who has wonderful tact and patience in watching a covert."

"He is good at watching other game than foxes, your Jean Oullier," remarked the general.

"Yes, yes; he's clever at all game, no doubt."

"Marquis, I wish you would take a fancy to fox-hunting."

"Why?"

"Because England is the land for it; and I have a fancy that the air of England would be very good just now for you and your young ladies."

"Goodness!" said the marquis, sitting up in bed.

"Yes, I have the honor to tell you so, my dear host."

"Which means that you are advising me to emigrate? No, thank you."

"Do you call an agreeable little trip emigration?"

"My dear general, those little trips, I know what they are, — worse than a journey round the world; you know when they begin, but nobody knows when they'll end. And, besides, there is one thing — you will hardly, perhaps, believe it — "

"What is that?"

"You saw yesterday, I may say this morning, that in spite of my age I have a very tolerable appetite; and I can certify that I never had an indigestion in my life. I can eat anything without being made uncomfortable."

"Well?"

"Well, that devilish London fog, I never could digest it. Isn't that curious?"

"Very good; then go to Italy, Spain, Switzerland, wherever you please, but don't stay at Souday. Leave Machecoul; leave La Vendée."

"Ha! ha! ha!"

"Yes, yes."

"Can it be that I am compromised?" said the marquis, half to himself, and rubbing his hands cheerfully.

"If you are not now, you will be soon."

"At last!" cried the old gentleman, joyously.

"No joking," said the general, becoming serious. If I listened to my duty only, my dear marquis, you would find two sentries at your door and a sub-lieutenant in the chair where I am now sitting."

"Hey!" cried the marquis, a shade more serious.

"Yes, upon my word, that's the state of things. But I can understand how a man of your age, accustomed as you are to an active life in the free air of the forests, would suffer cooped up in a prison where the civil authorities would probably put you; and I give you a proof of my sympathetic friendship in what I said just now, though in doing so I am, in a measure, compromising with my strict duty."

"But suppose you are blamed for it, general?"

"Pooh! do you suppose I can't find excuses enough? A senile old man, worn-out, half-imbecile, who tried to stop the column on its march —"

"Of whom are you speaking, pray?"

"Why, you, of course."

"I a senile old man, worn-out, half-imbecile!" cried the marquis, sticking one muscular leg out of bed. "I'm sure I don't know, general, why I don't unhook those swords on the wall and stake our breakfast on the first blood, as we did when I was a lad and a page forty-five years ago."

"Come, come, old child!" cried Dermoncourt; "you are so bent on proving I have made a mistake that I shall have to call in the soldiers after all."

And the general pretended to rise.

"No, no," said the marquis; "no, damn it! I am senile, worn-out, half-imbecile, wholly imbecile, — anything you like, in short."

"Very good; that's all right."

"But will you tell me how and by whom I am, or shall be, compromised?"

"In the first place, your servant, Jean Oullier —"

"Yes."

"The fox man —"

"I understand."

"Your servant, Jean Oullier, — a thing I neglected to tell you last night, supposing that you knew as much about it as I did, — your man, Jean Oullier, at the head of a lot of seditious rioters, attempted to stop the column which was ordered to surround the château de Souday. In attempting this he brought about several fights, in which we lost three men killed, not counting one whom I myself did justice on, and who belongs, I think, in these parts."

"What was his name?"

"François Tinguy."

"Hush! general, don't mention it here, for pity's sake. His sister lives in this house, — the young girl who waited on you at table last night, — and her father is only just buried."

"Ah, these civil wars! the devil take them!" said the general.

"And yet they are the only logical wars."

"Maybe. However, I captured your Jean Oullier, and he got away."

"He did well, — you must own that?"

"Yes; but if he falls into my grip again —"

"Oh, there's no danger of that; once warned, I'll answer for him."

"So much the better, for I shouldn't be indulgent to him. I haven't talked of the great war with him, as I have with you."

"But he fought through it, though, and bravely, too."

"Reason the more; second offence."

"But, general," said the marquis, "I can't see, so far, how the conduct of my keeper can be twisted into a crime of mine."

"Wait, and you will see. You said last night that imps came and told you all I did between seven and ten o'clock that evening."

"Yes."

"Well, I have imps, too, and they are every bit as good as yours."

"I doubt it."

"They have told me all that happened in your castle yesterday."

"Go on," said the marquis, incredulously; "I'm listening."

"On the previous evening two persons came to stay at the château de Souday."

"Good! you are better than your word. You promised

to tell me what happened yesterday, and now you begin with the day before yesterday."

"These two persons were a man and a woman."

The marquis shook his head, negatively.

"So be it; call them two men, though one of them had nothing but the clothes of our sex."

The marquis said nothing, and the general continued:

"Of these two personages, one, the smaller, spent the whole day at the castle; the other rode about the neighborhood, and gave rendezvous that evening at Souday to a number of gentlemen. If I were indiscreet I would tell you their names; but I will only mention that of the gentleman who summoned them, — namely, the Comte de Bonneville."

The marquis made no reply. He must either acknowledge or lie.

"What next?" he said.

"These gentlemen arrived at Souday, one after the other. They discussed various matters, the most calming of which was certainly not the glory, prosperity, and duration of the government of July."

"My dear general, admit that you are not one whit more in love than I with your government of July, though you serve it."

"What's that you are saying?"

"Eh? good God! I'm saying that you are a republican, blue, dark-blue; and a true dark-blue is a fast color."

"That's not the question."

"What is it then?"

"I am talking of the strangers who assembled in this house last night between eight and nine o'clock."

"Well, suppose I did receive a few neighbors, suppose I even welcomed two strangers, where's the crime, general? I've got the Code at my fingers' ends, — unless, indeed, the old revolutionary law against suspected persons is revived."

"There is no crime in neighbors visiting you; but there

is crime when those neighbors assemble for a conference in which an uprising and resort to arms is discussed."

"How can that be proved?"

"By the presence of the two strangers."

"Pooh!"

"Most certainly; for the smaller and fairer of the strangers, the one who, being fair, wore a black wig to disguise herself, was no less a person than the Princess Marie-Caroline, whom you call regent of the kingdom, — her Royal Highness Madame la Duchesse de Berry, who is now pleased to call herself Petit-Pierre."

The marquis bounded in his bed. The general was better informed than he, and what he was now told entered his mind like a flash of light. He could hardly contain himself for joy at the thought that he had received Madame la Duchesse de Berry under his roof; but, unhappily, as joy is never perfect in this world, he was forced to repress his satisfaction.

"Go on," he said; "what next?"

"Well, the next is that just as you had reached the most interesting part of the discussion, a young man, whom one would scarcely expect to find in your camp, came and warned you that I and my troops were on our way to the château. And then you, Monsieur le marquis (you won't deny this, I am sure), you proposed to resist; but the contrary was decided on. Mademoiselle, your daughter, the dark one—"

"Bertha."

"Mademoiselle Bertha took a light. She left the room, and every one present, except you, Monsieur le marquis, who probably set about preparing for the new guests whom Heaven was sending you, — every one present followed her. She crossed the courtyard and went to the chapel; there she opened the door, passed in first, and went straight to the altar. Pushing a spring hidden in the left forepaw of the lamb carved on the front of the altar, she tried to open a trap-door. The spring, which had probably not been used for some time, resisted. Then she took the bell used for the mass, the handle of which is of wood, and pressed it on the button. The panel instantly yielded, and opened the way to a staircase leading to the vaults. Mademoiselle Bertha then took two wax-tapers from the altar, lighted them, and gave them to two of the persons who accompanied her. Then, your guests having gone down into the vault, she closed the panel behind them, and returned, as did another person, who did not immediately enter the house, but, on the contrary, wandered about the park for some time. As for the fugitives, when they reached the farther end of the subterranean passage, which opens, you know, among the ruins of the old château that I see from here, they had some difficulty in forcing their way through the piles of stones that cover the ground. One of them actually fell. However, they managed to reach the covered way which skirts the park wall; there they stopped to deliberate. Three took the road from Nantes to Machecoul, two followed the crossroad which leads to Légé, and the sixth and seventh doubled themselves, — I should rather say, made themselves into one — "

"Look here! is this a fairy tale you are telling me, general?"

"Wait, wait! You interrupt me at the most interesting part of all. I was telling you that the sixth and seventh doubled up; that is, the larger took the smaller on his back and went to the little brook that runs into the great rivulet flowing round the base of the Viette des Biques. Now as they are the ones I prefer among your company, I shall set my dogs of war on them."

"But, my dear general," cried the Marquis de Souday, "I do assure you all this exists only in your imagination."

"Come, come, my old enemy! You are Master of Wolves, are not you?"

"Yes."

"Well, when you see the print of a young boar's paw

sharply defined in soft earth, — a clear trail as you call it, — would you let any one persuade you into thinking it was only the ghost of a tusker? Well, marquis, that trail, I have seen it, or rather, I should say, I have read it."

"The devil!" cried the marquis, turning in his bed with the admiring curiosity of an amateur; "then I wish you 'd just tell me how you did it."

"Willingly," replied the general. "But we have still a good half-hour before us. Order up a pâté and a bottle of wine, and I 'll tell you the rest between two mouthfuls."

"On one condition."

"And that is?"

"That I may share the meal."

"At this early hour?"

"Real appetites don't carry a watch."

The marquis jumped out of bed, put on his flannel trousers, slipped his feet into his slippers, rang, ordered up a breakfast, covered a table, and sat down before the general with an interrogating air."

The general, put to the test of proving his words, began, as he said, between two mouthfuls. He was a good talker, and a better eater than even the marquis.

XXXVII.

WHICH SHOWS THAT IT IS NOT FOR FLIES ONLY THAT SPIDERS' WEBS ARE DANGEROUS.

"You know, my dear marquis," began the general, by way of exordium, "that I don't inquire into any of your secrets. I am so perfectly sure, so profoundly convinced that everything happened precisely as I tell you, that I'll excuse you from telling me that I am mistaken or not mistaken. All I want to do is to prove to you, as a matter of self-respect, that we have as good a nose for a scent in our camp as you have in your forest, — a small satisfaction of vanity which I am bent on getting, that's all."

"Go on, go on!" cried the marquis, as impatient as if Jean Oullier had come to tell him on a fine snowy day that he had roused a wolf.

"We'll begin with the beginning. I knew that M. le Comte de Bonneville had arrived at your house the night before last, accompanied by a little peasant, who had all the appearance of being a woman in disguise, and whom we suspect to be Madame. But this is only a report of spies; it does n't figure in my own inventory," added the general.

"I should hope not; pah!" said the marquis.

"But when I arrived here in person, as we military fellows say in our bulletin French, without being, I must assure you, at all misled by the extreme politeness which you lavished upon us, I at once remarked two things."

"What were they?"

"First, that out of ten places laid at the supper-table, five had napkins rolled up, evidently belonging to certain regular guests; which fact, in case of a trial, my dear marquis — don't forget this — would be an eminently extenuating circumstance."

"Why so?"

"Because if you had known the rank and quality of your guests you would hardly have allowed them to roll their napkins like ordinary country neighbors, would you? The linen closets of Souday can't be so short of napkins that Madame la Duchesse de Berry could n't have a clean one for every meal. I am therefore inclined to believe that the blonde lady disguised in the black wig was nothing more to your mind than a dark young lad."

"Go on, go on!" cried the marquis, biting his lips at this revelation of a perspicacity so far exceeding his own.

"I intend to go on," said the general. "So, as I say, I noticed five rolled napkins, which proved that the supper, or dinner, was not so entirely prepared for us as you tried to make me believe, and that you simply gave us the places of Monsieur de Bonneville and his companion and others, who had judged it best not to wait for our arrival."

"Now for your second observation?" said the marquis.

"Mademoiselle Bertha, whom I suppose and believe to be a very neat young lady, was, when you did me the honor to present me to her, singularly covered with cobwebs; they were even in her beautiful hair."

"Well?"

"Well, certain as I was that she had not chosen that style of adornment out of coquetry, I looked about this morning for a part of the château that was well supplied with the toil of those interesting insects, the spiders."

"And you discovered — ?"

"Faith! what I discovered does n't redound to the honor of your religious sentiments, my dear marquis, or, at any rate, to your practice of them; for it was precisely across the doorway of your chapel that I found a dozen spiders working with unimaginable zeal to repair the damage done last night to their webs, — a zeal no doubt inspired by the belief that the opening of the door where they had fixed their homes was only an accident not likely to occur again."

"You must allow, my dear general, that all these indications are somewhat vague."

"Yes, but when your hounds turn their noses to the wind and strain at the leash, that is nothing more than a vague indication, is it? And yet on that indication you beat the woods with care, and very great care, too."

"Certainly," said the marquis.

"Well, that's my way also. Then, on your paths (where, by the bye, gravel is essentially lacking), I have discovered some very significant tracks."

"Steps of men and women?" exclaimed the marquis. "Pooh! they are everywhere."

"No, there are not everywhere steps crowded together and going in one direction, according to what I suppose to be the number of actors on the scene, — steps, too, of persons who were not walking, but running together."

"But how in the world could you tell that those persons were running?"

"Why, marquis, that's the A B C of the business."

"Tell me, quick!"

"Because their footmarks are more from the toes than the heels, and the earth is pushed backward. Is n't that the way to tell, my dear Master of Wolves?"

"Right," said the marquis, with the air of a connoisseur; "quite right. What next?"

"Next?"

"Yes."

"I examined the footprints; there were men's steps of various sizes and shapes, boots, shoes, and hob-nail soles. Then in the midst of all these masculine feet what did I see but the print of a woman's foot, slender and arched, Cinderella's foot, — a foot to put all the Andalusian women to shame from Cordova to Cadiz; and that, too, in spite of the heavy nailed shoes which contained it."

"Well, well! skip that."

"Skip it! why?"

"Because, if you say another word you'll be in love with that delicate foot in a hobnailed shoe."

"The truth is, I would give anything to hold it. Perhaps I shall. It was on the steps of the chapel and on the pavement within it that these traces were most observable; mud had left its own marks on the polished floor. I also found, near the altar, droppings from wax-tapers close to a long, thin footprint, which I would swear to be Mademoiselle Bertha's; and as other droppings were close to the outside of the trap-door, I concluded that your daughter held the light in her left hand, while she put the key with her right into the lock. However, without this last proof, the cobwebs — in fragments at the door, and tangled in her hair — proved to me conclusively that it was she who aided the escape."

"Very well; continue."

"The rest is hardly worth telling. The lamb's paw was broken, and left exposed a small steel button which worked a spring; therefore I had no merit in that discovery. It resisted my efforts as it did those of Mademoiselle Bertha, who, by the bye, scratched her finger and drew blood, leaving a little fresh trace of it on the carved wood. Like her, I looked for some hard thing to push in the little button, and like her again, I spied the wooden handle of the bell, which retained not only the marks of the pressure of the night before but also a little trace of blood."

"Bravo!" cried the marquis, evidently beginning to take a double interest in the narration.

"So, as you will readily believe," continued Dermoncourt, "I went down into the vault. The footprints of the fugitives were perfectly distinct on the damp, sandy soil. One of the party fell as they went through the ruins; I know this because I saw a thick tuft of nettles bruised and beaten down, which we may be sure, considering the unamiable nature of that plant, was not done intentionally.

In a corner of the ruins, opposite to the door, stones had been moved, as if to facilitate the passage of some delicate person. Among the nettles growing beside the wall I found the two tapers, thrown away as soon as the party reached the open air. Finally, and in conclusion, I found footsteps in the road, and then, as they separated there, I was able to class them in the manner I have already described to you."

"No, no; that's not the conclusion."

"Not the conclusion? yes, it is."

"No; who told you that one of these persons took another on his back?"

"Ah, marquis, you want to catch me tripping in discernment. The pretty little foot in the hobnailed shoe, — that charming foot that captivates me so much that I have neither peace nor rest till I have overtaken it, that delicate little foot, no longer than a child's nor wider than my two fingers, — well, I saw it in the vaults, also in the covered way behind the ruins, and at the place where they all stopped and deliberated before they parted. Then, suddenly, close to a huge stone, which the rain must usually keep clean, but which, on the contrary, I now found covered with mud, those dainty footsteps disappeared. From that moment, like the hippogriffs who no longer exist in our days, Monsieur de Bonneville, I presume, took his companion on his back. The footprints of the said Monsieur de Bonneville became suddenly heavier; they were no longer those of a lively, active youth, such as you and I were at his age, marquis. Don't you remember how the wild-sows when with young make heavier tracks, and their hoof-marks, instead of just pricking the earth, are placed flat with the two points separate? Well, from the stone I spoke of, M. de Bonneville's footsteps grew heavier in the same way."

"But you have forgotten something, general."

"I think not."

"Oh! I sha'n't let you off yet. What makes you think

that Monsieur de Bonneville spent the day riding about to summon my neighbors to council?"

"You told me yourself you had not gone out."

"Well?"

"Well, your horse, the one you always ride, — as that pretty little wench who took my bridle told me, — your favorite horse, which I saw in the stable when I went to make sure that my own Bucephalus had his provender, was covered with mud to the withers. Now, some one had ridden that horse, and you would never have lent him to any one for whom you did not feel some special consideration."

"Good! Now another question."

"Certainly; I am here to answer questions."

"What makes you think that Monsieur de Bonneville's companion is the august personage you named just now?"

"Partly because she is evidently made to pass first, before others, and the stones are moved out of her way."

"Can you tell by a mere footprint whether the person who made it is fair or dark?"

"No; but I can find it out in another way."

"How? This shall be my last question; and if you answer it —"

"If I answer it, what?"

"Nothing. Go on."

"Well, my dear marquis, you were so good as to give me the bedroom occupied the night before by Monsieur de Bonneville's companion."

"Yes, I did so; what of it?"

"Well, here is a pretty little tortoise-shell comb, which I found at the foot of the bed. You must admit, my dear marquis, that it is too dainty and coquettish to belong to a peasant lad. Besides, it contained, and still contains, as you may see, some long meshes of light brown hair, not at all of the golden shade that adorns your younger daughter's head, — the only blond head in your house."

"General!" cried the marquis, bounding from his chair,

and flinging his knife and fork across the room, "arrest me if you like, but I tell you, once for all, I won't go to England; no, I won't, I won't, I won't!"

"Well, well, marquis, what's the matter with you, hey?"

"The devil! You've stimulated my ambition, you've spurred my pride and my self-love. Though I know, if you come to Souday — as you've promised, mind you, after the campaign is over — I shall have nothing to tell you equal to your own performances."

"Listen to me, my old and excellent enemy," said the general. "I have given you my word not to arrest you, this time at least, and whatever you may do, or rather, whatever you may have done, I shall keep my word; but I do entreat you, in the name of the interest you have inspired in me, in the name of your charming daughters, do not commit the folly on which you are bent, and if you will not leave France, at least stay quietly at home."

"And why?"

"Because the memories of those heroic times, which are making your heart beat now are but memories; because the emotions of the great and glorious actions you would like to see renewed are gone forever; because the day of great deeds of arms, of devotion without conditions, of deaths sublime in constancy, are passed without recall. Oh! I knew her, I knew her well, that unconquerable Vendée. I can say so, — I who bear the scars of her steel upon my breast. Well, I have been for the last month in the midst of her, in the midst of the places of the past, and I tell you I look for her old self in vain; I cannot find it, and no one can find it. My poor marquis, count up the few young gallant fellows, whose brave hearts dare to face the struggle, count up the veteran heroes who, like you, think that the duty of 1793 is still a duty in 1832, and see for yourself that a struggle so unequal is sheer madness."

"It will not be less glorious for that, my dear general," cried the marquis, forgetting in his enthusiasm the political position of his companion.

"No, no; it will not be glorious in any sense. All that happens, — you'll see, and when you do, remember that I foretold it to you, — all that is now about to happen will be colorless, barren, puny, stunted; and on both sides, too. Yes, my God! with us as well as with you: with us, petty motives, base betrayals; with you, self-seeking compromises, contemptible meannesses, which will cut you to the heart, my poor marquis, which will kill you, — you, whom the balls of the Blues have left untouched."

"You see things as a partisan of the established government, general; you forget that we have many friends even in your own ranks, and that when we say the word this whole region will rise as one man."

The general shook his shoulders.

"In my time, old comrade, — allow me to call you so," he said, — "all that was Blue was Blue; all that was White was White. There was, to be sure, something red, — the executioner and his guillotine; but don't let us speak of that. You had no friends in our ranks, we had none in yours; and it was that which made us equally strong, equally great, equally terrible. At a word from you La Vendée will rise, you say? You are mistaken. La Vendée, which went to its death in 1795, relying on the coming of a prince whose word she trusted, and who failed her, will not rise now; no, not even when she sees the Duchesse de Berry within her borders. Your peasants have lost that political faith which moves human mountains, which drives them one against another, clashing together until they sink in a sea of blood, — that faith which begets and perpetuates martyrs. We ourselves, marquis, — I am forced to acknowledge it, — no longer possess that passion for liberty, progress, glory, which shook the old worlds to their centres, and gave birth to heroes. The civil war which is about to break out — if, indeed, there must be a civil war, and if it must break out — will be just such a war as Barême describes: a war in which victory is certain to be on the side of the big battalions, the best exchequer. And that is why I say to you, count the cost, count it twice over, before you fling yourself into this mad folly."

"You are mistaken; I tell you, general, you are mistaken. We are not without an army, without soldiers; and, more fortunate than in former times, we have a leader whose sex will electrify the cautious, rally all devotions, and silence contending ambitions."

"Poor, valorous young woman! poor, noble, poetic spirit!" said the old soldier, in a tone of the deepest pity, dropping his scarred brow upon his breast. "Presently she will have no more relentless enemy than myself; but while I am still in this room, on neutral ground, I will tell you how I admire her resolution, her courage, her persistent tenacity, and how truly I deplore that she was born in an epoch that is no longer of the measure of her soul. The times have changed, marquis, since Jeanne de Montfort had but to strike the soil of Brittany with her mailed heel for warriors to spring up fully armed from it. Marquis, remember what I predict to you this day, and repeat it to that poor woman, if you see her,— namely, that her noble heart, more valiant even than that of Comtesse Jeanne, will receive, as the reward of her abnegation, her energy, her devotion, her sublime elevation of soul as princess and mother, only indifference, ingratitude, baseness, cowardice, treachery of all kinds. And now, my dear marquis, make your decision, say your last word."

"My last word, general, is like my first."

"Repeat it, then."

"I will not go to England," said the old man, firmly.

"Listen," continued Dermoncourt, laying a hand on the marquis's shoulder, and looking him in the eyes. "You are as proud as a Gascon, Vendéan though you be. Your revenues are small, I know that, — oh, don't begin to frown in that way; let me finish what I have to say, — damn it, you know I wouldn't offer you anything I wouldn't accept myself."

The marquis's face returned to its first expression.

"I was saying," continued the general, "that your revenues are slender; and in this cursèd region of country it is not enough to possess revenues, great or small, — you must also collect them. Well, that's difficult; and if you can't get the money to cross the straits and hire a little cottage somewhere in England, — well, I'm not rich, I have only my pay, but I have managed to lay by a few hundred louis (a comrade accepts such things, you know); won't you take them? After the peace, as you say, you can pay them back."

"Stop! stop!" said the marquis; "you know me only since yesterday, and you treat me like a friend of twenty years' standing." The old Vendéan scratched his ear, and added, as if speaking to himself, "How could I ever show my gratitude for such an act?"

"Then you accept it?"

"No, no; I refuse it."

"But you will go?"

"I stay."

"God keep you then in health and safety!" said the old general, his patience exhausted. "Only, it is likely that chance, the devil take it! will bring us face to face together once more, as we were formerly; and now that I know you, if there is a hand-to-hand fight, such as there used to be in the old days, at Laval, hey? I swear I'll seek you out."

"And I'll seek you," cried the marquis; "I'll shout for you with all my lungs. I'd be thankful and proud to show these greenhorns what the men of the old war were."

"Well, there's the bugle sounding; I must go. Adieu, marquis, and thank you for your hospitality."

"*Au revoir*, general, and thanks for a friendship which I must prove to you I share."

The two old men shook hands, and Dermoncourt went away. The marquis, as he dressed himself, watched the little column disappearing up the avenue in the direction of the forest. At a couple of hundred paces from the château the general ordered a half-turn to the right; then, stopping his horse, he gave a last look at the little pointed turrets of his new friend's abode. Seeing the marquis at a window, he waved him a last adieu, and then, turning rein, he rejoined his men.

After following with his eyes, as long as they were visible, the detachment and the man who commanded it, the marquis turned from the window, and as he did so he heard a slight scratching on a little door behind his bed, which communicated, through a dressing-room, with the backstairs.

"Who the devil is coming this way?" he thought, drawing the bolt.

The door opened immediately, and gave entrance to Jean Oullier.

"Jean Oullier!" cried the marquis, in a tone of actual joy. "Is it you? are you really here, my good Jean Oullier? Ha! faith! the day has begun under good auspices."

He held out his hand to his keeper, who pressed it with a lively expression of respect and gratitude. Then, disengaging his hand, Jean Oullier produced from his pocket and gave to the marquis a piece of coarse paper folded into the shape of a letter. M. de Souday opened and read it. As he read his face beamed with joy unspeakable.

"Jean Oullier," he said, "call the young ladies; assemble all my people! No, no; stop! don't assemble any of them yet. Polish up my sword, my pistols, my carbine, all my war accoutrements; give Tristan oats. The campaign opens! My dear Jean Oullier, the campaign is opening! Bertha! Mary! Bertha!"

"Monsieur le marquis," said Jean Oullier, calmly, "the campaign has been opened for me since yesterday at three o'clock."

The sisters now rushed in, hearing their father's call. Mary's eyes were red and swollen. Bertha was radiant.

"Young ladies! girls!" cried the marquis; "you are in it! You are to come with me! Here, read this."

And he held out to Bertha the letter Jean Oullier had just given him. The letter was thus worded: —

MONSIEUR LE MARQUIS DE SOUDAY, — It is desirable for the cause of King Henri V. that you hasten by several days the call to arms. Have the goodness, therefore, to assemble all the most devoted men that you have in the district which you command, and hold yourself and them, especially yourself, at my immediate orders.

I think that two more amazons in our little army will help to spur on the love and the self-love of our friends, and I ask you, my dear marquis, to be so very kind as to grant me your beautiful and charming huntresses as my aides-de-camp.

Your affectionate

PETIT-PIERRE.

"Well," said Bertha, "are we to go?"

"Of course!" exclaimed the marquis.

"Then allow me, papa," said Bertha, "to present to you a recruit."

"As many as you like."

Mary was silent and motionless. Bertha left the room, and returned in a few moments, leading Michel by the hand.

"Baron Michel de la Logerie," said the girl, dwelling on the title, "wishes to prove to you papa, that his Majesty Louis XVIII. was not mistaken in granting his family a patent of nobility."

The marquis, who had frowned at the name of Michel, softened his aspect.

"I shall follow with interest any efforts Monsieur Michel may make with that object in view," he said, at last, uttering those dignified words in a tone the Emperor Napoleon might have used on the eve of the battle of Marengo.

XXXVIII.

IN WHICH THE DAINTIEST FOOT OF FRANCE AND OF NAVARRE
FINDS THAT CINDERELLA'S SLIPPER DOES NOT FIT IT AS
WELL AS SEVEN-LEAGUE BOOTS.

HERE we are obliged to double in our tracks, as Jean Oullier would say in hunting parlance, and ask our reader's permission to retrograde a few hours, and follow the Comte de Bonneville and Petit-Pierre, who, as we have probably made it clear, are not the least important personages of our history.

The general's suppositions were perfectly correct. When the fleeing party left the subterranean passage, the Vendéan gentlemen crossed the ruins, entered the covered way, and there deliberated for a few moments on the proper course to pursue. The one whose identity was concealed under the name of Gaspard[1] thought it advisable to move cautiously. Bonneville's excitement when Michel announced the approach of the column had not escaped him; he heard an exclamation the count could not restrain, — "We must put Petit-Pierre in safety!" Consequently, he watched during their flight (as well as the feeble gleam of the torches would allow) the features of the little peasant, the result being that his manners became not only reserved but profoundly respectful.

"You said, monsieur," he now exclaimed, addressing the Comte de Bonneville, "that the safety of the person who accompanies you was to be considered before our own, being of the utmost importance to the cause we are resolved to sustain. Ought we not therefore to remain as a body-

[1] I refer those of my readers who would like to have a key to the real names of these men to the careful and interesting book of General Dermoncourt entitled "La Vendée and Madame."

guard to that person, so that if any danger threatens him, — and we are likely now to meet danger everywhere, — we may be at hand to make a rampart of our bodies for him."

"You would be right no doubt, monsieur, if the question were one of fighting," said the Comte de Bonneville. "But just now our object is flight, and for that the fewer we are in number, the easier and more certain our escape."

"Remember, count," said Gaspard, frowning, "that you take upon yourself at twenty-two years of age the responsibility of a very precious treasure."

"My devotion has already been judged, monsieur," replied the count, haughtily. "I shall endeavor to be worthy of the confidence with which I am honored."

Petit-Pierre, who had hitherto held his place silently in the midst of the little group, now thought the time had come to interfere.

"Come, come," he said; "the safety of a poor little peasant must not be made an apple of discord between the noblest champions of the cause you mention. I see it is necessary that I should say a word; we have no time to lose in useless discussion. But I wish, in the first place, my friends," said Petit-Pierre, in a tone of grateful affection, "to ask your pardon for the disguise I have thought best to keep up, even with you, for one purpose only, that of hearing your real thoughts, your frank opinions, unaffected by your desire to comply with what is known to be my most ardent desire. Now that Petit-Pierre has gained the information he sought, the regent will take part in your discussions. Meantime, let us separate here; the poorest place is all I need to pass the rest of the night, and Monsieur de Bonneville, who knows the country well, can easily find it for me."

"When may we be admitted to confer with her Royal Highness?" asked Pascal, bowing low before Petit-Pierre.

"As soon as her Royal Highness can find a suitable abode for her wandering majesty, Petit-Pierre will summon you; it will not be long. Remember that Petit-Pierre is firmly resolved never to abandon his friends."

"Petit-Pierre is a gallant lad!" cried Gaspard, gayly, "and his friends will prove, I hope, that they are worthy of him."

"Farewell, then," said Petit-Pierre. "Now that the mask is off, I thank you heartily, my gallant Gaspard, for not being deceived by it. Come, it is time to shake hands and part."

Each gentleman, in turn, took the hand that Petit-Pierre held out to him and kissed it respectfully. Then they all separated on their different ways, some to the right, others to the left, and soon disappeared from sight. Bonneville and Petit-Pierre were left alone.

"Well, what shall we do?" said the latter.

"Follow a direction diametrically opposed to those gentlemen."

"Forward, then, without losing another minute," cried Petit-Pierre, running toward the road.

"Oh! wait, wait a moment!" cried Bonneville. "Not in that way, if you please. Your Highness must — "

"Bonneville," said Petit-Pierre, "don't forget our agreement."

"True; Madame must please excuse — "

"Again! why, you are incorrigible!"

"I was about to say that Petit-Pierre must allow me to take him on my back."

"Very good; here's a great stone that seems planted here for the very purpose. Come nearer, count; come nearer."

Petit-Pierre was already on the stone as he spoke. The young count approached, and Petit-Pierre mounted astride his shoulders.

"You take to it famously," said Bonneville, starting.

"*Parbleu!*" exclaimed Petit-Pierre. "Saddle-my-nag was a fashionable game when I was young; I have often played at it."

"A good education, you see, is never wasted," said Bonneville, laughing.

"Count," said Petit-Pierre, "it is n't forbidden to speak, is it?"

"On the contrary."

"Well, then, as you are an old Chouan, and I am only beginning my apprenticeship at Chouannerie, do tell me why I am perched on your shoulders."

"What an inquisitive little person is Petit-Pierre!" said Bonneville.

"No; for I did as you requested, instantly, without discussion, though the position is a rather questionable one, you must admit, for a princess of the House of Bourbon."

"A princess of the House of Bourbon! Is there any such person here?"

"Ah! true. Well then, please to tell me why Petit-Pierre, who can walk and run and jump ditches, is perched on the shoulders of his friend Bonneville, who can't do any of those things with Petit-Pierre on his back."

"Well, I'll tell you; it is because Petit-Pierre has such a tiny foot."

"Tiny, yes; but firm, too!" exclaimed Petit-Pierre, as if his vanity was ruffled.

"Yes, but firm as it may be, it is too small not to be recognized."

"By whom?"

"By those who are on our traces."

"Good heavens!" exclaimed Petit-Pierre, with comic sadness; "who would ever have told me that some day, or some night, I should regret that my foot was not as large as that of Madame la Duchesse de ——"

"Poor Marquis de Souday, who was so fluttered by what you told him of your court acquaintances," said Bonneville, laughing, "what would he think now if he heard you talking with such assurance and experience of the feet of duchesses?"

"He would set it down to my rôle of page." Then after a moment's silence, "I understand very well that you should want them to lose my tracks; but you know we can't travel long in this way. Saint Christopher himself would get tired; and, sooner or later, that wretched little foot will leave its imprint on a patch of mud."

"We'll baffle the hounds for a short time, at any rate."

The young man bore to the left, attracted by the sound of a brook.

"What are you about?" asked Petit-Pierre. "You will lose the path; you are knee-deep in water now."

"Of course I am," said Bonneville, hoisting Petit-Pierre a little higher on his shoulders; "and now let them look for our traces!" he cried, hurrying up the bed of the brook.

"Ha, ha! that is clever of you!" cried Petit-Pierre. "You have missed your vocation, Bonneville; you ought to have been born in a primeval forest, or on the pampas of South America. The fact is that, to follow us, a trail is needed, and here there is none."

"Don't laugh. The man who is after us is an old hand at such pursuits; he fought in La Vendée in the days when Charette, almost single-handed, gave the Blues a terrible piece of work to do."

"Well, so much the better," cried Petit-Pierre, gayly; "better far to fight with those who are worth the trouble."

But in spite of the confidence he thus expressed, Petit-Pierre, after uttering the words, grew thoughtful, while Bonneville struggled bravely against the rolling stones and fallen branches which impeded him greatly, for he still followed the course of the brook.

After another quarter of an hour of such advance the brook fell into a second and a wider stream, which was really the one that circles at the base of the Viette des Biques. Here the water came to Bonneville's waist, and presently, to his great regret, he was forced to land and continue his way along one or the other bank of the little stream.

But the fugitives had only gone from Scylla to Charybdis, for the shores of the mountain-torrent, bristling with thorns, interlaced with trunks and roots of fallen trees, soon became impassable.

Bonneville placed Petit-Pierre on the ground, finding it

impossible to carry him further, and struck boldly into the thicket, requesting Petit-Pierre to follow closely through the opening made by his body; and thus, in spite of all obstacles, in spite too of the darkness of the night and the deeper darkness of the woods, he advanced in a straight line, as none but those who have constant experience in forests can succeed in doing.

The plan succeeded well, for after going some fifty yards they struck one of those paths called "lines," which are cut parallel to each other through forests, partly to mark the limits of felling, and partly to facilitate the transportation of the wood.

"Oh, what a good find!" said Petit-Pierre, who found it hard to walk through the tangle of underbrush and briers which rose at times above his head. "Here, at least, we can stretch our legs."

"Yes, and without leaving tracks," replied Bonneville, striking the ground, which was hard and rocky.

"Now all we want to know is which way to go," said Petit-Pierre.

"As we have, I believe, thrown those who are after us off the scent, we can now go whichever way you think best," replied Bonneville.

"You know that to-morrow night I have a rendezvous at La Cloutière with our friends from Paris."

"We can get to La Cloutière from here almost without leaving the woods, where we are safer than we should be in the open. We can take a path I know of to the forest of Touvois and the Grandes-Landes, to the west of which is La Cloutière; only, it is impossible for us to get there to-day."

"Why not?"

"Because we should have to make a number of detours, which would take us at least six hours; and that is very much more than you have strength for."

Petit-Pierre stamped his foot impatiently.

"I know a farm-house," continued Bonneville, "about

three miles this side of La Benaste, where we should be welcome, and where you could rest awhile before doing the remainder of the way."

"Very good," said Petit-Pierre; "then let us start at once. Which way?"

"Let me precede you," said Bonneville. "We must go to the right."

Bonneville took the direction he named, and stalked on with the persistency he had shown on leaving the banks of the stream. Petit-Pierre followed him.

From time to time the Comte de Bonneville stopped to reconnoitre the way and give his companion time to breathe. He warned him of the various obstacles in the path before they came to them, with a minuteness which showed how thoroughly familiar he was with the forest of Machecoul.

"You see I am avoiding the paths," he said to his companion, during one of their halts.

"Yes; and why do you do so?"

"Because they will be certain to look for us in the paths where the ground is soft; whereas here, where there has not been so much trampling, our steps are less likely to be observed."

"But perhaps this way is the longer."

"Yes, but safer."

They walked on for ten minutes in silence, when Bonneville stopped and caught his companion by the arm. The latter asked what the trouble was.

"Hush! or speak very low," said Bonneville.

"Why?"

"Don't you hear anything?"

"No."

"I hear voices."

"Where?"

"There, about five hundred yards in that direction. I fancy I can distinguish through the branches a ruddy gleam of light."

"Yes, and so can I."

"What do you suppose it is?"

"I ask you that."

"The devil!"

"Can it be charcoal-burners?"

"No; this is not the time of year when they start their kilns. And if they were charcoal-burners, I should not like to trust them; I have no right, being your guide, to run any risks."

"Is there any other road we could take?"

"Yes."

"Then suppose we try it."

"I don't want to take it till reduced to the last extremity."

"Why not?"

"Because it crosses a marsh."

"Pooh! you who can walk on the water like Saint Peter! Don't you know the marsh?"

"I know it very well. I have often shot snipe there; but —"

"But?"

"It was by daylight."

"And this marsh —"

"Is a bog where, even in the daytime, I have come near sinking."

"Then let us risk an encounter with these worthy people. I should not be sorry to warm myself at their fire."

"Stay here; and let me go and reconnoitre."

"But —"

"Don't be afraid."

So saying, Bonneville disappeared noiselessly in the darkness.

XXXIX.

PETIT-PIERRE MAKES THE BEST MEAL HE EVER MADE IN HIS LIFE.

PETIT-PIERRE, left alone, leaned against a tree, and there, silent, motionless, with fixed eyes and straining ears, he waited, striving to catch every sound as it passed him. For five minutes he heard nothing except a sort of hum which came from the direction of the lights.

Suddenly the neighing of a horse echoed through the forest. Petit-Pierre trembled. Almost at the same moment a light sound came from the bushes, and a shadow rose before him; it was Bonneville.

Bonneville, who did not see Petit-Pierre leaning against the trunk of a tree, called him twice gently. Petit-Pierre bounded toward him.

"Quick! quick!" said Bonneville, dragging Petit-Pierre away.

"What is it?"

"Not an instant to lose! Come! come!"

Then, as he ran, he said:—

"A camp of soldiers. If there were men only I might have warmed myself at their fire without their seeing or hearing me; but a horse smelt me out and neighed."

"I heard it."

"Then you understand; not a word. We must take to our legs, that's all."

As he spoke they were running along a wood-road, which fortunately came in their way. After a time Bonneville drew Petit-Pierre into the bushes.

"Get your breath," he said.

While Petit-Pierre rested, Bonneville tried to make out where they were.

"Are we lost?" asked Petit-Pierre, uneasily.

"Oh, no danger of that!" said Bonneville. "I'm only looking for a way to avoid that horrid marsh."

"If it leads us straight to our object we had better take it," said Petit-Pierre.

"We must," replied Bonneville; "I don't see any other way."

"Forward, then!" cried Petit-Pierre; "only, you must guide me."

Bonneville made no answer; but in proof of urgency, he started at once, and instead of following the "line" path on which they were, he turned to the right and plunged into the thicket. At the end of ten minutes' march the underbrush lessened. They were nearing the edge of the forest, and they could hear before them the swishing of the reeds in the wind.

"Aha!" cried Petit-Pierre, recognizing the sound; "we are close to the marsh now."

"Yes," said Bonneville; "and I ought not to conceal from you that this is the most critical moment of our flight."

So saying, the young man took from his pocket a knife, which might, if necessary, be used as a dagger, and cut down a sapling, removing all the branches, but taking care to hide each one as he lopped it off.

"Now," he said, "my poor Petit-Pierre, you must resign yourself and go back to your former place on my shoulders."

Petit-Pierre instantly did as he was told, and Bonneville went forward toward the marsh. His advance under the weight he carried, hindered by the long sapling which he used to test the condition of the ground at every step, was horribly difficult. Often he sank into the slough almost to his knees, and the earth, which seemed soft enough as it gave way under him, offered a positive resistance when he sought to extricate himself. It was, in fact, with the utmost difficulty that he could get his legs out of it; it seemed as though the gulf that opened at their feet was unwilling to relinquish its prey.

"Let me give you some advice, my dear count," said Petit-Pierre.

Bonneville stopped and wiped his brow.

"If, instead of paddling in this mire, you stepped from tuft to tuft of those reeds which are growing here, I think you would find a better foothold."

"Yes," said Bonneville, "I should; but we should leave more visible traces." Then, a moment later, he added, "No matter. You are right; it is best."

And changing his direction a little, Bonneville took to the reeds. The matted roots of the water-plants had, in fact, made little islets of a foot or more in circumference, which gave a fairly good foothold over the boggy ground. The young man felt them, one after the other, with the end of his stick and stepped from each to each.

Nevertheless, he slipped constantly. Burdened with Petit-Pierre's weight, he had great difficulty in recovering himself; and before long this toilsome struggle so completely exhausted him he was forced to ask Petit-Pierre to get down and let him rest awhile.

"You are worn out, my poor Bonneville," said Petit-Pierre. "Is it very much farther, this marsh of yours?"

"Two or three hundred yards more, and then we re-enter the forest as far as the line-path to Benaste, which will take us direct to the farm."

"Can you go as far as that?"

"I hope so."

"Good God! how I wish I could carry you myself, or at any rate, walk beside you."

These words restored the count's courage. Giving up his second method of advancing from tuft to tuft, he plunged resolutely into the mire. But the more he advanced, the more the slough appeared to move and deepen. Suddenly Bonneville, who had made a mistake and placed his foot on a spot he had not had time to sound, felt himself sinking rapidly and likely to disappear.

"If I sink altogether," he said, "fling yourself either to right or left. These dangerous places are never very wide."

Petit-Pierre sprang off at once, not to save himself, but to lighten Bonneville of the additional weight.

"Oh, my friend!" he cried, with an aching heart and eyes wet with tears as he listened to that generous cry of devotion and self-forgetfulness, "think only of yourself, I command you."

The young count had already sunk to the waist. Fortunately, he had time to put his sapling across the bog before him; and as each end rested on a tuft of reeds sufficiently strong to bear a weight, he was able, thanks to the support they gave, and aided by Petit-Pierre, who held him by the collar of his coat, to extricate himself from the dangerous place.

Soon the ground became more solid; the black line of the woods which had all along marked the horizon came nearer and increased in height. The fugitives were evidently approaching the end of the bog.

"At last!" cried Bonneville.

"Ouf!" exclaimed Petit-Pierre, slipping off Bonneville's shoulders as soon as he felt that the earth was solid beneath their feet. "Ouf! you must be worn out, my dear count."

"Out of breath, that's all," replied Bonneville.

"Good heavens!" cried Petit-Pierre; "to think that I should have nothing to give you, — not even the flask of a soldier or pilgrim, or the crust of a beggar's loaf!"

"Pooh!" said the count; "my strength does n't come from my stomach."

"Tell me where it does come from, my dear count, and I will try to be as strong as you."

"Are you hungry?"

"I'll admit that I could eat something."

"Alas!" said the count; "you make me regret now what I cared little for a moment ago."

Petit-Pierre laughed; and then, for the purpose of keeping up his companion's heart, he cried out gayly: —

"Bonneville, call the usher and let him notify the chamberlain on duty to order the stewards to bring my lunch-basket. I would like one of those snipe I hear whistling about us."

"Her Royal Highness is served," said the count, kneeling on one knee, and offering on the top of his hat an object which Petit-Pierre seized eagerly.

"Bread!" he cried.

"Black bread," said Bonneville.

"Oh, no matter! I can't see the color at night."

"Dry bread! doubly dry!"

"But it is bread, at any rate."

And Petit-Pierre set his handsome teeth into the crust, which had been drying in the count's pocket for the last two days.

"And when I think," said Petit-Pierre, "that General Dermoncourt is probably at this moment eating my supper at Souday, is n't it aggravating?" Then, suddenly, "Oh! forgive me, my dear guide," he went on, "but my stomach got the better of my heart; I forgot to offer you half my supper."

"Thanks," replied Bonneville; "but my appetite is n't strong enough yet to munch stones. In return for your gracious offer, I'll show you how to make your poor supper less husky."

Bonneville took the bread, broke it, not without difficulty, into little bits, soaked it in a brook that was flowing quite near them, called Petit-Pierre, sat down himself on one side the brook, while Petit-Pierre sat on the other, and taking out one by one the softened crusts, presented them to his famished companion.

"Upon my honor!" said the latter, when he came to the last crumb, "I have n't eaten such a good supper for twenty years. Bonneville, I appoint you steward of my household."

"Meantime," said the count, "I am your guide. Come, luxury enough; we must continue our way."

"I'm ready," said Petit-Pierre, springing gayly to his feet."

Again they started through the woods, and half an hour's walking brought them to a river which they were forced to cross. Bonneville tried his usual method; but at the first step, the water came to his waist, at the second to his shoulders. Feeling himself dragged by the current he caught at the branch of a tree and returned to the bank.

It was necessary to find a way to cross. At a distance of about three hundred yards Bonneville thought he had found one; but it was nothing more than the trunk of a tree lately blown down by the wind, and still bearing all its branches.

"Do you think you can walk over that?" he asked Petit-Pierre.

"If you can, I can," replied the latter.

"Hold on to the branches, and don't have any conceit about your powers; don't raise one foot till you are quite sure the other is firm," said Bonneville, climbing first on to the trunk of the tree.

"I'm to follow, I suppose?"

"Wait till I can give you a hand."

"Here I am! Goodness! what a number of things one ought to know in order to roam the wilds; I never should have thought it."

"Don't talk, for God's sake! pay attention to your feet. One moment! Stop where you are; don't move. Here's a branch you can't get by; I'll cut it."

Just as he stooped to do as he said, the count heard a smothered cry behind him and the fall of a body into the water. He looked back. Petit-Pierre had disappeared.

Without losing a second, Bonneville dropped into the same place; and his luck served him well, for going to the bottom of the river, which was not more than eight feet deep at this place, his hand came in contact with Petit-Pierre's leg.

He seized it, trembling with emotion, and paying no heed to the uncomfortable position in which he held the body he struck out for the bank of the stream, which was, happily, as narrow as it was deep. Petit-Pierre made no movement. Bonneville took him in his arms and laid him on the dry leaves, calling, entreating, even shaking him.

Petit-Pierre continued silent and motionless. The count tore his hair in his anguish.

"Oh, it is my fault! my fault!" he cried. "O God, you have punished my pride! I counted too much on myself; I thought I could save her. Oh, my life,— take my life, O God! for one sigh, one breath — "

The cool night air did more to bring Petit-Pierre to life than all Bonneville's lamentations; at the end of a few minutes he opened his eyes and sneezed.

Bonneville, who, in his paroxysm of grief, swore not to survive the being whose death he thought he had caused, gave a cry of joy and fell on his knees by Petit-Pierre, who was now sufficiently recovered to understand his last words.

"Bonneville," said Petit-Pierre, "you did n't say 'God bless you!' when I sneezed, and now I shall have a cold in my head."

"Living! living! living!" cried Bonneville, as exuberant in his joy as he was in his grief.

"Yes, living enough, thanks to you. If you were any other than you are, I would swear to you never to forget it."

"You are soaked!"

"Yes, my shoes especially, Bonneville. The water keeps running down, running down in a most disagreeable manner."

"And no fire! no means to make one!"

"Pooh! we shall get warm in walking. I speak in the plural, for you must be as wet as I am; in fact, it's your third bath, — one was of mud."

"Oh, don't think of me! Can you walk?"

"I believe so, as soon as I empty my shoes."

Bonneville helped Petit-Pierre to get rid of the water which filled her shoes. Then he took off his own thick jacket, and having wrung the water from it, he put it over her shoulders, saying: —

"Now for Benaste, and fast, too!"

"Ha! Bonneville," exclaimed Petit-Pierre; "a fine gain we have made by trying to avoid that camp-fire which would be everything to us just now!"

"We can't go back and deliver ourselves up," said Bonneville, with a look of despair.

"Nonsense! don't take my little joke as a reproach. What an ill-regulated mind you have! Come, let us march, march! Now that I use my legs I feel I am drying up; in ten minutes I shall begin to perspire."

There was no need to hasten Bonneville. He advanced so rapidly that Petit-Pierre could barely keep up with him; and from time to time she was forced to remind him that her legs were not as long as his.

But Bonneville could not recover from the shock of emotion caused by the accident to his young companion, and he now completely lost his head on discovering that, among these bushes he once knew so well, he had missed his way. A dozen times he had stopped as he entered a "line" path and looked about him, and each time, after shaking his head, he plunged onward in a sort of frenzy.

At last Petit-Pierre, who could scarcely keep up with him, except by running, said, as she noticed his increasing agitation: —

"Tell me what is the matter, dear count."

"The matter is that I am a wretched man," said Bonneville. "I relied too much on my knowledge of these localities, and — and — "

"We have lost our way?"

"I fear so."

"And I am sure of it. See, here is a branch I remember breaking when we passed here just now; we are turning in a circle. You see how I profit by your lessons, Bonneville," added Petit-Pierre, triumphantly.

"Ah!" said Bonneville; "I see what set me wrong."

"What was it?"

"When we left the water I landed on the side we had just left, and in my agitation at your accident, I did not notice the mistake."

"So that our plunge bath was absolutely useless!" cried Petit-Pierre, laughing heartily.

"Oh! for God's sake, Madame, don't laugh like that; your gayety cuts me to the heart."

"Well, it warms me."

"Then you are cold?"

"A little; but that's not the worst."

"What is worse?"

"Why, for half an hour you have not dared to tell me we are lost, and for half an hour I've not dared to tell you that my legs seem to be giving way and refusing to do their duty."

"Then what is to become of us?"

"Well, well! am I to play your part as man and give you courage? So be it. The council is open; what is your opinion?"

"That we cannot reach Benaste to-night."

"Next?"

"That we must try to get to the nearest farm-house before daylight."

"Very good," said Petit-Pierre. "Have you any idea of where we are?"

"No stars in the sky, no moon —"

"And no compass," added Petit-Pierre, laughing, and trying by a joke to revive her companion's nerve.

"Wait."

"Ah! you have an idea, I'm sure!"

"I happened to notice the vane on the castle just at dusk; the wind was east."

Bonneville wet his finger in his mouth and held it up.

"What's that for?"

"A weathercock. There's the north," he said, unhesitatingly; "if we walk in the teeth of the wind we shall come out on the plain near Saint-Philbert."

"Yes, by walking; but that's the difficulty."

"Will you let me carry you in my arms?"

"You have enough to carry in yourself, my poor Bonneville."

The duchess rose with an effort, for during the last few moments she had seated herself, or rather let herself drop, at the foot of a tree.

"There!" she said; "now I am on my feet, and I mean that these rebellious legs shall carry me. I will conquer them as I would all rebels; that's what I'm here for."

And the brave woman made four or five steps; but her fatigue was so great, her limbs so stiffened by the icy bath she had taken, that she staggered and came near falling. Bonneville sprang to support her.

"Heart of God!" she cried; "let me alone, Monsieur de Bonneville. I will put this miserable body that God has made so frail and delicate on the level of the soul it covers. Don't give it any help, count; don't support it. Ha! you stagger, do you? ha! you are giving way? Well, if you won't march at the common step you shall be made to charge, and we'll see if in a week you are not as submissive to my will as a beast of burden."

So saying, and joining the action to the word, Petit-Pierre started forward at such a pace that her guide had some difficulty in overtaking her. But the last effort exhausted her; and when Bonneville did rejoin her, she was once more seated, with her face hidden in her two hands. Petit-Pierre was weeping, — weeping with anger rather than pain.

"O God!" she muttered; "you have set me the task of a giant, but you have given me only the strength of a woman."

Willing or not, Bonneville took Petit-Pierre in his arms and hurried along. The words that Gaspard had said to him as they left the vaults rang in his ears. He felt that so delicate a body could not bear up any longer under these violent shocks, and he resolved to spend his last strength in putting the treasure confided to him in a place of safety. He knew now that a few moments wasted might mean death to his companion.

For over fifteen minutes the brave man kept on rapidly. His hat fell off, but no longer caring for the trail he left behind him, the count did not stop to pick it up. He felt the body of the duchess shuddering with cold in his arms, he heard her teeth chattering; and the sound spurred him as the applause of a crowd spurs a race-horse, and gave him superhuman energy.

But, little by little, this fictitious strength gave way. Bonneville's legs would only obey him mechanically; the blood seemed to settle on his chest and choked him. He felt his heart swell; he could not breathe; his breath rattled; a cold sweat poured from his brow; his arteries throbbed as if his head must burst. From time to time a thick cloud covered his eyes, marbled with flame. Soon he staggered at every slope, stumbled at every stone; his failing knees, powerless to straighten themselves, could only go forward by a mighty effort.

"Stop! stop! Monsieur de Bonneville," cried Petit-Pierre; "stop, I command you!"

"No, I will not stop," replied Bonneville. "I have still some strength, thank God! and I shall use it to the end. Stop? stop? when we are almost into port? when at the cost of a little further effort I shall put you in safety? There! see that; look there!"

And as he spoke they saw at the end of the path they were following a broad band of ruddy light which rose above the horizon; and on that glow a black and angular shape stood out distinctly, indicating a house. Day was dawning. They had now reached the end of the wood and were at the edge of fields.

But just as Bonneville gave that cry of joy, his legs bent under him; he fell to his knees. Then, with a last supreme effort, he cast himself gently backward as if at the moment when his consciousness left him he meant to spare his precious burden from the dangers of a fall. Petit-Pierre released herself from his grasp and stood at his feet, but so feebly that she seemed scarcely stronger than her companion. She tried to raise the count, but could not do it. Bonneville, for his part, put his hands to his mouth, — no doubt to give the owl's cry of the Chouans; but his breath failed him, and he scarcely uttered the words, "Don't forget —" before he fainted entirely.

The house they had seen was not more than seven or eight hundred steps from the place where Bonneville had fallen. Petit-Pierre determined to go there and ask at all risks for assistance to her friend. Making a supreme effort she started in that direction. Just as she passed a crossway Petit-Pierre saw a man on one of the paths that led to it. She called to him, but he did not turn his head.

Then Petit-Pierre, either by a sudden inspiration or because she gave that meaning to Bonneville's last words, utilized a lesson the count had taught her. Putting her hands to her mouth she uttered, as best she could, the cry of the screech-owl.

The man stopped instantly, turned back, and came to Petit-Pierre.

"My friend," she cried, as soon as he came within reach of her voice, "if you need gold, I will give it to you; but, for God's sake, come and help me save an unfortunate man who is dying."

Then, with all her remaining strength, and seeing that the man was following her, Petit-Pierre hurried back to

Bonneville and raised his head by an effort. The count was still unconscious.

As soon as the new-comer reached them and glanced at the prostrate man, he said: —

"You need not offer me gold to induce me to help Monsieur le Comte de Bonneville."

Petit-Pierre looked at the man attentively.

"Jean Oullier!" she cried, recognizing the Marquis de Souday's keeper in the dawning light, — "Jean Oullier, can you find a safe refuge for my friend and for me close by?"

"There is no house but this within a mile or two," he said.

He spoke of it with repugnance, but Petit-Pierre either did not or would not notice the tone.

"You must guide me and carry him."

"Down *there?*" cried Jean Oullier.

"Yes; are not they royalists? — the persons who live in that house, I mean."

"I don't know yet," said Jean Oullier.

"Go on; I put our lives in your hands, Jean Oullier, and I know that you deserve my utmost confidence."

Jean Oullier took Bonneville, still unconscious, on his shoulders, and led Petit-Pierre by the hand. He walked toward the house, which was that belonging to Joseph Picaut and his sister-in-law, the widow of Pascal.

Jean Oullier mounted the hedge-bank as easily as though he were only carrying a game-bag, instead of the body of a man. Once in the orchard, however, he advanced cautiously. Every one was still sleeping in Joseph's part of the house; but it was not so in the widow's room. In the gleam from the windows a shadow could be seen passing to and fro behind the curtains.

Jean Oullier seemed now to decide between two courses.

"Faith! weighing one against the other," he muttered to himself, "I like it as well this way."

And he walked resolutely to that part of the house which

belonged to Pascal. When he reached the door he opened it. Pascal's body lay on the bed. The widow had lighted two candles, and was praying beside the dead. Hearing the door open, she rose and turned round.

"Widow Pascal," said Jean Oullier, without releasing his burden or the hand of Petit-Pierre, "I saved your life to-night at the Viette des Biques."

Marianne looked at him in astonishment, as if trying to recall her recollections.

"Don't you believe me?"

"Yes, Jean Oullier, I believe you; I know you are not a man to tell a lie, were it even to save your life. Besides, I heard the shot and I suspected whose hand fired it."

"Widow Pascal, will you avenge your husband and make your fortune at one stroke? I bring you the means."

"How?"

"Here," continued Jean Oullier, "are Madame la Duchesse de Berry and Monsieur le Comte de Bonneville, who might have died, perhaps, of hunger and fatigue, if I had not come, as I have, to ask you to shelter them; here they are."

The widow looked at all three in stupefaction, yet with a visible interest.

"This head, which you see here," continued Jean Oullier, "is worth its weight in gold. You can deliver it up if you so please, and, as I told you, avenge your husband and make your fortune by that act."

"Jean Oullier," replied the widow, in a grave voice, "God commands us to do charity to all, whether great or small. Two unfortunate persons have come to my door; I shall not repulse them. Two exiles ask me to shelter them, and my house shall crumble about my ears before I betray them." Then, with a simple gesture, to which her action gave a splendid grandeur, she added: —

"Enter, Jean Oullier; enter fearlessly, — you, and those who are with you."

They entered. While Petit-Pierre was helping Jean

Oullier to place the count in a chair, the old keeper said to her in a low voice: —

"Madame, put back your own fair hair behind your wig; it made me guess the truth I have told this woman, but others ought not to see it."

XL.

EQUALITY IN DEATH.

THE same day, about two in the afternoon, Courtin left La Logerie to go to Machecoul under pretence of buying a draught-ox, but in reality to get news of the events of the night, — events in which the municipal functionary had a special interest, as our readers will fully understand.

When he reached the ford at Pont-Farcy, he found some men lifting the body of Tinguy's son, and around them several women and children, who were gazing at the dead body with the curiosity natural to their sex and years. When the mayor of La Logerie, stimulating his pony by a stick with a leathern thong, which he carried in his hand, made it enter the river, all eyes were turned upon him, and the conversation ceased as if by magic, though up to that moment it had been very eager and animated.

"Well, what's going on, *gars?*" asked Courtin, making his animal cross the river diagonally so as to reach land precisely opposite to the group.

"A death," replied one of the men, with the laconic brevity of a Vendéan peasant.

Courtin looked at the corpse and saw that it wore a uniform.

"Luckily," he said, "it is n't any one who belongs about here."

"You're mistaken, Monsieur Courtin," replied the gloomy voice of a man in a brown jacket.

The title of *monsieur* thus given to him, and given, too, with a certain emphasis, was in no wise flattering to the farmer of La Logerie. Under the circumstances and in the phase of public feeling La Vendée had just entered, he knew that this title of monsieur, in the mouth of a peasant, when it was not given as a testimony of respect, meant either an insult or a threat, — two things which affected Courtin quite differently.

In short, the mayor of La Logerie did himself the justice not to take the title thus bestowed upon him as a mark of consideration, and he therefore resolved to be prudent.

"And yet I think," he said, in a mild and gentle voice, "that he wears a chasseur's uniform."

"Pooh! uniform!" retorted the same peasant; "as if you did n't know that the *man-hunt*" (this was the name the Vendéan peasantry gave to the conscription) "does n't respect our sons and brothers more than it does those of others. It seems to me you ought to know that, mayor as you are."

Again there was silence, — a silence so oppressive to Courtin that he once more interrupted it. "Does any one know the name of the poor *gars* who has perished so unfortunately?" he asked, making immense but fruitless efforts to force a tear to his eye.

No one answered. The silence became more and more significant.

"Does any one know if there were other victims? Was any one killed among our own *gars*? I hear a number of shots were fired."

"As for other victims," said the same peasant, "I know as yet of only one, — this one here; though perhaps it is a sin to talk of such victims beside a Christian corpse."

As he spoke the peasant turned aside and, fixing his eyes on Courtin, he pointed with his finger to the body of Jean Oullier's dog, lying on the bank, partly in the water which flowed over it. Maître Courtin turned pale; he coughed, as if an invisible hand had clutched his throat.

"What's that?" he said; "a dog? Ha! if we had only to mourn for that kind of victim our tears would be few."

"Nay, nay," said the man in the brown jacket; "the

blood of a dog must be paid for, Maître Courtin, like
everything else. I'm certain that the master of poor
Pataud won't forget the man who shot his dog, coming out
of Montaigu, with leaden wolf-balls, three of which entered
his body."

As he finished speaking the man, apparently thinking
he had exchanged words enough with Courtin, did not wait
for any answer, but turned on his heel, passed up a bank,
and disappeared behind its hedge. As for the other men,
they resumed their march with the body. The women and
children followed behind tumultuously, praying aloud.
Courtin was left alone.

"Bah!" he said to himself, jabbing his pony with his
one spur; "before I pay for what Jean Oullier lays to my
account, he'll have to escape the clutches which, thanks
to me, are on him at this moment, — it won't be easy,
though, of course, it is possible."

Maître Courtin continued his way; but his curiosity
was greater than ever, and he felt he could not wait
till the amble of his steed took him to Machecoul before
satisfying it.

He happened at this moment to be passing the cross of
La Bertaudière, near which the road leading to the house
of the Picauts joined the main road. He thought of
Pascal, who could tell him the news better than any one,
as he had sent him to guide the troops the night before.

"What a jackass I am!" he cried, speaking to himself.
"It will only take me half an hour out of my way, and I
can hear the truth from a mouth that won't lie to me.
I'll go to Pascal; he'll tell me the result of the trick."

Maître Courtin turned, therefore, to the right; and five
minutes later he crossed the little orchard and made his
entrance over a heap of manure into the courtyard of
Pascal's dwelling.

Joseph, sitting on a horse-collar, was smoking his pipe
before the door of his half of the house. Seeing who his
visitor was he did not think it worth while to disturb him-

self. Courtin, who had an admirably keen faculty for seeing all without appearing to notice anything, fastened his pony to one of the iron rings that were screwed into the wall. Then, turning to Joseph, he said: —

"Is your brother at home?"

"Yes, he is still there," replied Picaut, dwelling on the word *still* in a manner that seemed a little strange to the mayor of La Logerie; "do you want him again to-day to guide the red-breeches to Souday?"

Courtin bit his lips and made no reply to Joseph, while to himself he said, as he knocked at the door of the other Picaut: —

"How came that fool of a Pascal to tell his rascally brother it was I who sent him on that errand? Upon my soul, one can't do anything in these parts without everybody gabbling about it within twenty-four hours!"

Courtin's monologue hindered him from noticing that his knock was not immediately answered, and that the door, contrary to the trustful habits of the peasantry, was bolted.

At last, however, the door opened, and when Courtin's eyes fell upon the scene before him he was so unprepared for what he saw that he actually recoiled from the threshold.

"Who is dead here?" he asked.

"Look!" replied the widow, without leaving her seat in the chimney-corner, which she had resumed after opening the door.

Courtin turned his eyes again to the bed, and though he could see beneath the sheet only the outline of a man's form, he guessed the truth.

"Pascal!" he cried; "is it Pascal?"

"I thought you knew it," said the widow.

"I?"

"Yes, you, — you, who are the chief cause of his death."

"I? — I?" replied Courtin, remembering what Joseph had just said to him, and feeling it all-important for his own safety to deny his share in the matter. "I swear to you, on the word of an honest man, that I have not seen your husband for over a week."

"Don't swear," replied the widow. "Pascal never swore; neither did he lie."

"But who told you that I had seen him?" persisted Courtin. "It is too bad to blame me for nothing!"

"Don't lie in presence of the dead, Monsieur Courtin," said Marianne; "it will bring down evil upon you."

"I am not lying," stammered the man.

"Pascal left this house to meet you; you engaged him as guide for the soldiers."

Courtin made a movement of denial.

"Oh! I don't blame you for that," continued the widow, looking at a peasant-girl, about twenty-five to thirty years of age, who was winding her distaff in the opposite corner of the fireplace; "it was his duty to give assistance to those who want to prevent our country from being torn by civil war."

"That's my object, my sole object," replied Courtin, lowering his voice, so that the young peasant-woman hardly heard him. "I wish the government would rid us once for all of these fomenters of trouble, — these nobles who crush us with their wealth in peace, and massacre us when it comes to war. I am doing my best for this end, Mistress Picaut; but I daren't boast of it, you see, because you never know what the people about here may do to you."

"Why should you complain if they strike you from behind, when you hide yourself in striking them?" said Marianne, with a look of the deepest contempt.

"Damn it! one does as one dares, Mistress Picaut," replied Courtin, with some embarrassment. "It is not given to all the world to be brave and bold like your poor husband. But we'll revenge him, that good Pascal! we'll revenge him. I swear it to you!"

"Thank you; but I don't want you to meddle in that, Monsieur Courtin," said the widow, in a voice that seemed almost threatening, so hard and bitter was it. "You have meddled too much already in the affairs of this poor household. Spend your good offices on others in future."

"As you please, Mistress Picaut. Alas! I loved your good husband so truly that I'll do anything I can to please you." Then, suddenly turning toward the young peasant-woman, whom he had seemed not to notice up to that time, "Who is this young woman?" he said.

"A cousin of mine, who came this morning from Port-Saint-Père, to help me in paying the last duties to my poor Pascal, and to keep me company."

"From Port-Saint-Père this morning! Ha, ha! Mistress Picaut, she must be a good walker, if she did that distance so quickly."

The poor widow, unused to lying, having never in her life had occasion to lie, lied badly. She bit her lips, and gave Courtin an angry look, which, happily, he did not see, being occupied at the moment in a close examination of a peasant's costume which was drying before the fire. The two articles which seemed to attract him most were a pair of shoes and a shirt. The shoes, though iron-nailed and made of common leather, were of a shape not common among cottagers, and the shirt was of the finest linen cambric.

"Soft stuff! soft stuff!" he muttered, rubbing the delicate tissue between his fingers; "it's my opinion it won't scratch the skin of whoever wears it."

The young peasant-woman now thought it time to come to the help of the widow, who seemed on thorns and whose forehead was clouding over in a visibly threatening way.

"Yes," she said; "those are some old clothes I bought of a dealer in Nantes, to make over for my little nephew."

"And you washed them before sewing them? Faith, you're right, my girl! for," added Courtin, looking fixedly at her, "no one knows who has worn the garments of those old-clothes dealers, — it may have been a prince, or it may have been a leper."

"Maître Courtin," interrupted Marianne, who seemed annoyed by the conversation, "your pony is getting restless."

Courtin listened.

"If I did n't hear your brother-in-law walking in the garret overhead I should think he was teasing it, the ill-natured fellow!"

At this new proof of the essentially detective nature of the mayor of La Logerie, the young peasant-woman turned pale; and her paleness increased when she heard Courtin, who rose to look after his pony through the casement, mutter, as if to himself: —

"Why, no; there he is, that fellow! He is tickling my horse with the end of his whip." Then, returning to the widow, he said, "Who have you got up in your garret, mistress?"

The young woman was about to answer that Joseph had a wife and children, and that the garret was common to all; but the widow did not give her time to begin the sentence.

"Maître Courtin," she said, standing up, "are not your questions coming to an end soon? I hate spies, I warn you, whether they are white or red."

"Since when is a friendly talk among friends called spying? Whew! you have grown very suspicious, all of a sudden."

The eyes of the younger woman entreated the widow to be more cautious; but her impetuous hostess could no longer contain herself.

"Among friends! friends, indeed!" she said. "Find your friends among your fellows, — I mean among cowards and traitors; and know, once for all, that the widow of Pascal Picaut is not among them. Go, and leave me to my grief, which you have disturbed too long."

"Yes, yes," said Courtin, with an admirably played good-humor; "my presence must be unpleasant to you. I ought to have thought of that before, and I beg your pardon for not having done so. You are determined to see in me the cause of your husband's death, and that grieves me; oh! it grieves me, Mistress Picaut, for I loved him heartily and wouldn't have harmed him for the world. But, since you feel as you do, and drive me out of your house, I'll go, I'll go; don't take on like that."

Just then the widow, who seemed more and more disturbed, glanced rapidly at the younger woman and showed her by that glance the bread-box, which stood beside the door. On that box was a pocket-inkstand, which had, no doubt, been used to write the order Jean Oullier had taken in the morning to the Marquis de Souday. This inkstand was of green morocco, and with it lay a sort of tube, containing all that was necessary for writing a letter. As Courtin went to the door he could not fail to see the inkstand and a few scattered papers that lay beside it.

The young woman understood the sign and saw the danger; and before the mayor of La Logerie turned round she had passed, light as a fawn, behind him, and seated herself on the bread-box, so as to hide the unlucky implement completely. Courtin seemed to pay no attention to this manœuvre.

"Well, good-bye to you, Mistress Picaut," he said. "I have lost a comrade in your husband whom I greatly valued; you doubt that, but time will prove it to you."

The widow did not answer; she had said to Courtin all she had to say, and she now seemed to take no notice of him. Motionless, with crossed arms, she was gazing at the corpse, whose rigid form was defined under the sheet that covered it.

"Ho! so you are there, my pretty girl," said Courtin, stopping before the younger woman.

"It was too hot near the fire."

"Take good care of your cousin, my girl," continued Courtin; "this death has made her a wild beast. She is almost as savage as the she-wolves of Machecoul! Well, spin away, my dear; though you may twist your spindle or turn your wheel as best you can, and you'll never weave such fine linen as you've got there in that shirt." Then he left the room and shut the door, muttering, "Fine linen, very fine!"

"Quick! quick! hide all those things!" cried the widow. "He has gone out only to come back."

Quick as thought the young woman pushed the inkstand between the box and the wall; but rapid as the movement was, it was still too late. The upper half of the door was suddenly opened, and Courtin's head appeared above the lower.

"I've startled you; beg pardon," said Courtin. "I did it from a good motive; I want to know when the funeral takes place."

"To-morrow, I think," said the young woman.

"Will you go away, you villanous rascal!" cried the widow, springing toward him, and brandishing the heavy tongs with which she moved the logs in her great fireplace.

Courtin, thoroughly frightened, withdrew. Mistress Picaut, as Courtin called her, closed the upper shutter violently.

The mayor of La Logerie unfastened his pony, picked up a handful of straw, and cleaned off the saddle, which Joseph, maliciously and out of hatred, — a hatred which he inculcated to his children against the "curs," — had smeared with cows' dung from pommel to crupper. Then, without complaining or retaliating, as if the accident he had just remedied was a perfectly natural one, he mounted his steed with an indifferent air, and even stopped on his way through the orchard to see if the apples were properly setting, with the eye of a connoisseur. But no sooner had he reached the cross of La Bertaudière and turned his horse into the high-road toward Machecoul than he seized his stick by the thick end, and using the leather thong on one flank, and digging his single spur persistently and furiously into the other flank of his beast, he contrived to make that animal take a gait of which it looked utterly incapable.

"There, he's gone at last!" said the younger peasant-woman, who had watched his movements from the window.

"Yes; but that may be none the better for you, Madame," said the widow.

"What do you mean?"

"Oh! I know what I mean."

"Do you think he has gone to denounce us?"

"He is thought to be capable of it. I know nothing personally, for I don't concern myself in such gossip; but his evil face has always led me to think that even the Whites didn't do him injustice."

"You are right," said the young woman, who began to be uneasy; "his face is one that could never inspire confidence."

"Ah! Madame, why did you not keep Jean Oullier near you?" said the widow. "There's an honest man, and a faithful one."

"I had orders to send to the château de Souday. He is to come back this evening with horses so that we may leave your house as soon as possible, for I know we increase your sorrow and add to your cares."

The widow did not answer. With her face hidden in her hands, she was weeping.

"Poor woman!" murmured the duchess; "your tears fall drop by drop upon my heart, where each leaves a painful furrow. Alas! this is the terrible, the inevitable result of revolutions. It is on the head of those who make them that the curse of all this blood and all these tears must fall."

"May it not rather fall, if God is just, on the heads of those who cause them?" said the widow, in a deep and muffled voice, which made her hearer quiver.

"Do you hate us so bitterly?" asked the latter, sadly.

"Yes, I hate you," said the widow. "How can you expect me to love you?"

"Alas! I understand; yes, your husband's death — "

"No, you do not understand," said Marianne, shaking her head.

The younger woman made a sign as if to say, "Explain yourself."

"No," said the widow, "it is not because the man who for fifteen years has been my all in life will be to-morrow in his bed of earth; it is not because when I was a child I witnessed the massacres of Légé, and saw my dear ones killed beneath your banner, and felt their blood spattering my face; it is not because for ten whole years those who fought for your ancestors persecuted mine, burned their houses, ravaged their fields, — no, I repeat, it is not for that, nor all that, that I hate you."

"Then why is it?"

"Because it seems to me an impious thing that a family, a race, should claim the place of God, our only master here below, — the master of us all, such as we are, great and small; impious to declare that we are born the slaves of that family, to suppose that a people it has tortured have not the right to turn upon their bed of suffering unless they first obtain permission! You belong to that selfish family; you have come of that tyrant race. It is for that I hate you."

"And yet you have given me shelter; you have laid aside your grief to lavish care not only upon me, but also upon him who accompanies me. You have taken your own clothes to cover me; you have given him the clothes of your poor dead husband, for whom I pray here below, and who, I hope, will pray for me in heaven."

"All that will not hinder me, after you have once left my house, after I have fulfilled my duty of hospitality, — all that will not prevent me from praying ardently that those who are pursuing you may capture you."

"Then why not deliver me up to them, if such are really your feelings?"

"Because those feelings are less powerful than my respect for misfortune, my reverence for an oath, my worship of hospitality; because I have sworn that you shall be saved this day; and also because, perhaps, I hope that what you have seen here may be a lesson not wholly lost upon you, — a lesson that may disgust you with your projects. For you *are* humane; you *are* good. I see it!"

"What should make me renounce projects for which I have lived these eighteen months?"

"This!" said the widow.

And with a rapid, sudden movement, like all she made, she pulled away the sheet that covered the dead, disclosing the livid face and the ghastly wound surrounded by purple blotches.

The younger woman turned aside. In spite of her firmness, of which she had given so many proofs, she could not bear that dreadful sight.

"Reflect, Madame," continued the widow; "reflect that before what you are attempting can be accomplished, many and many a poor man, whose only crime is to have loved you well, — many fathers, many sons, many brothers, — will be, like this one, lying dead. Reflect that many widows, many sisters, many orphans will be weeping and mourning, as I do, for him who was all their love and all their stay!"

"My God! my God!" exclaimed the princess, bursting into tears, as she fell on her knees and raised her arms to heaven; "if we are mistaken, — if we must render an account to thee for all these hearts we are about to break —"

Her voice, drowned in tears, died away in a moan.

XLI.

THE SEARCH.

A KNOCK was heard on the trap-door leading to the garret.

"What is the matter?" cried Bonneville's voice.

He had heard a few words of what had passed, and became uneasy.

"Nothing, nothing," said the young woman, pressing the hand of her hostess with an affectionate strength that showed the impression the poor widow's words had made upon her. Then, giving another tone to her voice, she cried out cheerfully, going a few steps up the ladder to speak more easily, "And you — ?"

The trap-door opened, and the smiling face of Bonneville looked down.

"How are you getting on?" said the peasant-woman, ending her sentence.

"All ready to do it over again, if your service requires it," he replied.

She thanked him by a smile.

"Who was it came here just now?" asked Bonneville.

"A peasant named Courtin, who did n't seem to be one of our friends."

"Ah, ha! the mayor of La Logerie?"

"That's the man."

"I know him," continued Bonneville; "Michel told me about him. He is a dangerous man. You ought to have had him followed."

"By whom? There is no one here."

"By Joseph Picaut."

"You know our brave Jean Oullier's repugnance to him."

"And yet he's a White," cried the widow, — "a White, who stood by and let them kill his brother."

The duchess and Bonneville both gave a start of horror.

"Then it is far better we should not mix him in our affairs," said Bonneville. "He would bring a curse with him. But have you no one we could put as sentry near the house, Madame Picaut?"

"Jean Oullier has provided some one, and I have sent my nephew on to the moor of Saint-Pierre; he can see over the whole country from there."

"But he is only a child," said the pretended peasant-woman.

"Safer than certain men," said the widow.

"After all," remarked Bonneville, "we have n't long to wait; it will be dark in three hours, and then our friends will be here with horses."

"Three hours!" said the young woman, whose mind had been painfully pre-occupied ever since her talk with the widow. "Many things may happen in three hours, my poor Bonneville."

"Some one is running in," cried Marianne Picaut, rushing from the window to the door, which she opened quickly. "Is it you, nephew?"

"Yes, aunt; yes!" cried the boy, out of breath.

"What is it?"

"Oh, aunt! aunt! the soldiers! They are coming up; they surprised and killed the man who was on the watch."

"The soldiers?" cried Joseph Picaut, who from his own door heard the cry of his boy.

"What can we do?" asked Bonneville.

"Wait for them," said the young peasant-woman.

"Why not attempt to escape?"

"If Courtin, the man who was here just now, sends them or brings them, they have surrounded the house."

"Who talks of escaping?" asked the Widow Picaut.

"Did I not say that this house was safe? Have I not sworn that so long as you are within it no harm should happen to you?"

Here the scene was complicated by the entrance of another person. Thinking, probably, that the soldiers were coming after him, Joseph Picaut appeared on the threshold of the widow's door. The house of his sister-in-law, who was known to be a Blue, may have seemed to him a safe asylum. Perceiving the widow's guests, he started back in surprise.

"Ha! so you have White gentlefolk here, have you? I see now why the soldiers are coming; you have sold your guests."

"Wretch!" cried Marianne, seizing her husband's sabre, which hung over the fireplace, and springing at Joseph, who raised his gun and aimed at her.

Bonneville sprang down the ladder; but the young peasant-woman had already flung herself between the brother and sister, covering the widow with her body.

"Lower your gun!" she cried to the Vendéan, in a tone that seemed not to come from that frail and delicate body, so male and energetic was it. "Lower your gun! in the king's name I command it!"

"Who are you who speak thus to me?" asked Joseph Picaut, always ready to rebel against authority.

"I am she who is expected here, — who commands here."

At these words, said with supreme majesty, Joseph Picaut, speechless, and as if bewildered, dropped his weapon to the ground.

"Now," continued the young woman, "go up in the loft with monsieur."

"But you?" said Bonneville.

"I stay here."

"But —"

"There's no time to argue. Go; go at once!"

The two men mounted the ladder, and the trap-door closed behind them.

THE SEARCH. 377

"What are you doing?" the young woman asked with surprise, as the widow began to disarrange the bed on which the body of her husband lay and to drag it from the wall.

"I am preparing a hiding-place where no one will seek you."

"But I don't mean to hide myself. No one will recognize me in these clothes. I choose to await them as I am."

"And I choose that you shall not await them," said the Widow Picaut, in so firm a tone that she silenced her visitor. "You heard what that man said; if you are discovered while in my house it will be thought that I sold you, and I do not choose to run the risk of your being discovered."

"You, my enemy?"

"Yes, your enemy, who would lie down on this bed and die if she saw you made prisoner."

There was no reply to make. The widow of Pascal Picaut raised the mattress on which the body lay, and hid the clothes and shirt and shoes, which had so awakened Courtin's curiosity, beneath it. Then she pointed to a place between the mattress and the straw bed, on the side toward the wall, wide enough for a small person to lie, and the young woman glided into it without resistance, making for herself a breathing-space at the edge. Then the widow pushed the bedstead back into its place.

Mistress Picaut had barely time to look carefully into every corner of the room to make sure that nothing compromising to her guests was left about, when she heard the click of arms, and the figure of an officer passed before the casement.

"This must be the place," she heard him say, addressing a companion who walked behind him.

"What do you want?" asked the widow, opening the door.

"You have strangers here; we wish to see them," replied the officer.

"Ah, *ça!* don't you recognize me?" interrupted Marianne Picaut, avoiding a direct reply.

"Yes; of course, I recognize you. You are the woman who served us as guide last night."

"Well, if I guided you in search of the enemies of the government, it is n't likely I should be hiding them here now, is it?"

"That's logical enough, is n't it, captain?" said the second officer.

"Bah! one can't trust any of these people; they are brigands from the breast," replied the lieutenant. "Did n't you notice that boy, a little scamp not ten years old, who in spite of our shouts and threats ran across the moor at full speed? He was their sentinel; they have been warned. Happily, they have not had time to escape; they must be hidden somewhere here."

"Possibly."

"Certainly." Then, turning to the widow, he said, "We shall not do you any harm, but we must search the house."

"As you please," she said, with perfect composure.

Seating herself quietly in the corner of the fireplace, she took her shuttle and distaff, which she had left upon a chair, and began to spin.

The lieutenant made a sign with his hand to five or six soldiers, who now entered the room. Looking carefully about him, he went up to the bed.

The widow grew paler than the flax on her shuttle. Her eyes flamed; the distaff slipped from her fingers. The officer looked under the bed, then along the sides of it, and, finally, put out his hand to raise the sheet that covered the body. Pascal's widow could contain herself no longer. She rose, bounded to the corner of the room where her husband's gun was leaning, resolutely cocked it, and threatening the officer, exclaimed: —

"If you lay a hand on that body, so sure as I am an honest woman, I will shoot you like a dog."

THE SEARCH. 379

The second lieutenant pulled away his comrade by the arm. The Widow Picaut, without laying down the weapon, approached the bed, and for the second time she raised the sheet that covered the dead.

"See there!" she said. "That man, who was my husband, was killed yesterday in your service."

"Ah! true; our first guide, — the one that was killed at the ford of the river," said the lieutenant.

"Poor woman!" said his companion; "let us leave her in peace. It is a pity to torment her at such a time."

"And yet," replied the first officer, "the information of the man we met was precise and circumstantial."

"We did wrong not to oblige him to come back with us."

"Have you any other room than this?" said the chief officer to the widow.

"I have the loft above, and that stable over the way."

"Search the loft and the stable; but first, open all the chests and closets, and look carefully in the oven."

The soldiers spread themselves through the house to execute these orders. From her terrible hiding-place the young woman heard every word of the conversation. She also heard the steps of the soldiers as they mounted the ladder to the loft, and she trembled with greater fear at that sound than when the officer had attempted to remove the death-sheet that concealed her, for she thought, with terror, that Bonneville's hiding-place was far less safe than her own.

When, therefore, she heard those who had gone to search the loft coming down, without any sound of a struggle or cry to show that the men were discovered, her heart was lightened of a heavy load.

The first lieutenant was waiting in the lower room, and was seated on the bread-box. The second officer was directing the search of eight or ten of the soldiers in the stable.

"Well," asked the first lieutenant, "have you found anything?"

"No," said a corporal.

"Did you shake the straw, the hay, and everything?"

"We prodded everywhere with our bayonets. If there was a man hidden anywhere it is impossible he should have escaped being stabbed."

"Very good; then we will go to the adjoining house. These persons must be somewhere."

The men left the room, and the officer followed them.

While the soldiers continued their exploration the lieutenant stood leaning against the outer wall of the house, looking suspiciously at a little pent-house he resolved to search carefully. Suddenly a bit of plaster, no bigger than a man's finger, fell at his feet. He raised his head and fancied he saw a hand disappearing under the roof.

"Here!" he cried to his men, in a voice of thunder.

The soldiers surrounded him.

"You are a pretty set of fellows!" he said; "you do your business finely!"

"What's happened, lieutenant?" asked the men.

"It has happened that the men are up there in the very loft you pretend to have searched. Go up again, quick! and don't leave a spear of straw unturned."

The soldiers re-entered the widow's house. They went straight to the trap-door and tried to raise it; but this time it resisted. It was fastened from above.

"Good! now the matter is plain enough," said the officer, putting his own foot upon the ladder. "Come," he cried, raising his voice to be heard in the loft, "out of your lair, or we'll fetch you."

The sound of a sharp discussion was heard; it was evident that the besieged were not agreed as to their line of action. This is what had happened with them: —

Bonneville and his companion, instead of hiding under the thick hay, where the soldiers would, of course, chiefly look for them, had slipped under a light pile of it, not more than two feet deep, which lay close to the trap-door. What they hoped for had happened; the soldiers almost walked over them, prodding the places where the hay lay thicker, but neglecting to examine that part of the loft where it seemed to be only a carpet. The searching party retired, as we have seen, without finding those they were looking for.

From their hiding-place, with their ears to the floor, which was thin, Bonneville and the Vendéan could hear distinctly all that was said in the room below. Hearing the officer give the order to search his house, Joseph Picaut grew uneasy, for in it was a quantity of gunpowder, the possession of which might get him into trouble. In spite of his companion's remonstrances, he left his hiding-place to watch the soldiers through the chinks left between the wall and the roof of the loft. It was then that he knocked off the fragment of plaster which fell near the officer and re-awakened his attention; and it was Joseph's hand the lieutenant had noticed, which he had rested against a rafter, while leaning forward to look into the yard.

When Bonneville heard the officer's shout and knew that he and his companion were discovered, he sprang to the trap-door and fastened it, bitterly reproaching the Vendéan for the folly of his conduct. But reproaches were useless now that they were discovered; it was necessary to decide on a course.

"You saw them, at any rate," said Bonneville.

"Yes," replied Joseph Picaut.

"How many are there?"

"About thirty, I should say."

"Then resistance would be folly. Besides, they have not discovered Madame, and our arrest would take them away from here, and make her safety with your brave sister-in-law more secure."

"Then your advice is?" questioned Picaut.

"To surrender."

"Surrender!" cried the Vendéan. "Never!"

"Why not?"

"Oh, I know what you are thinking of! You are a gentleman; you are rich. They'll put you in a fine prison, where you'll have all your comforts. But me! — they'll send me to the galleys, where I've already spent fourteen years. No, no; I'd rather lie in a bed of earth than a convict's bed, — a grave rather than a cell."

"If a struggle compromised ourselves only," said Bonneville, "I swear I would share your fate, and, like you, they should not take me living; but it is the mother of our king that we must save, and this is no moment to consult our own likings."

"On the contrary, let us kill all we can; the fewer enemies of Henri V. we leave alive, the better. Never will I surrender, I tell you that!" cried the Vendéan, putting his foot on the trap-door, which Bonneville was about to raise.

"Oh," said the count, frowning, "you will obey me, and without replying, I presume!"

Picaut burst out laughing.

But in the midst of his threatening mirth, a blow from Bonneville's fist sent him sprawling to the other end of the loft. As he fell he dropped his gun; but in falling he came against the loft window, which was closed by a wooden shutter. A sudden idea struck him, — to let the young man surrender, and profit by the diversion to escape himself.

While, therefore, Bonneville opened the trap-door, he himself undid the shutter, picked up his gun, and as the count called down from the top of the ladder, "Don't fire; we surrender!" the Vendéan leaned forward, discharged his gun into the group of soldiers, turned again, and sprang with a prodigious bound from the loft to a heap of manure in the garden; and after drawing the fire of one or two soldiers stationed as sentinels, he reached the forest and disappeared.

The shot from the loft brought down one man, dangerously wounded. But ten muskets were instantly pointed on Bonneville; and before the mistress of the house could fling herself forward and make a rampart with her body for him, as she tried to do, the unfortunate young man, pierced by seven or eight balls, rolled down the ladder to the widow's feet, crying out with his last breath: —

"Vive Henri V!"

To this last cry from Bonneville came an echoing cry of grief and of despair. The tumult that followed the explosion and Bonneville's fall hindered the soldiers from noticing this second cry, which came from Pascal Picaut's bed, and seemed to issue from the breast of the corpse, as it lay there, majestically calm and impassible amid the horrors of this terrible scene.

The lieutenant saw, through the smoke, that the widow was on her knees, with Bonneville's head, which she had raised, pressed to her breast.

"Is he dead?" he asked.

"Yes," said Marianne, in a voice choking with emotion.

"But you yourself, — you are wounded."

Great drops of blood were falling thick and fast from the widow's forehead upon Bonneville's breast.

"I?" she said.

"Yes; your blood is flowing."

"What matters my blood, if not a drop remains in him for whom I could not die as I had sworn?" she cried.

At this moment a soldier looked down through the trap-door.

"Lieutenant," he said, "the other has escaped through the loft; we fired at him and missed him."

"The other!" cried the lieutenant; "it is the other we want!" — supposing, very naturally, that the one who had escaped was Petit-Pierre. "But unless he finds another guide we are sure of him. After him, instantly!" Then reflecting, "But first, my good woman, get up," he continued. "You men, search that body."

The order was executed; but nothing was found in Bonneville's pocket, for the good reason that he was wearing Pascal Picaut's clothes, which the widow had given him while she dried his own.

"Now," said Marianne Picaut, when the order was obeyed, "he is really mine, is he not?" and she stretched her arm over the body of the young man.

"Yes; do what you please with him. But thank God that you were useful to us last night, or I should have sent you to Nantes to be taught there what it costs to give aid and comfort to rebels."

With these words, the lieutenant assembled his men and marched quickly away in the direction the fugitive had taken. As soon as they were well out of sight the widow ran to the bed, and lifting the side of the mattress, she drew out the body of the princess, who had swooned.

Ten minutes later Bonneville's body was laid beside that of Pascal Picaut; and the two women, — the presumptive regent and the humble peasant, — kneeling beside the bed, prayed together for these, the first two victims of the last insurrection of La Vendée.

XLII.

IN WHICH JEAN OULLIER SPEAKS HIS MIND ABOUT YOUNG BARON MICHEL.

WHILE the melancholy events we have just related were taking place in the house where Jean Oullier had left poor Bonneville and his companion, all was excitement, movement, joy, and tumult in the household of the Marquis de Souday.

The old gentleman could hardly contain himself for joy. He had reached the moment he had coveted so long ! He now chose for his war-apparel the least shabby hunting-clothes he could find in his wardrobe. Girt, in his quality as corps-commander, with a white scarf (which his daughters had long since embroidered for him in anticipation of this call to arms), with the bloody heart upon his breast, and a rosary in his button-hole, — in short, the full-dress insignia of a royalist chief on grand occasions, — he tried the temper of his sabre on all the articles of furniture that came in his way.

Also, from time to time, he exercised his voice to a tone of command, by drilling Michel, and even the notary, whom he insisted on enrolling into the number of his recruits, but who, notwithstanding the violence of his legitimist opinions, thought it judicious not to manifest them in a manner that was ultra-loyal.

Bertha, like her father, had put on a costume which she intended to wear on such expeditions. This was composed of a little overcoat of green velvet, open in front, and showing a shirt-frill of dazzling whiteness; the coat was trimmed with frogs and loops of black gimp, and it fitted the figure closely. The dress was completed by enormously wide trousers of gray cloth, which came down to a pair of high huzzar boots reaching to the knee. The young girl wore no scarf about her waist, the scarf being considered among Vendéans as a sign of command; but she was careful to wear the white emblem on her arm, held there by a red ribbon.

This costume brought out the grace and suppleness of Bertha's figure; and her gray felt hat, with its white feathers, lent itself marvellously well to the manly character of her face. Seen thus, she was enchanting. Although, by reason of her masculine ways, Bertha was certainly not coquettish, she could not prevent herself, in her present condition of mind or rather of heart, from noticing with satisfaction the advantages her physical gifts derived from this equipment. Perceiving, too, that it produced a great impression upon Michel, she became as exuberantly joyful as the marquis himself.

The truth is that Michel, whose mind had by this time reached a certain enthusiasm for his new cause, did not see without an admiration he gave himself no trouble to conceal the proud carriage and chivalric bearing of Bertha de Souday in her present dress. But this admiration, let us hasten to remark, came chiefly from the thought of what his beloved Mary's grace would be in such a costume, — for he did not doubt the sisters would make the campaign together in the same uniform.

His eyes had, therefore, gently questioned Mary, as if to ask her why she did not adorn herself like Bertha. But Mary had shown such coldness, such reserve, since the double scene in the turret chamber, she avoided so obviously saying a word to him, that the natural timidity of the young man increased, and he dared not risk more than the appealing look we have referred to.

It was Bertha, therefore, and not Michel, who urged Mary to make haste and put on her riding-dress. Mary did not answer; her sad looks made a painful contrast to the general gayety. She nevertheless obeyed Bertha's behest and went up to her chamber. The costume she intended to wear lay all ready on a chair; but instead of putting out her hand to take it, she merely looked at the garments with a pallid smile and seated herself on her little bed, while the big tears rolled from her eyes and down her cheeks.

Mary, who was religious and artless, had been thoroughly sincere and true in the impulse which led her to her present rôle of sacrifice and self-abnegation through devotion and tenderness to her sister; but it is none the less true that she had counted too much on her strength to sustain it. From the beginning of the struggle against herself which she saw before her, she felt, not that her resolution would fail, — her resolution would be ever the same, — but that her confidence in the result of her efforts was diminishing.

All the morning she kept saying to herself, "You ought not, you must not love him;" but the echo still came back, "I love him, love him!" At every step she made under the empire of these feelings, Mary felt herself more and more estranged from all that had hitherto made her joy and life. The stir, the movement, the virile excitements, which had hitherto amused her girlhood, now seemed to her intolerable; political interests themselves were effaced in presence of this deeper personal preoccupation which superseded all others. All that could distract her heart from the thoughts she longed to drive from her mind escaped her like a covey of birds when she came near it.

She saw, distinctly, at every turn, how in this fatal struggle she would be worsted, isolated, abandoned, with no support except her own will, with no consolation other than that which ought to come from her devotion itself; and she wept bitter tears of grief as well as fear, of regret as much as of apprehension. By her present suffering she measured the anguish yet to come.

For about half an hour she sat there, sad, thoughtful,

and self-absorbed, tossing, with no power of escape, in the maelstrom of her grief, and then she heard on the outside of her door, which was partly open, the voice of Jean Oullier, saying, in the peculiar tone he kept for the two young girls, to whom he had made himself, as we have seen, a second father: —

"What is the matter, my dear Mademoiselle Mary?"

Mary shuddered, as though she were waking from a dream; and she answered the honest peasant with a smile, but also with embarrassment: —

"Matter, — with me? Why, nothing, my dear Jean, I assure you."

But Jean Oullier meanwhile had considered her attentively. Coming nearer by several steps, and shaking his head as he looked at her fixedly, he said, in a tone of gentle and respectful scolding: —

"Why do you say that, little Mary? Do you doubt my friendship?"

"I? — I?" cried Mary.

"Yes; you must doubt it, since you try to deceive me."

Mary held out her hand. Jean Oullier took that slender and delicate little hand between his two great ones, and looked at the young girl sadly.

"Ah! my sweet little Mary," he said, as if she were still ten years old, "there is no rain without clouds, there are no tears without grief. Do you remember when you were a little child how you cried because Bertha threw your shells into the well? Well, that night, you know, Jean Oullier tramped forty miles, and your pretty sea-baubles were replaced the next day, and your pretty blue eyes were all dry and shining."

"Yes, my kind Jean Oullier; yes, indeed, I remember it," said Mary, who just now felt a special need of expression.

"Well," said Jean Oullier, "since then I've grown old, but my tenderness for you has only deepened. Tell me your trouble, Mary. If there is a remedy, I shall find it; if there is none, my withered old eyes will weep with yours."

Mary knew how difficult it would be to mislead the clear-sighted solicitude of her old servant. She hesitated, blushed, and then, without deciding to tell the cause of her tears, she began to explain them.

"I am crying, my poor Jean," she replied, "because I fear this war will cost me, perhaps, the lives of all I love."

Mary, alas! had learned to lie since the previous evening. But Jean Oullier was not to be taken in with any such answer, and shaking his head gently, he said: —

"No, little Mary; that's not the cause of your tears. When old fellows like the marquis and I are caught by the glamor and see nothing in the coming struggle but victory, a young heart like yours does n't go out of its way to predict reverses."

Mary would not admit herself beaten. "And yet, Jean," she said, taking one of the coaxing attitudes which she knew by long practice were all-powerful over the will of the worthy man, "I assure you it is so."

"No, no; it is not so, I tell you," persisted Jean Oullier, still grave, and growing more and more anxious.

"What is it, then?" demanded Mary.

"Ah!" said the old keeper; "do you want me to tell you the cause of your tears? Do you really want me to tell you that?"

"Yes, if you can."

"Well, your tears, — it is hard to say it, but I think it, I do, — they are caused by that miserable little Monsieur Michel; there!"

Mary turned as white as the curtains of her bed; all her blood flowed back to her heart.

"What do you mean, Jean?" she stammered.

"I mean to say that you have seen as well as I what is going on, and that you don't like it any more than I do. Only, I 'm a man, and I get in a rage; you are a girl, and you cry."

Mary could not repress a sob as she felt Jean Oullier's finger in her wound.

"It is not astonishing," continued the keeper, muttering to himself; "*wolf* as they call you, — those curs, — you are still a woman, and a woman kneaded of the best flour that ever fell from the sifter of the good God."

"Really, Jean, I don't understand you."

"Oh, yes; you do understand me very well, little Mary. Yes; you have seen what is happening the same as I have. Who would n't see it ? — good God ! One must be blind not to, for she takes no pains to hide it."

"But whom are you speaking of, Jean ? Tell me; don't you see that you are killing me with anxiety ? "

"Whom should I be speaking of but Mademoiselle Bertha ? "

"My sister ? "

"Yes, your sister, who parades herself about with that greenhorn; who means to drag him in her train to our camp; and, meantime, having tied him to her apron-strings for fear he should get away, is exhibiting him to everybody all round as a conquest, without considering what the people in the house and the friends of the marquis will say, — not to speak of that mischievous notary, who is watching it all with his little eyes, and mending his pen already to draw the contract."

" But supposing all that is so," said Mary, whose paleness was now succeeded by a high color, and whose heart was beating as though it would break, — ". supposing all that is so, where is the harm?"

" Harm ! Do you ask where 's the harm ? Why, just now my blood was boiling to see a Demoiselle de Souday — Oh, there ! there ! don't let 's talk of it ! "

" Yes, yes; on the contrary, I wish to talk of it," insisted Mary. " What was Bertha doing just now, my good Jean Oullier ? "

And the girl looked persuasively at the keeper.

" Well, Mademoiselle Bertha de Souday tied the white

scarf to Monsieur Michel's arm, — the colors borne by Charette on the arm of the son of him who — Ah! stop, stop, little Mary; you'll make me say things I mustn't say! Little she cares — Mademoiselle Bertha — that your father is out of temper with me to-day, all about that young fellow, too."

"My father! Have you been speaking to him — "

Mary stopped.

"Of course I have," replied Jean, taking the question in its literal sense, — "of course I have spoken to him."

"When?"

"This morning: first, when I brought him Petit-Pierre's letter; and then when I gave him the list of the men who are in his division, and who will march with us. I know they are not as numerous as they should be; but he who does what he can does what he ought. What do you think he answered me when I asked him if that young Monsieur Michel was really going to be one of us?"

"I don't know," said Mary.

"'God's death!' he cried; 'you recruit so badly that I am obliged to get some one to help your work. Yes, Monsieur Michel *is* one of us; and if you don't like it go and find fault with Mademoiselle Bertha.'"

"He said that to you, my poor Jean?"

"Yes; and I mean to have a talk with Mademoiselle Bertha, that I do."

"Jean, my friend, take care!"

"Take care of what?"

"Take care not to grieve her, not to make her angry. She loves him, Jean," said Mary, in a voice that was scarcely audible.

"Ah! then you do admit she loves him?" cried Jean Oullier.

"I am forced to do so," said Mary.

"Love a little puppet that a breath can tip over!" sneered Jean Oullier, — "she, Mademoiselle Bertha, change her name, one of the oldest in the land, one of the names that make our glory, the peasants' glory, as they do that of the men who bear them, — change a name like that for the name of a coward and a traitor!"

Mary's heart was wrung in her bosom.

"Jean, my friend," she said; "you go too far, Jean. Don't say such things, I entreat you."

"It shall not be," continued Jean Oullier, paying no heed to Mary's interruption, and walking up and down the room; "no, it shall not be. If all the rest are indifferent to the family honor I will watch over it, and rather than see it tarnished I, — well, I will — "

And Jean Oullier made a threatening gesture, the meaning of which was unmistakable.

"No, Jean; no, you would never do that," cried Mary, in a heart-rending voice. "I implore you with clasped hands."

And she almost fell forward on her knees. The Vendéan stepped back, horrified.

"You, — you, too, little Mary?" he cried; "you love — "

But she did not give him time to end his sentence.

"Think, Jean, only think of the grief you would cause to my dear Bertha."

Jean Oullier was looking at her in stupefaction, only half-relieved of the suspicion he had just conceived, when Bertha's voice was heard ordering Michel to wait for her in the garden and on no account to go away. Almost at the same moment she opened the door of her sister's room.

"Well!" she exclaimed; "is this how you get ready?" Then, looking closer at Mary and noticing the trouble in her face, she continued, "What is the matter? You have been crying! And you, Jean Oullier, — you look as cross as a bear. What's going on here?"

"I'll tell you what's going on, Mademoiselle Bertha," replied the Vendéan.

"No, no!" exclaimed Mary; "I entreat you not, Jean. Hold your tongue; oh, do be silent!"

"You scare me with such preambles," cried Bertha; "and Jean is looking at me with an inquisitorial air as if

I had committed some great crime. Come, speak out, Jean; I am fully disposed to be kind and indulgent on this happy day, when all my most ardent dreams are realized, and I can share with men their noblest privilege of war!"

"Be frank, Demoiselle Bertha," said the Vendéan; "is that the true reason why you are so joyful?"

"Ha! now I see what the matter is," said Bertha, boldly facing the question. "Major-General Oullier wants to scold me for trenching on his functions." Turning to her sister, she added, "I'll bet, Mary, that it is all about my poor Michel."

"Exactly, mademoiselle," said Jean Oullier, not leaving Mary time to answer.

"Well, what have you to say about him, Jean? My father is delighted to get another adherent, and I can't see anything in that to make you frown."

"Your father may like it," replied the old keeper, "but it does n't suit the rest of us; we have other ideas."

"May I be allowed to know them?"

"We think each side should stay in its own camp."

"Well?"

"Well what?"

"Go on; finish what you mean to say."

"I mean to say that Monsieur Michel's place is not with us."

"Why not? Monsieur Michel is royalist, is n't he? I think he has given proof enough during the last two days of his devotion to the cause."

"That may be; but all the same, Demoiselle Bertha, we peasants have a way of saying, 'Like father, like son,' and therefore we don't believe in Monsieur Michel's royalism."

"He will force you to believe in it."

"Possibly; meanwhile—"

The Vendéan frowned.

"Meanwhile, what?" said Bertha

"Well, I tell you, it will be painful to old soldiers like me to march cheek by jowl with a man we don't respect."

"What possible blame can you put on him?" asked Bertha, beginning to show some bitterness.

"Much."

"Much means nothing unless you specify it."

"Well, his father, his birth —"

"His father! his birth!" interrupted Bertha; "always the same nonsense! Let me tell you, Jean Oullier," she cried, frowning darkly, "that it is precisely on account of his father and his birth that he interests me, that young man."

"Why so?"

"Because my heart revolts against the unjust reproaches which he is made to endure from all our party. I am tired of hearing him blamed for a birth he did not choose, for a father he never knew, for faults he never committed, and which, perhaps, his father never committed. All that makes me indignant, Jean Oullier; it disgusts me. And I think it a noble and generous action to encourage that young man and help him to repair the past, — if there is anything to repair, — and to show himself so brave and so devoted that calumny will not dare to meddle with him in future."

"I don't care," retorted Jean Oullier; "he will have a good deal to do before I, for one, respect the name he bears."

"You must respect it, Jean Oullier," said Bertha, in a stern voice, "when I bear it, as I hope to do."

"Oh, yes! so you say," cried Jean Oullier; "but I don't yet believe you mean it."

"Ask Mary," said Bertha, turning to her sister, who was listening, pale and palpitating, to the discussion, as though her life depended on it; "ask my sister, to whom I have opened my heart, and who knows my hopes and fears. Yes, Jean, all concealments, all constraints are hateful to me; and I am glad, especially with you, to have thrown off mine and to speak openly. Well, I tell you boldly, Jean Oullier, — as boldly as I say everything, — I love him!"

"No, no; don't say that, I implore you, Demoiselle Bertha. I am but a poor peasant, but in former days — it is true you were but a little thing — you gave me the right to call you my child; and I have loved you, and I do love you both as no father ever loved his own daughters: well, the old man who watched over you in childhood, who held you on his knee, and rocked you to sleep, night after night, that old man, whose only happiness you are in this low world, flings himself on his knees to say, Don't love that man, I implore you, Bertha!"

"Why not?" she said, impatiently.

"Because, — and I say this from the bottom of my heart, on my soul and conscience, — because a marriage between you and him is an evil thing, — a monstrous, impossible thing!"

"Your attachment to us makes you exaggerate everything, my poor Jean. Monsieur Michel loves me, I believe; I love him, I am sure, and if he bravely accomplishes the task of distinguishing his name, I shall be most happy in becoming his wife."

"Then," said Jean Oullier, in a tone of deep depression, "I must look in my old age for other masters and another home."

"Why?"

"Because Jean Oullier, poor and of no account as he may be, will never make his home with the son of a renegade and a traitor."

"Hush! Jean Oullier, hush!" cried Bertha. "Hush, I say, or I may break your heart."

"Jean! my good Jean!" murmured Mary.

"No, no," said the old keeper; "you ought to be told the noble actions which have glorified the name you are so eager to take in exchange for your own."

"Don't say another word, Jean Oullier," interrupted Bertha, in a tone that was almost threatening. "Come, I'll tell you now, I have often questioned my heart to know which I loved best, my father or you; but if you say another word, if you utter another insult against my Michel, you will be no more to me than — "

"Than a servant," interrupted Jean Oullier. "Yes; but a servant who is honest, and who all his life has done his duty without betraying it, — a servant who has the right to cry shame on the son of him who sold Charette, as Judas sold Christ, for a sum of money."

"What do I care for what happened thirty-six years ago, — eighteen years before I was born? I know the one who lives, and not the one who is dead, — the son, not the father. I love him; do you hear me, Jean? I love him as you yourself have taught me to love and hate. If his father did as you say, which I will not believe, but if he did, we will put such glory on the name of Michel — on the name of the traitor and renegade — that every one shall bow before it; and you shall help in doing so, — yes, you, Jean Oullier, — for I repeat, I love him, and nothing but death can quench the spring of tenderness that flows to him from my heart."

Mary moaned almost inaudibly; but slight as the sound was, Jean Oullier heard it. He turned to her. Then, as if crushed by the plaint of one and the violence of the other, he dropped on a chair and hid his face in his hands. The old Vendéan wept, but he wished to hide his tears. Bertha understood what was passing in that devoted heart; she went to him and knelt beside him.

"You can measure the strength of my feelings for that young man," she said, "by the fact that it has almost led me to forget my deep and true affection for you."

Jean Oullier shook his head sadly.

"I comprehend your antipathies, your feelings of repugnance," continued Bertha, "and I was prepared for their expression; but, patience, my old friend, patience and resignation! God alone can take out of my heart that which he has put there; and he will not do that, for it would kill me. Give us time to prove to you that your prejudices are unjust, and that he whom I have chosen is indeed worthy of me."

At this instant they heard the marquis calling for Jean Oullier in a voice that showed some new and serious event had happened. Jean Oullier rose and went to the door.

"Stop!" said Bertha; "are you going without answering me?"

"Monsieur le marquis calls me, mademoiselle," replied the Vendéan, in a chilling tone.

"*Mademoiselle!*" cried Bertha; "*mademoiselle.* Ah! you will not listen to my entreaties? Well, then, remember this: I forbid you — mark, I forbid you — to offer any insult of any kind to Monsieur Michel; I command that his life be sacred to you. If any evil happens to him through you I will avenge it, not on you but on myself; and you know, Jean Oullier, whether or not I do as I say."

Jean Oullier looked at the girl; then taking her by the arm, he said: —

"Maybe it would be better so than to let you marry that man."

The marquis now called louder than ever, and Jean Oullier rushed from the room, leaving Bertha bewildered by his resistance, and Mary bowed down beneath the terror which the violence of her sister's love inspired in her.

XLIII.

BARON MICHEL BECOMES BERTHA'S AIDE-DE-CAMP.

JEAN OULLIER went down, as we have said, in haste; perhaps he was more anxious to get away from the young girl than to obey the call of the marquis. He found the latter in the courtyard, and beside him stood a peasant, covered with mud and sweat.

The man had just brought news that Pascal Picaut's house was surrounded by soldiers; he had seen them go in, and that was all he knew. He had been stationed among the gorse on the road to Sablonnière, with orders from Jean Oullier to come to the château at once if the soldiers should go in the direction of the house where the fugitives had taken refuge. This mission he had fulfilled to the letter.

The marquis, to whom of course Jean Oullier had told how he left Petit-Pierre and the Comte de Bonneville in Pascal Picaut's house, was terribly alarmed.

"Jean Oullier! Jean Oullier!" he kept repeating, in the tone of Augustus calling, "Varus! Varus!" "Jean Oullier, why did you trust others instead of yourself? If any misfortune has happened my poor house will be dishonored before it is ruined!"

Jean Oullier did not answer; he held his head down gloomily, in silence. This silence and immovability exasperated the marquis.

"My horse! my horse, Jean Oullier!" he cried; "and if that lad, whom yesterday, not knowing who he was, I called *my young friend*, is made prisoner by the Blues, let us show by dying to deliver him that we were not unworthy of his confidence."

But Jean Oullier shook his head.

"What!" exclaimed the marquis; "don't you mean to fetch my horse?"

"Jean is right," said Bertha, who had come upon the scene and had heard her father's order and Jean Oullier's refusal; "we must not risk anything by precipitate action." Turning to the scout, she asked, "Did you see the soldiers leave Picaut's house with prisoners?"

"No; I saw them knock down the *gars* Malherbe, whom Jean Oullier stationed on the rise of the hill, and I watched them till they entered Picaut's orchard. Then I came here at once, as Jean Oullier ordered me to do."

"Are you sure, Jean Oullier," said Bertha, "that you can answer for the faithfulness of the woman in whose charge you left them?"

"Yesterday," he said, giving Bertha a reproachful look, "I should have said of Marianne Picaut that I could trust her as myself; but —"

"But?" questioned Bertha.

"But to-day," said the old man, with a sigh, "I doubt everything."

"Come, come!" cried the marquis; "all this is time lost. My horse! bring my horse! and in ten minutes I shall know the truth."

But Bertha stopped him.

"Ha!" he exclaimed; "is this the way I am obeyed in this house? What can I expect from others if in my own family no one obeys my orders?"

"Your orders are sacred, father," said Bertha, — "to your daughters, above all; but your ardor is carrying you away. Do not forget that those for whose safety we are so anxious are merely peasants in the eyes of others. If the Marquis de Souday goes himself in search of two missing peasants their importance will be known directly, and the news will reach our enemies."

"Mademoiselle Bertha is right," said Jean Oullier; "it is better for me to go."

"Not you, any more than my father," said Bertha.

"Why not?"

"Because you run too great a risk in going over there."

"I went there this morning; and if I ran that risk to find out whose ball killed my poor Pataud, I can certainly do the same to learn news of M. de Bonneville and Petit-Pierre."

"I tell you, Jean," persisted Bertha, "that after all that happened yesterday you must not show yourself where the soldiers are. We must find some one who is not compromised, and who can get to the heart of the matter without exciting suspicion."

"How unlucky that that animal of a Loriot would go back to Machecoul!" said the marquis. "I begged him to stay; I had a presentiment that I should want him."

"Well, have n't you Monsieur Michel?" said Jean Oullier, in a sarcastic tone; "you can send him to the Picaut's house, or anywhere else, without suspicion. If there were ten thousand men guarding it. they 'd let him in; and no one, I am sure, would imagine he came on any business of yours."

"Yes; he is just the person we want," said Bertha, accepting the support thus given to her secret purpose, and ignoring Jean Oullier's malicious intention in making it. "Is n't he, father?"

"On my soul, I think so!" cried the marquis. "Though he is rather effeminate in appearance, the young man may turn out very useful."

At the first rumor of alarm Michel had approached the marquis, as if awaiting orders. When he heard Bertha's proposition, and saw it accepted by her father, his face became radiant. Bertha herself was beaming.

"Are you ready to do all that is necessary for the safety of Petit-Pierre, Monsieur Michel?" she said.

"I am ready to do anything you wish, mademoiselle, in

order to prove my gratitude to Monsieur le marquis for the friendly welcome I have received from him."

"Very good. Then take a horse — not mine; it would be recognized — and gallop over there. Go into the house unarmed, as though curiosity alone brought you, and if our friends are in danger light a fire of brush on the heath. During that time Jean Oullier will assemble his men; and then, in a body and well-armed, we can fly to the support of those so dear to us."

"Bravo!" cried the Marquis de Souday; "I have always said that Bertha was the strong-minded one of the family."

Bertha smiled with pride and looked at Michel.

"And you," she said to her sister, who had now come down and joined them quietly, just as Michel departed to get his horse, — "and you, don't you mean to dress and go with us?"

"No," replied Mary.

"Why not?"

"I mean to stay as I am."

"Oh! you can't mean it!"

"Yes, I do," said Mary, with a sad smile. "In an army there are always sisters of mercy to care for the fighting men and comfort them; I shall be the sister of mercy."

Bertha looked at Mary with amazement. She may have been about to question her as to this sudden change of mind; but at that instant Michel, already mounted on the horse provided for him, re-appeared, and approaching Bertha stopped the words upon her lips. Addressing her as the one to whom he looked for orders, he said: —

"You told me what I was to do in case some misfortune has happened at the Picaut house, mademoiselle; but you have not told me what to do in case I find Petit-Pierre safe and well."

"In that case," said the marquis, "come back here, and set our minds at ease."

"No, no," said Bertha, who was determined to give the man she loved some important part to play; "such goings

VOL. I. — 26

to and fro would excite suspicion in the various troops now stationed about the forest. You had better stay at the Picauts' or in the neighborhood till nightfall, and then go and wait for us at the July oak. You know where that is, don't you?"

"I should think so!" said Michel; "it is on the road to Souday."

Michel knew every oak and every tree on that road.

"Very good!" said Bertha; "we will be in the woods near by. Make the signal, — three cries of the screech-owl and one hoot, — and we will join you. Go on, dear Monsieur Michel."

Michel bowed to the marquis and to the two young ladies. Then, bending forward over the neck of his horse, he started at a gallop. He was, in truth, an excellent rider, and Bertha called attention to the fact that in turning short out of the *porte cochère*, he had very cleverly made his horse change step.

"It is amazing how easy it is to make a well-bred gentleman out of a rustic like that," said the marquis, re-entering the château. "It is true that women must have a finger in it. That young man is really passable."

"Oh, yes; well-bred gentlemen, indeed! They are easy enough to make; but men of heart and soul are another thing," muttered Jean Oullier.

"Jean Oullier," said Bertha, "you are forgetting my advice. Take care."

"You are mistaken, mademoiselle," replied Jean Oullier. "It is, on the contrary, because I have forgotten nothing that you see me so troubled. I thought my aversion to that young man might be remorse," he muttered; "but I begin to fear it is presentiment."

"Remorse! — you, Jean Oullier?"

"Ah! did you hear what I said?"

"Yes."

"Well, I don't unsay it."

"What remorse have you about him?"

"None about him," said Jean Oullier, in a gloomy voice: "I meant his father."

"His father?" said Bertha, shivering in spite of herself.

"Yes," said Jean Oullier. "My name was changed in a day because of him; I was no longer Jean Oullier."

"What were you then?"

"Chastisement."

"On his father?"

Then, remembering all that was told in the region, of the death of Baron Michel the older, she exclaimed: —

"His father! found dead at a hunt! Ah, miserable man! what do you mean?"

"That the son may avenge his father by bringing mourning for mourning upon us."

"In what way?"

"Through you, and because you love him madly."

"What of that?"

"I can myself assure you of one thing."

"And that is?"

"That he does not love you."

Bertha shrugged her shoulders disdainfully; but the blow nevertheless reached her heart. A feeling that was almost hatred to the old Vendéan came over her.

"Employ yourself in collecting your men, Jean Oullier," she said.

"I obey you, mademoiselle," replied the Chouan.

He went toward the gate. Bertha returned to the house, without giving him another look. But before leaving the château, Jean Oullier called up the peasant who had brought the news.

"Before the soldiers got to Picaut's house did you see any one else go in there?"

"To Joseph's place, or Pascal's?"

"Pascal's."

"Yes, I saw one man go in."

"Who was he?"

"The mayor of La Logerie."

"You say he went into Pascal's part of the house?"

"I am sure of it."

"You saw him?"

"As plain as I see you."

"Which way did he go when he left it?"

"Toward Machecoul."

"The same way by which the soldiers came soon after, was n't it?"

"Exactly; it was n't half an hour after he left before they came."

"Good!" ejaculated Jean Oullier. Shaking his clenched fist in the direction of La Logerie, he muttered to himself, "Ah, Courtin! Courtin! you are tempting God. My dog killed yesterday, this treachery to-day, — you try my patience too far!"

XLIV.

MAÎTRE JACQUES AND HIS RABBITS.

To the south of Machecoul, forming a triangle round the village of Légé, stretch three forests. They are called respectively the forests of Touvois, Grandes-Landes, and La Roche-Servière.

The territorial importance of these forests is not great if considered separately; but standing each within three kilometres of the others, and connected by hedges and fields full of gorse and brambles, even more numerous there than elsewhere in La Vendée, they form a very considerable agglomeration of woodland. The result has been that in times of civil war they became a very hot-bed of revolt, where insurrection was fostered and concentrated before it spread through the adjacent regions.

The village of Légé, besides being the native place of the famous physician Jolly, was, almost continuously, Charette's headquarters during the great war. It was there, in the thick belt of woodland surrounding the village that he took refuge if defeated, reformed his decimated battalions, and prepared for other fights.

In 1832, although a new road from Nantes to the Sables-d'Olonne, which runs through Légé, had modified in a measure its strategic strength, the wooded neighborhood was still the most formidable centre of the insurrectionary movement then organized. The three forests hid, in their impenetrable undergrowth of holly and ferns which grew under the shadow of the great thickets, those bands of refractories (conscripts escaping service) whose ranks were daily increasing and forming the kernel of the insurrectionary divisions in the Retz region and on the plains.

The clearings made by government, even the felling of a considerable portion of the wood, had no perceptible result. It was rumored that the deserters had excavated underground dwellings, like those the first Chouans burrowed in the forests of Gralla, in the depths of which they had so often defied the closest search. In this particular case rumor was not mistaken.

Toward the close of the day when, as we have seen, Michel started on horseback from the château de Souday toward the Picaut cottage, any one who had stood concealed behind one of the huge centennial beeches that surround the glade of Folleron in the forest of Touvois, would have seen a curious sight.

At the hour when the sun, sinking toward the horizon, left a sort of twilight behind it, — an hour when the wood-paths were already in a shadow that seemed to rise from the earth, while the tree-tops were still burnished with the last rays of the dying sunlight, — this concealed spectator would have seen in the distance, and coming toward him, a personage whom, with a very slight stretch of fancy, he might have taken for some uncanny or impish being. This personage advanced slowly, looking cautiously about him, — a matter which seemed to be the more easy because, at first sight, he appeared to have two heads, with which to keep a double watch over his safety.

He was clothed in the sordid rags of an old jacket and the semblance of a pair of breeches, the original cloth of which had completely disappeared beneath the multifarious patches of many colors with which its decay had been remedied; and he appeared, as we have said, to belong to the class of bicephalous monsters who occupy a distinguished place among the choice exceptions which Nature delights to create in her fantastic moments.

The two heads were entirely distinct the one from the other, and though they apparently came from the same trunk there was no family resemblance between them. Beside a broad and brick-dust colored face, seamed with small-pox and covered with unkempt beard, appeared a second face, less repulsive, very astute, and rather malign in its ugliness, whereas the other countenance expressed only a sort of idiocy which might at times amount to ferocity.

These two distinct countenances did, in truth, belong to two men, whose acquaintance we have already made at Montaigu on the day of the fair; namely, to Aubin Courte-Joie, the tavern keeper, and — if the reader will pardon an almost too expressive name, but one we think we have no right to change — to Trigaud the Vermin, the beggar, whose herculean strength, it will be remembered, played a noted part in the riot at Montaigu by lifting the general's leg from the stirrup and throwing him out of his saddle.

By a judicious arrangement, which we have already mentioned, Aubin Courte-Joie had supplemented, or re-completed, his own personality by the help of this species of beast of burden whom he had, by good luck, encountered on his path through life. In exchange for the two legs he had left on the road to Ancenis, the truncated cripple had obtained a pair of steel limbs, which resisted all fatigue, feared no task, and served him as his own original legs never did and never could have done, — legs, in short, which did his will with passive obedience, and had reached, after a certain period of association, such adaptability that they instinctively guessed the very thoughts of Aubin Courte-Joie, if conveyed by a mere word, a single sign, or even a slight touch of a hand on the shoulder or a knee on the flank.

The strangest part of this affair was that the least satisfied partner in the firm was not Trigaud-Vermin; quite the contrary. His thick brain knew that Aubin Courte-Joie was directing his physical strength in the direction of his sympathies. The words "White" and "Blue," which dropped into his large ears, always pricked up and listening, proved to him that he supported, in his quality of locomotive to the tavern-keeper, a cause whose worship was the one glimmer of light which had survived the collapse of his brain. He made it his glory. His confidence in Aubin Courte-Joie was boundless; he was proud of being linked body and soul to a mind whose superiority he recognized, and he was now attached to the man who might indeed be called his master, with the self-abnegation that characterizes all attachments which instinct governs.

Trigaud carried Aubin sometimes on his back, sometimes on his shoulders, but always as affectionately as a mother carries her child. He took the utmost care of him; he showed him little attentions which seemed to disprove the poor devil's actual idiocy. He never thought of watching his own feet or guarding them from the cutting and wounding of stones and briers; but he carefully held aside, as he walked along, the bushes or branches which he thought might rub the body or scratch the face of his rider.

When they had advanced about a third of the way into the open, Aubin Courte-Joie touched Trigaud on the shoulder, and the giant stopped short. Then, without needing to speak, the innkeeper pointed with his finger to a large stone lying at the foot of an enormous beech-tree, in the right-hand corner of the clearing.

The giant advanced to the beech, picked up the stone, and awaited orders.

"Now," said Aubin Courte-Joie, "strike three blows."

Trigaud did as he was told, timing the blows so that the second followed the first rapidly, and the third did not sound until after a certain interval.

At this signal, which was made on the trunk of the tree, a little square of turf and moss rose from the ground, and a head beneath it.

"Ho! it's you, is it, Maître Jacques? What's the watch-dog doing at the mouth of the burrow?" asked Aubin, visibly pleased at meeting with an intimate acquaintance.

"Hey! my *gars* Courte-Joie, this is the hour for business, don't you see; and I never like to let my rabbits out till I make sure myself the hunters are not about."

" And you are right, Maître Jacques; you are right," replied Courte-Joie; " to-day, especially, for there are lots of guns on the plain."

" Hey, how 's that, tell me ? "

" That 's what I want to do."

" But first, won't you come in ? "

"Oh, no; no, Jacques. It is hot enough where we are, — is n't it Trigaud ? "

The giant uttered a grunt which might, at a pinch, pass for an affirmation.

"Goodness! why, he 's speaking!" remarked Maître Jacques. "They used to say he was dumb. You are in luck 's way, *gars* Trigaud, to be taken into Aubin's good graces; do you know that ? Why, you are almost a man, not to speak of having your board and lodging sure; and that 's more than all dogs can say, — even those at the castle of Souday."

The beggar opened his large mouth and began a chuckle of laughter, which he did not end, for a motion of Aubin's hand stopped in the cavities of his larynx that impulse to hilarity which his powerful lungs rendered dangerous.

"Hush! lower! lower, Trigaud!" he said, roughly. Then turning to Maître Jacques, "He thinks he is in the market-place of Montaigu, poor innocent!"

"Well, as you won't come in, I 'll call out the *gars*. You 're right, my Courte-Joie; it is devilish hot inside. Some of 'em say they are roasted; but you know how such fellows grumble."

"That 's not like Trigaud," replied Aubin, pounding with his fist, by way of a caress, on the head of the elephant who served him as steed; "he never complains, — not he!"

Trigaud gave a nod of gratitude for the signs of friendship with which Courte-Joie honored him.

Maître Jacques, whom we have just presented to our readers, but with whom it remains for us to make them fully acquainted, was a man of fifty to fifty-five years of age, who had all the external appearance of a worthy farmer of the Retz region. Though his hair was long and floated on his shoulders, his beard, on the contrary, was cut close and shaved with the utmost care. He wore a perfectly clean jacket of gray cloth, cut in a shape that was almost modern compared with those that were still in use in La Vendée, and a waistcoat, also of cloth, in broad stripes, alternately white and fawn-colored. Breeches of coarse brown cloth and gaiters of blue twilled cotton were the only part of his costume which resembled that of his compatriots.

A pair of pistols, with shining handles, stuck into his jacket, were the only military signs he bore at this moment. But in spite of his placid, good-humored face, Maître Jacques was really the leader of the boldest band in the whole region, and the most determined Chouan to be found in a circuit of fifty miles, throughout which he enjoyed a very formidable reputation.

Maître Jacques had never seriously laid down his arms during the whole fifteen years that Napoleon's power lasted. With two or three men — oftener alone and isolated — he had managed to make head against whole brigades detailed to capture him. His courage and his luck were something supernatural, and gave rise to an idea among the superstitious population of the Bocage that his life was invulnerable, and that the balls of the Blues were harmless against him. When, therefore, after the revolution of July, in fact, during the very first days of August, 1830, Maître Jacques announced that he should take the field, all the refractories of the neighborhood flocked to his standard, and it was not long before he had under his orders a considerable body of men, with whom he had already begun the second series of his guerilla exploits.

After asking Aubin Courte-Joie to excuse him for a few moments, Maître Jacques, who, for the purposes of conversation had put first his head and then his bust above the trap-door, now stooped down into the opening, and gave a curiously modulated whistle. At this signal a hum arose from the bowels of the earth, much like that of a hive of bees. Then, close by, between two bushes, a wide sort of lid or skylight, covered only with turf and moss and dried leaves, exactly like the ground beside it, rose vertically, supported on four stakes at the four corners. As it rose it revealed the opening to a sort of grain-pit, very broad and very deep; and from this pit about twenty men now issued, one after another, in succession.

The dress of these men had nothing of the elegant picturesqueness which characterizes brigands as we see them issue from pasteboard caverns at the Opéra-Comique, — far, very far from that. Some wore uniforms which closely resembled the rags on Trigaud-Vermin's person; others — and these were the most elegant — wore cloth jackets. But the jackets of the greater number were of cotton.

The same diversity existed in their weapons. Two or three regulation muskets, half a dozen sporting guns, and as many pistols formed the entire equipment of firearms. The display of side-arms was far from being as respectable; it consisted solely of Maître Jacques's sabre, two pikes dating back to the old war, and eight or ten scythes, carefully sharpened by their owners.

When all the braves had issued from the pit into the clearing, Maître Jacques walked up to the trunk of a felled tree, on which he sat down. Trigaud placed Aubin Courte-Joie beside him, after which the giant retired a few steps, though still within reach of his partner's signals.

"Yes, my Courte-Joie," said Maître Jacques, "the wolves are after us; but it gives me pleasure to have you take the trouble to come and warn me." Then, suddenly, "Ah, ça!" he cried; "how happens it that you can come? I thought you were caught when they took Jean Oullier? Jean Oullier got away, I know, as they crossed the ford, — there's nothing surprising in his escape; but you, my poor footless one, — how, in Heaven's name, did you get off?"

"You forget Trigaud's feet," replied Aubin Courte-Joie, laughing. "I pricked the gendarme who held me, and it seems it hurt him, for he let go of me, and my friend Trigaud did the rest. But who told you that, Maître Jacques?"

"Maître Jacques shrugged his shoulders with an indifferent air. Then, without replying to the question, which he may have thought an idle one, —

"Ah, *ça!*" he said; "I hope you have n't come to tell me that the day is changed?"

"No; it is still for the 24th."

"That 's good," replied Maître Jacques; "for the fact is I 've lost all patience with their delays and their shufflings. Good Lord! where 's the need of such a fuss to pick up one 's gun, say good-bye to one's wife, and be off?"

"Patience! patience! you won't have long to wait now, Maître Jacques."

"Four days!" said the other, in a tone of disgust.

"That 's not long."

"I think it is too long by three. I did n't have Jean Oullier's chance to do for some of them at the springs of Baugé."

"Yes; the *gars* told me about that."

"Unhappily," continued Maître Jacques, "they have taken a cruel revenge for it."

"How so?"

"Have n't you heard?"

"No; I have just come straight from Montaigu."

"Ah, true; then you can't know."

"What happened?"

"They caught and killed in Pascal Picaut's house a fine young man I respected, — I, who don't think any too much of his class usually."

"What was his name?"

"Comte de Bonneville."

"Did they really ? When was it ? "

"Why this very day, damn it ! about two in the afternoon."

"How, in the devil's name, did you hear that, down in your pit, Maître Jacques ? "

"Don't I hear everything that is of use to me ? "

"Then I don't know that there's any use in my telling you what brings me here."

"Why not ? "

"Because you probably know it."

"That may be."

"I should like to be sure whether you do or not."

"Pooh ! "

"Faith ! yes, I should. It would spare me a disagreeable errand, which I only accepted against my will."

"Ah ! then you have come from *those gentlemen ?* "

Maître Jacques pronounced the words we have underscored in a tone that varied from contempt to menace.

"Yes, I do, in the first instance," replied Aubin Courte-Joie; "but I met Jean Oullier on my way, and he, too, gave me a message for you."

"Jean Oullier ! Ah ! anything that comes from him is welcome. He is a *gars* I love, — Jean Oullier ! He has done a thing in his life which made me his friend forever."

"What was that ? "

"That's his secret, not mine. But come; tell me, in the first place, what those lordly gentlemen want of me ? "

"It is your division leader who has sent me."

"The Marquis de Souday ? "

"Yes."

"Well, what does he want ? "

"He complains that you attract, by your constant sorties, the attention of the government soldiers, and that you irritate the population of the towns by your exactions, and also that you paralyze the general movement by making it more difficult."

"Pooh ! why haven't they made their movement sooner?

We have waited long enough, God knows! For my part, I've been waiting since July 30."

"And then —"

"What! is there any more of it?"

"Yes; he orders you —"

"Orders me!"

"Wait a moment; you can obey or not obey, but he orders you —"

"Listen to me, Courte-Joie; whatever he orders I here make a vow to disobey it. Now, go on; I'm listening."

"Well, he orders you to stay quietly in your quarters till the 24th, and, above all, to stop no diligence nor any traveller on the highroad, as you have been doing lately."

"Well, I swear, for my part," replied Maître Jacques, "to capture the first person that goes to-night from Légé to Saint-Étienne or from Saint-Étienne to Légé. As for you, stay here, *gars* Courte-Joie, and then you can tell him what you have seen."

"Oh, no! no!" exclaimed Aubin.

"Why not?"

"Don't do that, Maître Jacques."

"Yes, by God! I will, though."

"Jacques! Jacques!" insisted the tavern-keeper; "can't you see it will compromise our sacred cause?"

"Possibly; but it will prove to him — that old fox I never chose for my superior — that I and my men are outside his division, and that here, at least, his orders shall never be obeyed. So much for the *orders* of the Marquis de Souday; now go on to Jean Oullier's message."

"I met him as I reached the heights near the bridge at Servières. He asked where I was going, and when I told him, '*Parbleu!*' said he; 'that's the very thing! Ask Maître Jacques if he can move out and let us have his earth-hole for some one we want to hide there.'"

"Ah, ha! Did he say who the person was, my Courte-Joie?"

"No."

"Never mind ! Whoever it is, if he comes in the name of Jean Oullier, he 'll be welcome; for I know Jean Oullier would n't turn me out if it were not for some good reason. He is not one of the crowd of lazy lords who make all the noise and leave us to do the work."

"Some are good, and some are bad," said Aubin, philosophically.

"When is the person he wants to hide coming ? " asked Maître Jacques.

"To-night."

"How shall I know him ? "

"Jean Oullier will bring him."

"Good. Is that all he wants ? "

"No; he wishes you to capture all doubtful persons in the forest to-night, and have the whole neighborhood watched, more especially the path toward Grand-Lieu."

"There now ! just see that ! The division commander *orders* me to arrest no one, and Jean Oullier wants me to clear the forest of curs and red-breeches, — reason the more why I should keep the oath I made just now. How will Jean Oullier know that I shall be expecting him ? "

"If he can come — that is, if there are no troops in the way at Touvois — I am to let him know."

"Yes; but how ? "

"By a branch of holly with fifteen leaves upon it in the middle of the road half-way along to Machecoul, at the crossways of Benaste, the tip end turned toward Touvois."

"Did he give you the password? Jean Oullier would surely not forget that."

"Yes; 'Vanquished' and 'Vendée.' "

"Very good," said Maître Jacques, rising and going to the middle of the open. There he called four of his men, gave them some directions in a low voice, and all four, without replying, went off in four different directions. At the end of about four minutes, during which time

Maître Jacques had ordered up a jug of what seemed to be brandy, and had offered some to his companion, four individuals appeared from the four directions in which the other men had been sent. These were the sentinels just relieved by their comrades.

"Any news?" asked Maître Jacques.

"No," replied three of the men.

"Good. You, — what do you say?" he inquired of the fourth. "You had the best post."

"The diligence to Nantes was escorted by four gendarmes."

"Ah, ha! your nose is good; you smell specie. Bless me! and when I think there are those who *order* us not to get it! However, friends, patience! we are not to be put down."

"Well, what do you think?" interrupted Courte-Joie.

"I think there's not a pair of red breeches anywhere about. Tell Jean Oullier he can bring his people."

"Good!" said Courte-Joie, who during this examination of the sentries was preparing a branch of holly in the manner agreed upon with Jean Oullier. "Very good; I'll send Trigaud." Turning toward the giant, "Here, Vermin!" he said.

Maître Jacques stopped him.

"Ah, *ça!*" he exclaimed; "are you crazy, to part with your legs in that way? Suppose you should need him? Nonsense! there are forty men here who would like no better than to stretch their legs. Wait, you shall see — Hi! Joseph Picaut!"

At the call, our old acquaintance, who was sleeping on the grass in a sleep he seemed much to need, sat up and listened.

"Joseph Picaut!" repeated Maître Jacques, impatiently.

That decided the man. He rose, grumbling, and went up to Maître Jacques.

"Here is a branch of holly," said the leader of the belligerents; "don't pluck off a single leaf. Carry it immediately to the crossway of La Benaste on the road to Machecoul, and lay it down in front of the crucifix, with its tip-end pointing toward Touvois."

Maître Jacques crossed himself as he said the word "crucifix."

"But —" began Picaut, objecting.

"But? — what do you mean?"

"I mean that, after four hours of such a run as I have just made, my legs are breaking under me."

"Joseph Picaut," replied Maître Jacques, whose voice grew strident and metallic, like the blare of a trumpet, "you left your parish and enrolled yourself in my band. You came here; I did not ask you. Now, recollect one thing: at the first objection I strike; at the second I kill."

As he spoke Maître Jacques pulled a pistol from his jacket, grasped it by the barrel, and struck a vigorous blow with the butt-end on Picaut's head. The shock was so violent that the peasant, quite bewildered, came down on one knee. Probably, without the protection of his hat, which was made of thick felt, his skull would have been fractured.

"And now, go!" said Maître Jacques, calmly looking to see if the blow had shaken the powder from the pan.

Without a word Joseph Picaut picked himself up, shook his head, and went off. Courte-Joie watched him till he was out of sight; then he looked at Maître Jacques.

"Do you allow such fellows as that in your band?" he said.

"Yes; don't speak of it!"

"Have you had him long?"

"No, only a few hours."

"Bad recruit for you."

"I don't say that exactly. He is a brave *gars*, like his father, whom I knew well; only, he has to be taught to obey like my fellows, and to get used to the ways of the burrow. He 'll improve; he 'll improve."

"Oh, I don't doubt it! You have a wonderful way of educating them."

"God bless me! I've been at it a good while! But," continued Maître Jacques, "it is time for my round of inspection, and I shall have to leave you, my poor Courte-Joie. It is understood, isn't it, that Jean Oullier's friends are welcome to the burrow. As for the division commander, he shall have his answer to-night. You are sure that is all *gars* Oullier told you to say?"

"Yes."

"Rummage your memory."

"I am sure that is all."

"Very well. If the burrow suits him, he shall have it, — he and his friends. I don't bother myself about my *gars;* those scamps, they are like mice, — they have more than one hole. Good-bye for the present, *gars* Aubin; and while you are waiting, take a bite. I see them making ready for a stew down there."

Maître Jacques descended into what he called his burrow. Then he came out a moment later, armed with a carbine, the priming of which he examined with the utmost care; after which he disappeared among the trees.

The open was now very animated, and presented a most picturesque effect. A large fire had been lighted in the burrow, and the glare coming through the trap illumined the trees and bushes with fantastic gleams. The supper of the men, who were scattered about the open, was cooking at it, while the men waited. Some, on their knees, were telling their beads; others, sitting down, sang in low tones those national songs whose plaintive, long-drawn melodies were so in keeping with the character of the landscape. Two Bretons, lying on their stomachs at the mouth of the burrow, were betting, by means of two bones of different shades of color, for the possession of sundry copper coins, while another *gars* (who, from his pallid face and shrivelled skin, — shrivelled with fever, — was obviously a dweller among the marshes) employed himself, without much success, in cleaning a thick coat of rust from the barrel and match-lock of an old carbine.

Aubin Courte-Joie, accustomed to such scenes, paid no attention to the one before him. Trigaud had made him a sort of couch with leaves, and he was now seated on this improvised mattress, smoking his pipe as tranquilly as if in his tavern at Montaigu.

Suddenly he fancied he heard in the far distance the well-known cry of alarm, — the cry of the screech-owl, — but modulated in a certain long-drawn-out way which indicated danger. Courte-Joie whistled softly to warn the men about him to keep silence and listen; but almost at the same instant a shot echoed from a place about a thousand steps distant.

In the twinkling of an eye the water-pails, standing ready for this very use, had put out the fire; the roof was lowered, the trap closed, and Maître Jacques's belligerents, among them Courte-Joie, whom his physical partner remounted on his shoulders, were scattering in every direction among the trees, where they awaited the next signal from their leader.

XLV.

THE DANGER OF MEETING BAD COMPANY IN THE WOODS.

IT was nearly seven o'clock in the evening when Petit-Pierre, accompanied by Baron Michel, now her guide in place of poor Bonneville, left the cottage where she had escaped such dangers.

It was not, as we can readily believe, without a deep and painful emotion that Petit-Pierre crossed that threshold and left the cold, inanimate body of the chivalrous young man, whom she had known for a few days only, but already loved as an old and trusted friend. That valiant heart of hers had a momentary sense of weakness at the thought of meeting alone the perils that for four or five days poor Bonneville had shared with her. The royal cause had only lost one soldier, yet Petit-Pierre felt as though an army was gone.

It was the first grain of the bloody seed about to be sown once more in the soil of La Vendée; and Petit-Pierre asked herself in anguish if, indeed, nothing would come of it but regret and mourning.

Petit-Pierre did not insult Marianne Picaut by charging her to take good care of the body of poor Bonneville. Strange as the ideas of that woman may have seemed to her, she understood the nobility of her feelings, and recognized all that was truly good and profoundly religious beneath her rough exterior. When Michel brought his horse to the door and reminded Petit-Pierre that every moment was precious, the latter turned to the widow of Pascal Picaut, and holding out her hand, said:

"How can I thank you for all you have done for me?"

"I have done nothing for you," replied Marianne; "I have paid a debt, — fulfilled an oath, that is all."

"Then," said Petit-Pierre, with tears in her eyes, "you will not even accept my gratitude?"

"If you are determined to owe me something," said the widow, "do this: when you pray for those who are dead add to your prayers a few words for those who have died because of you."

"Then you think I have some credit with God?" said Petit-Pierre, unable to keep from smiling through her tears.

"Yes; because I know that you are destined to suffer."

"At least, you will accept this," said Petit-Pierre, unfastening from her throat a little medal hanging to a slender black silk cord. "It is only silver, but the Holy Father blessed it in my presence, and said when he gave it to me that God would grant the prayers uttered over it, if they were just and pious."

Marianne took the medal. Then she said: —

"Thank you. On this medal I will pray to God that our land be saved from civil war, and that He will ever preserve its grandeur and its liberty."

"Right!" said Petit-Pierre; "the last half of your prayer will be echoed in mine."

Aided by Michel, she mounted the horse which the young man led by the bridle, and with a last signal of farewell to the widow, they both disappeared behind the hedge.

For some minutes Petit-Pierre, whose head was bowed on her breast, swayed to the motions of the horse and seemed to be buried in deep and painful reflections. At last, however, she made an effort over herself, and shaking off the grief that overcame her, she turned to Michel, who was walking beside her.

"Monsieur," she said, "I already know two things which entitle you to my confidence: first, that we owed the warning that troops were surrounding the château de

Souday to you; second, that you have come to me to-day in the name of the marquis and his charming daughters. But there is still a third thing, about which I should like to know, and that is, who you are. My friends are rare under present circumstances, and I like to know their names that I may promise not to forget them."

"I am called Baron Michel de la Logerie," replied the young man.

"De la Logerie ! Surely this is not the first time I have heard that name ? "

"Very likely not, Madame," said the young man; "for our poor Bonneville told me he was taking your Highness to my mother — "

"Stop, stop ! what are you saying ? *Your Highness!* There is no highness here; I see only a poor little peasant-lad named Petit-Pierre."

"Ah, true; but Madame will excuse — "

"What ! again ? "

"Pardon me. Our poor Bonneville was taking you to my mother when I had the honor of meeting and conducting you to Souday."

"So that I am under a triple obligation to you. That does not disquiet me; for, great as your services have been, I hope the time will come when I can discharge my debt."

Michel stammered a few words, which did not reach the ears of his companion. But the latter's words seemed to have made an impression on him; for from that moment, while obeying the injunction to refrain from a certain deference, he redoubled his care and attention to the personage he was guiding.

"But it seems to me," said Petit-Pierre, after a moment's thought, "from what Monsieur de Bonneville told me, that royalist opinions are not altogether those of your family."

"No, they are not, Ma — mon — "

"Call me Petit-Pierre, or do not call me anything; that

is the only way to avoid embarrassment. So it is to a conversion that I owe the honor of having you for my knight?"

"An easy conversion! At my age opinions are not convictions; they are only sentiments."

"You are indeed very young," said Petit-Pierre, looking at her guide.

"I am nearly twenty-one."

Petit-Pierre gave a sigh.

"That is the fine age," she said, "for love or war."

The young man heaved a deep sigh, and Petit-Pierre, who heard it, smiled imperceptibly.

"Ah!" she said; "there's a sigh which tells me many things about the conversion we were speaking of just now. I will wager that a pretty pair of eyes knows something about it, and that if the soldiers of Louis-Philippe were to search you at this moment they would find a scarf that is dearer to you for the hands that embroidered it than for the principles of which its color is the emblem."

"I assure you, Madame," stammered Michel, "that is not the cause of my determination."

"Come, come, don't defend yourself; all that is true chivalry, Monsieur Michel. We must never forget, whether we descend from them or whether we seek to emulate them, that the knights of old placed women next to God and on the level of kings, combining all three in one device. Do not be ashamed of loving! Why, that is your greatest claim to my sympathy! *Ventre-saint-gris!* as Henri IV. would have said; with an army of twenty thousand lovers I could conquer not only all France, but the world! Come, tell me the name of your lady, Monsieur le Baron de la Logerie."

"Oh!" exclaimed Michel, deeply shocked.

"Ah! I see you are discreet, young man. I congratulate you; it is a quality all the more precious because in these days it is so rare. But never mind; to a travelling-companion we tell all, charging him to keep our secret inviolably. Come, shall I help you ? I will wager that we are now going toward the lady of our thoughts."

"You are right there."

"And I will further wager that she is neither more nor less than one of those charming amazons at Souday."

"Good heavens ! who could have told you ? "

"Well, I congratulate you again, my young friend. Wolves as I am told some persons call them, I know they have brave and noble hearts, capable of bestowing happiness on the husbands they select. Are you rich, Monsieur de la Logerie ? "

"Alas, yes ! " replied Michel.

"So much the better, and not alas at all ! You can enrich your wife, and that seems to me a great happiness. In all cases, in all loves, there are certain little difficulties to overcome, and if Petit-Pierre can help you at any time you have only to call upon him; he will be most happy to recognize in that way the services you have been good enough to render him. But, if I 'm not mistaken, here comes some one toward us. Listen; don't you hear a tread ? "

The steps of a man now became distinctly audible. They were still at some distance, but were coming nearer.

"I think the man is alone," said Petit-Pierre.

"Yes; but we must not be the less on our guard," replied the baron. "I shall ask your permission to mount that horse in front of you."

"Willingly; but are you already tired ? "

"No, not at all. Only, I am well known in the neighborhood, and if I were seen on foot leading a horse on which a peasant was riding, as Haman led Mordecai, it might give rise to a good deal of speculation."

"Bravo ! what you say is very true. I begin to think we shall make something of you in the end."

Petit-Pierre jumped to the ground. Michel mounted, and Petit-Pierre placed herself humbly behind him. They were hardly settled in their seats before they came within thirty yards of an individual who was walking in their direction, and whose steps now ceased abruptly.

"Oh! oh!" said Petit-Pierre; "it seems that if we are afraid of him, he is afraid of us."

"Who's there?" called Michel, making his voice gruff.

"Ah! is it you, Monsieur le baron?" replied the man, advancing. "The devil take me if I expected to meet you here at this hour!"

"You told the truth when you said that you were well known," whispered Petit-Pierre, laughing.

"Yes, unfortunately," said Michel, in a tone which warned Petit-Pierre they were in presence of a real danger.

"Who is this man?" asked Petit-Pierre.

"Courtin, my farmer, — the one we suspect of denouncing your presence at Marianne Picaut's." Then he added, in a vehement and imperative tone, which made his companion aware of the urgency of the situation, "Hide behind me as much as possible."

Petit-Pierre immediately obeyed.

"Oh! it is you Courtin, is it?" said Michel.

"Yes, it is I," replied the farmer.

"Where do you come from?" asked Michel.

"From Machecoul; I went there to buy an ox."

"Where is your ox? I don't see it."

"No, I could n't make a trade. These damned politics hinder business, and there's nothing now in the market," said Courtin, who was carefully examining, as well as he could in the darkness, the horse on which the young baron was mounted.

Then, as Michel dropped the conversation, he continued: —

"But how is it you are turning your back to La Logerie at this time of night?"

"That's not surprising; I am going to Souday."

"Might I observe that you are not altogether on the road to Souday?"

"I know that; but I was afraid the road was guarded, so I have made a circuit."

"In that case, — I mean if you are really going to Souday," said Courtin, — "I think I ought to give you a bit of advice."

"Well, give it; sincere advice is always useful."

"Don't go; the cage is empty."

"Pooh!"

"Yes, I tell you, it is empty; there's no use in your going there, Monsieur le baron, to find the bird who has sent you scouring the country."

"Who told you that, Courtin?" said Michel, manœuvring his horse so as to keep his body well before Courtin, and thus mask Petit-Pierre behind him.

"Who told me? Hang it! my eyes told me; I saw them all file out of the courtyard, the devil take them! They marched right past me on the road to Grandes-Landes."

"Were the soldiers in that direction?" asked the young baron.

Petit-Pierre thought this question rash, and she pinched Michel's arm.

"Soldiers!" replied Courtin; "why should you be afraid of soldiers? But if you are, I advise you not to risk yourself at this time of night on the plain. You can't go three miles without coming plump on bayonets. Do a wiser thing than that, Monsieur Michel."

"What do you advise me to do? Come, if your way is better than mine, I'll take it."

"Go back with me to La Logerie; you will give your mother great satisfaction, for she is fretting herself to death over the way you are behaving."

"Maître Courtin," said Michel, "I'll give you a bit of advice in exchange."

"What's that, Monsieur le baron?"

"To hold your tongue."

"No, I cannot hold my tongue," replied the farmer,

assuming an appearance of sorrowful emotion, — "no, it grieves me too much to see my young master exposed to such dangers, and all for — "

"Hush, Courtin!"

"For those cursed she-wolves whom the son of a peasant like myself would have none of."

"Wretch! will you be silent?" cried Michel, raising his whip.

The action, which Courtin had no doubt tried to provoke, caused Michel's horse to give a jump forward, and the mayor of La Logerie was now abreast of the two riders.

"I am sorry if I've offended you, Monsieur le baron," he said, in a whining tone. "Forgive me; but I haven't slept for two nights thinking about it."

Petit-Pierre shuddered. She heard the same false and wheedling voice that had spoken to her in the cottage of the Widow Picaut, followed, after the speaker's departure, by such painful events. She made Michel another sign, by which she meant, "Let us get rid of this man at any cost."

"Very good," said Michel; "go your way and let *us* go ours."

Courtin pretended to notice for the first time that Michel had some one behind him.

"Good heavens!" he exclaimed. "Why, you are not alone! Ah! I see now, Monsieur le baron, why you were so touchy about what I said. Well, monsieur," he said, addressing Petit-Pierre, "whoever you are, I am sure you will be more reasonable than your young friend. Join me in telling him there is nothing to be gained by braving the laws and the power of the government, as he is bent on doing to please those wolves."

"Once more, Courtin," said Michel, in a tone that was actually menacing, "I tell you to go. I act as I think best, and I consider you very insolent to presume to judge of my conduct."

But Courtin, whose smooth persistency we all know by this time, seemed determined not to depart without getting a look at the features of the mysterious personage whom his young master had behind him.

"Come," he said; "to-morrow you can do as you like; but to-night, at least, come and sleep at the farmhouse, — you and the person, lady or gentleman, who is with you. I swear to you, Monsieur le baron, that there is danger in being out to-night."

"There is no danger for myself and my companion, for we are not concerned in politics. What are you doing to my saddle, Courtin?" asked the young man suddenly, noticing a movement on his farmer's part which he did not understand.

"Why, nothing, Monsieur Michel; nothing," said Courtin, with perfect good-humor. "So then, you positively won't listen to my advice and entreaties?"

"No; go your way, and let me go mine."

"Go, then!" exclaimed the farmer, in his sly, sarcastic tone; "and God be with you. Remember that poor Courtin did what he could to prevent you from rushing into danger."

So saying, Courtin finally drew aside, and Michel, setting spurs to his horse, rode past him.

"Gallop! gallop!" cried Petit-Pierre. "That is the man who caused poor Bonneville's death. Let us get on as fast as we can; that man has the evil-eye."

The young baron stuck both spurs into his horse; but the animal had hardly gone a dozen paces before the saddle turned, and both riders came heavily to the ground. Petit-Pierre was up first.

"Are you hurt?" she asked Michel, who was getting up more slowly.

"No," he replied; "but I am wondering how — "

"How we came to fall? That's not the question. We did fall, and there's the fact. Girth your horse again, and as fast as possible."

"*Aïe!*" cried Michel, who had already thrown the saddle over his horse's back; "both girths are broken at precisely the same height."

"Say they are cut," said Petit-Pierre. "It is a trick of your infernal Courtin; and it is a warning of worse — Wait, look over there."

Michel, whose arm Petit-Pierre had seized, looked in the direction to which she pointed, and there, about a mile distant in the valley, he saw three or four camp-fires shining in the darkness.

"It is a bivouac," said Petit-Pierre. "If that scoundrel suspects the truth — and no doubt he does — he will make for the camp and set those red-breeches on our traces."

"Ah! do you think that knowing I am with you, I, his master, he would dare —"

"I must suppose everything, Monsieur Michel, and I must risk nothing."

"You are right; we must leave nothing to chance."

"Had n't we better leave the beaten path?"

"I was thinking of that."

"How much time will it take to go on foot to the place where the marquis is awaiting us?"

"An hour, at least; and we have no time to lose. But what shall we do with the horse? He can't climb the banks as we must."

"Throw the bridle on his neck. He'll go back to his stable; and if our friends meet the animal on the way, they'll know some accident has happened and will come in search of us. Hush! hush!"

"What is it?"

"Don't you hear something?" asked Petit-Pierre.

"Yes; horses' feet in the direction of that bivouac."

"You see it was not without a motive that your farmer cut our saddle-girths. Let us be off, my poor baron."

"But if we leave the horse here those who search for us will know the riders are not far off."

"Stop!" said Petit-Pierre; "I have an idea, an Italian

idea! — the races of the *barberi*. Yes, that's the very thing. Do as I do, Monsieur Michel."

"Go on; I obey."

Petit-Pierre set to work. With her delicate hands, and at the risk of lacerating them, she broke off branches of thorn and holly from the neighboring hedge. Michel did the same, and they presently had two thick and prickly bundles of short sticks.

"What's to be done with them?" asked Michel.

"Tear the name off your handkerchief and give me the rest."

Michel obeyed. Petit-Pierre tore the handkerchief into two strips and tied up the bunches. Then she fastened one to the mane, the other to the tail of the horse. The poor animal, feeling the thorns like spurs upon his flesh, began to rear and plunge. The young baron now began to understand.

"Take off his bridle," said Petit-Pierre, "or he may break his neck; and let him go."

The horse was hardly relieved of the snaffle that held him before he snorted, shook his mane and tail angrily, and darted away like a tornado, leaving a trail of sparks behind him.

"Bravo!" cried Petit-Pierre. "Now, pick up the saddle and bridle, and let us find shelter ourselves."

They jumped the hedge, Michel having thrown the saddle and bridle before him. There they crouched down and listened. The gallop of the horse still resounded on the stony road.

"Do you hear it?" said the baron, satisfied.

"Yes; but we are not the only ones who are listening to it, Monsieur le baron," said Petit-Pierre. "Hear the echo."

XLVI.

MAÎTRE JACQUES PROCEEDS TO KEEP THE OATH HE MADE TO AUBIN COURTE-JOIE.

THE sound which Baron Michel and Petit-Pierre now heard in the direction by which Courtin had left them changed presently into a loud noise approaching rapidly; and two minutes later a dozen chasseurs, riding at a gallop in pursuit of the trail, or rather the noise made by the running horse, which was snorting and neighing as it ran, passed like a flash, not ten steps from Petit-Pierre and her companion, who, rising slightly after the horsemen had passed, watched their wild rush into the distance.

"They ride well," said Petit-Pierre; "but I doubt if they catch up with that horse."

"They are making straight for the place where our friends are awaiting us, and I think the marquis is in just the humor to put a stop to their course."

"Then it is battle!" cried Petit-Pierre. "Well, water yesterday, fire to-day; for my part, I prefer the latter."

And she tried to hurry Michel in the direction where the fight would take place.

"No, no, no!" said Michel, resisting; "I entreat you not to go there."

"Don't you wish to win your spurs under the eyes of your lady, baron? She is there, you know."

"I think she is," said the young man, sadly. "But troops are scattered over the country in every direction; at the first shots they will all converge toward the firing. We may fall in with one of their detachments, and if, unfortunately, the mission with which I am charged should end disastrously I shall never dare to appear again before the marquis — "

"Say before his daughter."

"Well, yes, — before his daughter."

"Then, in order not to bring trouble into your love affairs I consent to obey you."

"Oh, thank you ! thank you ! " cried Michel, seizing Petit-Pierre's hand vehemently. Then perceiving the impropriety of his action, he exclaimed, stepping backward, "Oh, pardon me; pray, pardon me ! "

"Never mind," said Petit-Pierre; "don't think of it. Where did the Marquis de Souday intend to shelter me ? "

"In a farmhouse of mine."

"Not that of your man Courtin, I hope ? "

"No, in another, perfectly isolated, hidden in the woods beyond Légé. You know the village where Tinguy lived ? "

"Yes; but do you know the way there ? "

"Perfectly."

"I distrust that adverb in France. My poor Bonneville said he knew the way perfectly, but he lost it." Petit-Pierre sighed as she added, in a lower tone, "Poor Bonneville ! alas ! it may have been that very mistake that led to his death."

The topic brought back the melancholy thoughts that filled her mind as she left the cottage where the catastrophe that cost her the life of her first companion had taken place. She was silent, and after making a gesture of consent, she followed her new guide, replying only by monosyllables to the few remarks which Michel addressed to her.

As for the latter, he performed his new functions with more ability and success than might have been expected of him. He turned to the left, and crossing some fields, reached a brook where he had often fished for shrimps in his childhood. This brook runs through the valley of the Benaste from end to end, rises toward the south and falls again toward the north, where it joins the Boulogne near Saint-Colombin. Either bank, bordered with fields, gave a safe and easy path to pedestrians. Michel took to the brook itself, and followed it for some distance, carrying Petit-Pierre on his shoulders as poor Bonneville had done.

Presently, leaving the brook after following it for about a kilometre, he bore again to the left, crossed the brow of a hill, and showed Petit-Pierre the dark masses of the forest of Touvois, which were visible in the dim light, looming up from the foot of the hill on which they now stood.

"Is that where your farmhouse is?" asked Petit-Pierre.

"We have still to cross the forest," he said; "but we shall get there in about three quarters of an hour."

"You are not afraid of losing your way?"

"No; for we do not have to plunge into the thicket. In fact, we shall not enter the wood at all till we reach the road from Machecoul to Légé. By skirting the edge of the forest to the eastward we must strike that road soon."

"And then?"

"Then all we have to do is to follow it."

"Well, well," said Petit-Pierre, cheerfully, "I'll give a good account of you, my young guide; and faith, it shall not be Petit-Pierre's fault if you don't obtain the reward you covet! But here is rather a well-beaten path. Isn't this the one you are looking for?"

"I can easily tell," replied Michel, "for there ought to be a post on the right— There! here it is! we are all right. And now, Petit-Pierre, I can promise you a good night's rest."

"Ah! that is a comfort," said Petit-Pierre, smiling; "for I don't deny that the terrible emotions of the day have not relieved the fatigues of last night."

The words were hardly out of her lips before a black outline rose from the other side of the ditch, bounded into the road, and a man seized Petit-Pierre violently by the collar of the peasant's jacket which she wore, crying out in a voice of thunder:—

"Stop, or you're a dead man!"

Michel sprang to the assistance of his young companion by bringing down a vigorous blow with the butt-end of his whip on her assailant. He was near paying dear for his intervention. The man, without letting go of Petit-Pierre, whom he held with his left arm, drew a pistol from his jacket and fired at the young baron. Happily for the latter, in spite of Petit-Pierre's feebleness she was not of a stuff to keep as passive as her captor expected. With a rapid gesture she struck the arm that fired the weapon, and the ball, which would otherwise have gone straight to Michel's breast, only wounded him in the shoulder. He returned to the charge, and their assailant was just pulling a second pistol from his belt when two other men sprang from the bushes and seized Michel from behind.

Then the first assailant, seeing that the young man could interfere no longer, contented himself by saying to his companions: —

"Secure that fellow first; and then come and rid me of this one."

"But," said Petit-Pierre, "by what right do you stop us in this way?"

"This right," said the man, striking the carbine, which he carried on his shoulder. "If you want to know why, you will find out presently. Bind that man securely," he said to his men. "As for this one," he added contemptuously, "it isn't worth while; I think there'll be no trouble in mastering him."

"But I wish to know where you are taking us," insisted Petit-Pierre.

"You are very inquisitive, my young friend," replied the man.

"But — "

"Damn it! come on, and you'll find out. You shall see with your own eyes where you are going in a very few minutes."

And the man, taking Petit-Pierre by the arm, dragged

MAÎTRE JACQUES KEEPS HIS OATH.

her into the bushes, while Michel, struggling violently, was pushed by the two assistants in the same direction.

They walked thus for about ten minutes, at the end of which time they reached the open where, as we know, was the burrow of Maître Jacques and his bandits. For it was he, bent on sacredly keeping his oath to Aubin Courte-Joie, who had stopped the two travellers whom luck had sent in his way; and it was his pistol-shot which, as we have already seen at the close of a preceding chapter, put the whole camp of the refractories on the *qui vive*.

END OF VOL I.

Printed in the United States
47284LVS00001B/2